VINDICATION

CHRIS JANISH

VINDICATION

Edited by Christina Hart of Savage Hart Book Services
Proofread by Tina Torrest
Cover Illustration by Marilyn Church
Cover Design by Kat Savage of Savage Hart Book Services
Formatted by J.R. Rogue

ISBN: 9781092383301

TRIGGER WARNING: This book contains explicit content relating to violence, graphic sex, sexual abuse, crime, and suicide.

For Jules.

The one who continued to believe in me when everyone else walked out. The one who gave me the confidence to write when no one else did. The one who was the real writer in our family but gave it up to raise our boys. I love you, baby.

And to all the dudes who are locked up and could use a little hope.

PROLOGUE

RAY

I PICTURED THE DAY I'D FINALLY WALK OUT THAT GATE. IT'D be a warm spring day and a start so fresh that the thought both exhilarated and paralyzed me. I envisioned myself dropping to my knees once my feet crossed beyond the outside fence, but I stopped myself there. No one would ever have me on my knees again. Not the DA, not the parole board, not anyone. Freedom is not something you're grateful for until it's violently snatched from you.

The recent parole decision was the first break I got in four years. And after a grueling stretch behind bars, on March 19, 2010, I would finally get a new start in the world. Inmate #08-A-1075 would finally be free. That's what I was: A number. Not Raymond Jansen, not Ray. Just a number. Barely even human.

I was just a shade under 40 years old and had the latter part of my 30s taken away from me. But now, I could taste the freedom on my lips, hear it in my ears, see it through a twisted kaleidoscope of hope. And if my release wasn't all I imagined it would be, I thought I'd at least have my wife there waiting for me.

But there was no picturesque warmth or happiness to greet me. The day I got out, it was a typical western New York day—gray and windy, with snowflakes drifting off Lake Erie, even though spring was supposed to be in the air. I caught the prison bus to the airport, and for the first time in four years, my hands were not cuffed outside that wall. I had an E-ticket waiting for me to take me back to the city. My wife was there waiting for me when I got off the plane. She still looked beautiful to me with her freshly done blonde hair. The smile on her face told me she was relieved I was finally home. But that smile would soon fade, just like the love and compassion did after one year in prison turned to two years, until it was four years later with little to show for it. Some things just never return to the way they were, no matter how much you try to force it.

Being away, I was helpless for the first time, with no means to take care of her and our two boys. I wrote them letters, used the kids as a way to find the strength to keep going. But my fond memories with my wife were gone, buried. They started fading once she begged me to take the plea. She said she'd never leave me or stop loving me, even though I'd had some indiscretions as a young hedge fund manager before this whole mess. She had me convinced for a while there.

She knew that fighting for my innocence was one of the most important things in the world to me, but nothing was as important as my family. Or her. And she was right, I couldn't run the risk of blowing trial and doing 10 to 30 years while losing everything. She wanted me to see our kids grow up. She wanted our life back. I wanted that, too. And because of her willingness to endure the fight with me, I gave the government what they wanted from me: Time, and 13 years of a hard-earned fortune.

But after I went upstate, everything started to wane. Hurt and resentment reverberated on both sides, despite the efforts in holding on. Memories of my late nights working on Wall Street overcame her. My thoughts of what *she* was doing all those lonely nights while I was locked up…

They pulled us further apart emotionally. And now that I was officially out, every doubt surfaced and came to light. The fighting was too much. The decision to split was mutual on the surface, but I knew somewhere along the way that she fell out of love with me.

Throughout every injustice in my case, the torture in prison, the suicide of one of my co-defendants, the corruption of the DA and judges, she was always there for me. And with her officially gone, I felt that rock bottom hit, that low that people talk about. At least when I had her, I had something to fight for. Now, alone, in a tiny apartment with little money, it dawned on me that I had lost everything. Power, possessions, contacts. But losing my dignity hurt the most. I couldn't bear to have my kids see me like this, so I dealt with it how I'd learned to in the last few years. Internally. Isolated. Alone.

But quitting in life was not an option for me. Not even while fighting my case in the grueling, horrific conditions of Rikers Island. I knew things would be tough on the outside, but I never knew they could be even worse than being inside. One thing that stayed with me was once you hit bottom, you can only go up. So, I regrouped. I didn't mind being labeled as an outcast. I didn't need social satisfaction anymore, or fake friends filled with nights of designer drug use. I just wanted to start a new career and rebuild my life—slowly, brick by brick.

I worked as much as possible, saving whatever money I could to reinvest in my business, or for an occasional present for the boys. I got back on my feet, eventually. Old business contacts gradually came back, along with some friends who realized my downfall was over-exaggerated. I started to socialize again, strictly for business purposes. I think most people assumed I would just revert to my old ways of partying and the lifestyle I once knew intimately. But they were wrong. I was focused on my career, so despite being an eligible bachelor, dating along with everything else was secondary. I wasn't bitter anymore about losing my family, but nothing else could ever compare, so why bother trying? Beautiful women and passionate sex were things I had so many times in my 20s. I was no longer interested in chasing that. Something of substance. That was what I wanted.

It took me a good two to three years to get back on track and get my mind right. And then, before anyone could really notice, I was once again rising to the top of a niche specialty financing business and things were falling into place. I even learned to deal with the now ex-wife who had moved on in mere months. Now, in my early 40s, I started to toy with the idea that if I wanted, I could start over with someone else. But I only started to creak that door open.

I moved out of that shitty little apartment and into a nice place near Grammercy Park. I bought a black SUV to drive out to Jersey on the weekends to see the kids. I even started playing golf again at the new country club. Most exclusive clubs would never accept someone with a notorious felony rap like mine, but it was different in Essex County. My reputation was as good as gold—mainly because I kept my mouth shut when it mattered most, something that goes a long way on the streets of Jersey. Regardless of the pressure put on me, I never gave up those principles.

It was now 2015, five years from my release, and nine years from my original indictment. I was finally feeling like

I belonged in society again, without the constant need to look over my shoulder. And I was on a mission to get back everything the government had taken from me. Only this time, I'd do it right—by working the system the way it worked me.

CHAPTER ONE

RAY

I NEVER THOUGHT MY REDEMPTIVE RISE FROM A FELON AT rock bottom to a respected high earner would land me here —in the *Four Seasons Hotel* with an invitation to Ari Rohnstein's private penthouse for a special event. Ari Rohnstein wasn't only one of the most influential sports franchise owners in America, he was probably the most powerful media tycoon in New York today. And as it turned out, he was also the father of the girl I was seeing.

I had requested an early check-in at the hotel since I had plans with Nick Salerno, one of my oldest friends. And he wasn't just a friend, he was one of the key guys to ever support me in my case. Salerno was my key money man, or "nominee" as we say on Wall Street. Part of a powerful Broadway advertising family, he was worth in excess of $100MM. But still, the pittance of money he lost in the stock fraud scheme impacted him personally and he felt burned by the allegations during that time. Regardless, he helped me make my $5MM bail, the largest insurance bond ever posted in New York State criminal history at the time. And he didn't *just* visit me at Rikers Island, he also pledged financial support to my wife, even though it was done so begrudgingly.

Despite the financial damage Salerno went through—along with some lingering resentment—he wrote a glowing letter to the parole board on my behalf to advocate for my release. Our friendship was strained for a while thanks to outside influence from the government and parts of his involvement in my past dealings, but we were back on track and back to doing business together. We had an early liquid lunch planned to celebrate the success of our recent media launch party and discuss our future business prospects, which were looking bright on the horizon.

I booked us two massages at the spa in the hotel so we could relax and unwind before the evening ahead. Nick deserved it after being the dual advertising broker on the latest deal for my company, which also involved my new strategic partner, Isabella—who just so happened to be Rohnstein's daughter. She had recently founded *New Age Family* magazine, a new media publication platform built to empower people everywhere to better themselves regardless of their economic limitations, and I was in. More in than most people knew. I agreed to finance the entire digital platform and app that would be the key to future distribution for the growing number of millennials and the digital-centric world in general. By doing so, I created a strategic relationship between Isabella's venture and mine, with my company obtaining the national marketing exposure we desired. And Salerno's ad agency was the broker for both us—reaping double fees.

Over the last few weeks, we'd grown closer. Isabella never judged me for my past, which was something I'd gotten used to over the years. People hear you're an ex-con and instant assumptions fly. She didn't tell me who her father was, and I didn't put two and two together, despite knowing Ari was also one of Salerno's clients. Isabella's last name was Martin. How could I have guessed she was a Rohnstein by adoption?

I knew Ari partially offered the invite out of curiosity, and I couldn't blame him. If I had a daughter, I'd probably want to meet the guy who was getting close to her, too. I'd had enough of the badgering questions from Salerno. The hints and innuendos. The subtle drops of irritation and anger he'd toss my way about it all. He didn't want Isabella and me being romantically involved, that much was apparent. He had a festering fear of that budding romance manifesting, which I didn't understand then, but I poured salt in that wound before I even knew it was there. Isabella and I were both adults. And if we wanted to have a relationship that was a little beyond the realm of professional, that's exactly what we were going to do. And no one else needed to know.

I sat in the steam room with a nice buzz and reminisced about old times with Salerno, back when I was still a young Wall Street success story.

"You know, even after all these years, you haven't changed much," he said, laughing. "Hell, you still look like you did 15 years ago."

"Well, you know what they say, prison preserves you," I said, letting out a small laugh at how true it was. Salerno liked to ask me questions about it, what it was like being on the inside. How I got through it. And I'd tell him the same thing. It was mental, physical, and emotional survival, every single day.

"I can't believe you still shave down," he said.

He loved to rip on me for shaving my chest and arms. But I'd always done this. Call it a habit. "Why not? Some things never change."

"What'd you do in there when you couldn't shave?" he asked.

"I always did. Whatever you do on the outside, you do on the inside. You gotta keep as much of your routine as you can. Just for the sake of feeling some sense of normalcy."

He nodded, like he understood. But he didn't. He never would.

After our massages, I went back to my room to get ready. The anxiety about that night didn't hit me until later outside the penthouse when Salerno handed me my access credential and mentioned the level of security that would be at Rohnstein's. Including the bit about the pat-frisks due to the political guests and possible paparazzi trying to gain access. I tried to exhale the worry that was building inside me. But as I walked off the elevator to the enormous three-story loft penthouse, it came back. I wasn't sure if it was stemming more from the fact that I was about to meet Isabella's father, or if it was mere flashbacks of the pat-frisks in prison. I never got over them.

Before I could think any further on it, we were met by security personnel who did their jobs of vetting out who we all were. Ari's wife, Michele, eventually came to shoo the guards away and give us a heartfelt welcome to her home. Isabella appeared next, holding a glass of rosé champagne. She looked like a runway model in her cocktail dress and stilettos. Her long legs were tan, and paired with the white of her dress, she looked like she was glowing.

"Ray!" she said, pulling me in for a hug, her brown hair with streaks of blonde grazing my face.

I kissed her on the cheek and whispered so only she could hear me. "You look gorgeous, babe." I let go, being careful not to linger in the hug even a moment too long, and addressed her mom. "Mrs. Rohnstein, it's a pleasure to meet you. Thank you for having me."

"It's so nice to meet you, too! Anyone important to

Isabella is important to me. Please, come in," Michele said, smiling.

We went through the formalities and hellos and the initial welcome. Before we could leave the foyer, Michele went to get Ari to let him know Nick and I had arrived.

Ari appeared moments later, giving me a firm handshake and a once-over. "Welcome, boys," he said, with a tone that was less than welcoming. "Why don't I show you around a little bit?"

He took immediate control and walked us through just one section of the penthouse. The first stop was the men's lounge, fully equipped with a large, flat-screen TV, leather couches, a walk-in humidor stocked with the best cigars in the world, and a state-of-the-art airtight cigar ventilation system. And, of course, a large bar with a bartender behind it, ready to make our drinks. The Sutton Place neighborhood was an elitist address already. But the floor-to-ceiling windows, plus the view of the skyscrapers and East River, made it that much more impressive.

We ordered our drinks and I commented on how spectacular the place was, including the cigar collection. I mentioned my affinity for the Monte Cristo #2 from Havana.

"I'll make sure to send you a box or two next week," Ari said. "I have so many of them in here. I'll never smoke them all."

The conversation started off light. We talked about golf and sports as we sipped our drinks. But Ari quickly shifted the focus to more important matters.

"Why don't we take a walk over to the library where we can talk in private?" he asked quietly.

I could tell he wasn't the type to beat around the bush, and I could relate to that. Once we stepped into the library, filled with hundreds of leather-bound classics, Ari looked at me and I braced myself, wondering how much he knew and if Salerno had let anything slip in alcohol-fueled moments.

"Look, Ray, I hear my daughter is very fond of you, not only professionally but personally as well. And I don't want you to think I have anything against you because of your past."

"But?" I asked, knowing what was coming.

"You understand my concerns about your history right, being in the position I'm in?"

"Sure, Mr. Rohnstein," I said.

"Please, call me Ari."

"Okay, Ari. Just to be clear, I didn't come searching for this. I didn't even know you were Isabella's father until recently."

"My daughter never mentioned it to you?" he asked, surprised, with a questioning glance.

"No. She just said her dad was in the media and advertising business and that you had referred some investors to her publication. And actually, Salerno was the one who told me."

Ari stood there, taking this in. Eventually, he looked at me. Something in his tone changed when he spoke. "So, what happens if the press gets a hold of the fact that my daughter is a strategic partner with a convicted felon?"

"I haven't thought about that, to be honest," I said. "I guess I'm just used to it by now. At this point, what other people think doesn't faze me."

"Well, I guess we're different there. The media members that I'm not friendly with will use any leverage they can against me to make me or my daughter look bad. Purely from a business perspective, I always have to be concerned with damaging our brands. You understand that, right?"

"Yes," I said. "I get it. But we have Isabella's company positioned perfectly now after the success of the launch party, which I wanted to thank you for. You brought in tons of exposure for us."

"Thank you for acknowledging that. People take that for granted sometimes," Ari said.

I nodded, giving him room to finish his thoughts.

"Nick speaks highly of you. And from what I've heard, you're the kind of guy who delivers. Based on the recent transaction you pulled off, I'll admit I'm a little impressed."

"Thank you," I said.

"Look, I'm here to support you guys, and my daughter, in any way I can. However, your past concerns me and I need some time to think about the dynamics of all of this. Tonight is not the right night for this. I'll reach out to Salerno next week. Just stay available."

I nodded my head in agreement and we left the library where Ari moved on to meet his more important guests. Guests a bit higher on the social ladder than the scummy ex-con dating his daughter.

CHAPTER TWO

ISABELLA

I WAS BUZZED FROM THE PERPETUAL SERVING OF CHAMPAGNE cocktails that progressed from lunch to dinner, but also romanced with the fact that Ray was holding his own around my father. Well, adoptive father. I could never consider Ari a true dad. I watched Ray from across the room at times when I was mingling with other guests. His green eyes would catch me and send shivers up my spine. We'd been waiting for weeks to touch, and my patience was growing thin.

I introduced him to everyone, mostly making a home on his arm all night. I showed him different parts of the penthouse, and in private rooms, I'd sneak kisses. We were planning to spend the rest of the weekend together, but the time wasn't passing fast enough. I just wanted to be alone with him.

As the party wound down, only family and close friends were left. Including Ray. My father had gone to sleep. He had a business trip planned and had to leave early the next morning. Nick and his wife were getting ready to go to bed in the wing that had been arranged for them. I had my own apartment in the building, attached to the penthouse by a separate elevator, one floor above. I demanded it after coming home from college, needing privacy. So, my dad converted part of the outside terrace and fitness areas for me. Space. From this. From them.

For the time being, everyone stayed in the main quarters, finishing the last of their drinks and making small talk. My mom had been so hospitable to Ray—something I considered a bit of an act—and now showed concern with the stormy conditions outside. The recent May weather felt like summer, but also brought with it violent thunderstorms. News hit that power lines were down in the city, and the rain and lightning were both growing more severe. She insisted that Ray stay in the guest room in the opposite wing from where Nick was staying. He resisted at first, but she was persistent.

I gave him the final push he needed. "Just stay," I said, putting my arm around his shoulder. "It's bad out."

"All right, I will," he said, looking at me.

Everyone said goodnight, and I showed Ray to his guest room, bringing a bottle of water for him in case he got thirsty during the night. I kissed him goodnight, behind the closed door, then left. I was an adult, yes. 26 years old but still treated like a baby. I couldn't let anyone see me enter Ray's room and not leave. Not security, not my mother, not even Nick. So, I said goodnight to everyone and went to my apartment. For the sake of appearances.

I WAS IN MY BEDROOM, looking in the mirror. I had on a white negligee, the same one I had worn when I face-timed with Ray just a few days earlier. It was fun to tease him, to build the tension that was already growing. I knew I should wait until the next day—our arranged day to finally be together—but I couldn't. I put my robe on and snuck back down to the penthouse where his guest room was. I walked quietly, aware of my feet and the noise they were making, the creaking of the floor boards beneath my heels. I reached the door to his room and turned the knob, then locked it behind me once I was inside.

The lights were off, but the city streetlights dimly illuminated the room. I took my robe off and waited for him to notice me there. My heart was racing. I hadn't been touched in longer than I'd like to admit. Sex was not something that came completely naturally to me, or even ever yearned for. In fact, I usually avoided it. It was easier that way. But not with him. Not having him, that was not easy. And with everyone trying to push us apart lately—Salerno, my father, their business partners—it only made me want him more. Especially since he had refused to succumb to that. I climbed on top of him in the bed and he sat up.

"Is this cool here?" he asked.

His nervousness was cute—always so collected and cool, it was endearing on him.

I bent down, rubbing my hands over his shoulders. "Relax," I whispered. "This room is isolated. And I took the emergency stairs right outside here so no one would see me."

He grabbed my thighs and squeezed. "I want you so bad, baby, but what about waiting until tomorrow?"

I picked up his presidential Rolex that was on the nightstand and showed it to him. "It is tomorrow," I said with a smirk. "See? It's past midnight. I don't want to wait anymore." I put the watch down and got comfortable on his lap while he lay on his back. I leaned forward and kissed him deeply.

And here, it wasn't rushed. It didn't have to be like it was when we met in obscure places, hiding from prying eyes. I grinded against him as his hands made their way over my body. My back, my hips, my neck.

He lowered the delicate straps of my negligee, exposing my breasts. The patient kissing turned more aggressive, more passionate. I held him down to try to slow him a little, but he guided my hand down onto him. I could feel him getting hard for me. His pants and shirt came off quickly. I knew he kept himself in good shape, but I wasn't fully expecting this. The abs, the biceps. I kissed his shoulders, his chest, still holding his arms down with my hands. I wanted to have control. No, *needed* to, but it wasn't working. I felt the rush of fluid under me and at that point, I let go.

I sat up and lifted my arms in the air, signaling for him to pull the negligee off.

"You sure?" he asked.

I nodded and closed my eyes.

Before I knew it, we were both fully naked. He moved my head down on him for a little bit. I could feel him fully hard now that he was in my mouth. It made me slightly uncomfortable, but I did it for him. And then, in one fluid motion, he had me on my back. I tried to stop him, the anxiety taking over as he pushed my legs apart. As much as I wanted to please him, and for him to please me, his dominance made me uneasy.

This position was not good for me. I fought the feeling, trying to enjoy it as his mouth made contact. I had fallen in love with him. I wanted this. Hell, I begged for it. Started it. In the beginning, and even now. I closed my eyes and let him take over. I could feel how strong he was, and as he put his hands on the back of my thighs and pushed my legs open even wider, I felt powerless. I started breathing in frantic gasps as his tongue lightly licked my clit, a finger penetrating me simultaneously.

He was gentle at first, but then the pressure with his

tongue and fingers got harder. I was wet, and moaning, repeating his name, but the pleasure mixed into pain and it started to hurt. My thoughts became disjointed. Dizziness started to take over. Caught between fear and ecstasy, I tried to brush it off. I pushed him for more, grabbing his hair.

My moans got increasingly louder, and he asked me to climax for him. I was out of breath, practically paralyzed, both mentally and physically. I wanted to orgasm, for me, for him, but the anxiety came back. My head was flush and I felt almost unconscious lying there. I couldn't move. I just needed to breathe for a moment. My whole body was shaking. *From pleasure?* But my head, it started to spin. Fear. Anxiety. Memories. I felt him climb on top of me. His body felt so big, suffocating, all consuming.

Out of instinct I put my hands on his chest, pushing him away. But he was too strong. And he was ready. I could feel how hard he was on top of me. I became lightheaded, my heart pounding furiously. Something was happening. I couldn't move, couldn't speak. I felt the tip of him start to enter me, slowly.

And then came the stench of the beer in the frat house.

I mumbled something under my breath.

And something snapped.

I scratched at his neck and chest violently and started thrashing underneath him. "No!" I yelled. I swung at him with both hands on the sides of his head, just as I learned in the self-defense classes I had taken.

He was shocked, quiet, calm. He did not fight back; he did not try to stop me. I think I heard him say something, maybe a "shh" or a "what's wrong?" or "Iz".

But I was screaming. And crying. I couldn't quite hear him.

"He raped me!" I screamed. "He raped me!"

In a desperate attempt to cover myself, I grabbed my

robe from the floor and ran out of the room, needing to get away from him, continuing to yell.

"He raped me!" I screamed at the top of my lungs.

The cries turned to sobs and I couldn't breathe. I fell to the ground somewhere in the hallway after I felt far enough away from him. "He raped me," I whispered to myself, hugging my knees to my chest. "He raped me…"

CHAPTER THREE

RAY

I SAT THERE, STUNNED, THINKING THIS HAD TO BE SOME SORT of nightmare. I could still hear the echoes of her screams, coming from somewhere in the halls.

"He raped me!"

Her voice was getting farther and farther away. The door was still ajar from her sudden episode and subsequent escape. I couldn't wrap my mind around what just happened. But I didn't have time to. My jailhouse instincts took over and told me to get the fuck out of there.

I got dressed, quickly. I grabbed my watch, trying to plan my escape route. I was in a power player's penthouse, surrounded by people who would take her word over mine without hesitation. The ex-con. I was the one with the colored past here. The one with a record. And I wasn't naïve enough to think otherwise, no matter how innocent I was. I'd played that game once before—and lost.

I was in a panic, surrounded by impending chaos soon to ensue. Thoughts flew in and out of my mind, and the confusion would have crippled me had I not needed to move. I wanted to find Isabella, to ask her what happened, what went wrong. But I couldn't. Not now. Not in the state she was in and certainly not with all the security around. All I could hear was her voice, yelling the same thing, over and over again. *He raped me.*

She must have gone to the side of the penthouse where Salerno and his wife were, as well as some of the live-in staff. I started to hear some additional screaming, faint rustling of feet, becoming hurried. I rushed into the hallway and was about to turn right into another hallway toward the elevator, but a staff member sounded an alarm in the kitchen area, which told me there was no way of getting out without the security credential Salerno had given me. I had to go back for it.

I turned back into the room and saw the security pass sitting next to the alarm clock, and as I did, I noticed something else blending into the sheets. Isabella's white negligee. I remembered my jailhouse friend, Cuba.

"You're going to walk out of prison thinking and acting like a criminal," he had said. "You'll see. You'll develop Spiderman-type senses behind these walls and things will come to you without even thinking."

With the alarm blaring, I felt the pressure to run even more. As if second nature, I grabbed the negligee and stuffed it into my pocket then headed to the hallway. I could hear people starting to run toward my part of the penthouse, undoubtedly coming to confront me. I left the room before they could get too close. Instead of heading right toward the elevator, I quickly glanced left and less than five feet away was an obscure door with a small window pane. Something told me these were the emergency stairs that Isabella took to my room.

I was on my way, racing the sounds above me, but had almost 50 floors to go to get to the bottom. The pace I went down the stairs fainted the alarm sound above me with each floor I passed. As my feet took the steps, thoughts of my kids ran through my head. Their father, accused of rape. I couldn't allow it.

As I reached the lobby, I took a quick glance outside the small window pane of the stairwell. Four beefy security guards were waiting by the elevator with an auxiliary gate they'd set up to block the front entrance. I had no choice but to go down another flight of stairs. There was a sign that pointed around a hallway that said "Service Entrance" and a bright red sign that said "EXIT". I slammed through the door with all my force and realized I was at the side of the building on 56th Street. The rain was coming down hard, with lightning crashing through the air, creating low visibility. *Just what a criminal on the run would hope for.*

I shook my head and ran through the cold rain as if it were a race. *Should I go to the Four Seasons or will they be there waiting for me?* If I didn't go there for the stack of cash I had in the hotel safe, I wouldn't be able to make it very far anyway. I couldn't think about what just happened, I could only focus on what was in front of me. Having some physical evidence eased me as much as it could, but thoughts raced in my mind of the corruption I would face in a Manhattan courtroom as an already convicted felon. If I surrendered they wouldn't give me bail, so there was no sense in thinking about that.

I reached the *Four Seasons* and walked in, slowly, into the front entrance on 57th Street. I was dripping wet, but being that it was NYC on a Saturday night, no one would think much of it. I got to my room and grabbed only what was important, leaving the rest behind. Most of the hotel guests had retired for the night. I calmly hit the down button on the elevator, and when I walked out, I noticed some additional staff waiting around the front desk. They didn't seem too alarmed, so I kept walking.

"Sir!" one of the male managers yelled. "We need to check your ID."

Just as I started to hightail out the front door to reach a cab, I could hear the walkie-talkies coming from the main lobby area. If I had never stayed at that hotel before, I may have been caught, but I knew there was a back entrance on 58th Street. The rest of the female staff members ran to the front of the lobby to alert the police.

"Here he is, officer!" one of them yelled.

The cops looked slightly confused as they reached the check-in desk, but I didn't have time to study their movements. I slipped outside and across the street through a crowd of people waiting in line to get into a nightclub, even though it was pouring rain. *Only in New York.*

I knew this part of the city pretty well since I used to have a crash pad on the Upper East Side back in the heydays of the late 90s. I also knew that with Ari's connections, and my past criminal record, a manhunt would be on for me immediately.

I wasn't scared to go back to prison. I figured based on recidivist rates that it could always be a possibility. But as a rapist—or rape-o, as we say in prison—no. I couldn't fathom that thought. I wasn't running to avoid being caught, I was running to save evidence and try to prove my innocence. Once convicted, twice shy. I knew I'd be presumed guilty. This was just the norm in America now.

I crossed Park Avenue and headed east. Park was busy, with a ton of traffic. I could see multiple police cars with their sirens blaring, red and blue lights flashing. I exited Park down 61st Street, my old block. This was a street I had walked many times. As I meandered down 61st, each time I saw a headlight I didn't like the looks of, I would drop into one of the townhouse basement entryways until it passed. I continued to check to make sure I had Isabella's white negligee still stuffed in my pocket, and while taking some time tucked away, I gathered my thoughts. I needed to start building my defense.

I knew the negligee and past texts corroborating her desires for me would be a good start. I also knew, within a matter of time, the NYPD would have my cell phone number and trace it through GPS tracking. So I turned it off, hoping it would be enough to stop them from getting a quick trace on me.

I continued east on 61st and the further I got from the *Four Seasons*, I could sense that I was almost in the clear. But just as I thought that, a cop with his lights on turned down the top of 3rd Avenue. I figured I was about to be caught, but I didn't panic. I refused to.

Instead, I jumped down into one of the brownstone basement stairwells and tried to get low behind a few garbage cans. But there were two large rats sitting there, and I hated rats—both the real and metaphorical kind. I thought of the rat, JB, in my indictment, and kicked one of them so hard they both went running.

The cop was driving awfully slowly now, creeping up the block, shining bright lights up and down each side of the sidewalk. It was a quiet neighborhood street; traffic was heading west toward Lexington. He was shining lights on all the stragglers walking in the rain. I got parallel to the basement stoop, behind the garbage cans. I heard the sirens getting closer, watched the lights move up the block in tandem with the methodical movement of the car, which was now approaching me. The lights moved slower, too, almost to a stop. My heart pounded so hard I thought they could hear it. Then I felt the light's heat against my skin and knew the cops wouldn't be able to miss me. But finally, the light was brightest now, just above my head, the car slowly rolling up near me. I could hear the police radio frequency with the car window down. The car stopped, and then, as if frozen in time, the light passed me by.

I would make a beeline to 3rd Avenue, which was only 150 yards or so away. I gathered everything I had tightly in my hand and dashed like I was back in high school playing football again. I didn't look back. I was going through whatever was in front of me at that point, cop or no cop. I reached 3rd Avenue and saw a couple trying to get a cab. I jumped in front of them, which was beyond rude on a night when the city was so rainy and cabs were at a premium. The guy didn't take kindly to it. His knee jerk reaction was to jump back and look at me like he was ready to square up.

"I'm sorry, man," I blurted out. "It's an emergency." I jumped in the cab, but the driver didn't want to leave. I took out a wad of cash. "Here's a hundred for you," I said, handing the bill to the driver. I took another hundred and crumpled the bill so it wouldn't fly away in the wind. I handed it to the guy I stole the cab from. "Here, for your troubles. I'm very sorry. Really."

The couple looked stunned, but the man nodded.

I had no more time to waste. The cabbie wasn't moving fast enough so I closed the door hard. "Now take me to Wall Street!"

Then, the cabbie hit the gas and peeled off.

I leaned my head against the window, refusing to look behind me. All I could hear now was the rain thundering against the cab and Isabella's voice in my head.

He raped me.

He raped me.

He raped me.

CHAPTER FOUR

ISABELLA

In the penthouse, it was complete chaos. I thought I heard someone say there wasn't a citywide man hunt out for Ray—yet—but that the police would be apprehending him for questioning. My father was already hell-bent on getting justice for this. Having Ray's head on a spike.

There's no way to tell if a crime has actually occurred, sir.

I could hear it on loop. The detective's voice in my head. His calm, monotone response to my father's outbursts and threats. People were awake, already taking sides. I tuned them out. All of them. My mother, as usual, was distant. She played the part—the concerned and caring mother—to the cops. But me? I was always just something slightly more than invisible to her. Something she knew was there but pretended not to see. I didn't even care anymore. And now, in this moment, I cared about absolutely nothing. Numbness, I think that's what I was feeling.

I sat in the kitchen at the table, staring. Robe still on. A blanket slung over my shoulders. A steaming mug of tea in front of me, untouched. My mother sat across from me. She had tried to hold my hand—I think for show—but I snatched it out of her reach without a word. I wouldn't talk. To anyone. My mother, my father, the police. No one. I didn't want to speak to any of these people. I sat. I stared. I thought. At times, I wasn't even thinking. It was just a cloud through me. A foggy haze of a distant memory. A question as to what just happened. And they all kept asking me about it.

How could I answer them when I didn't have an answer for myself? Trauma. Your response to it. It slides in sometimes when you least expect it. I thought I was over my fight or flight response to sex and romantic encounters. I thought I was past all that.

"Why isn't she moving, huh? Why is she just sitting there, staring?" my father wondered aloud. "Aren't you gonna do something?" he asked, tone increasingly louder.

"This isn't atypical. Sometimes, rape victims go into shock after crimes like this occur," the detective said.

I tuned them out again. I heard my mother and father start arguing. Right there. In front of everyone. The Special Victims Unit detective tried to speak to me again. He tried to urge me to go to the trauma center with them to be checked. He said something about wanting to administer a rape kit, to get a *thorough sexual assault forensic exam.* And *the sooner we go, the better.*

The Salernos said their goodbyes to my parents, telling them they were going back to their home in Short Hills to get *out of the way.* They didn't say goodbye to me. No one wants to talk to you when you're damaged. When you're clearly suffering a slight disconnect with reality.

When you've just accused someone of rape.

I heard the one cop mention that Ray was an ex-con, and a high-profile one at that. And then the vultures started circling. More showed up. More police, more detectives, more questions. More everything. They seemed eager to start *cracking the case*, as the one had said. I heard him say it'd be much easier to convict an ex-con *in a case like this.* That they had a big story on their hands and a chance to land Raymond Jansen in state prison *for the next 20 years, plus.* What was that I heard in his tone? Joy? It almost seemed like the cops were happy about all this.

The lead investigator on the case arrived and I looked up at him. He was an older, Irish-looking man, wearing a rain hat and what looked like old clothes. He had a wet, unlit cigar hanging from his lips. I found him typical and unimpressive. He walked over to my father and held out his hand. I dropped my eyes but kept my ears open.

"Stu O'Neill," he said.

"Ari Rohnstein."

Stu's voice lowered when he spoke again. "Look, we know this guy pretty well in our office. He's a bad guy, but pretty sophisticated with the law in his own right. Thinks he's smart. So, if we don't follow protocol to a T, I'm sure he'll dig up some scum lawyer to expose us at trial. We need to get your daughter to the hospital. Immediately."

My mother heard this, seeming to notice the mounting pressure building in the room around us. "Ari, we need to do something. Now," she said. "Get your daughter up and convince her she has to go. She won't listen to me. She never has."

"I got this, Michele," my dad said, authoritative as always, regardless of the situation. "Just stay calm."

She cursed under her breath at him and walked away, angry footsteps heading the direction opposite of him.

My father leaned in toward Stu as I picked my eyes up.

"I don't care what you have to do. I want him paying for this. Do you hear me?" my dad said.

Stu nodded. "Let's get her to the hospital."

I looked up in time to see Stu walk away, into another

conversation with another nameless uniformed cop. I stared across the room, hatred burning through me. My parents were across the kitchen, speaking in hushed and hurried tones.

"We need to get that test done. We need to make sure she's okay," my mom insisted, frenzy in her voice.

"Hang on a minute," my dad said. "We cannot have the media catch wind of this and spin it in a certain way. How do you think we'll look when they find out our daughter was in bed with an ex-con? Figuratively and literally speaking."

He spat the last words out and I could almost taste the disgust on his tongue.

I knew then, I had no choice.

They tried to convince me to go to their hospital in Harlem, the one that specializes in sex crimes forensics, but I refused at first. It took them hours of poking and prodding, as if I was being interrogated, but I finally agreed to go.

CHAPTER FIVE

RAY

I RODE IN THE CAB DOWN THE FDR IN THE POURING RAIN, taking in the blurry city lights and thundering raindrops over the East River, wondering if this would be my last ride as a free man. I felt like this was my worst nightmare coming true. Having to possibly go back to prison, but as a sex offender. I knew what it was like in there. Regardless of the circumstances, if I lost this case, I'd have zero respect on the inside this time around. I knew one thing. If I had any shot at beating this rap, I had to stay one step ahead of the DA.

I asked the cabbie to drop me off at Battery Park, knowing it would be a ghost town on a rainy Friday night. And I was right. Not a soul in sight, just the Statue of Liberty looming in the foggy harbor. Exactly as I'd hoped. I figured it was about 1:30AM at this point, and I had to hurry. My iPhone was off, but I slammed it into the ground and stomped on it to disable any semblance of its computing system, then threw it into the harbor for good measure.

I walked over to Broadway, just south of the big bull, and turned down Stone Street to head toward *Nebraska Steakhouse*, a place where I used to have Friday power lunches with the boys. The owners and employees in this neighborhood bar were like family to me, especially the manager, Mike, who I knew would be closing the place around 2AM before making the long trek home to Connecticut.

Mike was a family man, but also an ex-con. He did a five-year bid at Otisville for stabbing some guy that disrespected his family, something unacceptable to an Albanian. We had our pasts and one shared trait in common—loyalty—among other things that the normal Joe couldn't relate to unless he'd been upstate like we had. When you're among your people like this, you don't have to speak certain things. There's a mutual understanding. And I knew if there was one place in Manhattan I could go right now and be safe, it was there.

Mike seemed surprised to see me in the alley in the rain, where he was smoking his customary Marlboro red. "Jansen, how the hell are you?" he asked in his slow and heavy accent.

His face changed when he saw I wasn't here for a regular old visit, and I didn't have time to shoot the shit. "Mike, I need your help. I'm in some trouble."

"What happened?"

"It has to do with that girl Isabella I was telling you about a few weeks ago. It's a long story, but all I can say is you have to believe me. What she's claiming I did, you know I would never do. I'll leave it at that. I can't talk about it, but by the end of the weekend it'll be all over the papers."

Mike took in the words and nodded. "What can I do for you?"

"I need you to keep the back door unlocked when you leave so I can hide out here overnight. They're looking for me. If anyone finds me here, I'll say I broke in. You have my word."

"No problem, Jansen," Mike said, holding out his hand, as if consummating a deal.

I explained my plan to him to be out of there in the morning. I didn't know the specifics beyond that. "Just don't mention this to anyone," I reminded him.

He promised, gave me a brief hug, then went inside to close down the restaurant.

I LAY on the long booth that wrapped around the upstairs lounge, grateful to finally be able to rest my body and mind and plot my next move. I didn't get far though. Sleep took me rapidly.

AS THE SUN rose from the east and began to make its way over the New York Harbor to the south, the first rays of light began to creep into the front of *Nebraska*, startling me awake. I shot up and went downstairs to make a phone call to one of the guys I knew I could trust. Andy, my friend who had just come home from serving 17 years of an 8 to 25 for manslaughter.

Andy and Frankie were my two main friends in prison. Both were downstate city guys like me. Frankie was part of a crew from the Bronx who was part of the Fiore crime family, and his ties were closest to mine in Jersey. We had mutual friends from Howard Beach and Wall Street. Andy's crew, on the other hand, was based out of Brooklyn, and the Balboni family was going through some tough times on the street with defections of rats at the top of the family. Andy's family was even stripped of their representation on the five-family membership committee during his time in prison.

This led to a power struggle between Frankie and Andy, with me constantly in the middle trying to mediate. The issue being we were all white with Italian blood—at least me in part—forced to stick together on the inside as one. It was just the way it was, regardless of any personal differences.

I pulled out their numbers that I had written down while in the cab and dialed Andy's house in Staten Island where he was living with his wife. I dialed twice, with the ringing echoing in my ears. No answer. I knew he had to be there based on his parole guidelines. I called again, cursing under my breath. Third time was the charm.

"Hello?" Andy asked, annoyed. "Who the fuck is this?"

"Andy, it's Ray. I'm in trouble. I need your help."

"No talking on the phone. You know that. Where you at?"

"I'm at the steakhouse downtown. The one we met at when you came home."

"I'll be there in an hour," he said, hanging up.

When he got there, he came in through the back and I gave him the rundown. Andy was good in these situations. Despite his volatility in prison which often led to violence, when it came to others he was eerily calm in tense moments. I assured Andy I didn't do it. Whether he believed me or not was undetermined. There was a certain amount of skepticism in his eyes, in the way he watched me when he listened. When I swore to him that I did nothing wrong. He told me he wouldn't turn his back on me—unless proof showed otherwise.

He offered to hide me out at his home in South Amboy that was being renovated, just over the Outerbridge Crossing on the Jersey side. We both knew he had strict parole guidelines not to associate with felons or commit new crimes, and the fact that he would soon be harboring the most wanted man in New York could easily land him back in prison on a parole remand for the final eight years of his 25-year max. He didn't care though. That was just the way it was when you created a jailhouse bond. You stuck together—inside and outside—and you expected the same favors in return. No questions asked. Even though, the crime in this case that was being questioned was on an entire other level. You don't associate or side with a rape-o, period.

As we headed through the Brooklyn Battery Tunnel toward Jersey, I started to instruct Andy on what to do in order to find me a lawyer.

I pulled Isabella's negligee out of my pocket and gave it to him. "Here. This should have her DNA on it. I think it'll help exonerate me.

Andy wasn't dumb. He knew I was nice with the law, especially after spending countless hours in the law library and becoming a bona fide jailhouse lawyer. He mostly listened, until he voiced his concerns.

"Look pal, this might not be easy for me to do. If this girl is Ari Rohnstein's daughter, I don't know how many lawyers in the city will want to bang against the DA and Ari alongside an ex-con and now accused rape-o," Andy said flat out, in his brutally honest thick Brooklyn accent.

"I understand that, but I need you to go out on a limb for me here," I said. "I'm innocent, Andy, you have the evidence right there. I can't come forward yet. Not until I get a good lawyer."

"I got you," he said, "but you gotta realize my family won't condone getting one of our house lawyers on this for a potential sex offender. Murd'a, yeah, but not this type of case." He took his eyes off the road and looked at me to make sure I understood. "You feel me, cuz?"

I knew this was typical jailhouse logic, or illogic. Murderers are viewed as men of honor in certain instances whereas sex offenders never are. We both lived it and understood it, but I also knew there was some defense lawyer out there who would love to get his face on TV, especially if he had a shot at winning. It was just the way it worked. And if Andy advocated for me, it would only help.

"Look, here's what you do. Go see my ex-bail bondsman, Ira Judleson. He's right by the courthouse in Tribeca," I said.

I knew that Ira, "The Bail Bondsman to the Stars" as he was billed in the papers, would do his best to get me the perfect lawyer. After all these years, I was still one of the biggest clients of Ira's career. Sure, he handled all the celebrities with large bails, including ex-NY Giants' Plaxico Burress when he shot himself, but it was my original $5MM bail that Ira wrote about in his novel as his biggest commission ever, and the largest insurance bond ever posted in New York State criminal history.

My family paid Ira a $250K fee for his efforts in getting me released after 120 days on Rikers, and I knew he'd never forget that. We even stayed in touch after my release. He knew the Manhattan DA and the judges well, and he knew how to play the system. It was part of his job, knowing every lawyer in the city. They all sent him business and he referred them cases, too. If there was anyone who could help get me the right lawyer, it was Ira.

"Call Frank and ask him to go see Ira with you. I'm gonna need his help, too. He owes me," I said to Andy.

"I'll try, but you know how he is. He might say you gotta clear your name on your own first."

"Just tell him I don't have it in my paperwork yet," I said. "I'll make it up to you guys. I promise."

Frankie's motto with accepting a guy in prison or not was, "Whatever his paperwork says he is, he is," meaning he wasn't going to take in a sex convict and try to justify it in any way. It was kind of similar to the famous quote from

NFL football coach Bill Parcells when talking about a team's reputation: "You are what your record says."

Andy nodded, agreeing to everything just as we pulled up outside his home. "Fine. I'll call him. I'll be back on Monday. Don't use the phone and don't go out of the house. I'll bring back some more food then. You got enough snacks in here for now. I just want you to know we don't want any payback for helping a friend, but you understand that if we go out on a limb for you and you're guilty, then you're going to have a problem bigger than the DA when you get back up top?" he said harshly.

"Yeah, Andy, I know," I said. "I wouldn't come to you if I wasn't innocent. You gotta know that."

Andy gave me a kiss on the cheek. "Hang in there, kid."

And with that, he left. And I was left imagining what would happen to me in prison if I *was* found guilty.

THE NEXT DAY, Andy called me from his burner phone to tell me my name was in the Sunday papers. By Monday, the full-blown story was out. The New York tabloids blew it up and before long, it became a national story, especially since Rohnstein was such a big media player. My picture was splattered everywhere. The *Post* was the least kind to me with their headline, "Convicted Stock Scum, Now Alleged Rapist".

One blogger linked Isabella's appearance to that of my ex-wife, calling her a "younger-looking, prettier version" of the kind of women I "target". I cursed to myself, hoping my kids hadn't gotten wind of any of this shit. What kind of role model would they view me as if they saw these headlines? And worse, would they believe it? Even if just for a second?

I worked hard as a father to make sure my boys had a good example. I wasn't about to let this bullshit break that mold.

I didn't have much time to think about that, though. The pressure was on to find me. There was an evening press conference in which the DA said that I could be "armed and dangerous". I watched in horror from the drawn shades of the South Amboy hideout, wondering if Andy would be back today like he said he would, or if he saw the headlines and was bailing on me now. I was getting paranoid that the NYPD was planning to murder me, based on that armed and dangerous comment. The more that was mentioned, the more I thought I needed to turn myself in.

I rationalized that going back to prison—even as a sex offender—would be better than being dead. I knew my paranoia and conspiracy theories were getting the best of me, but there was no mistaking it. The more I evaded this, the worse I would look in the public eye. I remembered the public's perception of OJ Simpson in the famous white Bronco chase in the summer of 1994 and could almost feel the stifling heat inside that truck, the cameras on me, the public outcry for justice. The only difference being my actual innocence here.

I felt like I was already in prison again, only this was a different kind of prison, and the only choice I had now was to lay up and be patient. And wait. For whatever would transpire next.

CHAPTER SIX

AP

AS A LAWYER, YOU NEVER KNOW WHAT YOU'RE GOING TO get on any given day. I wouldn't necessarily say anything is ever *typical* in the common sense of the word. But the firm I worked for was about to be involved with a high-profile case involving an accused rapist. And not just your typical guy off the street, but a guy who had been down this road before, only the last time for stock fraud. Rape and fraud were two totally different things, and I was hesitant to be part of his defense team without meeting the guy first. Raymond Jansen. I Googled him prior to introductions, before even agreeing to be on the case. When it came to celebrities or wealthy and well-known clients, you needed to do your homework or you'd look like a damn fool. And me? I'd worked too hard for that.

Raymond Jansen—known as just "Ray" or "Jansen" to his friends—seemed hard to pin. There wasn't much online I could find about him regarding his recent personal life. There was one picture of him and his wife in the Winners Circle with one of his thoroughbreds at Monmouth Park. The picture was from September 2001, a week before 9/11, and the couple looked happy at the time.

He had no social media, making him seem more like a mystery than anything. Did he strike me as your quintessential bad guy? Nah. Based strictly off his looks, this guy didn't seem like he'd have a hard time getting the attention of women, but you learn quickly in my field that you can't judge someone's character off their good looks. I'd met some people who were pretty attractive at first glance, only to discover they were some of the most hideous people I'd ever encountered.

The articles relating to his stock scam arrest were littered all over the web from every major newspaper and financial publication. Through research, it seemed that back in the late 90s and early 2000s the mob had their hands in a bunch of the smaller firms on Wall Street. My guess was that he had some part in it, eventually pleading guilty to State RICO after his 2006 indictment. Not my case. Not my problem. And quite frankly, none of my business at this point in my representation.

My boss, and head attorney at his firm, Anthony Mika, received a cautionary heads up phone call from Ira Judleson, who said he referred two of Ray's buddies to us after they stormed into his office earlier that day demanding his help. I overheard the phone call. Anthony's responses, anyway. Ira suggested to Anthony that he may be interested in taking this on since Ari Rohnstein was involved. And that was all he had to hear.

Ari Rohnstein and Anthony had a business dispute almost two decades ago. It seemed that Rohnstein needed to be "straightened out" as we'd say in Pittsburgh.

We left an important court appearance for another client just to get back to the office to meet with Raymond Jansen's associates. Anthony's call. We'd been following the story in the news since it broke over the weekend, and the tension and heat were only building since then.

The building our office was in was considered an "A" real estate building, located right on Madison Avenue, only a few train stops away from the courthouse. But Anthony Mika & Partners, in particular, needed a makeover. And maybe not just the office, which had old press clippings dating back to more than 20 years ago strewn about. One was about the 1988 big mob acquittal when Anthony was still an unknown lawyer on his way up. Unfortunately for us, the office décor hadn't changed much since the dates on those articles.

When drinking, Anthony liked to tell me there was a time in the late 90s when the market was rolling, when he had substantially grown his net worth and began dabbling in commercial, personal injury, and real estate law. He said he had his hands in everything by the time he hit his 40s. *The sky was the limit,* he'd say, with a faraway look in his eyes. He reached celebrity status—well, for lawyers anyway—and not only in New York, but nationwide.

But also when drinking, he liked to talk about how the market crumbled in 2000. How his business was highly leveraged as he got further away from criminal law, which was always his bread and butter revenue stream. He was a fighter though—his words. He thought he could pull through with a major commercial transaction that he was assured would make him bigger than ever. Of course that was *before* Ari Rohnstein pulled a fast one on him that ruthlessly cut Anthony out of the deal, basically stealing his non-refundable deposit while at it.

Anthony tried to report it to the DA at the time, but they had no interest since he was a defense lawyer, and they insisted that he *should have known better*. Sometimes he mumbles this while cursing out the DA. He didn't have the money or energy then to sue Rohnstein.

After his business started to crumble, Anthony spiraled. Then 9/11 happened. He says his financial future collapsed almost as quickly as the towers downtown did. He not only lost his money, but he almost lost his mind, too.

But I still had faith in him. Anthony Mika, the once great and powerful, was now in his 60s. And while he clearly had lost a step somewhere and his mind wasn't as sharp, he still had all the drive in the world. That, in addition to common sense and a firm belief in defending his clients, was enough to make me stay with him. Education. Growth. Experience. That was what I got with Anthony.

There was no denying that his reputation was gone, though. All the new hot shot lawyers in the city were now taking the big cases that used to come his way. He'd gotten rid of most of his staff, but he couldn't let go of the office. Plus, he said it was cheaper to stay than to move at this point. He was in the process of trying to rebuild his practice and reputation, and the only way he could do that was by going back to *only* criminal law and proving he could win big cases again. On a small-scale level, it was working. But when he got the call about Mr. Jansen, that was it. He insisted we drop everything for this. I couldn't tell if it was more to get Ari or his legacy back.

We walked into the reception area in the office and spotted the two hulking figures that Ira had described to a T. Anthony walked straight up to them and cut right to the chase, excusing any formalities.

"Anthony Mika," he said, shaking both their hands. "Come on in, gentlemen, right to my office."

He shot me a look and I saw it there. The subtle grin, playing on the corners of his mouth. This was making him happy. I couldn't help but fight a smile back. I followed

Anthony and both men into his office, then closed the door behind me. We all sat. Anthony in his chair behind his desk, the two men in the two chairs in front. And me, I took the seat against the wall in the center where I could see everything while still going largely unnoticed.

"Thanks for seeing us on such short notice," the one man said. "I'm Frankie." He nodded his head to the side. "This is Andy. We're friends of Ray."

"Look, boys," Mika said, "I'm not gonna bullshit you. You need to get Jansen in here immediately. I'll take the case initially just so he gets a little representation at arraignment, but if I don't feel that he's innocent, I'm dropping the case. And that's all there is to it."

"All due respect, Mr. Mika, but if Ray is guilty, we'll deal with him on our own, whether he's on the street or locked up," Andy said. "But I can tell you one thing. He's a good guy. And we have evidence that will exonerate him."

Anthony's ears perked up. He was leaning back in his chair but leaned forward a bit at this. The interest grew, just like that. But he played it well. "Don't tell me anything about the case right now. I don't want to hear anything until I have him retained. Get him in here tomorrow and tell him he needs to be ready to surrender." Then, he stopped for a moment, seemingly collecting his thoughts before he stood up. "And tell your friend he's coming to the right place. Let's just say I'm not so fond of Rohnstein."

Frankie and Andy stood up as well. They all shook hands again, and Frankie assured Anthony they would have Ray at his office the next day.

Then, Andy pulled something out and held it up. It looked like a women's nightie. Some little white, sheer number. Looked expensive, too. Something a Rohnstein daughter might purchase.

"Mr. Mika, I think it'd be best if you hold onto this

evidence and discuss it with Ray. To tell you the truth, I don't know how I feel carrying something like this in my pocket anymore. Although it wouldn't be the first time, if you catch my drift. Just, different circumstances." Andy said, smiling, sending a wink my way.

I tried not to smile and shook my head. I hated to admit it, but these street guys did have a certain charm to them. No bullshit, no pretentiousness. A certain bluntness and wit that usually got them what they wanted. In all areas of life, I imagined.

"Lovely," Anthony said dryly. Then he looked at me. "Alexandra, could you put that in the file cabinet behind you?"

I nodded, getting up and retrieving the apparently-used women's garment from Andy, holding it out so as not to get any, uh, fluids on me.

"We'll wait for Ray to get here before we take that out again," Anthony said.

I scrunched my face and nodded. Something told me *this* would be interesting.

We didn't know what was on that negligee, or where it came from. And I'm sure Mr. Jansen didn't know he just got his first big break in his case before the cuffs even went on him.

CHAPTER SEVEN

RAY

It was early Tuesday when I heard the rumbling of an engine outside the house that had become my fugitive hideout. I jumped up and peered through the blinds, thinking it was the cops. Instead, I saw Andy and Frankie walking up to the door. I didn't feel the warmest of welcomes from Frankie.

"Sorry I couldn't get back here last night," Andy said. "We spent the whole day working on your case. We got some good news, though."

I sat up. "Let me hear it."

"We saw the bail bondsman," Frankie said. "He referred us to Anthony Mika."

"Are you serious?" I asked. "That guy is a dinosaur."

"Hey, pal, beggars can't be choosers. And let me tell you something, you got lucky even getting him," Frankie said.

"Why?" I asked, curiosity settling in.

"He had a beef with Rohnstein years ago. Otherwise I doubt he'd have been interested. A thank you would be nice." Frankie folded his hands and looked at me with a solemn face.

"Thank you," I said, not understanding why Frankie seemed so perturbed, but I knew better than to poke the bear.

"And there's one condition, *pal,*" Frankie said, with some sharpness in his tone. "You need to be a hundred percent innocent, you hear me? Not just for him, but for us, too. You understand? Because if you're playing me, you know what the result will be. You remember what happened to Los upstate in the yard, right?"

I stood up. "C'mon, you saw the negligee, Frankie. I didn't do this shit. Not even close. You wanna help me or not?"

Frankie narrowed his eyes at me, like he was deciphering whether or not I was telling the truth, then sighed. "Yeah. I'll help you. I'll talk to my boss, Tony Annello, make sure Mika takes the case. But you understand you cannot take a plea?"

"Geez, Frank. I know. It's innocence or bust," I said.

Andy interrupted us, probably trying to stop wherever this was going. "Look, Ray, we gotta get you back to the city now so go get ready. Take this stuff to disguise yourself." He tossed me a bag. "We'll be taking you right to Mika's office and he'll turn you in after you sign the retainer agreement with him."

I looked at the bag with a Yankee flat-cap and oversized shades inside, then at Frankie. The way he was looking at me, questioning my innocence, even as my friend, I knew I'd better get used to that. And I knew it'd be worse from strangers. All I could do now was ride this out. At least I had a lawyer. At least I had one person on my side. Even if he doesn't give a shit about me, he might pretend like he does.

CHAPTER EIGHT

AP

Anthony scheduled a 4:30PM press conference outside the courthouse, right before the five o'clock news—the high time for media exposure. It was my first buzz-worthy case, and maybe the biggest Anthony had in almost 20 years. He still had some loyal contacts in the media world, and for a hot story like this, they were all in. He only let his key media members know the purpose of it, the ones he *knew* didn't like Ari and his own media hounds. Anthony wasn't dumb. He knew they were the only reporters he could use to counteract what Ari and the DA would undoubtedly do. It was only a matter of time before they tried to assassinate our client's character in the press. But after we saw the physical evidence, and after Anthony met Ray, he said he was feeling pretty good about the case.

I hadn't gotten a chance to meet the infamous Ray Jansen yet. Anthony liked to remind me that I "wasn't ready" for certain things. That he needed to introduce certain elements slowly. Feel his clients out first before bringing me in. I got it. I also thought there was a small chance he didn't want to bring me around a potential rapist, which I could appreciate.

Although, from what I gathered, he didn't seem to think Ray was guilty—yet.

Nothing could have prepared me for the media frenzy. It was bigger than even Anthony expected, but he stood up there, dressed his best. He ditched his dated suits for a younger, sharper one, and stood tall at the podium, looking attentive in his navy suit, almost like he did 20 years ago. He was prepared to set the tempo of his defense from the word "go". He explained to me that so many Manhattan cases were fought through the newspapers, and he needed to take the fight to them. The goal? To immediately put doubt in the minds of potential jurors. His statement was brief, and he didn't take any questions.

I watched him, mentally taking notes. Anthony started the press conference with the fact that he had been retained by Raymond Jansen, and that Mr. Jansen would be turning himself in within a few hours to begin the process of proving his innocence. He then read the statement he prepared.

"My client is 100% innocent, and there will be no pleas in this case. Either the charges will be dismissed or fought in front of a fair jury. Due to the high-profile nature of this case, my team of lawyers and I will be closely monitoring it for any possible corruption." Then he made eye contact with the cameras. "All we ask is that our client gets a fair trial without the influence of any outside forces."

And I knew that was directed at Ari. I grinned, proud of him. To some, it may have been perceived as an unnecessary statement and a bold defense maneuver, especially considering he was representing a possible sex offender *and* an ex-con. But it certainly set the tone, showcasing just how deep Anthony was willing to go to win this case. And anyone that knew his history with Ari knew *exactly* what he was referencing.

No matter what the legal eagles were saying about the

case, the stage was set for one of the biggest heavyweight legal fights on Centre Street that Manhattan had seen in some time. And I was here for it, counting my blessings for the opportunity to be involved.

Later that night, Anthony surrendered Ray to the DA's offices at 7PM. After treating him to a nice steak dinner and a few glasses of red wine, he'd be expected to endure the grueling bull pen therapy at the bottom of the Manhattan Detention Center, aka "The Tombs" as Ray called it. Of course I wasn't invited, and I didn't push to be. It was a night for the "big boys" to talk and engage in private conversation. As a young woman in this industry, you get used to that. I no longer felt insulted by it. Infuriated, though? Maybe a little. I just used it to further my ambition and drive. To show the boys who could really wear the pants in the courtroom.

Anthony called me that night after Ray was in custody. He said they briefly discussed the case, and Ray assured him he never ejaculated—a key element in defending a case like this. Without a semen sample, it made proving motive much harder. I could hear the sense of excitement in Anthony's voice, the feeling that we just may be victorious in this thing. In the beginning, it was palpable. Contagious, even.

CHAPTER NINE

RAY

NOW THAT I WAS IN CUSTODY, THE DA ONLY HAD A LIMITED amount of days to bring an indictment. It was a constitutional right under the habeas corpus rule, in Latin meaning "you should have the body". But securing an indictment was typically a formality whenever the DA wanted it, so much so that an old Manhattan chief judge coined the famous phrase: "You can indict a ham sandwich." Knowing this, I didn't think the DA would try to overextend the facts, considering they'd potentially be exposed later at trial.

It was a stark contrast to what was going on in New York City at the same time, where a Staten Island Grand Jury failed to indict the officer who killed Eric Garner. The public wanted the transcripts of the hearings, but they were denied. Moreover, witnesses who were there to assist the DA in securing an indictment—as was their public duty—were actually discredited by the DA himself, by disparaging their character. Not only was the public starting to take notice, but they were shaking their heads in disgust. And all races and religions were starting to protest in Manhattan at impromptu marches.

My indictment got the headlines the DA probably wanted, but there were already issues with it—mainly that they were all untrue, not like they gave a shit. In the end, the only statement used to indict me in front of the Grand Jury was: "Perp forcibly threw victim to bed when she was bringing him some water. He pulled her robe and underwear off and then forcibly put his penis in her mouth, then forcibly spread her legs and began penetrating and raping her. Victim attempted to fight off perp by pushing his chest off her, while scratching him and pulling his hair as hard as she could. Victim was able to eventually fight perp off. Victim then ran for help, while perp fled on foot."

It was pretty straightforward. False, but straightforward. They would inevitably place me at the scene through a hair follicle or two, a DNA match a given.

The DA's strategy seemed cut and dry like usual, in most cases. Get the indictment and force a plea. It's too easy, especially when you have an ex-con facing too much prison time to risk taking the case to trial.

When it came to securing a conviction, the Manhattan DA's offices were the best in the business. They didn't win 93% of their indicted cases because 93% of the people were actually guilty. They won them because they knew how to manipulate each case to increase their probability in winning. Force people to plead, and wear them down with pre-trial detention on Rikers. It was as simple as that, especially when the DA could convince a judge to effectively deny bail.

Although by 2015—finally—the public was starting to notice as many innocent inmates from all five boroughs were winning appeals, due to gross misconduct from detectives and prosecutors, but only after doing decades of prison time already. Regardless of the advances in DNA technology, the DA never had the same zeal to free someone that was wrongly accused as they did to convict them. It was a gross contradiction to the premise of our Constitution—to protect innocent people from malicious prosecution at all costs.

I witnessed it firsthand in my former case. Every time I found a slight strategic edge, I was smacked back to reality with a new angle by the DA or judges. I never stood a chance, whether I was innocent or not. And after two rough years of enduring the brutal conditions on Rikers Island, I reluctantly took their shitty deal, just like so many others before me.

I always knew the system in New York was flawed, if not outright corrupt. It was common knowledge in the city that judges were always in the DA's pocket. They viewed every defendant that walked into the courtroom with contempt, unless of course they were cooperators. In addition, there was motivation for the judges to remain friendly with the DAs because New York judges are appointed from a nominee process, a process highly dependent on political clout. In essence, the judges who played ball with the DAs and their donors got to stay on the bench for a long career. And so, the defendant's constitutional right to have an impartial judge in New York City was pretty much a complete sham. At least this time, I knew that going in.

The morning of my arraignment, I could faintly see the endless media trucks and vans parked outside 111 Centre Street through the double caged wire and shackles of the Rikers prison bus.

Walking into the courtroom with heavy feet, I looked around me. The familiarity struck me. The bright lights. The hostility. The tension. I never wanted to be back here again. In these cuffs, in this court. In a situation like this.

Anthony Mika greeted me and brought me up front with him, giving me an encouraging nod. I stood to face the court.

"Mr. Jansen, how do you plead to the charges of Rape in the First and Third Degree, Criminal Sexual Act in the First and Third degree, and a Misdemeanor for Resisting Arrest for the fleeing?" the Honorable Katy Beekman asked.

"I'm innocent, judge," I said.

I saw the cartoonist sketching me from the corner of my eye, knowing she was probably drawing me with a mean-looking face that everyone would see in the morning papers the next day. They *wanted* me to look guilty. All of them.

Since the DA broke the bail barrier in my first case, I expected no less this time around, but I felt myself cringe hearing it.

"The people are requesting a $15MM bail," the DA said. "We are dealing with a convicted felon who was the mastermind in a large fraud, which he pled guilty to. We have knowledge that he still has banking relationships abroad and represents a severe flight risk."

I started to chuckle in the court, to publicly make a mockery of the procedure. I would dictate the action this time around, and not let the DA, judges, or media break me. In this case, I'd play fast and loose.

The DA and judge looked at me in contempt, but the media throngs were curious. The bail argument didn't last long at all since Mika didn't really contest bail; he only requested a low bail for me for the sake of putting it on the record. The judge completely ignored it and set bail at $10MM—a number that was simply unattainable for me. I knew in that moment I'd have to fight the case from the inside—again—and leave my kids for a second time.

"Now let's move on to the discovery issues," Judge Beekman said. "The DA is asking for a two-month delay for any documents, statements, etc. Are you willing to grant this request, Mr. Mika?"

"No, Your Honor," Mika said. "My client maintains his innocence 100%, and he'll be invoking his 30.30 right under the Sixth Amendment of the US Constitution for a speedy trial. The DA has indicted Mr. Jansen, they have effectively denied him bail, and we are entitled to discovery by law. We will remain vigilant in requiring the delivery of these reports, including the initial witness statements, which we *expected* to receive at this hearing," he said, loud and incredulous in what looked like an effort to theatrically play to the media. "Where is it, by the way? All we have is an indictment outlining the charges," he added, looking at the ADAs.

I watched their smug faces drop in embarrassment, glad they'd have their hands full with Mika. He wasn't a new breed defense attorney who knew their relationships in the DA's office were more beneficial to their career than fighting hard for their defendants. No, I lucked out because Mika was a throwback defense attorney. He didn't believe in representing cooperators, and by the looks of it, he took his job in zealously defending his clients very seriously. And in this particular case, it was personal to him, which only made him go harder. I counted my blessings that moment in the courtroom.

I looked over at Ari, who was sitting in his seat. A certain level of discomfort washed over him, turning his face almost the same shade as his pale green tie. I couldn't help but look for Isabella and wonder where she was. Something told me Ari was behind the pressing of the charges. Much more so than her. I felt a quick jab to the heart, in the hope that she was okay.

The judge was flustered when she called the parties to the bench for an ex-parte hearing—off the record. I was close enough to listen.

"Now, lawyers, this case is just starting. Can't we work something out here?" she asked, voice low.

Before the DA could respond, Mika jumped in, voice not quite as low. "This is a case in which we will be defending the charges, and I need to be proactive in protecting my client's due process rights to ensure we are dealing with a level playing field. I want all of you to know that the case needs to be fast-tracked. He's not sitting on Rikers for two years. This is a simple case to try and there's absolutely no reason we should be waiting any longer for basic discovery material. If we don't get what is needed, I *will* file motions to compel what I need to defend him."

Judge Beekman sighed. "Okay, you've made your point, Mr. Mika. Let's all try to play nice, especially with the media here, okay? I'll make a ruling on the record." She paused, waiting for the DA and defense attorney to leave the bench. When everyone was back in their places she spoke again, only this time it was loud enough for the entire courtroom to hear. "We are back on the record. In light of Mr. Mika's argument, I'm going to allow a delay in the standard reports for 30 days, however, the time will be charged to the People once I get Mr. Mika's speedy trial motion. We will have another status hearing at that time to ensure that all the documents are provided in a timely manner. Are we all on the same page with this?"

I glanced over at two young ADAs who were assigned to prosecute the case. They looked perplexed about how to deal with the pressure Mika was putting on them regarding the speedy trial motion.

"Your Honor, may I?" the male ADA asked, unsurely. "The People are still doing forensic DNA testing and there is a bit of sensitivity to the victim's rights on some of the medical reports at this time. We will do our best to get this within 30 days, but a lot of it is out of our hands."

"Your Honor," Mika butted in, "these are serious charges levied against my client, and although we have tremendous respect for the alleged victim in this matter, my client has rights. And it is my job to defend him against false accusations. He has a constitutional right to all discovery material that exists right now."

Some snickering was heard in the court, along with muffled laughs and audible gasps, causing the judge to become visibly annoyed.

"Okay, Mr. Mika," she said. "We are not going to turn this case into some media circus with long-winded statements. That's what trials are for. I have given the People 30 days, and I believe in a sex crime like this, they are able to get some latitude on discovery, but considering you have stated your 30.30 request, we will do our best to move the case along quickly. Is that understood to the People?" She glanced over at them.

"Yes, Your Honor. Thank you," the ADA said, respectfully.

"Thank you, Your Honor," Mika said.

"We'll go back on the calendar in 30 days, which should be interesting," Judge Beekman said, the second part under her breath. Then, she looked directly at me. "Now, I want to say something to you, Mr. Jansen. Do you understand the charges against you?"

I nodded.

"Just so we are clear, you have been charged with four felony counts, Rape in the First and Third Degree, and a Criminal Sexual Act in the First and Third Degree as well." And then her voice started to trail. "And you are also charged with a Misdemeanor for fleeing the police and resisting arrest."

Hearing it all made me sick. But I knew exactly why they structured the indictment like they did, including the misdemeanor. I knew then, right out of the gate, what I was up against.

She looked at me with a look of disgust on her face, then continued in a nasty voice. "I just want to advise you—and as I say this, I know you are no stranger to the courtroom—that in the event you go to trial on these charges and you are convicted on the top two counts, you are facing up to 50 years in state prison if I decide to charge you consecutively. And although I am here to provide you with a fair trial, I can tell you to check my history of giving away prison time to repeat felons for violent crimes. I just want you to be aware of this."

"Oh, I'm well aware of it, Your Honor. You're basically a household name on Rikers," I said, with a slight smile.

Interestingly enough though, my comment got a few chuckles out of some of the media members, which only infuriated the judge further. But regardless of how cool and calm I appeared, my heart was racing. Anxiety was spreading, taking off. I lit the match and waited for the familiar burn. And what was driving it was that I was aware that an ex-cop was recently sentenced to 75 years on three consecutive 25-year sentences in New York City for a brutal courtyard rape.

I knew the DA had judge-shopped my case to Katy Beekman. It made sense. She was known for scaring defendants into taking pleas or giving them the maximum if they blew trial. And I wasn't joking with what I said to her. She really did have a reputation throughout the prisons as the one judge you didn't want to go in front of at sentencing. DAs were smart. They often found ways to win in the end, whether it was by hook or by crook.

But this fact also told me something about the DA's case. And in some strange way, I found comfort in that.

CHAPTER TEN

ISABELLA

RAY'S RECENT INDICTMENT AND ARRAIGNMENT BROUGHT A lot of media attention my family's way, even more than usual. My father detested the amount of exposure we were getting over this. I wasn't sure what made him madder. The fact that he was getting negative press, or that he had to stand by his decision with prosecuting Ray in order to look like the *strong father* who *just wanted justice for his daughter.*

By any means necessary.

I didn't want this either. The press. The questions. The cameras in my face. I never even wanted to go to their hospital. It was forced. It seemed like everyone cared less about me and more about the actual potential of getting rid of Ray, once and for all. Even if it was this way, possibly sending him to prison. I closed my eyes and remembered the hospital. The sleek shine of the floors. Everything so clinical. The cold instruments against my body. Inside me. *This won't hurt much.*

Have you ever stood naked in front of someone while they examine you to determine whether or not you've just been raped? Have you ever seen the look of pity in someone's eyes when they look at you like you're a victim? And nothing else?

There are certain things people in my life will never understand. Not my father. Not my mother. Not the reporters. No one.

Ever since the night in question, I kept repeating the same thoughts in my head. *What really happened? What did I even tell them happened? Was I drunk? Did I black out? Do I believe that Ray raped me? Did he rape me? Was my mind playing tricks on me? Am I finally going insane, after all these years?*

It's never too late to crack, I guess. To allow your demons to drown you. Some part of you giving in, giving up. You know it's always been just around the corner. Maybe sometimes it sneaks out and grabs you when you least expect it.

I saw his face on the news a few times. Ray. Each time, I had to turn off the TV. I couldn't look. His sad face. The green eyes, wondering how he got there. I couldn't bear it. I was in the kitchen again, sitting, staring. Hot tea in front of me. I was here most nights. It was where I could still feel him, somewhere. In the penthouse. In my parents' kitchen.

The ring of a telephone distracted me from my thoughts and I heard my father's voice, booming.

"Yeah, but at what cost?" he shouted. "Screw a plea deal. I want him to get all 50 years. Do what you have to do!"

Something slammed. A chair, maybe. Maybe he punched a wall.

50 years. Could he really do that much time?

Initially, I felt violated by Ray. Then, I felt violated again by being forced to get the post-rape kit testing. All of it, so damaging. So invasive.

I watched the steam from the tea and counted my issues

I'd been dealing with all these years. The murder of my biological mother. Being adopted by one of New York's most elite families soon after, only to feel shunned and alone. My own "mother" here, never being a mother. Never seeing me. Never wanting to acknowledge me.

My therapist was right. I should see her more often. I'd been ignoring her emails, checking in on me. She'd heard of the indictment on the news and wanted to know if I was okay.

I got up and got dressed for the first time in what felt like years, though only days had passed. I couldn't escape the paparazzi, the media. The lights, the questions on loop. I put on a hoodie and large sunglasses and left the penthouse, telling my mother I wanted to go for a walk in the park to clear my head. I knew she wouldn't ask too many questions anyway. She never cared about what I did. If anything, she seemed to always take satisfaction in my leaving, especially in my younger years.

I called Dr. Morgan on the way down, who told me she would move some of her patients around to find time to fit me in. And when I got there, I walked into the familiar office and nearly collapsed in her arms when she hugged me.

"I'm so sorry you're going through this," Dr. Morgan said. She grabbed me by the shoulders and looked at me. "Are you okay?"

I wiped my eyes and nodded. "Yeah. I'm okay. I'm fine. Just, confused by everything."

"What do you mean you're confused?" she asked.

I sat in the chair across from her. "I don't know," I said, starting to cry. "I just have all these conflicting emotions. I can't really remember what happened and I don't know what's real and what isn't anymore."

"Isabella," she said, "are you sure you're safe?"

"Yes," I said. "100%. But I need your help."

"You know that I'm here for you, not only as a professional, but also as a friend," she said, pausing, forcing my eyes to meet hers. "But, if you need my help, I need you *here.* It would be best for you to see me two to three times a week until we get through this critical period. I need you to be flexible, though, because you know my schedule is always booked solid."

I nodded, then dove right in. I explained to Dr. Morgan that everyone was tailing me. Not only private investigators, but detectives from the DA's office. At least, that's who I thought they were. I didn't know anymore. But she wouldn't hear it.

"Look, I don't care about any of that," she said. "And you shouldn't either. You should only put your energy into getting some clarity from the inside out. As always, I'll do my best to keep our conversations private, but you understand that if the defense hears about us meeting, they'll do everything they can to get my notes. And I can only protect you so far when it comes to a criminal trial. Do you understand that?"

I nodded. I didn't care anymore. About anything. "I understand. We just, we need to be as discreet as possible. Like we always have."

"I'll try," she said, taking out her calendar book. "How about we meet again early next week, in the evening?"

"Okay," I said, getting up. "I know you have patients to get to, so, I'm gonna get out of here. Thanks for seeing me on such short notice."

"Always," she said. "And take care of yourself, okay? Make sure you call me."

I promised her I would, and left. Hiding my puffy eyes and face with my sunglasses. Blocking out the sunlight. I put my hoodie up and headed back to the penthouse. Back to the luxury in the middle of all this loss.

CHAPTER ELEVEN

RAY

I WAS HOUSED IN THE RIKERS ISLAND'S CLOSED CUSTODY Unit and once again living in the torturous conditions there, a place I never wanted to go back to. Closed Custody was the worst block on "The Rock". It was located in the basement of the "4 building", reserved only for the most high-profile cases and institutional risks of any kind.

I'd been here before, against my will. During my first bid I was kept here on lockdown for a little bit. It wasn't necessarily cozy. This time, I felt nothing going back. It felt more like business as usual. The fact that it didn't scare me was subtly frightening in itself. I kept busy, praying, meditating, and took my half-hour of rec a day, even though the recreation was merely another larger pen that had open air to the outside.

I would go out there, close my eyes, and inhale. Try to tan my face for vitamin D. Fresh air was a luxury, even if it only lasted for 30 minutes. The conditions broke the barrier of cruel and unusual punishment as outlined in the US Constitution. 23 hours a day on lockdown was supposed to be the constitutional max, but Rikers didn't give a shit. They pushed it to 23 1/2 on their own. These conditions were designed to break people down, even drive them to suicide. But for me, I used it as motivation. For strength, determination. To get the fuck out.

The two things that vexed me were that I had no legal work to attack to keep my mind busy. No discovery whatsoever; no medical reports, victim statements, police reports, etc. Nothing. All I had was a basic indictment to breeze through. The second concerning factor was how the hell I would raise the $25K that Mika needed for his staff and his best private investigator. Considering Salerno took a strong stand against me this time, with the circle we hung in following suit, it made it nearly impossible to get any financial support. My mom offered, but seeing the aging on her face at the arraignment, I decided to leave her fully out of it this time. To make matters worse, my business partner in Arizona had a freeze on our company assets from the civil forfeiture department, in case restitution needed to be paid to the victim. *Funny.*

It worked for the DA in my first case, so I wasn't surprised they were trying again, despite it being an unusual play. This left Frankie and Andy as the only people I could reach out to on the street to possibly make a deal with. But I knew this move would cost me in the end.

I got a visit from my lawyer, Mika, and one of his young associates, Alexandra. I couldn't help but notice her. A young brunette, hair up in a bun. She looked serious, but even when she was doing her best to appear solemn and professional, she looked cute. I didn't remember her being *that* cute when we briefly met at the arraignment. Shackles and cuffs don't necessarily keep your blood from pumping. I reminded myself of the situation at hand. And even though I was happy to see them—happy to see any faces, really—I was disappointed that they still had no other discovery material as of yet. They were there, empty-handed but full of encouragement. After our greeting, and asking how I was holding up in here, Mika cut to the chase and did his best to assure me.

"I'm drafting a motion to dismiss the indictment on numerous issues, including the fact that they're withholding Brady material."

Before he could finish, Alexandra jumped in eagerly. "Brady material is any exculpatory or potentially exculpatory evidence that can help your defense. And the DA is required to disclose if they have it in their possession. No questions asked."

I tried to be polite, gave a slight laugh, and said, "Thank you, I am very familiar with Brady."

After a discussion, neither I nor Mika thought it would be enough to dismiss the case, but we agreed that it was the right move to make. The fact that the DA was playing possum with the initial investigative and medical reports only made me think more cynically about their case.

The visit was brief, but succinct. It was nice that they took the ride out and got prepared for the next upcoming court appearance. I truly did appreciate it. It wasn't always easy for a Manhattan lawyer to deal with visiting a client on Rikers, especially a cute, young female attorney who was just a few years out of law school. It was a place that no one needed to see if they didn't have to. And the truth was, most lawyers would prepare to meet you at court and give you a brief update on the defense, never really covering any ground while doing so.

I shook their hands and told them I'd see them in court. But upon their leaving, I thought more of my legal team. We seemed to have good chemistry between the three of us, but I knew that might not always last as lawyers can be headstrong—like me. It was hard for me to butt heads with anyone at this point, let alone Anthony Mika, the man defending me. The man who basically had my life in his hands. I was blessed to have any lawyer take my case, especially one like Mika, so I stayed quiet regarding the defense —for now.

CHAPTER TWELVE

AP

After meeting Ray, I still didn't have much of an opinion on him. Our interaction was minimal, the meeting short. Even just visiting Rikers felt like I was temporarily caged in some musty dungeon. The smell in there, less than ideal. The atmosphere not nearly as poetic as one's first true meeting with their new client could be. Part of me wondered how many men died in there on an annual basis. Whether by choice or not.

I hung around Mika like some sidekick for the most part. Taking notes, keeping my eyes and ears open. Writing down the things he told me to. Occasionally, I'd chime in with a suggestion. It was too early, though. Mika didn't usually let me have much of a say until I was familiar enough with the case to actually form an opinion. I'd gotten used to that. Used to the way he operates, the way attorneys move. Or the way they *should* move, rather.

We both agreed driving out to Rikers would be the right thing to do so that we could have some basic preparation for our next court appearance. Almost a month had flown by since the arraignment, but since we still didn't have the discovery reports, this was not going to be a status quo appearance.

Mika, in good Mika fashion, continued to play up the media about his belief in our client. He did this not only for Ray, but for the good of the firm, to showcase our dedication to our clients. But just over the course of the first month since taking the case, I thought it was happening a little too quickly. We didn't know much about how we would build our defense yet. Anthony did trust in some of Ray's thinking, though. Our client was no stranger to the injustices in our system, so my boss started to believe Ray was right to be skeptical of the DA's intentions. Anthony's response was to keep the pressure on the DA, even if it was just to set himself up for appellate grounds later.

On the other hand, the DA's team seemed like they knew very well that they had egg on their faces for failing to produce timely reports, and they continued to try and get us to voluntarily extend the deadline for delivery of the discovery. Anthony refused all their phone calls, telling them the motion would be filed before the next court hearing, and he'd request a dismissal, which we all knew he had legitimate grounds for.

Judge Katy Beekman was not in a good mood. I imagined it had something to do with the tabloids stating that public perception was shifting since many legal experts were on the record saying what was happening in the case was bizarre at minimum, if not downright unconstitutional. I just wondered if she was willing to ruin her pristine career by being party to the nefarious behavior obviously occurring in the DA's office. Judging by the looks of it, she was now in a bad position. And I wasn't the only one to notice.

I was still pretty new to the law scene, but I'd learned in a short time that corruption could only take you so far. Just as easily as a defendant could feel the wrath of a 50-year prison sentence in her court part, the DA could be found guilty if they were discovered obviously ignoring clear-cut procedural issues. This was the catch-22 everyone knew of when judge-shopping to Katy Beekman. If you won a conviction, she'd make you shine with a lengthy prison term. But as a DA you'd have to get there somewhat fairly, at least without making a show of a blatant disregard for the rules. And with this much public attention, and an over-zealous defense attorney like my boss, there was little wiggle room. Especially now that our 30.30 speedy trial motion was officially filed.

"Mr. Mika," Honorable Beekman started, "I have read your discovery request and motion to dismiss, and I agree with it in part. However, I confirmed specific case law in sexual assault cases that gives the DA some latitude. So, the motion is denied at this time. But, and this is a *big* but, if we don't have the bare essential reports that were taken within the first 48 hours of the alleged crime, then I will encourage Mr. Mika to renew his motion."

"Thank you, Your Honor," the ADAs replied in what sounded like sincere relief.

She wasn't done with her lecture though. She stared at them. "The People should be keenly aware that we have rules in this country that are to be followed in this court-room, regardless of your personal preferences on how to present a case. I suggest that you follow them, or you will see how I enforce them. Do you understand me?"

"Yes, Your Honor," the ADAs said in unison.

I watched the younger one's face flash with a rosy hue and fought back a smile. It was nice to hear, pleasant to think that perhaps she would be impartial here. But a big part of me knew it was only a façade to placate the public and media and make it *seem* like she was being impartial. I looked at Ray, who didn't show much emotion. He seemed accustomed to whatever was going on.

"We will be back on the calendar in two weeks to resolve this," Judge Beekman said. Then, she looked to the DA's table again. "I expect you attorneys to work together and have Mr. Mika what he wants before our next appearance. Good day."

She banged her gavel and within seconds, the state correctional officers were cuffing Ray to head back to the holding cells in preparation for his return to Rikers. A look of relief washed over his face now that court was over, at least for today. As I watched them take him away, he turned around once and made eye contact with me before fully disappearing from my sight.

On our way back to the Madison Avenue office, Mika wondered aloud as to why the DA was withholding the reports.

"It's just, it's beyond curious at this point," he said.

"Who knows what they're doing," I said.

Once inside, before we could even get settled, the phone rang. Instantly, I recognized the number, as I'd seen it many times on our caller ID. It was the DA's office.

"That was quick," I said.

He motioned for me to follow into his office where he picked up and put the call on speaker. As the male ADA went through his customary speech on how we all needed to work together as colleagues, I rolled my eyes.

Anthony cut him off mid-sentence. "Can you please get to the point already? Because as you heard, your time is very limited, so if you don't have those reports in the next two weeks your career is over."

"All right, all right. There's no need for hostility, Mr. Mika," the younger male ADA said. "I think we should meet. You'd be interested to know that we are prepared to make your client a very fair offer prior to turning over the reports. The family is extremely sensitive to the victim and they want the case resolved without the media sensationalizing it."

Mika looked at me and laughed out loud so they could hear. "Sensationalizing it? Really? And where does that come from? Ari Rohnstein?" The question was rhetorical in nature, so Mika continued before they could answer. "Before you say something to insult me, put me on speaker so your bosses can hear me as well."

"Are you serious?" the young ADA asked, seemingly unaware that he was about to be taken to school.

Anthony sat in his chair and leaned back. "Oh, yes. Very serious." He paused a moment, giving the young ADA time to follow his instructions. "Now, listen up, and Ari, I know you're there, so you better listen to this, too. Do *not* call me to waste one more minute of my time between now and the trial. My only goal here is to vindicate my client of all charges. So, the only reasonable deal here is dismissal. And quite frankly, from what I see in this case, that would be a bargain. For all of you."

There was a brief silence. Anthony and I made eye contact, and I nodded my silent approval.

"So, this is about some unsettled business between us," a voice said.

I looked at Anthony, trying to read his face.

But he leaned forward, his eyes narrowing. "Call it what you want, Ari, but I got a job to do for my client, just like you told me you had a job to do for your real estate partners years ago, *remember*?"

But someone else butted in. A new voice. A stern one,

full of warning. "Now you listen, Anthony, and you listen good. You and I have been in this game a long time and you better watch yourself with your client. I've been in touch with Robby who prosecuted him on the Wall Street case and he said to warn you that you shouldn't put your career on the line for him."

"Warn me of what, chief? Of how you guys don't want to give him a fair trial?" Anthony asked defiantly.

"Now you watch yourself, Mika," he said.

"No, I won't. You're out of line trying to dictate how I run my firm and represent my clients," Anthony shot back. "Years ago, that would have never happened."

I looked at Anthony and mouthed *who is that?* as he jotted something down on a post-it and slid it to me.

Sex crimes chief atty.

"Look, all I'm telling you is if your client goes down in Katy Beekman's part she's going to hang him. And if you're as good of an attorney as you *think* you are, you'd do him a service and at least consider a great plea before this gets out of hand," the chief said.

"No thanks on any deals," Mika said. "This is the type of case we need to go all the way with."

"Well you have a duty to inform your client of any pleas, so with that said, we are willing to settle the case right now for a flat five. Your client will be home in four years without seeing the parole board."

Mika chuckled. "Wow, what a generous offer," he said sarcastically. "And then he gets to live in prison and for the rest of his life as a registered sex offender, too?"

The young ADA chimed in and responded earnestly. "Yes, Mr. Mika, that would be a contingency to the plea."

Mika shook his head in disgust. "When will you people understand that some defendants have dignity? You guys are just the DA's office. You cannot play god and dictate what everyone should or shouldn't do in this life." Then he sat up, closer to the phone. "Oh, and chief, I don't have a duty to disclose anything to my client. He has given me strict instructions not to discuss any pleas whatsoever. Period."

"Before you go, Anthony, I need to make sure you understand that the five-flat is only based on a plea without the documents," the chief said with a mocking tone. "Once we move forward with full discovery, tell your client the next plea will be north of ten years."

Mika stood up and picked up the phone. "You're clearly not listening, so once and for all, take your five years and your threats and shove it!" And with that, he slammed the phone down, ending the conversation with a figurative and literal bang.

CHAPTER THIRTEEN

RAY

THE TWO WEEKS BETWEEN HEARINGS WERE QUIET. I HAD been keeping up with the newspapers, although they were sometimes coming to me a day or two late while in lockdown. I was noticing some interesting things playing out in the media. Ari Rohnstein was apparently not a well-liked man, which was causing a certain lack of sympathy for Isabella in some of the national publications. And because this was now a national story, the NY State procedural law was starting to be called into question. I smirked when I read some of the articles, the headlines. It gave me just enough hope that I may walk out of this thing. And that was all I needed to keep going. Hope. I thought about my boys, too, knowing I had to be strong—for them.

As time passed, the local tabloids moved on to the next big story in the city, but it was just the calm before the storm. I awaited my next court hearing, anxiously, hoping and praying that Iz would come to her senses and end this fucking madness.

But the morning was here. I got ready as well as I could,

trying to look presentable despite the cuffs and limited wardrobe I had.

It didn't matter though. I knew this position all too well. Once the DA had secured an indictment along with their grip on me, they wouldn't let me go. It was analogous to a pit bull clamping down its jaws on its prey.

I rode the Rikers bus to the 111 Centre Street holding cells, and my 9:30AM status hearing was delayed because my bus was late. A common occurrence for Rikers. Mika came to see me in the pens behind the courtroom. He informed me that the DA had emailed him a few days earlier, letting him know they would have all the required discovery information delivered in person at the hearing, therefore having no need for him to file another dismissal motion.

Finally, I was in the courtroom, and Judge Beekman started the hearing by asking the ADA if they had the minimum discovery material that was requested of them, which they began handing over to my defense team.

"I want to thank both legal teams for your professionalism in handling this per my request," Judge Beekman said.

During the exchange of the documents, the male ADA spoke to the judge. "Your Honor, we would like the court to know that since the defense has requested a speedy trial, we have also garnered all the DNA results in this case from the lab, which is rather difficult to obtain this quickly. Additionally, the lab has told us that there are two positive DNA matches based on samples given by Mr. Jansen from his last felony conviction in 2008."

That was the bombshell none of us wanted to hear. Especially Mika. He shot me a look with a quick glance of incredulousness.

What DNA? It was all I could think. I searched my brain wondering what the hell they were talking about considering we never actually had intercourse. Almost immediately, rumblings in the courthouse were heard followed by some reporters running out of the room, as this could possibly be the linchpin in securing my conviction. I closed my eyes, momentarily, and took a deep breath before opening them. I just needed to stay calm.

Judge Beekman attempted to grab control of the courtroom again. "Okay, we don't need the grandstanding, just hand the documents over to the defense and let's see if there are any other issues at this point."

As the lawyers finished handing the documents over to the associates seated with my defense team, Mika started to speak. "Your Honor, we have no issues at this time. We need to analyze all the material and determine if any hearings are warranted or if we should proceed directly to trial."

"And do the People want to add anything on the record?" she asked.

"Just that the People are ready to set a trial date at this time. We feel we have a simple case to present to the jury. And with other cases also slated for trial, the sooner the better for us," the ADA said with conviction.

I looked at Mika, who stood with the straightest face he could muster, but my plan was backfiring, and we both knew it. A wave of anxiety overcame me as I tried to remain calm. All I could think of was the 50 years that Judge Beekman would give me. And then my thoughts ran rampant. *What DNA? What fucking DNA? Hair follicles? Okay, fine. Semen? No way. That is physically impossible. I never came! I never penetrated her. They have to be bluffing. It doesn't matter. None of it matters. They're going to find a way to make me guilty, even though I'm not.*

The judge's voice broke me from my thoughts. She set the next status conference after Labor Day to see if motions would be filed for pre-trial hearings.

"I now have approximately 30 days of the 180 charged to

the People in respect to the defense's 30.30 motion. However, if the defense needs to have hearings, then those days will not be charged to the People. So, I am not quite ready to set a trial date," Judge Beekman said. She looked at Mika. "Does your client understand that any hearings under your request will not be charged to the People?"

"Yes, Your Honor," Mika said. "I will have a conference with my client right after this and will then advise the court if there is need for an earlier court date. Thank you."

Then, as I was being whisked away in what felt like a major momentum shift to the People's side of the case, Mika looked at me angrily.

"I'll come back to the pens to see you," he said.

Judging by his tone and his face, I could tell he was not happy. But fuck, neither was I. I let the guards take me away. I just needed to get the hell out of there.

BACK IN THE holding pens at 111 Centre Street, I felt like my world was falling apart—one thread at a time. I spoke to no other inmates in the holding pens, figuring the DA had a snitch in there somewhere, even if only to gauge my mood. I always acted like it was status quo on the inside, never wanting to have another prisoner try to use my emotions against me. I couldn't trust anyone. And the more time went on, the more people proved it to me.

"Jansen," the CO called out. "Attorney call."

I tried to think positive, but unfortunately, when I saw Mika, he did nothing to allay the negative feelings building inside me.

"What the hell did you get me into?" he asked, spitting saliva on the glass partition separating us.

"What the fuck is that supposed to mean?" I shot back.

"On the night you surrendered, you guaranteed me that there was no god damn semen in this case," Mika said. "Now how the hell are we getting around this? They have two of your DNA samples!"

"I don't know, Anthony. Maybe they're framing me?" I said.

"Oh, would you please stop with your paranoid delusional thoughts!" he yelled.

"What, you don't think it's possible?" I asked, remaining calm.

"Not if it's fucking semen!" Mika yelled even louder.

I wasn't one to be yelled at, especially in my face. Mika was lucky there was a partition separating us. But I kept my cool. Now was no time to fight with my lawyer. "I never came. I told you that already."

"Yeah, well, this is the quote from the ADA in today's *Times*," he said, holding up his phone.

I didn't want to read it, not at that moment. But my eyes scrolled down to their quote in the article:

"We have statements from the victim that now coincide with the positive hair and semen DNA evidence linked to the defendant, along with physical evidence found at the scene and to her person. The citizens of this city should know that we will not tolerate sex crimes of any nature, whether on the streets or in private homes. At this time, we are prepared to go to trial and bring justice to both the victim and her supporting family."

They portrayed it as an open and shut rape case. And of course, I was sure the reporters had enough to run wild with, with the help of Ari's media cohorts.

Mika slammed his phone down as I started shaking my head.

"Unbelievable," I said.

"Yeah, unbelievable is right. So, are you still going to sit here and tell me there's no way they have your semen?" Mika asked. "Because the ADA would *not* have made a statement like that if they didn't have it. I need to know the truth here. Before we go any further."

"I'm going to tell you for the last time, I never came close to getting off. It just never went that far from what I remember," I said, looking into Mika's eyes with a straight face. "Maybe they're talking about, I don't know. I don't know anymore." I failed to think of anything else to say. The anxiety became so strong that my brain was having a hard time articulating words. I just sunk my head. I was at a loss, knowing I looked like a liar.

Mika tapped the glass to get my attention back on him. "Hey, look. If they have a semen sample of you, I'm telling you, you're *done.* At the very minimum, they'll try the case, and with your record, you got less than a puncher's shot to defend yourself. So, I need the truth now. And if you're lying to me, let me go back over to the DA's office with my tail between my legs and beg for that five-flat back for you."

"Wait, what five?" I asked, taken aback. "Hold on a minute, did you start plea negotiations?" My voice rose to a suspicious pitch before I could stop myself.

"No, but the head DA called me after the last hearing and offered you a five-flat without turning over any documents. I told them to screw off, that you didn't want to entertain any deals. That it was dismissal or nothing," Mika said. Then he looked at me, his tone softening. "Is that still the case, Ray?"

"Damn right it is! I didn't do this shit! When the fuck are you going to believe me?" I yelled, angrily pounding on the glass partition.

CO Burns, who knew me from the countless visits on my last case, came over to me. "Is everything all right over here?" he asked.

"Yeah, Burnsy. My bad, it won't happen again," I said, calmly, which got him to nod once and walk away.

Anthony Mika looked at me, and I felt like I was watching my lawyer try to figure out some sort of plan, mentally. "I believe you, okay. I do. But the truth is, I'm not the one who needs convincing, those 12 jurors do. And as of tomorrow morning, the whole city is going to want you executed in Times Square. So, we need to do some damage control here."

"I don't disagree," I said.

"I think we need to make some statement to stem the tide of emotion after what the DA just pulled. The problem is, I don't know what's in that discovery. And to be perfectly honest, I have an issue going out on a limb for you right now," he said.

"So, what, you gonna do me dirty now, too?" I asked him.

"I'm not going to leave you hanging, but I have a career and a reputation, and you have to respect that."

"C'mon, how long you been in this game?" I asked him. "The DA is manipulating your mind like the rest of the public. I've read this book already. I'm just not buying the dog and pony show today. You gotta trust me. I didn't do it. They're trying to fit a round peg in a square hole."

"You're looking at 50 years, Ray," he said softly.

"I know what I'm facing."

"Okay, let me go through the evidence and think this all through. I'm sorry, I just can't commit to anything right now. Not until I know the facts."

And with that, he left. And I watched my lawyer walk away from me and the dirty pens around me, wondering if I would even see this guy again.

CHAPTER FOURTEEN

ISABELLA

I HAD THE DREAM AGAIN. THE SAME DREAM THAT'S HAUNTED me for years. I spoke with my Aunt Bianca last night just before I fell asleep. The same aunt I lived with when I moved to California to get away from my parents. There was less pressure on me on the West Coast than there was in New York, where I always had to play the part of the perfect daughter. Talking with my aunt always brought the memories back. We were close once. As close as an aunt and niece could be. My last tie to my actual bloodline, Aunt Bianca was one person I actually trusted. One person I *knew* cared for me. Still, my new parents feigned shock when I said I wanted to live with her in LA as a teenager—or should I say runaway.

They weren't surprised, and in reality, I thought my mom would've been happy to get rid of me. Instead, they requested Aunt Bianca to watch over me. Living in our California mansion with me, working for Ari. Aunt Bianca jumped at the chance. At the *favor*. The *gift*. Because my dad is just so generous. Such a loving father. Whatever it was, it gave me separation from them while they were back in NY.

Eventually, my aunt became romantically involved with a man from back home in South America. She took trips back and forth to see him, leaving her with less time for me. And leaving me more time to get in trouble. Drugs weren't rare in California, and when I enrolled—and my dad had me accepted—at the highly regarded Annenberg School for Communications and Journalism at USC, I found out just how commonplace they were. And how much I liked them. The way they made me forget. The way they made me feel beautiful, for once. See, it doesn't matter how many people tell you you're beautiful, if you don't believe it yourself, it means nothing. *Looks* mean nothing when you see something different staring back at you in the mirror.

I was never comfortable. In my body. In my skin. With this appearance that got me attention that I often didn't ask for. Even though I commuted to school my first year, the idea of going into a new environment terrified me. Aunt Bianca gave me advice, tried to comfort me. Told me I would prosper and bloom. Become the woman I was meant to be. I wanted to believe it all. I tried to.

On the first day of orientation, I ran into the first guy I ever met in Los Angeles. A pleasant surprise. An ally. A friend. I was 18 then, an adult. What I always craved. Freedom. But age doesn't necessarily guarantee you that. I learned that the hard way. When you're in a prominent, well-known family like mine, freedom isn't something you know. It's not something you can earn. You play the role. Dress the part. Become the character. A wealthy girl, with everything. That's what I looked like from the outside.

Bryant showed me the ropes. Took me to parties. Having a gay best friend in LA was a blessing. He was better than any girlfriend I could have had. He helped me buy clothes, taught me what to say, what not to say. "How to be a diva," as he called it.

"You got the looks, now you just need the attitude," he'd remind me.

I'd laugh it off, shrug it away. What I didn't shrug away, though, was the drugs. The cocaine. The ecstasy. The molly. We'd go to parties together, including frat and sorority parties. A few sororities tried to get me to pledge. They wanted the Rohnstein name. In this life, if you live one of privilege, you get used to people wanting things from you. It was a given. An understanding. Most of the time, people didn't even have to say it, although they did. They'd take whatever they could get. Ask for favors, for *an in.*

That's something else the drugs were good for; I didn't have to play a role that wasn't built for me. They numbed everything. And I loved it.

It was my sophomore year, the night of the incident. The one that I still dream about. Have nightmares about, really. I had dyed my hair blonde, a stark change from the dark brown it had always been. A new look for who I wanted to be. A new person, trapped in the same damaged skin. I was 19 then.

It was a popular fraternity's annual Halloween party which they dubbed their "Pimp and Ho Party". My new beau at the time, Jeff—a wholesome California surfer looking frat boy—had invited me as his date. God, we looked like the perfect pair. He'd been wanting sex, as almost all college guys do, and I was starting to want it, too. Or at least, I started convincing myself I did. It was the normal next step of any adult relationship. And that's what I was then. An adult.

I wore a sexy outfit that night, glammed myself up for him. The more shots we took, the more fun I had. At some point, everything started getting fuzzy. The mixture of the alcohol and weed were getting to me. I remember Jeff leading me by the hand back to his room, where he slipped me a molly. Before long, we were back in the main party room, where Tu Pac's "California Dreaming" was bumping through the speakers. The dance floor was packed. And we slithered in with the rest of the sexy couples, dancing and grinding like the rest of them. After the molly kicked in, it didn't matter who was around. We were kissing, sliding our hands along each other's bodies. I remember his hands, the way they felt sliding up my short skirt. The way he began to rub me. When he slipped his fingers inside me and then moved the same fingers on my lips. I was aroused, moaning. Taken over by the ecstasy.

He didn't wait another moment after that. Seizing the opportunity for us to finally physically be together, he took me back to his room. The pitch black surrounded us. My head started to spin as he threw me down on the bed and ripped my panties off while kissing me with a desperate urgency. The arousal I felt started to dissipate and fear took over. Anxiety. My heart pounded in my chest. Everything happened so fast. His pants were off and he pressed against me before I could tell him to slow down. I remember trying to mumble something. Something to get him to stop for a second. My head felt flush the more forceful he became. I started to try to push him off, but the last thing I remembered was the stench of stale beer.

And then everything went black.

CHAPTER FIFTEEN

RAY

I ENDURED THE LONG BULLPEN THERAPY BACK TO CLOSED custody in the "4 building", which was officially known as C-74 to civilians. The long waiting and shuffling from pen to pen and on buses, shackled, was physically exhausting. It typically started with a 4:15AM wakeup call at Rikers, with a return sometime before midnight after court. The physical part was just one aspect of it, but on the days where the court hearing didn't go your way, it was emotionally draining as well. But throughout all my years in the system, with the constant shuffling back and forth to court in my first case, none of the trips were as grueling as this one.

I could envision going in front of KB—as Judge Beekman was known to the prisoners on Rikers and in the tombs—and her basically putting an end to my natural life on earth. The only solace I found in the ordeal I was facing was that nothing could get worse at this point. But still, I refused to complain about the DA not playing fair. I just needed to find a way to rise above it all. I saw so many innocent people in prison just give up. The people who couldn't handle the gravity of it all. They crumbled. I watched young minorities, with little or no education, go to the law library to try to save themselves. I had tremendous respect for them. I even noticed that some of them eventually won their cases. I took it as motivation. I had to keep fighting. That was all I knew.

When I returned to Rikers that evening, some of the COs taunted me.

"Yo, Jansen, they're saying all over the news that you're going down for this shit."

I just made a face and kept my mouth shut. It didn't faze me. They wanted a reaction. They wanted me to explode. Instead, I patiently waited to get back to my cell. A few of the COs who remembered me from last time took up some compassion and tended to believe that I was innocent—even though everyone in prison claims they are. Of course, there were also the COs who liked to talk to me *just* because I was considered a celebrity inmate.

"Don't believe what you read in the papers," was always my response to them.

But I used my prison notoriety to my advantage, whether it was with the COs or the inmates. I knew from my first time inside as the head of a $30MM Wall Street fraud case the kind of attention the headlines bring you. For whatever reason, the money or the fame, people inside gravitated toward me. Some wanted things. Some probably just wanted to say they knew me, to use it to their advantage in some way. Some wanted me to sign their newspapers next to the articles. That's just the way it goes in jail.

I learned how to move on the inside. How to get what I wanted by manipulating a female CO or civilian worker who needed a little attention. It was commonplace in prison and I figured out how to get a cigarette, some stamps, food, or something else of value to use for barter. But in closed custody, on virtual lockdown, there wasn't much maneuvering I could do. However, tonight was different. I needed a favor.

"Yo, Flowers, let me holler at you, my dude," I yelled down the cell block to the CO on duty.

I watched Flowers take his slow stroll from the CO station to cell #23 where he asked me what I was bothering him with.

"What are they saying on the news about my case?" I asked him as he stopped at the gate.

"Well, it ain't good, I can tell you that," Flowers said, laughing, half mocking me and half playing with me.

It was the kind of relationship we always had on my first tour on "The Rock". Flowers was the type of CO that would ride you hard one day, and then stay up all hours of the next night bullshitting with you like he was your friend. He'd often bring in food for the inmates he liked. I never knew where I stood with him, but that was fine as long as I could get something small out of him when I needed it.

"Can you do me a solid?" I asked him. "I've been in the pens all day. Can you crack my cell and let me take a shower?" I needed to gauge his mood to see if I could ask for a bigger favor next.

"Yeah, no problem. You know I hate germs on my block," he said.

"You already know," I said. "Listen, do you think I can watch the 11 o'clock news right after my shower? I need it for my defense. I didn't do this shit, Flowers. I ain't no rape-o."

"All right, I'll crack your cell at 10:45, then you can change and go into the TV room right after your shower until they talk about your case. But don't make it a habit," he said.

"Good looks, man. I really appreciate it," I said.

At 10:45, Flowers cracked my cell.

"On the rec, Jansen 23," he yelled out.

I left my cell and took a cold shower out of the single pipe flowing in the Closed Custody Unit. It was a deplorable rusted shower pipe which only had ice cold water, along with a window that was perpetually left open to make it even colder in winter months. But the shower always made me feel better, especially after a long day going back and forth to Manhattan, lying around in filthy pens for 20 hours or so.

Afterwards, Flowers came into the TV room to watch the news with me and gave me half a sandwich and a soda as a small token of compassion.

The fact that the local stations were carrying the latest development in the case as the lead story was not a good sign. The story wasn't going away, but actually picking up steam with the DA's newfound aggressiveness to convict me through the media. Reporters were still camped at the courthouse when they broke to the first live reporter, who read the DA's statement and further identified that the DNA results "have confirmed a positive DNA match of both hair and semen samples of the defendant, Raymond Jansen".

A chill ran through my body when I heard the words DNA and semen linked together. *How? How do they have this?* I beat myself up in my head over it and kept watching. The reporter mentioned that Anthony Mika declined an interview request, citing that he needed time to review the documents first, which was also a bad sign for me.

And then the reporter added, "This looks like a tough case to defend at this point. You have a convicted felon who was clearly at the scene, and now a positive DNA semen match to go with it. So, Anthony Mika will have to try and turn back the clock and see if he can once again be the top-notch attorney he was back in the 90s."

After that, I went back to my cell where I had a restless night. The main thing that got me through it was knowing the sun would come up in the morning, and it would be a new day.

By the time the weekend came, I could relax a little since the courts were now closed and there would be no media talk about the case over the weekend. But I was woken early on Saturday morning by a voice at my cell door.

"Jansen, you got a VI, you gotta get up," the CO said.

"Yo, I ain't gotta do shit," I said. "I didn't expect anyone to come, so I don't want to see anyone. For all I know it's a media member or something."

"It's an attorney visit," the CO said. "You want to go or refuse it?"

I sat up. "No, I'll go. Can you crack my cell so I can take a quick shower?"

The CO responded by nodding, then went back to the bubble and cracked it.

While I was in the shower, my mind was racing, wondering what Mika's direction would be, and if I would need a new lawyer. But when I stepped out to the visit floor, Mika looked up at me like he was in a rather jovial mood.

"Hey, how are you holding up?" he asked, in a friendly tone.

"I'm doing the best I can," I said, halfheartedly. "I'm happy you took the time to come out here so I can at least get some legal work."

Along with Mika was the young lawyer, Alexandra. She was wearing her casual attire again, especially since it was the weekend. Tight jeans. With her dark brown hair pulled up and very little makeup on. Whether dressed up in the courtroom or casual like today, damn was she pretty. I tried to fight the thoughts so I wouldn't come off as the accused rapist I now was.

We had become familiar with each other now since her first visit and seeing her in court this week. But we hadn't formally conversed about my case yet directly. Still, needless to say, I was happy to see her, but I wasn't quite sure what her and Mika's plan was today. So, I braced myself for the worst—that they were here to drop me as a client.

CHAPTER SIXTEEN

AP

RAY SEEMED CONFUSED WHEN HE CAME OUT TO GREET US IN the visitor's section. Judging by the look on his face, he was wondering why we were there. Me, especially. I wanted to tell him Rikers Island wasn't my ideal location for a Saturday morning either.

"Ray, I wanted to bring Alexandra again," Anthony said, getting to the point. "She's going to be working on this case moving forward now."

Ray didn't say much. He kept his face locked. "It's nice to see you again. Thank you for coming today."

"It's nice to see you again, as well," I said, offering a smile. Because while this wasn't my preferred Saturday activity, I was there because I wanted to be there. I genuinely wanted to work on this case and know more about it. And knowing more meant knowing our client.

We sat down and Anthony started the conversation for us all.

"Look, Ray, I didn't make a statement about the evidence," he said. "I just thought with everything already being said about the semen, that maybe I should take a full look myself before saying anything. I hope you understand."

"Okay," Ray said, listening intently.

"Here's the good news," Anthony continued. "Alexandra went through all the reports on her own two nights ago. And it looks like the semen reports they're referencing are only on the inside of your underwear that you left at the scene."

"Fuck," Ray said, putting his hand on his head like he was massaging a headache. "I didn't realize I left them there."

"The contents of the semen found are negligible and nothing was found on her clothes or the sheets of any kind. It is Alexandra's theory, and I concur, that the semen could have been a stain from a prior sexual encounter who knows when, which simply didn't fully wash out."

"Kinda like the Monica Lewinsky dress that even after being washed still had President Clinton's semen on it?" Ray asked.

"Exactly," I said, finally chiming in. "I believe you that you didn't orgasm with her based on the evidence that I've seen in this case so far. In fact, the sample size and place where it was found is so damn minimal that I think it actually *helps* our case. *Really* helps, actually."

Ray looked at me, really looked at me, maybe for the first time. "Thank you, Alexandra. And your gut is right. I never did. We never had intercourse. That night, or any other night."

Anthony took control of the conversation again and addressed Ray. "I'm sorry for yelling and drawing conclusions. I should have looked more deeply into it first before reacting and doubting you."

"It's fine. I understand. So, does this mean you guys are going to remain my counsel?" Ray asked, with a little uncertainty.

I looked at Anthony for his approval before I answered, and then looked Ray in the eyes. "Yes, it does. I told Mr. Mika that I am committed to doing whatever is needed to help win this case. And that we are *not* turning our backs on you. No matter what the media says."

"Well, thank you. I really appreciate that," Ray said.

I thought I saw a hint of emotion there. Possibly a glassy look that could indicate tears, or the potential for them. But Ray tried to play it off without me noticing. It was my first glimpse into the man I would be defending. And what I saw was authenticity.

"You're welcome," I said to him.

"Ray, we have a good team with Alexandra on the case with me," Anthony said. "I think we can beat this thing, but I want to lay low for a little bit. I don't believe the judge is going to consider a dismissal right now, so let's just work on our defense for the time being."

"I understand," Ray said. "Not much else matters right now anyway."

"Alexandra put together a nice file for you in this folder," Anthony said to Ray. "Go through everything and take some notes. Don't call or talk on the phone, unless it's to confirm court dates or something not related to our defense. Even be careful with what you are sending in 'legal mail'. I don't trust the DA on this case at all, especially with Rohnstein pulling the strings."

"Oh, I know. Trust me," Ray said.

"And I know I don't need to tell you this," Anthony said, "but don't talk to anyone at all about the case. We're going to war here and I'm sure they have snitches trying to get to you in here or on your way to court."

"Of course. This isn't my first rodeo," Ray said. "But truthfully, who would I even talk to? This place is so brutal.

They got me on 23 1/2-hour lockdown in here. I haven't seen a blade of grass since I've been locked up."

My mouth was agape at this but I tried to hide my shock. I knew the conditions on Rikers were bad, but I didn't know they were that deplorable.

"Also," Anthony continued, "if we are going to move forward, we will need the $25K that we discussed to start with the defense. Have you thought about that?"

"Yes," Ray said. "I've reached out to Andy and Frankie and I think I'll be able to get it for you."

"Great," I said. "I'll call them myself Monday morning and let them know we are feeling confident in the case."

Mika nodded. "You, me, and Alexandra are going to have to meet to start discussing the facts of the case. You both know we have an uphill battle here, because we aren't only fighting the DA's office, but Rohnstein too."

"I know," Ray said. "And Ari is bad news. Isabella doesn't really have a good relationship with him, regardless of how the media is portraying it."

I jotted that down, taking note of the valuable tidbit. "Okay," I said. "I want to know more about all of this, as well as your relationship with her leading up to this, but not today."

"Okay," Ray said, before laughing. "Well, I'm definitely not going anywhere. And if it's easier to produce me to Manhattan, then I'll deal with it."

"No, no," I said. "I'm not gonna put you through that DOC torture. I'm not that kind of lawyer. I'll come to you, even if I have to come here by myself."

The look in Ray's eyes told me he appreciated this and he thanked me once again. This time he got up and hugged us both before returning to his cell.

I watched him walk away, more curious than ever about

what exactly got him into this mess in the first place. I knew one thing though. I'd get to the bottom of it.

CHAPTER SEVENTEEN

RAY

AFTER THE LAST VISIT WITH MY LAWYERS, I STARTED TO FEEL better. Things were looking up. At least with Mika and Alexandra in my corner, I'd have my day in court. And if I lost, I'd lose fighting, with all my dignity and pride in hand. This time, I wasn't going out like a sucker.

I looked at the small file of documents that Alexandra put together for me, excited to tackle it. It was a stark difference from my last case where there was so much paper evidence it was nearly impossible to store it all while detained.

Upon going through it, I quickly noticed deficiencies and inconsistencies in the documents that I knew would be exploited as such at trial. I was even puzzled by the statement that was made regarding the specific act. After reading it, I realized some part of Isabella was deranged. It was the first time my feelings for her started to wane. I closed the folder and paced back and forth in my 5x9 cell, half thinking, half steaming.

I thought what we had was real. How could she do this to me? All of this. It's because of her. Why hasn't she just come forward to clear my name? She knows nothing fucking happened. She knows I wouldn't do that. To anyone.

As confident as the reports made me feel in going to trial, obtaining the legal work left my mind unable to shut off. I tried to keep up with the meditation and staying balanced, but with so many things beyond my control, it wasn't easy. What the fuck were my boys thinking and hearing?

On top of all of this, I didn't know if Andy and Frankie would pull their support after the bombastic news reports made me look guilty in the press. How would their crews feel, helping out an alleged rapist, with DNA and semen now linking me to the crime?

And forget about making too many calls outside these walls. I knew the prison line was tapped. My strategy for now was to completely shut the DA out and frustrate them with the unknown. I could only hope it was working.

WITH LITTLE CONTACT with the outside world for a couple of weeks, I didn't know what was going on with my defense. The calendar turned to August, and I had an unexpected visitor. And when Flowers cracked my cell so I could take a shower, I asked him to find out who the visitor was. I didn't want a media member showing up, and I'd rather refuse the visit than have to go through all the strip searches. But Flowers was in a cranky mood after just completing his overnight shift and working a double this morning.

"Jansen, just take your shower and go to the visit floor. I'm not calling up there for you. I'm tired," Flowers barked.

I was in no mood for him either, but I knew from experience that it would be best to be agreeable today. However, I also knew that it was customary in closed custody for the

COs to alert the inmates who their visitors were. The reason being that there were some of the worst types of criminals on the block in all of New York City, and the wrong visitor showing up could turn into a combustible situation. Still, I remained calm when approaching this.

"Flowers, I ain't new to this shit. You gotta call up there 'cause I don't know if I can legally see the person that's here. Man, I'm just asking you to do your job. This ain't pop, this is closed custody."

"Take your fucking shower," Flowers yelled back, waking up the block.

I didn't respond with words. I just went to take my shower.

And on the way out, Flowers told me the visitor was Frank Demaio.

As I got dressed, I wondered why the hell Frankie was here, reflecting on all the time we spent together upstate and then on the street following our release. I thought maybe he was here to cut ties with me once and for all, just like I'd seen him do with many others in prison after their paperwork came back bad.

When I got out to the visit floor, I saw Frankie—all 500 pounds of him—sitting there. His bald head was sweating profusely after having to go through the entire Rikers experience of getting on the bus to cross the bridge on to the island. It was a steamy hot day in August, and Frankie was crabby to say the least at having to see me this Saturday morning instead of heading out east to his Hamptons house. One glimpse at him told me he was there to talk business.

"I'm off parole now and I was sent here by our mutual friends," Frankie said bluntly. "We need to know what happened, to ensure you are 100% innocent. You know we can't support no rape-o, and the reports in the media ain't helping here."

"I understand your position, but I just need to beat this shit. Then I can make things right on the street," I said.

"Well, you're asking for a lot," Frankie said. "Mika's firm reached out to my boss trying to raise $25K for legal costs, but of course, due to confidentiality they can't discuss the case with any of us. So, Andy calls a sit-down with me and we reached out to your Jersey crew. 'Cause Andy says, 'this guy ain't even with us, he's with yous, and my balls are twisted over here in Brooklyn because my people want nothing to do with this guy.'"

At the "my balls are twisted" line, I start laughing with Frankie, as this was Andy's favorite line in the can, and the one Frankie and I would mimic behind his back all the time.

Frankie continued on a more serious note. "Look, you're gonna need a bare minimum of $25K just to get the case off the ground. The only thing your defense team would tell us is that they think they got a good shot of beating the case and getting your assets unfrozen at some point to pay everyone back." Frankie paused for a moment, looked at me, and then added, "I hope there *is* enough to pay everyone back, and then some."

"Oh," I said. "And you guys want a vig on top?"

Frankie sat back in his chair, folded his hands, and smiled. "Hey, what are friends for?"

"Unbelievable," I said, with a slight chuckle, not the least bit surprised.

"Seriously, I'm here to help you in whatever way I can. But the people upstairs," Frankie said as he motioned to the roof, meaning the bosses of the family, "they don't know you and they need to know you're innocent. And more importantly, that you're not going to forget about them if you beat the case."

Frankie's crew in the Bronx sent him. Apparently, Mika's team reached out to Tony Anello directly. Andy's crew didn't want any part of supporting me, according to Frankie, so Andy deferred to Frank to see if his crew could help get the $25K to secure Jay Johnstone, the best private investigator in the five boroughs. With me being on lockdown, I had no idea any of this was transpiring, until now.

"Yeah, I know. What's your favorite line? Don't invite me to the funeral if I wasn't invited to the wedding? I gotcha," I said, making a mockery of the typical mob jargon. "You already know what happened. It's pretty much a simple defense at this point. And I'm sure my friends in Jersey told you that I'll do the right thing when the time comes."

"Of course they put in a solid word for you. They didn't even want us to send anyone to disrespect you like this, but that wasn't enough for the guys in the X, ya heard?"

"Yeah, Frankie. I heard."

"Plus, the truth is, I wanted to come see you anyway," Frankie said, genuinely. "See how you were doing, you know."

"Yeah, I'm fine. I'm lucky to have Mika and his associate. This broad, Alexandra. She's like a cute little angel sent from above. She's a couple of years out of law school and still thinks there's justice in our court system, and that's exactly what I need on this case. I just can't believe I'm back in here over this bullshit," I said, shaking my head.

"So tell me what happened," Frankie said.

I got a little closer to Frankie and started to whisper. You could never be sure if they had a bug in the visit room. My words seemed to satisfy him for the moment, but he made some things clear before he left.

"You know you *cannot* take a plea," he said, emphasizing that fact.

"I know. I'm not taking shit. I can't have any type of sex crimes on my jacket. I didn't mind pleading to the Wall

Street bullshit, but I'm not letting them take my dignity," I said.

"Yeah, plus the assets," Frankie said, looking at me sternly.

"I understand, Frank. Geez. Let's not get ahead of ourselves. You know I'm not into all the wise guy politics, but I will do the right thing if we win. You know that. I just can't have you guys in my pocket for the rest of my life."

At that, Frankie nodded, got up, and gave me a kiss on the cheek. Then he headed out east for the rest of the weekend.

I walked back to my cell knowing that Frankie got what he wanted from me, my word that I would not forget his help. He knew that already, but that was what the bosses above him needed to hear. I just hoped it was enough.

CHAPTER EIGHTEEN

AP

THE DOG DAYS OF SUMMER SLOWED THE COURTS DOWN. AND with the next status hearing pushed off until September, it gave me and Anthony the opportunity to go back to Rikers and visit with Ray. We wanted to get some more information about the case so we could start to plan our defense strategy. While it wasn't uncommon to represent clients prior to knowing the full details of the incident that made them need us, it was an element of the law world I wish I could change. It just seemed backwards to me. But my job wasn't to rearrange the way things worked. My job was to arrange a clear and concise defense to clear my client of the outrageous charges against him. And in Ray's case, charges that were clearly fabricated.

I didn't look forward to the hungry eyes on me. The sunken, solemn faces of the convicts on Rikers, some of whom were allowed to walk around a little too freely. Ray didn't look like he belonged there. With his bright green eyes, focused and determined. When he saw us, his face changed. Especially when I handed him the chocolate I brought for him. Not only a treat, but a peace offering. I wanted him to know I was on his side, here.

Anthony started the conversation as we sat down. "Ray, let me tell you the good news and the bad news. These reports are weak. For starters, the statements and blood-alcohol tests were taken close to 18 hours after the alleged assault, yet the police were on the scene immediately." He flopped down a paper on the table. "Doubt." He then flipped to the next one. "The injuries to the vaginal wall are practically non-existent with just mild abrasions, which could be normal for any girl. Doubt." He plopped the paper next to the other. "Next, the semen sample they're referring to, as you know, came from the inside of your briefs and is so de minimis that it had to be from a past sexual encounter. Doubt." He placed the paper next to the others. "Lastly, they have the DNA match with additional hair follicles, but we concede that you were there, so that proves nothing." He placed the paper next to the others. "And one other telling omission is that their key rape investigator didn't do the report, which is very curious to me. So, we're going to get to the bottom of that."

Ray listened to Anthony, watching the papers get arranged on the table in front of him. "Okay, so what's the bad news?"

"The bad news is that they put together a semblance of an alleged crime that is just enough to establish a prima facie case and get this to a jury. And they're going to continue to play chicken and do everything they can to hang the 50 years over your head and hope you plead. My concern is that with your record, we can't put you on the stand. And since this is a 'he said, she said' case, the jury is only going to hear her side."

"But what about the negligee?" Ray asked. "You don't

think that would be enough to get a dismissal at some point?"

"In Manhattan, probably not, but maybe an appeal," Anthony said.

I jumped in to add my two cents. "Quite frankly, I don't believe there's enough from what I see to make a prima facie case if we can prove she was wearing that."

Anthony looked at me with a scolding look. "Well that's because you still believe what you learned in law school applies to real life," he said sarcastically.

Fucker. I kept quiet after that, taking notes and observing instead of offering my opinion. I became sidetracked with the whole aura that Ray carried. He stood out in this hell hole. An attractive man, intelligent. I wondered how he kept looking so fit in here. Maybe with all his time, he spent a good portion of it exercising. My eyes wandered to the top of his gray jumpsuit where part of his bare chest was peeking out. He had a set of a white rosary beads draped around his neck and I wondered if he prayed often. If he prayed at all. If he believed there was a god out there that was just. One that would see to it that he gets out of this mess.

"The negligee will be a major help at trial," Anthony said. "Especially if we can get a DNA match on her. But that might not be as easy as we think."

"I understand," Ray said. "This is going to fall under procedural rules of evidence at trial, correct?"

Hearing him say this surprised me. How did he know more about criminal law than perhaps even I did, even after all my years at law school? My hand paused from taking notes and I looked at him, finally getting the nerve to ask the question lingering in my mind. "How do you know about this stuff?"

He smiled at me. "I'm what they call a jailhouse lawyer, sweetheart. Let me tell you, don't believe the real lawyers that say jailhouse lawyers don't know what they're talking about, because I've seen a lot of good ones in my day."

I smiled back and nodded.

But Ray turned his attention back to Anthony. "I found a good cited case regarding a similar issue on how to get it into evidence," Ray said. He then scribbled the name of the case on my legal pad for me to look up for Anthony.

Anthony seemed to like what he was hearing, and nodded his head before speaking. "Good stuff, Ray. I had my concerns with going to trial at one point there with the DNA, but as long as we don't let them sneak in your past felony convictions somehow and get the jury to hate you, then we should be okay on the evidence. But, I will say this, many times, to both of you, it is rarely about the evidence at trial."

But I had a different feeling on how the jury would respond to this case. "Well, from a woman's point of view, I'm not sure anyone will hate him as much as they hate her," I said. "Especially with her text messages to him. I don't think older women will be able to identify with that and someone who is claiming they were raped by the man they were seducing. Especially with the distorted 'facts'. Just my view though."

Anthony put his hand up to stop me there so we could shy away from potential jury issues. "Okay, okay. We are not doing voir dire yet, kids."

But Ray responded differently. He didn't shut me down. Instead, he looked at me thoughtfully. "Thank you, Alexandra. I appreciate that."

With the way he was looking at me, I felt the heat on my face and looked away. *God, did he just make me blush?*

"Look," Anthony said, pulling me back into what was at stake here, "we want to make the case *before* we get in front of the jury so the DA is so afraid of being embarrassed that they dismiss the case. It is imperative that we get our private investigator digging up as much as he can on Isabella, as well as anything else that can help the case."

"Oh, speaking of that," Ray said, looking at Anthony, "Frankie came to visit me last weekend."

"Yeah," Anthony said. "I made a personal call on your behalf to a friend who knows Frankie. They've agreed to help with funding some of the expenses. I'm gonna need more, Ray, but it's a start."

"Yeah well, they're good friends for sure, but there's no such thing as a free lunch, you know what I mean?" Ray said.

"Get what you can now," Anthony said to him. "Your life is on the line. Worry about dealing with the payback later. It beats the alternative of dealing with prison."

"I agree with you there," Ray said.

I noticed the genuine chemistry between Ray and Anthony and had a good feeling about how this would all play out. That was vital when dealing with legal strategy on a big case like this.

"Now tell us more about the whole relationship and what led you here," Anthony said to Ray, then he looked at me. "Alexandra, please take notes."

CHAPTER NINETEEN

RAY

I TRIED NOT TO LET MY MIND GO HERE. TO TAKE ME BACK TO the beginning where this all started. When I met Iz. My feelings for her. How we got here—with me behind bars, and her accusing me of rape. I still wasn't sure how it escalated like this. But when Mika asked me to tell him and AP about my relationship with Isabella, everything was forced back to the surface as if I were living it all over again.

And it all started when I reached out to Nick Salerno to see if he was interested in getting back in business together, even after he had to walk away from $500K of his personal investments in the Wall Street mess. I closed my eyes, took a deep breath, and took Mika and Alexandra back to the start, recounting the details that led up to the here and now of it all, starting with what I felt was important:

I hadn't spoken with Nick Salerno in months. We had lost touch after the changes in my life. So, I think he was surprised to hear from me, but within minutes it felt like we hadn't missed a beat.

"I'm gonna book *Nobu* for us next week," Salerno had said to me. "I'm interested to hear what you're up to."

Nobu was a trip down memory lane. Back in the day, it was where we'd meet after a big score. Salerno would take the train down to Tribeca from his midtown advertising agency and I'd take the train up from my Wall Street offices. Being back there, after all these years, was a good bit of nostalgia. And even though we were there to talk business, we wound up catching up like the old friends we were.

After that night, we spent a few weeks exchanging emails, texting, and talking real budget numbers over the phone. I was serious about my need for major advertising exposure, and Nicky was coming around. He invited me out to an event he was throwing for some of his advertising contacts and office staff, and I accepted. I didn't know my life would change so quickly after that.

The night of the party, I stood across from Salerno. We each had a drink in our hands. Across the room, I caught the eye of a sexy 20-something-year-old woman. I looked away, bringing my attention back to Salerno. But a few minutes later, we were interrupted.

"Hi, Nick," a female's voice said.

I turned my head to find the same woman standing there, in a slim black dress that stopped just above her knee. I couldn't help but notice how gorgeous she was, with a body to die for. She had everything. The looks, the body, the allure. If there was any woman who would make me change my mind about my single status, it might be her.

Salerno gave her a quick kiss on the cheek. "Isabella," he said, smiling, though he seemed slightly taken aback. "This is Ray." He motioned his hand from me to her. "Ray, Isabella."

Isabella smiled and held out her hand for me to shake, and I caught a whiff of her floral perfume. That scent, along with her smile, almost knocked the wind right out of me. I couldn't help the way my eyes traveled down her body in that dress. And when my eyes caught hers again, she was looking at me in the same way.

I grabbed her hand, while looking into her eyes. "Pleasure to meet you," I said.

"Likewise," she said.

"Uhh, excuse us, Isabella," Salerno cut in. "I want to introduce Ray to a potential advertising partner." He smiled and grabbed a hold of my arm, leading me away from the bombshell.

I turned around to look at her once more. "Wow, who is that?" I asked him.

"Oh, she's just a client," Salerno said, leaving it at that.

"Just a client?" I said incredulously.

Later that evening, while Salerno was off mingling with other guests and getting a little toasty, I took it upon myself to seek out Isabella. I had to talk to her again. I didn't waste time breaking the ice with some light conversation, which made her laugh. Before long, we were talking business. She was prodding to know more about my company —and me.

"So, tell me, what kind of advertising partner are you looking for?" she asked me.

I explained what I was currently doing with my business model and how the company I ran was gaining a lot of traction at this juncture. How I was looking for more exposure to grow the brand on a national platform now, as opposed to my regional markets.

Isabella listened intently, intrigued by my target market, which was primarily geared toward minorities in the middle market segment between working class and professionals. I discussed the change in demographics occurring in the country and told her how my company was thriving in the market due to the changes in the traditional banking industry.

"Wow," Isabella had said. "Sounds like you're pretty determined to execute on this."

"If you only knew," I said, chuckling. "And what about you? How do you know my boy Nicky so well?"

"Well, I'm a client of his, and he's working on a women's magazine project that I plan on launching sometime this year, god willing," she said.

As more people gathered to get to the bar, I toasted her and we clanged each other's glasses as I looked her in the eyes. "Well, that sounds very exciting," I said. "Here's to us both having a great year."

And with that, a rush of people began to congregate toward the bar, and we were pulled in other directions, although, inwardly, I don't think either of us wanted to separate.

CHAPTER TWENTY

ISABELLA

I SAT IN THE CHAIR ACROSS FROM DR. MORGAN, FINALLY ready to talk about what happened between me and Ray. After her insistence that I come in and open up about the situation by giving her every detail I could remember, I agreed. I'd rehearsed things in my head. What I could say. What I could convince myself of believing. Between the pestering of my parents, the police, the DAs, and my friends, I just wanted to be alone. I isolated myself, mostly. But Dr. Morgan was the one person I could talk to. The one person who wouldn't judge me, who would just listen.

"Are you ready to talk about what happened?" she asked me, notebook in hand.

I bit my lip and looked down. *Am I?*

"Isabella?" she asked. "If you're not ready, we can…"

"No. I am," I said. "I need to do this for myself. I need to retrace our steps, mine and Ray's. See how this happened. I'm so confused. Some things are still so blurry."

"Okay. When you're ready," Dr. Morgan said.

I nodded and closed my eyes. Bringing myself back to the party that night. The night we first met:

I still remember seeing him from across the room. This handsome stranger in a room of faces I knew. He wasn't in the circle I usually ran in. I didn't recognize him. But there was something about him. I couldn't explain it. I just *needed* to know who he was. Instantly, I was drawn to him. Like a moth to a flame.

And after our hands touched, he was all I could think about.

My father entrusted my magazine launch to Nick Salerno's ability to attract his A-list clientele to the magazine. And Nick was no dummy; he knew if he didn't make my magazine launch a success, there would be no future projects for him from my father.

I had always been strictly business with Nick, aside from occasional light joking. I never mixed business with pleasure, especially when it came to my father's contacts. I didn't date much, if ever. And I was *not* interested in any males in the crowd that Nick Salerno mixed with. They were all too tangled up with my father and wanting his approval—and business.

I paid a visit to Nick in his office the day after the party. And after some small talk, I cut to the chase.

"What's up with your friend?" I asked him.

Nick leaned back in his chair, pretending to dig for recollection.

I rolled my eyes. He was going to make this hard. "You know, your friend from home. Geez, Nick. The one *you* introduced me to last night."

"Oh, Ray. He's an old friend. He's had it pretty hard in life for a while, but he really is a sharp businessman. He's looking to do some business with me in a new company he's running."

"What do you mean he's had it hard in life?" I asked.

Nick shrugged, shifting in his chair.

"Tell me."

"He's been through some stuff, okay," Nick said. "Let's just leave it at that."

"Is he married?" I asked.

Nick paused and looked down for a moment, then looked at me like he was trying to see what I was after here. "He actually just got divorced, why?"

I shrugged, seeming nonchalant. "Just wondering. Hey, why don't you pitch him to be an advertising feature in my magazine? He was telling me a bit about his business. I like his vision and focus. I think there could be a fit."

"Yeah?" he asked, eyes narrowing a bit. "All right, I'll give him a call and see what he says."

I cocked my head to the side. "Actually, why don't you let *me* call him? After all, it is my magazine."

"Okay," Nick said, with hesitation in his tone, "just let Ray know we discussed this, because he is *my* client."

I wasn't sure where the subtle concern was coming from, but something about it irked me. Additionally, it made me even *more* curious about Ray. More intrigued about him as both a businessman and a person. "Oh don't worry. I'm sure he can handle himself just fine," I said, holding out my hand. "Business card, please."

Nick sighed, and handed it to me, almost like he didn't want to.

I took it and left the office, then emailed Ray from the Starbucks downstairs and included my cell number. I wasn't the type to wait around. When I wanted something, I went for it. Well, that was the motto for the new me, at least. He called me rather quickly, seeming excited about reconnecting with me. Instantly, it made me laugh. And I could tell from his reaction that I hadn't been the only one of us thinking about the other. Before long, I told him that I was going to reserve a table for two at *Glow* for us. To talk business. If there was any place that would impress him, that place would be it.

Glow was an ultra-chic spot reserved for mostly celebrities and New York's elite crowd. It was a place you were expected to look your best, and the night we met up, we both did.

My long hair was down and straight, and the cocktail dress I had on was meant to get his attention—and keep it. He was already waiting by the hostess when I got there. In a dark blue windowpane suit, looking even better than he did at the party.

I walked toward him, trying to keep my nerves at bay. "Ray," I said, leaning into him and giving him a kiss on the cheek. I looked him up and down, grinning. "My, someone cleans up nice."

He laughed. "Well, you look just as stunning as I remember, if not more. Let's go grab some drinks."

He grabbed my hand and led me through the crowded lounge to a private cocktail table for two. I remember feeling the electricity pulse between us when his hand touched mine, and staring down at my hand in his. As silly as it sounded, it was almost like a movie moment. The music faded. Everyone else became blurs. It was only us.

When we reached the table, I snapped back to reality and sat down. Typically, I didn't like men who were forward like that. But with Ray, it was different. He wasn't aggressive or overbearing. It just felt natural. Like we were meant to be there together. And I think we both felt it, almost immediately.

As foreign as it was for me, I liked it. We were technically there on business, but the comfort level and attraction wouldn't let it be *just business*. On some level, I think we were both aware of that.

We first sat in the lounge, had drinks, small talk. We

laughed. He casually touched me, and I touched back, following his lead.

It was never *meant* to be a date. But that's what it felt like. Until he brought it back to business.

"So, tell me more about your idea for the *New Age Women* magazine," he said. "It sounds intriguing."

"Well, I want a magazine that can reach many demographics of women, not just wealthy New York women, or one specific minority. I want it to be relatable and helpful, to empower women everywhere to better themselves regardless of their economic limitations."

"That's interesting," he said. "It's similar to what I believe is happening regarding the demographic changes in this country."

"It definitely is. That's why I thought it would be worth it for us to meet and discuss," I said.

"Well, our funding model is not based only on women decision makers, but on bettering the entire family, so there could be a fit on a small-scale level to do some test marketing to see what type of results we get," Ray said. "But on better thought, have you done the statistical analysis of minority families and the changes in social status and income levels for the ones clearly above the poverty line?"

"Not really," I said, a little embarrassed, knowing I probably should have done my research.

"Well, I have, and I can give you all the data if you're interested," he offered. "The reason I bring this up to you is because, well, why would you want to limit your market to *just* women? It would seem to me that your vision is great, especially if you expand it to families where the decision makers are not always the women of the house, but in more cases, the men. This is what I would think advertisers are looking for regarding the bigger ticket items."

I stopped at the thought, watching the way his green eyes

lit up when he spoke about my project. My instincts all felt validated in that moment. "No, I actually never thought of that until you just said it. That's…that's actually brilliant," I said, looking at him. Something about his passion, our connection, it overwhelmed me. "Excuse me," I said, gently touching his arm. "I need to go to the ladies' room. I'll be right back." I wanted to appear as unaffected and normal as possible, but inside, something was screaming. I knew I had to step away and try to put myself back together.

He nodded and tossed me a small smile as he watched me walk away.

I felt his eyes on me as I headed toward the bathroom in a rush, pushing past bystanders in all their sparkles and celebrity glory. Once I reached the restroom, I found an empty stall, shut the door and locked it, then leaned against the wall. I closed my eyes, letting out a few deep breaths, trying to hold it together. *Don't cry, you asshole. You're fine. You're having fun. You do not like him. This is just business.* I tried to steady my breaths, to collect my thoughts. *You're fine. Breathe. Do not ruin your makeup.*

But I never felt this way before. This strong, immediate connection with a man. I felt so comfortable with him that it was abnormal for me. And it made my anxiety spike instantaneously. I stayed in that cold stall for a few minutes longer, working on my breathing. Eventually, I calmed myself down and got rid of the panic attack that was building inside me. I reminded myself I was a strong, capable, intelligent woman. Not a little girl. And I made my way back to the table, resuming the business talk with Ray as though nothing ever happened in that bathroom stall.

The place was already busy when our booth was finally ready. And as we pushed through the crowd as one, Ray grabbed my hand again. And I didn't stop him.

The hostess sat us at our booth and smiled. "You two are such a cute couple."

Neither of us corrected her. Instead, we smiled and laughed in unison. As dinner wound down, we discussed our philosophies on both our directions with our companies. Ray offered to pay the tab; in fact, he insisted, unlike some of the younger generation men did nowadays. But I wouldn't have it.

"Nope," I said. "Technically you're *my* client, and I asked you here. But maybe I'll take you up on the offer someday."

"Okay, fine," he said, laughing. "I'm going to run to the bathroom before we leave."

As I waited for the waitress to drop the tab off I reflected on our evening. And how excited I was.

Ray came back but didn't sit back down. Instead he grabbed me by the hand and said, "Let's go. Tab is paid."

I gave him a friendly punch in the arm and thanked him. Before I knew it, we found ourselves standing on the street corner, our hands still together. A light rain started to fall as he hailed me a cab. Between the warmth of our closeness, the moonlight, and the budding attraction between us, I wondered if I should try to kiss him. Or if *he* would try. But when the cab pulled up, and our bodies were drawn even closer together, I kissed him on the cheek.

"Thank you for such a lovely evening," I said to him, then I turned to get in the cab. He grabbed me for a second, to pull me back in before I jumped in the waiting cab. My heart fluttered.

"Hey, let's do this again soon," he said sincerely. And then he backed away.

It killed me inside to walk away from him in that moment. And it always would, in every moment we ever had to part ways in the future.

CHAPTER TWENTY-ONE

RAY

THE DAY FOLLOWING THAT INITIAL MEETING WITH ISABELLA, I checked in with Nick to ensure him that the meeting went well and we would keep him up-to-speed on any developments. And over the next few weeks, things remained professional between me and Isabella—except for the occasional innuendo in an email or text, mostly at her doing. Things started to come together in our business deal rather quickly and there was an obvious strategic fit between our two companies. As far as our personal relationship, part of me wanted to pick up that pace. Although I knew it probably wasn't for the best. Not now at least.

Isabella had even taken my advice and changed the name of her magazine from *New Age Women* to *New Age Family*, or NAF for short. The transaction between us made more sense then. I also insisted she shy away from print-only media and develop a web-based platform and internet app to be in line with the sign of the times.

And I didn't know who her dad was then, but I knew he was giving her a hard time about working with a virtually unknown entity. Worse, he didn't like the unique terms of the deal. But as far as I knew, it was *her* magazine, and he was simply an investor and business resource. She made it seem like she was the one calling the shots. But her father wasn't the only one who seemed unhappy with our new relationship.

Salerno called me one day, with an irritated and accusatory tone, questioning the entire deal with me and Isabella.

I kept my voice even, diplomatic. "I understand your trepidation, Nick. I really do."

Nick let out a sarcastic laugh on the other end. "Actually, you don't."

"Why's that?"

"It's hard to explain," Nick said. "Let's have a meeting with everyone to discuss this."

"Okay, but if there's a problem I should know about, then let me know. Because I'm making a big commitment here, and to be honest, you haven't presented me with any other options to consider."

"Yeah, fine. I'll send you the details of where to meet." And with that, Nick hung up.

I was perplexed by the entire conversation, but I didn't show it. And I couldn't tell Isabella. She had enough anxiety over the entire thing, another aspect that confused me. She was a grown woman, starting her own business. I noticed she had already emailed me about it.

Hey hun, we need to be firm on our deal. It seems like Nick and maybe some other people are going to try to kill it. I need to know you are 100% committed to me on this prior to us presenting it next week. Let me know, please.

. . .

Iz

It was the first time she ever signed her name like that. The nickname I called her. And my feelings were confirmed that there was more to all of this than *just* business. But I wasn't into the head games or corporate posturing that went on in the business world. Prison does that to you, where you just don't have time for petty stuff anymore. Even worse, I started feeling like a pawn, and hated the idea of being played in *any* way, no matter how miniscule. Instead of emailing her back, I called her.

"What's going on?" I asked her when she answered.

"There are some concerns from my investors. They seem to be directing them to Nick, and they all want to have a meeting." She was being vague. Too vague.

Since she didn't open up, I remained coy about my conversation with Nick. "I guess it'll all come out in the wash next week, right?"

I heard her sigh.

"I'm sorry," I said. "I just don't understand the issue here. This is a great deal, for both of us, so who exactly has a problem with any of it?"

But I was met with more silence.

I could tell she was bothered by something, but was keeping it to herself. Still, there was something about her that made me feel the need to look over her, guide her emotionally. Protect her, even. "Listen, relax. I'm not going anywhere. I believe in you, I believe in your product. It's exciting to me and I love the way we work together. We'll make it work in the end. And regardless, I'm always gonna be here for you. Whether we are business partners or friends. If this is important to you, then it's important to me. Okay, honey?"

"Okay," she said, exhaling a breath.

"Let's just agree to the meeting," I told her. "And don't worry, I'll handle the investors just fine. Now let me get back to work. I'll call you later to say goodnight."

And I did.

As the meeting drew closer, my Scottsdale business partner flew in from the west coast since our company was making our largest marketing commitment in history and becoming essentially a joint venture partner in Isabella's NAF. If the deal didn't go well, it could strap our company's cash flow moving forward. And my business partner wasn't only a good friend, but he was the majority shareholder on the books due to my felony conviction.

Throughout my first sentence, I kept busy, studying what was happening in the regulation of investment banking and the home mortgage markets. I was fixated on the circumstances of the recent market crash that almost sent the country into a modern-day depression. I remember faintly hearing the COs at Downstate Correctional Facility from my 23-hour-a-day cell, listening to CNBC in the dayroom on that historic September day in 2008 when Lehman Brothers had collapsed. As a market historian during my career on Wall Street, I knew it would be a day that lived in infamy. And in some strange way, I was *glad* to be on lockdown, rather than living through the hell on Wall Street—*really* glad.

I realized that when I went home, I wouldn't be the only one starting from scratch. So would a lot of other people who'd been wiped up. It fueled me. I got financial newspapers weekly to understand the changes that were immediately occurring in the banking system. And I knew there would be opportunities to try and break into a niche market.

Everything in my past led me to that meeting with Isabella's investors, and I pulled through. Against certain objections from the investors that had Isabella nervous the deal would fall apart, I overcame them all. For her. For us. My preparation, delivery, and overall business acumen were at an all-time high, and *she* was my motivation. The outcome of the meeting wasn't what everyone wanted, but they say a good deal is when everyone walks away disappointed. What hooked the investors was my agreement to finance the *entire* digital platform and app that would be the key to the future for them. And I felt confident that the money would be well spent, by connecting our funding model to the precise clientele we were looking to target.

But the real action would come later that night, a night out in the city that was expected to be a throwback of all the past good times the boys and I had spent together, but also celebratory of what the future held after agreeing to the mutual partnership with Isabella's NAF publication. I was more excited than I had been in ten years, finally optimistic that the new deal would get me my millions back. But above all, my energy stemmed from the feelings Isabella and I had for each other.

Nick showed up a half-hour late to *STK Meatpacking*, and set the tone early before any small talk. "Look guys, I'm just gonna say this now. My partners have some concerns with this deal."

I couldn't believe it. "I don't understand. You guys stand to make a lot of money off this deal without doing much work at all." I was fuming, but I refused to blow my lid. Instead, I shook my head and took a sip of my cabernet. Out of respect, my business partner got up to leave. "No, you can stay. Any business involving our company involves you, too."

Nick only engaged with me now, as if trying to signal that my business partner wasn't part of this conversation. "Okay. Has Isabella told you who her dad is?"

"No," I said. "Just that he's in the industry and he helped to bring investors to the magazine."

"Her father is Ari Rohnstein," Nick said.

Before I could respond, my business partner's eyes lit up. "Holy shit, Ray! You hit the jackpot! Our company is gonna be bigger than US Steel!"

But I knew by Nick's tone—plus all the weird circumstances going on with Isabella for the last two months—that this was *not* a good thing. My mind scattered in a million directions all at once. But mostly, I was mad at myself for not figuring this out. Even though I *knew* Salerno had a relationship with Rohnstein for years. While I was locked up upstate watching sports, I'd seen him sitting in Rohnstein's owner box. I could only think back then how far apart our worlds had become. And now, I found myself thinking it again. But I was done being left out of anything of importance. Especially with this project.

"How the fuck did I miss this?" I mumbled to myself. "Wait. But her cards and email say Isabella Martin."

"Isabella's last name in Argentina was Martin. She's adopted. It's a sad story. Maybe it would be better for you to hear coming from her," Nick said.

"Well, obviously she didn't tell me this whole time, so why would she care to now?" I asked, utterly in shock over all this, wondering if I could even trust her again.

"Look, her mom was murdered in Buenos Aires when she was a young girl. Ari and his wife adopted her, out of the goodness of their hearts. When Isabella started this magazine project, she wanted to conceal her name so that she could feel like she made it on her own, without her dad's influence," Nick said.

"I can respect all that, I just don't understand why she wouldn't mention any of this to me. We've talked about everything," I said.

The waitress came by to see if the table wanted another round of drinks or to put our orders in. It was a needed break in the heavy conversation. But my focus was now on where this all was going and how I could calm my emotions, which were spreading like wildfire. Anger was one emotion that I had very little impulse control over, especially after four years in prison. It changed me, made me more volatile. Time helped, but this was more. This was about me and Iz, and maybe that was just another type of emotion I couldn't control at the current moment.

I abruptly ordered my meal then looked around and gazed out to the restaurant. People were socializing, conducting business, while the wait staff rushed around to the patrons' beck and calls. I reflected to myself like I often did at times after a long journey in prison that took away simple pleasures in life. I had learned to always appreciate a good meal, but that night, I just felt sick.

Once the waitress left, Salerno wasted no more time getting back into it. "Look, this is a complicated situation we have on our hands. After you guys left, my partners and I met. They're real nervous that this is gonna end badly. They think it's gonna hurt our firm's pockets in the long run."

"I don't understand how you're gonna lose money in the long run when *we* are putting up 500 grand in pre-paid advertising for two years?" I said.

"You don't get what's going on here, do you?" Nick snapped. "Ari is behind everything. Behind *New Age Family*. Behind Isabella's investors. And behind my ad agency. Hell, he's directly responsible for my largest clients in LA!"

I didn't know if this pent-up frustration only had to do with my relationship with Iz or if the resentment here went further back. I sipped my wine and took a minute, making sure to keep calm, even though inside I was raging. "From the way I see it, you've done a good job for his daughter, so what's the real problem here?" I could feel not only the deal, but Iz, slipping through my grasp. Regardless, I wasn't going down without a fight. For both of us. *For us.*

Nick glared at me as though I was still not getting it. So, he drove the point home. "You aren't looking at the big picture."

"I'm not?" I asked. "I thought I was." Then, my anger took over like the flip of a light switch and it was like I was suddenly back in D-block. "You know, Nick, I'm about to get real offended with all this corporate double talk, so why don't you just say what the fuck you mean?"

Nick paused. And when he spoke, his tone was softer. "If Ari finds out that I got his daughter set up with you…"

"Oh, an ex-con," I said, finishing his sentence for him.

"He may pull out on us, not only on this deal, but on the financial support of our entire ad agency. One thing about Rohnstein is that he's paranoid about any bad press. It's a fucking obsession for that guy. And if he even *thinks* I double-crossed him, in *any* way, my career is finished," Nick said.

"And what if Isabella falls flat on her face, then what?" I asked.

"Well, at least then it isn't my doing," Nick said without hesitating.

I wasn't letting it go that easy, though. I'd gotten accustomed to dealing with people holding my past against me, I just couldn't believe Nick Salerno was going to be party to it this time. "So, this is all about you, Nick. After all these years, it comes down to money," I said.

Salerno wasn't an angry guy but at times he could be intensely passionate, especially in moments of moral conflict. And I pushed him there.

"Damn it, Ray!" Nick yelled, slamming his hand on the table. "This isn't only about me! I got business partners, too. And none of us ever thought this shit would progress like this. In the meeting, after you left, the partners said that some of our contacts are saying that you're fucking her and they got spooked by how this could affect all our livelihoods if Rohnstein blames us. So, no, it *isn't* all about me."

"Are you serious?" I raised my voice so loudly that the friendly waitress decided it wasn't the best time to check in. "How dare you? You think you deserve to know that?"

"Yeah, I think you do owe me that," Nick said, raising his tone to match mine.

The tables nearby stopped their conversations to eavesdrop. I realized things were spiraling out of control and tried to diffuse the situation as best I could. I assured Nick my relationship with Isabella up until now had been nothing but professional. And I explained the dilemma he and his partners would be in considering me, and most likely Isabella, were prepared to move forward without them or Ari's investors.

"You might have a point there," Nick said. "But we all know that if Ari and the investors are out then you guys can only go so far with $500K with what you need in the digital platform. Ari brings more to the table than your money."

I conceded that might be the case, and by the look of my business partner, he didn't seem comfortable with that either. We all had a gun to each other's head in this deal, and I'm sure we all knew it. Salerno was a simple guy. He liked to schmooze clients and hawk advertising packages. He wasn't one for the drama, but he did need resolution. I just needed to come up with something to ease his mind.

"I need your help here, Ray," Salerno said with sincerity. "My ad agency is willing to give you double exposure for your finance company if you guys walk away from this."

My business partner seemed interested in the bribe, but I was not. There was no way I was turning my back on Iz. "Let me talk to Isabella. Let's make this an issue between the family. Isabella and her dad. Why should you or I be getting in the middle of this?" My plan was simple. Isabella could either convince her dad to go along with it, or he could simply kill the deal and risk alienating his daughter, which begged my next question to Nick. "Do you really think Ari would risk his relationship with his daughter just to protect his precious public persona?"

"Without a doubt," Nick said without a moment's hesitation.

CHAPTER TWENTY-TWO

ISABELLA

I GOT A TEXT FROM RAY LATER THAT NIGHT, AFTER THE meeting had taken place.

We need to talk.

I replied quickly. *I know.*

Actually, maybe we should talk tomorrow, he said.

Why, are you mad? I asked him.

Should I be?

I didn't know what was going on, but I had an idea. *Please call me. I have been waiting to talk to you all night. I don't want there to be any issues with us.* I ended the message with a broken heart emoji, and hit send.

Okay. I promise. I'll call you when I get home. I'm in a cab at the moment.

I waited. I drank wine and waited. I showered. I drank. And I waited. I knew part of the reason he wanted to talk. I had gotten a call from Nick's partner after the meeting that they didn't think this was the "right fit" for NAF and wanted me to know that Nick would be discussing this with Ray that night at dinner. I knew the reasons behind it. It had nothing to do with the actual merits of the deal at hand. I was trapped. Once. Now. Possibly forever. I just wanted to separate myself from my adoptive family for good.

It was approaching 3AM when my phone finally rang.

"Hey," I started. "Look, we…."

"No, Iz. If we are gonna move forward together then you need to be 100% honest with me," he said.

"I have been! I have never lied to you. And I never will." I already knew where the conversation was going and my voice started to crack since I was holding back tears. "I'm sorry, Ray. I know I didn't tell you everything about my family, but why would it have mattered to you?" I didn't give him time to answer. "I didn't want to scare you away, tell you who my dad is. My family life is just so fucked up. My father is a complicated guy. He's always been so overprotective of me. It's suffocating. It's all about how he's portrayed to the rest of the world. A few years ago, I tried to leave the family because it got so bad."

I took a big sip of wine and remembered California. My Aunt Bianca. Trying to get out. Trying to *stay* away.

His voice softened. "I'm sorry to hear all this. You know I support you in any way I can, but what does all this have to do with you and I launching the app together?"

"Because no matter what I do, my father extends his tentacles in my life and it wasn't supposed to be this way with the magazine. After I threatened to leave the family years ago, he wouldn't let me. Neither of my parents would. He does everything he can to keep me and everyone around him under his control to get what he wants. That's not love. And my mom couldn't care less about anybody else in the world as long as she gets to do whatever she wants, whenever she wants. Typical rich housewife shit. She acts like I don't even exist. And to her, I might as well not. No one understands any of it, but the truth is, I never felt like I was part of their family. Ever since I was adopted and brought here." I fought back tears, but lost.

"I know it must have been hard for you coming to the states, especially after your mother was murdered. I'm so sorry about that. It sounds like they wanted to give you a better life here, though. Maybe that just didn't work out for you the way they planned," he said.

"With what? All the money? The high life? That means something to my mom, but not to me. I guess I believed in it for a while when I was young, because whether I was in school or traveling somewhere, we always got special treatment. But as I got older, I got so disgusted with it all." My emotions started to shift more toward anger as my tears subsided. "I grew up in a small cattle town in Argentina when I was a little girl. Then our extended family sold the farms and everyone moved away. We moved to Buenos Aires because my mom wanted a better life for our family. It was just me, my mom, and my dad. My *actual* parents. But once my birth mom started working at that bank, her and my birth dad would fight. It was like all she cared about was money and status. And it finally drove her apart from my dad because he was just a simple family guy. The truth is, the happiest times of my life were just being a little kid on that farm with my cousins. Then my mom was murdered and it was like, I had no family, overnight. I never wanted to be in the spotlight like her. Look where it got her."

I heard Ray let out an exhale, almost like this was a lot for him to hear, which I'm sure it was. It was a lot to say. But I kept going. I needed him to know. Everything.

"All my adoptive father cares about is his public image. He's obsessed over it almost to the point of paranoia, you have no idea. It's nothing but a complete fraud. The way they speak about him and our family on TV. Half the shit is released by his own PR people. I don't even know why the two of them are married, honestly. Him and my adoptive mom. They're both so distant. But she stays with him because she's so fucking helpless without him. I never want him to think I need him like she does. Because I don't. I swear to god I don't. Regardless of what *he* thinks."

"Wait, I'm a little confused," Ray said. "Isn't your dad a big part of the magazine?"

"No," I said. "He isn't. Or at least, he wasn't *supposed* to be."

"But if you knew that bringing in certain investors meant your dad would be watching over your shoulder with this, then why'd you agree to it?" he asked.

"It's a long story," I said, taking a big sip of wine.

"Iz, you gotta be honest with me here. I mean, you have to admit, having your dad involved is a big part of getting this thing to the point that you have. So, I just don't get it all?"

"Look," I said. "This is what happened. My dad wanted me to come home from California after college and work here in New York. My aunt, whom I reconnected with, had met a guy and was considering moving back to South America. I really didn't know what to do next with my life. He and my mom promised me that if I came back to New York, I would have my own place and we would all work on being more of a family. It only took 15 years for it to happen. It was hard to trust them, but honestly, I was scared of being on my own. So, I gave in and came home and decided to try to start fresh here. My last couple of years at USC weren't the easiest." I gulped a big sip of wine and it came back. The darkness. The stench of stale beer.

"So how did the magazine come about?" Ray asked, breaking my thoughts.

"When I came back from Cali, my parents weren't as bad as they were in the past. And I had sort of grown this new skin. I wanted more for myself. I saw an opportunity with the magazine, and I just went for it."

"But you still needed your dad to pull it off?" he asked.

"I didn't want to go to him, but he put his spin on how he would stay completely out of it and said the money wouldn't come from him. The original stipulation was that I would be calling all the shots. But of course, my dad put all his puppets in like he always does, like Salerno and his investors. And now I'm trapped. Like usual."

"You're not trapped if you control the bank accounts and the operations," he said.

"Well, I do…"

"Then all we need to do is get this thing launched and off the ground," he said. "At that point, no one will be able to control us if you're running the day-to-day operations and have full control of the money."

I smiled at his words. At the confidence in them. And the way "us" sounded coming from his lips. "But how do we proceed if everyone is against us?"

"We keep fighting for what we believe in. They took a shot and I told Nick—and his partners for that matter—that I was fully committed to partnering with your company. Period."

I felt the tears well up again, but for different reasons this time. "That's what you told them?"

"Well, that and a whole bunch of other shit that you don't need to hear."

"Thank you. I appreciate that. It's just a disgrace because you know this has nothing to do with our deal. It's about their greed with my dad. You see why I feel so trapped, everywhere I turn?" I said.

"I do, and you are dead on," he said.

I smiled at the sound of his sleepy, raspy voice. It was sexy. I tossed onto my side and grazed my thigh with my hand. I just wanted to hear him speak again. I closed my eyes and pictured him in bed, lying there with a white T-shirt on and boxer briefs. I imagined those briefs hugging him in all the right ways.

"I'm not turning my back on you," he said. "Your dad can't do anything to me. I've already been to hell and back in my career and I don't need him like these other guys do."

Hearing this made me smile. *Finally, a real man.* "I'm so fucking disgusted with all of them. We should both pull out from Salerno's agency."

"No," he said. "We need them to get through this launch. Plus, they can't do shit to us now since neither of us fell for their slimy tactics. If they walk, they risk your dad getting pissed at them. You just need to be honest with your dad about what you want and then see how it goes from there."

I sighed, the wine getting to my head. "I don't know why they care so much about your past. You've told me everything. It's not like you're a murderer or something." I paused, thinking about my next words, then smiled. "You make me feel so much better when we talk, you know that?"

"Aww, baby. All this drama and we aren't even fucking yet," he said, letting out a little laugh. "Your voice sounds so sexy right now, you know that?"

Sleepiness overcame me, and I think it did for him, too. We started talking a little softer, breathing a little heavier, both of us thinking about the other.

I loved how he was so tactful, yet so barbaric at times. Most men weren't like that. And the fact that he said we weren't sleeping together *yet* got me wet just by the mere thought of it.

"So," I said softly, "when do we drop the 'yet'?"

"I don't know," he said. "But I know I want you right now. I've been thinking about that sexy body all the time. I swear I can't take it anymore."

I stopped talking for a minute as I touched myself, thinking about him touching me. "I want you so bad too, babe. I don't want to wait anymore. I feel like all this business is just making us closer, but it's holding us back from what we both really want."

"I want you to touch yourself for me right now," he said.

I smiled as I bit my lip and let out a soft moan. "I already am. I've been touching myself every day just thinking about you. You, touching me, running your hands all over my body…"

"So have I," he said. "And the crazy thing is I know the real thing is gonna be so much better."

"I hope so. I'm just scared because I haven't felt so turned on like this by anyone. Ever. You just don't understand..."

"I know, I feel the same way," he said. "I just don't know how much longer I can be patient. I really couldn't give a fuck if this gets any more complicated."

"I don't want to be held back any longer either. By anything. I don't care about anyone else." And with that, I let out a deep breath.

"So, back to you touching yourself. I want you to tell me exactly how wet your pussy is for me right now."

I smiled. "Well…"

CHAPTER TWENTY-THREE

RAY

THE NEXT 45 DAYS AFTER THAT INTENSE PHONE CALL WERE A whirlwind. After Salerno's firm, or more importantly, Ari, finally acquiesced into allowing the deal between my company and Isabella's. Both of us had been traveling—separately—to see our key business contacts for our respective businesses as we planned for our big launch party. I had visited the Arizona and Southern California markets while she flew off to Miami and Chicago. We were hoping to meet in Vegas, but logistically it just didn't work out. We found time to get on calls with our teams on the road, and we caught up for lunch while we were back in the city to keep abreast of each other's progress.

In truth, the separation only made us want each other more. We had graphic conversations, detailing exactly what we would do to each other when finally given the opportunity. She was getting hot. I could tell. But I was more focused on the business side of things as the launch approached. Getting over that hurdle wasn't only big for her career, but mine as well. And *we* would never work if this didn't. It was my first big opportunity since being released from prison. And nothing would stand in the way of that. I saw it rationally, being almost 20 years older than her. I could tell she was getting jealous with my travels, especially my late nights in Scottsdale.

I hope you haven't forgotten about me in Arizona, she wrote in one of her emails.

Of course not. I'm just focused on getting this done. For both of us. Maybe after this we'll go to an island where no one can find us.

Ooohhh that sounds so good. You promise after the launch party it'll be our time to celebrate?

I promise.

And I meant it. I didn't make empty promises. I always kept my word.

The launch party was a smashing success. The buzz that was created around the magazine—mostly from Ari's clout—even got Isabella on a national morning talk show. The focus of the story was the empowerment of the magazine for minorities to make their lives better. And even though I was the visionary in the movement, it was Isabella that was the star of the show in the media and the apple of the public's eye with her stunning looks. And no one could have been happier for her than I was.

While in prison, I saw how the media—and the public—had really gravitated to the epic accomplishment of having the first black president in our country. I thought to myself that the country was going through a seismic change, whereas America no longer had the racial barriers it had in the past, with minorities clamoring to break the traditional stereotypes.

The goal of the magazine was to be a wealth of information and resources to assist minorities with their entrance into unchartered societal waters most hadn't seen before. Unfortunately, with the decline in the housing and stock market in 2008, the inability to obtain capital for small businesses and potential first-time home buyers began to erode the American dream.

My vision was to bridge the gap and provide the needed capital for so many Americans who were denied legitimate access to funds due to the overall credit tightening. It seemed that our typical client was the newly successful black or Latino business owner who was denied from the traditional banks at a higher rate than their white counterpart. It just wasn't fair. So, I used this niche to build an expanding and loyal client base. And they were the same type of clientele that Isabella was trying to empower and subscribe to her magazine. The synergy between our companies was effortless.

Even Ari acknowledged how our companies were positioned perfectly with each other. At least, that's what I heard from Salerno, whom he asked to bring me to the penthouse party. The night everything changed. For the worst.

I could still hear her screams when I closed my eyes at night.

He raped me. He raped me. He raped me.

CHAPTER TWENTY-FOUR

AP

I LISTENED TO RAY'S STORY INTENTLY FROM MY SEAT IN THE Rikers visiting room as he recounted the events leading up to now, taking notes. Jotting down anything I felt was of importance.

"Hold on," Anthony said. "Can Salerno corroborate any of this?"

"Can he?" Ray asked rhetorically. "Yes. But *will he* is the question. His firm is basically controlled by Ari."

"Seems like it," I said, shaking my head.

Ray continued to explain in detail the day and night in question. The *Four Seasons*, how he planned to stay there, but that Michele Rohnstein insisted he stay over due to the storm. "Isabella and I had emailed each other about finally getting to spend some alone-time together and be together for the first time. We weren't going to have to hide it any longer after the launch party. But of course, all that went down..."

"Can we prove this through the email chains?" I asked him.

"Sure, emails and texts," Ray said.

"Okay, hold it," Anthony said. "Alexandra, I want you to specifically address all these items because everything Ray just explained basically throws the Rape 1 charge out the window."

I was more than confused here. None of it added up as to why she would accuse him of rape when it clearly was not the case. I looked at Anthony. "I'm sorry. None of this makes sense to me from a woman's perspective. If we can show the court that there was no way that his actions met the higher elements needed to prove the first-degree charges, then he deserves another bail hearing."

"Easy, Alexandra," Anthony said. "They aren't just going to let him out because we *think* we have a good case."

"No. I'm not standing for it. This place is inhumane. And the strength of the case *does* matter when determining bail," I argued.

Anthony gave me a look that told me to slow down.

"Alexandra, it's okay," Ray said. "I'm fine here. I have trust in you guys. Bail is not the most important thing now. A good defense is."

"Let's go back to the night in question," Anthony said. "We're a little pressed for time, so tell me exactly what happened once the two of you were alone."

Ray let out a frustrated sigh. "You want every little detail? I was on my back while she was giving me a blow job. I flipped her over and went down on her. She was into it, moaning, the whole nine. She seemed like she wanted to have sex. She was the one who came into the room to initiate all this. So, I climbed on top of her. Her legs were still open. Then she put her hands on my chest as I was about to penetrate her and she just went ballistic, clawing at me, yelling that I raped her."

I was scribbling notes as fast as I could to get it all down.

"Did she pull your hair at any time?" Anthony asked him.

"No," Ray answered firmly.

"So, just to reiterate, you are telling me you *never* had sex with her or had an orgasm?" Anthony asked.

"That's correct," Ray said.

There was a brief silence as I finished jotting everything down. When I looked up, Anthony was staring off into space before he continued speaking.

"Okay. That's all we need for today. We just need to discredit her on the stand," Anthony said. "It's as simple as that. The key to being a great criminal defense attorney is the cross-examination. And we need the ammo to extract the truth from her guilt."

I looked at my boss. "I'm all ears on anything I can do," I said. I was already in the process of developing my own direction, but it was too early to think too far out of the box. Still, I couldn't help but notice the rosary beads again dangling around his neck, and the chiseled chest that was just barely exposed inside the gray jumpsuit.

Anthony got up to go use the bathroom, leaving me alone with Ray for the first time.

"So," Ray said awkwardly, seeming like he was trying to break the ice after all that graphic sex talk, "what have you been doing for the summer?"

"I'm in a group house again out at the Hamptons," I said, trying not to roll my eyes at how uninteresting and typical I sounded.

"That sounds like fun," he said.

"Not really. It's getting old to be honest. Those people are so pretentious out there. I'm not really like that. I'm just a simple girl from Pittsburgh, and now that everyone knows I'm your lawyer, everyone has something to say about the case. It's annoying." I should have stopped myself. I wanted to take back the dumb words that just came out. Me, complaining, to a man who was on Rikers Island accused of a rape he did not commit. My problems here were really first-world…

"You're like a celebrity now, huh?" he joked.

"Well I guess so, if you're a celebrity client," I said, smiling a little.

"I'm not famous, just infamous," he said, mocking himself.

Our conversation ended there as Anthony approached the table. He seemed like he was thinking the entire time in the bathroom, as he came back ready to speak again.

"Ray, could it be possible that you pre-ejaculated without knowing it? Or that you blacked out from the alcohol and did in fact penetrate her, even for a moment?" Anthony asked.

Ray kind of laughed. "No. I don't think that's possible with me, to be honest. And I can tell you for sure that I did not penetrate her at all, whatsoever. I vividly remember that we were just about to have sex, she was ready, and then boom. The chaos."

"She was ready, huh?" I asked, rolling my eyes. "Try not to say that in court, okay? No woman juror will respect that. Even though it sounds like she was. But something just isn't adding up here, unless of course this girl is a basket case."

"I'm sorry, you're right. That was inappropriate," Ray said.

"It's okay, Ray," Anthony said, holding out his hand for Ray to shake. "Thanks for all this. It's been really helpful. We'll figure this out. Just give us a little time."

Ray shook his hand and thanked him but I wasn't done here.

"Wait, what about bail?" I asked. "I could really use Ray's help preparing if he's at liberty."

"Fuck them," Ray said. "I don't even want to give them the satisfaction of another bail hearing. I'll just layup here."

I glared at him. "Seriously, what is wrong with you? I want to get you out of here and you want to stay in this hell hole?"

Ray looked at me for a moment, like he was a little stunned at how forward I was, and then he turned his gaze on Anthony. "Look, Anthony, you are steering the ship. You do what is best for the case, okay?"

But I cut them both off before Anthony could respond. "I'm sorry, no. I'm going to work on this personally."

On the way back to Manhattan, Anthony and I discussed the meeting, offering our opinions. I was more than confident about our defense, but he was somewhat skeptical and I couldn't pinpoint why.

"Criminal defense is never as easy as it seems," Anthony said.

"Why do you have to be such a pessimist?" I asked him. "I can see it in his eyes, he's innocent!"

He grinned. "That's sweet, Alexandra. But my advice to you is to never wholeheartedly believe in a client. It will burn you at some point, that trust. It's okay to defend them, but personally believing in them will throw off your ability to defend them properly."

Although I heard him, and was listening, it was always hard for me to let go of my gut feelings. My instincts were part of the reason I wanted to be a lawyer in the first place. I always felt like that aspect of my nature would make me *good* at this. "I know, but it was just two weeks ago that everyone had him convicted, and that wasn't reality either."

"Very true," Anthony said. "But what does that tell you? The tide can swing back and forth in a high-profile case like this. Stay even-keeled and skeptical. That's what good lawyers do."

I looked out the window. Regardless of his pessimistic advice, Anthony had a bounce in his step. And when we got back to the office, he called Jay—the private investigator—and put it on speaker.

"Jay, let's start right from the beginning. I need to know about the reports. And I need to know why their best detective out of the Special Victims Unit wasn't on the case."

"I'm on it," Jay said. "I also want you to know that I've already dug up some information on the girl. This isn't her first claim of an assault of some kind. The first instance happened while she was enrolled at USC. No charges, though. The word is that Ari thought it was best not to press charges. Things are a little fuzzy, but between what happened in California and how the original adoption came about, it might connect some dots."

"Interesting," Anthony said. "Do what you need to do. We're gonna have to secure more funds for trial at some point. But my gut is that there are people out there that have an interest in making sure he isn't locked up too long."

"That's good to know, 'cause this isn't gonna be cheap," Jay said. "How's everything looking from your standpoint?"

"It's okay. We met with him on Rikers today. He seems to be thinking clearly considering the archaic conditions he's dealing with. But I'd like you to go interview him and get a feel from your perspective."

"Okay, Ant," Jay said. "I'll get out to Queens as soon as I can."

And with that, the conversation was over. But I was still stuck on his words.

This isn't her first claim of an assault of some kind.

No charges, though.

No charges...

CHAPTER TWENTY-FIVE

RAY

The peaceful end of summer on lockdown was over and I knew the pace of the case would pick up in September. Anxiety had made a home in me again as I prepared to go back to 111 Centre Street. A little peace had crept in though, knowing my lawyers were doing the best they could for me. But I never knew what to expect in the three-ring circus of the Manhattan Supreme Court.

CO Burns greeted me when I got to the seventh floor.

"What's going on today, Jansen?"

"Just another status hearing, Burnsy."

"You sure?" he asked.

"What do you mean?" I asked, my anxiety reaching a fever pitch level.

"There was media all over the place when I got here this morning. They all said they were here for your case."

After being beat down so viciously in my first case, my mind immediately went to the worst conclusions. But I played it cool. "Well I guess we'll find out soon enough, right?"

He shrugged. "Good luck, man."

Within a half-hour, Alexandra came back to the pens to have a quick conference with me before the status hearing. I knew it was her once I heard the sound of her walk. The heels clattering down the hallway. The other inmates trying to holler at her.

"Yo, mami, what's up? You looking for me?" one inmate called out.

"I need a lawyer, shorty," yelled another.

Whistles. Cat calls. The like. I stood up. "Yo, my dudes, that's my attorney. Show some respect, please?"

With that, the guys fell back. It brought a grateful smile to Alexandra, who was dressed flawlessly in a tight navy-blue business suit, with her hair and makeup perfect. We exchanged a quick smile between the bars and our eyes locked—something I wasn't likely to forget. She brought a certain calmness to me. And in that moment, it didn't matter what she was about to say. I felt like everything would be all right.

"I'm so sorry I couldn't make it out there last night," she said. "We're filing a motion to dismiss the indictment. We think there was another Brady violation where they failed to deliver some key notes at the beginning of the investigation, and it could be big. Our private investigator uncovered that one of the key investigators' notes are curiously missing. Even though we know she was on the scene. We are confident that they were omitted from the initial reports. Anthony is running late, so he can fill you in once they produce you."

"Unbelievable, so they withheld notes from Isabella's initial interview?" I asked, shaking my head as I gripped the bars, flexing my forearm out of the anger building inside me.

She grabbed my hand. "Yes. Relax. We are on top of everything. I'll see you in a bit."

She walked away, my eyes unable to stray from her tight ass in that suit.

When I entered the courthouse, I realized my case was a big event because I saw that the newspapers had the cartoonist in to sketch me. The heat of the bright lights pressed against my face, irritating me yet again.

Mika asked the judge for a quick moment with me before they went on record and thankfully, she obliged. We huddled at the defense table and Mika told me his plan.

"Well, thanks for trying, but I don't think it's enough," I said.

"I don't either," Mika said. "But I need them to be put on notice, 'cause the only way I see us losing this case is if they stack the deck. They're putting you on trial, but *we* need to put *them* on trial, too."

"I'm impressed," I said with a laugh. "A lawyer actually doing his job!"

Alexandra shot me an angry look. "Why are you being so sarcastic? We're trying to help you."

"I'm sorry," I said. "I just got a bad taste in my mouth after what Litchfield did to me in my last case."

"Well, don't take it out on us," she said. Then she grabbed the cuffs on my wrist. "We're getting these off you."

I nodded, hoping she was right.

Judge Beekman returned from her chambers and told the bailiff she was now ready, and we all rose. The COs uncuffed me for my appearance.

There was a tense feeling in the air, I sensed it. You could cut through it with a fucking ax. I looked over my shoulder and saw my mother's stern look on her face as it always appeared. And my two sisters were there, too; one flew up from South Carolina to be there. I didn't want them there, seeing me like this. But in that brief moment, it felt good knowing they were. That some people in this room were actually on my side. I was just grateful my ex-wife didn't come and bring the kids with her. I would hate for them to see me in this position. Innocent or guilty. What father would want that? As a man, you spend your parenting days trying to instill in your boys' heads that they need to respect women, to never harm them. At least, that's what fathers should be doing. I couldn't help but flinch from the heartache of the possibility that my boys might see the headlines and wonder if their father would do something like this.

"Okay," Judge Beekman said. "The People vs. Raymond Jansen, we are now on the record." She looked at Anthony. "Mr. Mika, I understand that you have filed a motion for dismissal of the indictment, in which you allege another Brady breach and prosecutorial misconduct." She said the last two words rather slowly and deliberately, probably because it was common knowledge that it was an unwritten rule that you don't accuse that unless you want to kill your career.

Mika straightened his shoulders. "That is correct, Your Honor."

"Now, you're saying that there was some nefarious collusion between the Special Victims Unit investigators and the DA's office? I need some time on this one, as these are serious allegations. And I'm going to need a response from the People." She looked at them. "Can you tell me when you can reply to this or do you want to add anything further to this today?"

The ADA looked calm and spoke neutrally. "Well, Your Honor, the People knew of none of this until today."

Anthony let out a huge gasp.

"Mr. Mika, no theatrics please," the judge barked at him.

The ADA shot Mika a warning glance then faced the judge. "As I was saying, Your Honor, the investigative unit is separate from the DA and I can assure you there was no collusion on our end. We obviously deny any assertion of prosecutorial misconduct, and quite frankly, I find it offensive that Mr. Mika and his associate are accusing us of this. As far as the timing of missing reports, we need some time to investigate this."

"How long?" the judge asked.

"I would say a few weeks to be conservative, so that we can fully investigate. I'm not sure if this will require Internal Affairs to be involved," he said.

"May I, Your Honor?" Alexandra interrupted, jumping in without Mika's approval.

"Do you have something you want to add, Ms., um, Peterson?" the judge asked.

"I do," she said. "We don't have a few weeks. Our client is sitting in isolation on Rikers Island for a heinous crime he did not commit. This needs to be addressed and ruled on as soon as judicially possible. We have a speedy trial motion in for a reason, and this time doesn't get charged to the People, or we can stop the nonsense with the ridiculous bail and have a *real* bail hearing now that there are new facts."

Judge Beekman seemed unimpressed. "Well, thank you for your passion," she said in a monotone voice, although she may as well have swatted Alexandra away with her hand. And then she turned to her left. "I'm giving the DA 30 days to deliver a full report of any and all written correspondence—whether formal or informal—taken at any point in this investigation. Do you understand me?" she rhetorically questioned the ADAs. Then, she turned her attention back to the defense's side of the courtroom. "*Mr. Mika*, I would like to know why we cannot simply cure the Brady issue if something is missing and it is provided to the defense?"

"Because the entire integrity of the investigation is now rotten," Mika said honestly. "I'm not talking about the fruits of the poison tree doctrine here. It goes to fraud or prosecutorial misconduct. Regardless of the DA's position, the investigators are not the NYPD, they are a Special Victims

Unit within the DA's office, so it directly impugns everyone currently working on the case. I really don't know how we could ever proceed with a fair trial now if potential exculpatory evidence has been discarded forever."

"You let me worry about that one, Mr. Mika," the judge said.

"All I'm saying, Your Honor, is that there is nothing now that doesn't alter what may have really happened in those first crucial hours after the victim claimed rape," Mika said.

"Okay, okay," Judge Beekman said. "I've heard enough. Let's save all this for a later date. We are on the calendar in 30 days as a tentative motion hearing with papers and any oral arguments as well."

In that moment, I glanced at Mika and Alexandra and smiled. I knew the media, and now the entire country probably, was watching. And Anthony Mika, the once brash defense lawyer, was once again making headlines. And so was his young female protégé.

And my gut was right. The next morning, the *Post's* headline read "Lawyer Makes Passionate Plea for Client's Release". And Alexandra's sexy sketched photo was on the cover, with a cameo of me sitting at the defense table surrounded by beefy court officers.

CHAPTER TWENTY-SIX

AP

IT WAS THE DAY OF OUR NEXT COURT HEARING AND WHILE I wasn't particularly fond of the idea of facing that condescending judge again, I had hope for Ray. For our defense. And faith that what we were doing was the right thing. Justice still existed in our country. Even if it was miniscule, it was there. Somewhere. I just had to find it. For my client. And to solidify my belief in being a lawyer and fighting for others' rights. Otherwise, what was the point?

I walked into the courtroom with high hopes and gave a quick wink to Ray. But when I saw how confident the ADA looked, basically beaming, I felt a pang in my gut.

Still, I tried to comfort Ray. I put my hand on his thigh, without thinking, and spoke softly to him so only he could hear me. "Hey, don't expect much today, but at least now we'll have this on the record for any strong appellate grounds down the road."

He nodded, showing his understanding.

When Judge Beekman came out, we all rose, and I straightened my shoulders and stood before the judge with the rest of the court. As soon as she started speaking, it seemed clear by her tone that she had already made her ruling despite the fact that she said oral arguments would be heard as well.

"Mr. Mika," the judge started, "I have extensively read your motion to dismiss on the denial of Brady material, however, I believe the issue can be cured and your client will not be prejudiced in any way. The People answered the brief clear and convincing to me and they cited relevant case law. I think this is a harmless error that can be resolved before trial."

I tried to keep my face neutral instead of displaying the utter disgust I felt.

Anthony cut in. "But Your Honor…"

"I will let you know when it's your turn to speak," Judge Beekman said in a stern tone. "As I was saying, the matter does not seem to be deliberate *or* fraudulent. In fact, you have offered no proof to assert there was any misconduct at all. The DA has acknowledged mere negligence in the chain of command, however, as in their cited case, this falls very short of a dismissal at this stage. It seems to me as though it was simply a miscommunication between the various parties." she said, shrugging, showing her indifference to it.

"Your Honor, may I at least make an oral argument?" Anthony implored.

"No. I'm sorry, Mr. Mika, but sometimes these things happen in a hectic situation. And when they do, we don't cry foul. We address it and keep the fundamental fairness intact, for *both* parties. But, with that said, you are entitled to notes of any kind, or any official documents or statements that were made by the victim during that time, whether in the apartment or at the hospital."

"Well, thank you for that, Your Honor, but I'd like to make a point," Anthony said sarcastically.

The judge ignored him and continued. "The issues you

raised lend more to your defense at trial, and your attempt to discredit the People's case. So, the motion is denied, and the People are back on the clock."

"Thank you, Your Honor," the ADAs answered respectfully.

"Thank you both for your expeditious work in filing these papers and moving the case on the calendar. I will have my clerk go through the days, but it looks like we are now scheduled to start the trial in about three months," Judge Beekman said.

"Your Honor, may I?" Anthony asked.

"Sure," she said, uninterested.

"Your Honor, I'd like to note that it is impossible to know if these new documents are now fabricated," he said.

"We are not going there, Mr. Mika," she snapped. "If you have another issue, then come with a valid motion."

"I would simply like to reserve the right to revisit this issue after I receive the documents, because technically they should have been part of the initial discovery," he said.

The male ADA sat up. "We will have any notes pertaining to this in a week or so."

"Does that work for you, Mr. Mika?" the judge asked.

"Sure, Your Honor," Anthony said. "I'll wait to get the notes and if need be, I'll call the other investigator who interviewed the alleged victim to stand in a preliminary hearing to determine the veracity of the notes."

The ADAs looked perturbed by this as I glanced at them and tried not to smile. He was planting the seed. I knew it. They knew it. The judge knew it.

"Your Honor, may I?" the female ADA asked, standing up. "There is nothing to suggest that anything improper occurred. If Mr. Mika wants to file another motion or cross examine a detective in a preliminary hearing, then that's fine. But Mr. Mika is trying to make a mountain out of a mole hill, and this is exactly why we would request a full media gag going forward."

Beside me, Ray laughed out loud and I glared at him.

"They're requesting a media gag," he said, shaking his head.

I had to stop myself from elbowing him. I hissed a quick "shh" at him and listened for the judge's response.

"Hold on," the judge said. "One issue at a time here. The motion is denied today. If any issues arise, we can certainly revisit them later. Now as far as the media gag, I'm in agreement and this goes for strict adherence from both parties. No statements. No leaks. No nothing. The trial will be fought in this courtroom, *not* through the media. Does everyone understand this?"

"Yes," everyone said in unison.

"Good," she said. "We'll be back on the calendar Nov. 2nd, and hopefully all discovery material will be caught up by then. That's it for today."

And just like that, the hearing was over. Ray was cuffed and sent back to the holding pens to wait for a long journey back to the island. Anthony and I went back to the office, where he made a quick call to Jay Johnstone.

"Hey, we need to start preparing for a defense, so I need you to uncover things that can really exploit this girl at trial. We don't have much time, Jay. Cut out the vanilla stuff and just get the important things," Anthony said to him.

"I hear you loud and clear," Jay said. "I'll make sure I get to Ray this week."

I worked on the case some more at the office, then I went home and went straight online to see what the latest websites were reporting now.

It was clear that the DA's office had taken the case back over. The media and obviously DA-friendly writers made our firm's claims look like nothing more than a vile effort to detract the public from the fact that our client was on trial for rape.

But they needn't worry about that. I wasn't about to let *anyone* forget the serious crime our client was accused of. The crime he was fucking innocent of.

CHAPTER TWENTY-SEVEN

RAY

Jay Johnstone showed up without any warning, leaving me unprepared for any information he might want from me. But it seemed that's exactly how the private investigator wanted it. Like he *wanted* to catch me off guard. It immediately made me suspect him and I wondered if he even believed I was innocent here. When we sat down, he cut right to the chase.

"Jay Johnstone," he said, holding his hand out for me to shake, which I did.

"Ray Jansen," I said.

"So, I hear you and Isabella had a casual romantic relationship going for a few months?"

I nodded.

"And I've been briefed that Nick Salerno was the guy that set you two up?" he asked, taking notes.

"Well, not really. He introduced me to her at one of their advertising parties, and things progressed from there. But he didn't *want* us getting romantically involved. That was apparent from the start."

"Okay," he said. "I heard you mention to Anthony that

Ari Rohnstein was directly or indirectly behind Salerno's firm, is this correct?"

"Yes, and that's the problem," I said.

"So, we cannot assume Salerno will help you in any way here?" he asked.

"Nah," I said, shaking my head. "I heard he's had it with me. At least that's some of the feedback I've been getting in the mail from some of our mutual friends."

"What are you thinking about?" he asked, going off subject. "You seem conflicted."

I wasn't sure he really cared, but if he was going to help, I had to be honest with him. All the way. "I don't know. It's just, you grow up with a guy your whole life and you know he's a man of principle, but when the money becomes too big, he finds a way to outcast you. You know, Nick rationalized to himself that it was *me* who did wrong. In some ways I get it. I'm the root of all this. But I would never sell out a friend, for any amount of money."

"Ray, I've dealt with so many of these situations with people I have to go interview. And just when you think a guy isn't going to be helpful, I find something that gets him talking. So, don't worry about that. I know what you guys need from Salerno."

"Do you think he'll talk?" I asked.

"I think he probably wants to," Jay said, like it was a fact. "Now, let's move on to the accuser. This Isabella girl. What's her story?"

I gave him the rundown of exactly what our relationship started as and what it had flourished into. I gave Jay my cell phone number and carrier, as well as my email accounts and passwords so he could access all the texts and emails between me and Iz.

"Let's continue to follow the evidence," Jay said. "Tell me more about her background."

I gave him everything I could remember, from Isabella's family history in South America, to LA. The adoption. How she had a strained relationship with her adoptive parents. I covered as much ground as I could, with Jay scribbling everything down in a small black journal.

When he felt like he had enough from me—or with me—he thanked me and was gone. I watched his black coat disappear around the corner and hoped this guy was as good as advertised.

CHAPTER TWENTY-EIGHT

ISABELLA

After I left California to come back to New York, I wanted a fresh start. A way to try to deal with my shit. And through a friend's recommendation, I started seeing Dr. Morgan. At first, the sessions started with my childhood. My real family. Then the adoption. My new family. It eventually led to the trauma—as she called it—of what I experienced at the USC frat party. I didn't necessarily consider it trauma. I mean, after the incident, I was in a dark place. I needed someone to talk to. To open up to. I've heard before that you shouldn't let things fester inside you. The shit that keeps you up at night, I wanted it out. At least as out as it could get.

I didn't mind that I had to keep my therapy a secret. My adoptive parents—or "Dad" and "Mom" as I'm supposed to call them—didn't really believe in therapy. Especially my dad. He found it a weakness, insisting that a stranger listening to your problems wouldn't help you. Insisting that speaking things aloud wouldn't change the fact that they happened. In a sense, he was right. And I could hate him for that alone.

But I didn't care what he thought. Or my mom, for that matter. The "mother" who was never a mother. The "mother" who hardly ever saw me, and acted like she never did.

I didn't care anymore. Dr. Morgan helped me. And even though she understood that the USC incident was difficult to overcome, she always tried to rationalize with me that I should at least attempt to have an active sexual relationship in my adulthood. But every so often, when I was on the verge of what she called "a breakthrough", something in me would shut down. And any progress would be lost.

She often counseled me to "push the envelope with my actions" regarding relationships and intimacy. And with Ray, I tried. And look where it got us.

I still remembered the day I first spoke to her about him, telling her about the new guy in my blossoming business life. How he genuinely cared about my project, and me. And I told her about his checkered past, how I didn't care. How he didn't care what people thought of him. And some of that rubbed off on me. I started realizing his outlook was the one to have. Fuck what everyone else thinks. Fuck what anyone wants from you.

She had smiled. "Wow. Wait, Isabella, are you falling for this guy?"

"Oh no," I had said with a small smile. "I've already fallen."

After the news broke about the alleged rape, she was shocked. Her concern for me, paramount. She respected my wishes to remain quiet on the situation, but she was curious about the veracity of the allegations and questioned me. She also apologized, for pushing me to explore intimacy, and my sexuality, despite me never being comfortable with either.

She pushed me, after that, for more therapy sessions. I knew it was vital. I wanted to understand myself, too. I wanted to be fixed. She told me I had to face the things that were haunting me.

But I didn't know if I was ready to face any of that.

I didn't know if I ever would be.

CHAPTER TWENTY-NINE

AP

THE NEXT STATUS HEARING WAS JUST A FEW WEEKS BEFORE Thanksgiving, which meant the trial was on track to start within a few months. Of course that depended on how Judge Beekman was going to calculate the speedy trial motion days. The DA's office had turned over a half-filled-out police report from their initial investigative report, as well as some scribbled notes on a pad. It *looked* like the DA played it straight, but we couldn't be sure. We also couldn't be clear as to what was going on with Isabella during the first interview, and if she, or *anyone*, would admit to exactly what happened.

Anthony had a discovery request for all medical reports and notes from Isabella's therapist, Dr. Morgan, whom Jay had discovered she was seeing. At the mention of this during the hearing, I couldn't help but catch Ari Rohnstein's facial expression at the mention of Isabella having a therapist. The troubled, concerned look. If I didn't know better, I'd say he almost looked *angry*.

The medical reports from Isabella's therapist were something the judge would have to address, however, how deep we could go into any past sexual or psychological issues were going to be matters of law at trial. Our client was on trial for rape, and the bottom line with our position was that no medical reports were confidential any longer. We knew going into this that it was vitally important to obtain any information relating back to the USC incident that could indicate a pattern by the accuser. To create reasonable doubt.

The DA arranged to have any and all final evidence that they intended to use at trial available for us before the next court date. And conversely, Anthony would have to hand over any evidence that we were holding onto, including any witness statements that Jay Johnstone had obtained. We all agreed to meet in the DA's office to exchange the important information instead of in court.

And then the bomb fell out.

Anthony looked at the judge. "Your Honor, we would also like the People to know that we intend to present as evidence a negligee that the accuser was wearing the night in question. We would like to submit this for an agreed upon DNA testing, which we will pay for, to determine if this is indeed a positive match to Ms. Rohnstein, whether through hair follicles or vaginal secretion," he said.

There was silence in the courtroom when the moment I was waiting for came, as I stood and briefly held up the white negligee to show the judge and the ADAs. The stunned faces conveyed that no one expected this or knew what to think.

Anthony let the silence hold for a moment before he continued. "Your Honor, in light of this astonishing evidence…"

"Let me guess," Judge Beekman said, cutting him off, "you want to file another motion to dismiss?"

I tried my best not to roll my eyes at the arrogance of this woman. Instead, I stood up, confidently, refusing to allow her to bully me into silence this time. I needed to take control. Right now.

"No, Your Honor, we are not going to be filing a motion to dismiss just yet. But we *will* be making a motion to drop the two first-degree charges, and we will be turning over to the prosecution the email and text chains that we have just been able to retrieve between Mr. Jansen and the alleged victim. It has been a challenge to get this information with our client detained in isolation. The electronic communication between the two of them is uncontroverted, and clearly demonstrates that there is nothing in the discovery to substantiate the legal threshold of "forcible compulsion" on either of those top counts. In reality, those charges should never have been presented to the Grand Jury. In light of this, we would like to schedule another bail hearing as soon as possible. It's bad enough that our client is being unjustly charged, but with the exposure on the 2-E felonies and the misdemeanor—if even legally allowable to be charged consecutively—we are talking a maximum of nine years. Mr. Jansen is not a flight risk, and he deserves an unhampered defense at this point in the case," I said.

"Thank you, Ms. Peterson, for your *input*," the judge said in a demeaning manner. "Just put in your bail motion and I suppose I'll hear it."

I nodded, taking my small victory and sitting down again. *That's not all you'll hear from me, bitch.*

CHAPTER THIRTY

ISABELLA

AFTER HEARING ABOUT THE NEGLIGEE EVIDENCE, I retreated into myself. Amazingly, I had totally forgotten about wearing it. Dr. Morgan put me on the spot the last time we spoke, asking about it. I didn't talk with anyone for weeks, hardly left my apartment, sank further and further into the depression that had its grips on me.

I was spiraling, obsessing over what had actually happened to me. No matter how many times I tried to replay it in my head, I couldn't understand. My mind started playing tricks on me. My dreams, confusing me even more. I almost reached a point where I couldn't decipher fiction from reality. Above all, what I felt was the emotion of a broken heart. Despite all the hell I was going through, I still loved Ray. But I knew, after all this, he was gone forever. Worse, he was sitting in a jail cell somewhere because of me.

Did he deserve to be there? I couldn't remember. Couldn't pinpoint exactly what happened. Did he rape me? Did he try? Did he succeed? The large dosages of anti-depressants and Xanax I was now on only made matters foggier.

If I could only see him and try to talk it out. If I could look into his eyes, so he could tell me what went wrong, maybe this could all go away. Maybe it could be fixed. Maybe he could fix me. He had a way of calming me, making me feel safe in a strange way. I was at least sane enough to know it was too late for all that now. And then, my resentment started setting in. For the DA. The detectives. How they initially pressured me. And how they were now controlling me.

The only person I could talk to was Dr. Morgan, but I was shutting her out now, too.

But then, I thought of Ray. Ray and his fuck-the-world attitude. And how he just lived his life, for him. So, I started doing the same.

I went back to the gym and started to get my mind and body right. I didn't give a shit about the paparazzi. The media. The investigators. Enough was enough. I just needed strength, and I was drawing it from Ray. Even if it was only from the memory of him.

This was my life, and I would take charge. For once.

CHAPTER THIRTY-ONE

AP

THE EARLY DECEMBER MEETING AT THE DA'S OFFICES AT 80 Centre Street was just two days before the next status hearing. Anthony and I were hoping it would clear up any of the open discovery issues outside of the court. But when we showed up, we were both shocked to see Ari Rohnstein himself standing there.

"What the hell is *he* doing here?" Anthony quipped.

"He represents the victim—you know, his *daughter*—and we would need his approval if we were going to talk any deals," the head of the department said.

"Hold on," Anthony said, "I'm here to work out the open legal issues, not talk pleas."

"Come on, Anthony," Ari said. "I'm just here to try and get a resolution for my daughter's sake, and maybe for your client as well."

Just as I opened my mouth to say something, Anthony grabbed my arm to stop me.

"I know why you're here, Ari," Anthony said. "It's for your own interest. There is no sense in going through all this nonsense. You want it to end? Agree to dismiss the case and free my client."

The department head jumped in and positioned himself between the two men. "Look, I've already pre-warned you about your client, but just so you know, we're prepared to get this case to a jury unless he comes to his senses."

Anthony shook his head in disbelief. "Maybe you guys should consider the damage this case could do to your careers. At least one person on the staff was smart enough to jump ship," he said, referencing the female ADA who resigned from the case.

"You don't know what you're talking about," the male ADA said. "She got a great offer in the private sector."

"Right she did," I said with a smirk, being snarky.

Anthony, on the other hand, still had more to say, and kept going in. "We're in a unique position with this case. Neither I nor my client will settle for anything. Ari, as you know, my career has not amounted to much in the last 15 years. He and I don't have much to lose. You and your brands, on the other hand, do. I read in *Forbes* that your net worth is down a bil since the case started."

The conversation was taking a turn I didn't expect, something I don't think anyone else saw coming either. Least of all Ari, who most likely knew that Anthony's personal agenda against him was problematic for him here.

"Look," the head DA said, "if you don't make a motion to drop the first-degree charges we are willing to offer your client a flat three on the Criminal Sexual Act in the Third Degree."

"What don't you guys understand?" Anthony asked, his tone firm. "My client is not pleading to a sex crime of any sort. And what do you think, I'm an amateur?" He chuckled. "We all know the first-degree charges are 'overcharges', they don't meet the 'forcible compulsion' requirement from all the evidence we now have. They probably never should've been presented to a Grand Jury. So, either you drop it voluntarily, or you're going to look bad when I get it dismissed. The choice is yours."

"Anthony," the head DA said rationally, "your client is still facing nine years on the third-degree charges in addition to the fleeing, and you know as well as I do that Judge Beekman will give him all of it."

I heard enough. "You guys don't get it. Some clients have integrity and respect. You basically tortured him in his last case, forced some of his co-defendants to rat. Do you think he wants to live his life as a registered sex offender now?"

"If he doesn't want to risk nine years in prison, he should seriously consider it," the head DA said to me.

"So, innocence doesn't matter then?" I asked him directly.

The head DA shook his head and tried to stifle an arrogant laugh. "Some people never learn." And with that, he walked out, leaving the remaining matters to be handled by his staff that were still in the room, in the thick of the tension.

Anthony threw his hands up and looked at me. "I don't even know why we came here. I guess we'll deal with any motions at the next hearing."

"No," the young ADA said. "We have some latitude to work out these issues without wasting too much time. Let's just put any plea talks to bed for Monday and continue to work on the legal matters in front of us."

Eventually, we negotiated a mutual agreement to drop the top counts, and agreed to a $1MM bail package. It was a reasonable bail that Ira could arrange with much less out-of-pocket costs to Ray this time around. Aside from all the bull-shit, I was just happy Ray would be coming home. I wanted to drive out to Queens to tell him, but Anthony instructed me to stay in the city and work on the matters at hand.

And so I did. I had never worked on a bail package of this nature and size before. Million-dollar bails were rare, and it was even rarer that they were posted in Manhattan. Anthony and I were working the phones between Ira, the insurance company, and Ray's family members, and all of it was unbeknownst to Ray.

I worked until midnight the day before court to make it all happen. I couldn't wait to surprise Ray and finally get to work on the case in a real office setting or over a civilized lunch rather than on Rikers Island.

That day, when we got to the pens at 111 Centre Street, I could barely hold my excitement.

"We need to talk privately," Anthony told him as we approached the pens.

We went into one of the small phone booths with glass partitions. Well, I stood behind Anthony as he sat there, because there was only room for one to talk. But Anthony explained the scenario to Ray as I tried to listen. When Anthony told him he would be released today, and that the first-degree charges would be dropped, Ray was less than ecstatic.

"What about the 30.30?" Ray asked.

"The bail conditions require that we withdraw the speedy trial motion," Anthony said.

"I'm not doing it," Ray said.

"Come on, you're being difficult now. Your family is here. Alexandra and Ira worked all night on this."

"Sorry, no. It's a deal breaker. I don't trust the government. They did the same shit to me in my last case. I know they're up to something and if I drop that 30.30 it becomes harder to put it back in if they detain me again. I also lose tons of leverage on appeal."

I couldn't believe the conversation I was hearing. I knew he had a reputation of being a difficult client, but I hadn't really experienced it until now. And I was hurt. All this work to free him and he didn't care? I wanted to cry. But being in the raw environment of the underbelly of the courthouse made me stay strong. I moved in closer. "Ray, we need to get you out of here to win this case. You need to come home. Now."

"Alexandra, they're trying to trap us," he said. "And I'm not going for it. Fool me once, shame on you. Fool me twice, shame on me."

"Well they aren't letting you out unless you drop the 30.30. You want to go home or not?" Anthony said.

"Go back and see if you can keep the 30.30 open. I mean really, you spring this on me *now*?" Ray asked.

"That's because I spent the last two days working on this, without a minute to spare. I've hardly even slept. Way to show your appreciation," I yelled at him. I couldn't take it anymore. I walked out.

And Anthony followed me. But he knew me well enough by now to know he needed to let me be for a few minutes. He knew I could handle myself, but he also knew I had feelings.

We went on the record. Without Ray.

"Your Honor," Anthony said, addressing the judge, "we are going to request a recall in the afternoon. We haven't had ample time to discuss the bail package with our client in detail."

"I'm confused," Judge Beekman said. "Does he not want to be bailed out?"

There was a large gasp in the courtroom from Ray's family. *I fucking know, people. I know. It's unbelievable.*

"Your Honor," I said, "we just need to speak to the People about a few of the conditions, and to our client's family regarding the bail. Please allow us a little time and I think we can work this out."

"Okay, Ms. Peterson. I hope you're right," the judge said. "We will adjourn now and have a 2:30 recall in the People vs. Jansen."

The parties took a lunch break and after some consideration on how exactly to deal with Ray, I told his mom I was going to speak with him—alone.

I looked at him through the glass partition like I was looking at a stubborn child. "The DA is not willing to accept the bail package unless you stipulate that you waive your right to a speedy trial. It's not necessary if you're no longer detained. It's that simple. Do you want to stay on Rikers or do you want to come home? It's your call. I'm done fighting for it. Especially if it's not even what you want."

"I just have concerns with dropping the 30.30," he said nonchalantly.

I moved closer to the glass, putting my hand under the partition to grab his hand. Those damn feelings springing up again. I tried to blink back my tears. "Ray, listen to me. I can't fucking stand you being in there anymore. You're innocent. I know you are. But I need you out here, working on this with me from the street. You don't know half the shit I've been doing for you. You need to trust me. Stop fighting this."

Ray sat there and looked at me for a moment, not giving away his emotions. "I'm sorry. You're right. Go ahead and have me produced and get me the fuck out of here."

I smiled, squeezed his hand, nodded, and was on my way.

RAY, his mother, and I took the walk over to Ira's office to sign all the bail paperwork. During the walk, Ray had his arm around his mother, and he and his mom got to talk a little. Some of which, I overheard.

"You need to keep fighting, son," she said. "Everyone who loves you can see what's going on here. We know you would never do something like that. Just don't give up."

"I won't," he said, giving her a kiss on her head. "How are the boys? I haven't seen them since all this came up. I don't want to drag them into it any more than necessary."

"They're okay," she said. "They know you wouldn't do anything like this."

He nodded. "Yeah. We've been writing back-and-forth, but it's hard trying to explain something like this to kids."

"I read in the papers that you rejected a three-year plea, is that true?" she asked him, changing the subject.

"Yes, I did. Everyone needs to understand something here. I'm not pleading to a sex crime. I'm innocent, and I'm getting railroaded by this office *again.* I'm not living my life as a pariah just so I can ensure myself less jail time. It's not about three years, or even nine years. It's about what I stand for and what I believe in. It's that simple. You know me better than that, Ma."

"I'm just getting old, Ray," his mom said. "I don't want to lose you and die while you're in prison."

"If I take a plea, then my *soul* will die. Do you want that?" he asked.

I saw her shake her head from the corner of my eye and once again I fought back tears. I wanted to look at her and tell her she would *not* die while he was in prison. Because I would not allow him to go to prison. Not for this, anyway.

CHAPTER THIRTY-TWO

RAY

Now that I was on the street, neither of the two sides seemed to be in a rush to meet and progress the case, especially with the holidays approaching. I needed some time to reconnect with society and get some edible food for the first time in months. I missed my two boys so much, and in the short time away I felt like they were turning into men now. I refused to let them come visit me this time in prison. I wanted them solely focused on their own lives and taking care of themselves. The letters we shared kept us connected. But I knew that reuniting with them in person and talking to them as men was of the highest of priority as soon as I could make it happen. And I was grateful that Alexandra got me home just in time to spend Christmas with them.

New York State courts were very aggressive in tying up assets of white-collar cases, and I was no stranger to it. It was just another way to convict a defendant by cutting off all his money supplies before even going to trial. But this time, I knew how to fight it.

I did the necessary research to get some of my tied-up

assets released to get back on my feet, and I also had funds in my business partner's name that I could now gain access to since I was out. It wouldn't be long before I'd be able to get back to living an independent life while still fighting this thing.

My first item of business to handle was to get up to speed on the evidence. After some time in the office breaking down the case from the various DNA and toxicology reports, it became apparent to me that the case was circumstantial at best. The DA would try to paint a picture of semen and hair follicles putting me at the scene, but after that, there wasn't much substance. However, the DA was sticking to the company line that Isabella said no, and no means no, which constituted rape.

Mika came in to the part of his office I was working in. "We need you to go back through all your history with Isabella and see if you can uncover anything that can help us discredit her," he said.

The thought of trying to *discredit* the woman I loved went against everything I stood for. *She accused you of rape. Remember that.* "I've been out of commission for almost six months now," I told him. "I need to try and get reacquainted with my surroundings first. They took everything from me, especially my computers. Is there any way I can get access to a computer?"

But it was Alexandra that responded. "I have an old laptop at my apartment. You can swing by whenever and pick it up."

Mika looked at her with a slight question in his eyes. "Okaaay," he said, drawing the word out. "You two just figure out how to get me some more background info as soon as you can. I have to head out now."

I nodded. After he left, I looked at Alexandra. "Hey,

since it's getting late, do you want to finish this outside the office? We can go grab dinner and drinks."

"Sure," she said. "I've been stuck in here too often lately. Let's go."

We went to a local bar and ordered a couple of drinks. Our plan—to finish the meeting about my case—didn't work out. We didn't discuss a single thing about the case. Instead, Alexandra told me about her childhood growing up in Pittsburgh and working her way through law school. She spoke highly of her closeness to her family and friends. She asked me questions, interesting questions, about my time on Wall Street and my journey through the courts. I felt comfortable speaking freely with her, not just because she was my lawyer. There was just something easygoing about her, easy to talk to. Good at listening.

At some point, I started getting tired, and she must have noticed. She reached out and touched my arm and I looked at her hand.

"You look like you could use a fun night out," she said. "My friends are dying to meet you. Why don't you come out with me for some more drinks up in the meatpacking district?"

"I'm getting there, but I really need to sleep and work out in the morning to get my mind right. Can I take a rain check on that though?"

"Sure you can, and I'm gonna hold you to it," she said.

After we finished the last of our drinks, I walked her outside to a cab and she turned to me.

"I just have to tell you, I feel so alive working on this case. I want to thank you for putting your trust in me. This is the reason I went to law school. For people like you."

"Are you kidding me? I can't thank you guys enough. I feel so comfortable with you. It's like I've known you forever."

Maybe because I was getting older, I was getting more sensitive throughout the years. But now, standing here with Alexandra who was genuinely fighting for me, I couldn't help it. Something about what I'd been through in the last six months made me emotional. I pulled her close and gave her a hug. "Now, go tell your friends that I can't wait to meet them, just not tonight." Then I gave her a kiss on the cheek and fetched her a cab.

I WAS SURPRISED the next day when I got a call from Nick Salerno, although I wasn't opposed to conversing with him. We agreed to meet for a quiet lunch.

After some quick catch-up talk, Salerno got right to the point. "I'm worried about you, man. Is it a smart thing to do, turning down a three-year deal?"

"I know why you're here, but you know I can't talk about the case. If I accept that deal then I have to register as a sex offender. And you know I'd never accept that willingly," I told him.

"You are talking a *decade* of time, Ray," he said.

"It doesn't matter. I got respect on the inside. If I go up there on a plea like this, I'm finished."

"Damn it, Jansen, you don't get it! They will crush you worse than they did last time," he said.

I sat there calm as could be and just looked at him, remembering the man he used to be. "What happened to you, Nick?"

"What are you talking about?" he asked, almost annoyed.

"Remember when you were a man of principle and honor? That's what I always loved and respected about you."

"And?" Nick said, motioning with his hands. "Where are we going with this?"

"You stand for Ari Rohnstein, and your god is money

now. It's sad you don't see it." We always had deep conversations that sometimes would turn religious in nature, but I felt like this one in particular might lead to the end of the road in our lifelong friendship.

"We're getting off topic," he said. "I'm the only link between you guys and I want to help both of you and try to mediate some reasonable resolution."

"You want to help?" I asked, not letting him finish. "The real Nick would stand up for what he believes in. You knew what was going on with me and Iz from the start. The first time she called me and took me out to dinner, you knew. You don't think I could have slept with her the first night we went out?"

"I don't know," he said, shrugging.

"Oh, you do know. You knew so well that you tried to stop it. Email after email, text after text, she wanted to. But I didn't do it. Out of respect for *you* and your relationship with Rohnstein. And this is how you repay me? You come here trying to broker me into pleading to a three-year deal for a sex crime no less? Then what? You turn your back on me?"

"I don't know what happened between you and Isabella. I was in the dark for so long. Then the next thing I know, the police are at the apartment and she's claiming you raped her..."

"Nothing happened," I said. "There was no sex, never mind rape!"

"Look, okay, I've seen a change in Ari lately. The media articles disparaging his family are getting to him. I told you that was always his biggest fear. Maybe your lawyers and his can try and resolve this thing somehow, 'cause if you don't, be prepared for him and the DA to pull all their resources together to finish you. It's as simple as that," he said.

I could almost feel my eyes gloss over with anger. I was officially fed up with having to defend myself, to anyone.

But especially to people who were supposed to be my friends. "Well thanks for coming to see me. Please tell Ari that he's not the hunter, he's the hunted." I peeled off a crisp hundred-dollar bill and flipped it on the table and walked out, leaving Salerno there alone.

CHAPTER THIRTY-THREE

ISABELLA

I FELT A WEIGHT OFF MY SHOULDERS, KNOWING RAY WAS out of prison. Even if he was only out on bail. The pressure of an imminent trial was now off, especially over the holidays. Everything seemed to stop with the case. And the thought—or dream, rather—of connecting with him somehow, started to become a daily desire for me for the New Year. That, and getting myself right.

Then, almost suddenly, I made a breakthrough with Dr. Morgan. I told her, finally, the entire truth. What I've never spoken aloud. What I've never told anyone. I finally faced my demons like she had been encouraging me to. I even told her everything about the incident in college, as well as my childhood. It was a series of intensely emotional sessions, and trying at times for both of us. But she was right. It was what I needed in order to start to heal.

Liberated by this, even though it was hard, I decided I needed to go forward with testifying in the case against Ray. Dr. Morgan advised me that this testimony would be the final nail in the coffin, which would allow me to let go of my past, and that was what I wanted. But I was still harboring resentment against the DA. I didn't make myself readily available for them, leading them to accuse me of being a potential uncooperative witness. At least that's what my father said. And then, I couldn't take it. I *had* to get in touch with Ray.

So, I emailed him. And because I wasn't *allowed* to contact him, I created a bogus email address that only he would understand—Janedoeglow@gmail.com. "I still love you" was the subject line. I desperately wanted to hear back from him. To hear anything from him at all.

There was one status hearing in early February, just to get everyone reacquainted with where things stood. I didn't pay much attention to it until I was told there was going to be what they called a "suppression hearing" coming up in a month.

I didn't know much about what this meant, but all I was told was that on March 3rd I would have to testify to the veracity of the negligee. There was so much media attention around it, I couldn't stand it. I was told that after the hearing and circumstances, a trial date would be set.

On one particularly annoying day, my father went to the DA's office. When he came home, he warned me about testifying. He told me I could not admit to wearing it. That the DAs said it would be "inconsistent" with my first testimony, and that it showed "seduction" on my part. Hearing that word thrown around by them, regarding me, disgusted me. I hated them all. But I had no choice but to get on board with what they all wanted. Even if it meant ruining everything.

My dad was also back to being his brash self—after I agreed not to admit to wearing the negligee—bragging to me and my mother how Ray and his lawyers were about to "get theirs". He had a few smug remarks about them. But I was disinterested in the whole conversation, and felt even less comfortable having to testify in this pre-trial hearing about any of it, especially in front of everyone. Including the entire world.

CHAPTER THIRTY-FOUR

AP

THE NEGLIGEE HEARING WAS JUST DAYS AWAY. ANTHONY brought the whole team into his office. It was time to start focusing full-bore on the case and preparing for a general defense. But the magnitude of the hearing became too important and only complicated things. So, we knew we couldn't get ahead of ourselves. In the conference room that day, Anthony played CEO, while Ray, Jay Johnstone, some associates and paralegals, and I took notes and listened.

"We are about to embark on two months of hell," Anthony started. "First is the Mapp hearing regarding the negligee evidence, and depending on that outcome, we begin preparing a straight-forward defense for trial. Everyone in this room needs their attention on nothing but this case. Tell your husbands, wives, and significant others that you are on my time now. It's the only way we can win this case."

I nodded, knowing full well how committed I was. I couldn't help but think the timing of the evidentiary hearing and subsequent trial couldn't have been better for the DA. With the recent Bill Cosby arrest, public sentiment was shifting toward convicting anyone associated in any way with a sexual assault crime of any nature, and we just knew that the DA and media would try to connect the two events—Cosby and Ray's trial—to the naïve public. The timing for us, Ray mostly, couldn't have been worse. During times like this, when there's a public outcry for justice, no one even wants to believe a man could be innocent. Not when so many of them do such heinous things. And worse, get away with it. But Ray was innocent. That was the difference here. And I would go down with him if I had to.

"We need to be prepared for anything that comes our way," Anthony said. "We are not only dealing with a judge and DA that will push the envelope, to say the least, but also one of the most influential media titans in the world. We have the truth on our side, but we're still the underdogs. And sometimes, even the truth isn't enough. We cannot take anything for granted here."

"Are you saying that we can't start preparing a defense until after the judge rules on the negligee?" I asked.

"I think we should wait," Anthony said. Then he paused before speaking again. "I'm confident we will win, but let's just see what happens. I don't want to get ahead of ourselves."

I nodded in response.

Anthony then looked at the private investigator. "Jay, I have a basic opening statement outlined, but I need more to bring doubt to the jurors' minds. Do you have anything for me? Anything at all?"

Jay gave Anthony a subtle shake of his head. "No real movement, sir. The leads I got in South America were back-peddling. At first, $20 was going a long way there, but then it seemed like someone, somewhere, had gotten to some of the people in their state department. I'm not done just yet, but I need to think it through and decide if it's worth another trip there."

Time was ticking. And even though the adoption history was something that would be pertinent in a cross examination with both Isabella and Ari, if another trip there wouldn't be fruitful, there was no point in wasting time and money. No one needed to say it aloud. It was just a fact.

Anthony ended with one final statement. "I appreciate everyone being on board. This case means a lot to Ray, but also to this law firm. It represents a rare opportunity to work as a team on a high-profile case of this magnitude. It will live with all of us forever, win or lose. We need to make sure we leave nothing to chance or have any regrets when it's all over."

I nodded, taking in his words.

Then he dismissed us.

And I kept hearing his words, later that night. When I was home, thinking about the defense strategy. *This case means a lot to Ray.*

It meant a lot to me, too.

CHAPTER THIRTY-FIVE

RAY

DESPITE THE JUDGE TRYING TO KEEP THE TRIAL ON SCHEDULE at the February status hearing, there were still issues that were going to push it back. The two big items were the lingering discovery issues and the much-anticipated procedural hearing on how to deal with the negligee at trial.

The courts in New York City were already pathetically slow, but the trial couldn't proceed until the pre-trial hearing took place first. With a lot of time leading up to it, it felt like the calm before the storm.

I tried to continue my meditation rituals and keep my mind balanced, but for some reason I couldn't turn my thoughts away from Isabella.

I always believed my dreams told me things. And the crux of what I was feeling, whether I was daydreaming or sleeping, continued to make me feel like Isabella needed me. I felt helpless, not being able to see if she was okay. Insane, I know. Me, worrying about the woman who put me in the situation I was in. The woman who didn't seem to care I was in prison, for her.

Alexandra called me the night before the hearing and

suggested we walk into court together, so we met at the park adjacent to the courthouse. The media trucks were plentiful, yet again giving me a twinge of anxiety. But Alexandra placed a calming hand on my arm.

"Just keep your head up, and don't smile. Let me do the talking if we have to," she said.

I nodded. She kept my anxiety down as we headed to the courthouse. The media tried to get a statement from me, but Alexandra took charge.

"We have no comment," she said, pushing our way in through the circular doors to go inside the old court building.

I remained calm at the defense table, until Isabella strolled in and our eyes locked. I couldn't look away, despite how painful it was. Especially remembering the email I got recently, but ignored. I knew in my heart it was her. Jane Doe Glow. *I still love you.* I almost forgot how beautiful she was. I was still looking at her when Alexandra nudged me and gave me a subtle shake of her head.

I had no idea what Isabella would say. I hoped she would end this. If she was still the woman I knew—or thought I knew—she would. But I don't think anyone knew what she would say. Maybe even Isabella herself. But she was dressed like she was prepared for a media event. Conservative, but it didn't matter. Anything she wore would catch my interest. It wasn't about the clothes, or her looks at that point. It was so much more than that. The conflicting emotions must have been showing, because Alexandra tried again to get me to focus.

But Isabella's second glance at me brought back the same emotions. I almost smiled at her. I wanted to. But as I felt my lips turning up instinctively, I stopped myself and looked away. I looked at the floor, the ceiling. Reminded myself I was in court, accused of rape. By the woman I love.

The woman sitting right over there, looking at me with no sign of remorse.

Judge Beekman came in and set the tone of the hearing with a sharpness in her voice directed at the defense. "Mr. Mika, this hearing is going to have a narrow focus of the issue at hand regarding procedural law only. You cannot lead the witness in any manner whatsoever, do you understand?"

"Your Honor, I may need some latitude on credibility issues," Mika said.

"There is no jury here, that's what a trial is for. I will determine if the witness is credible or incredible in my final ruling. Now go ahead with your examination," the judge said.

After the typical informative questions that were required for the court record, I watched Mika straighten his shoulders and look at Isabella. "Ms. Rohnstein, is this your negligee?" he asked her, as he held it up for the court—and media—to see.

Everyone including me waited for her response, and it was ultimately short and sweet.

"Yes," she said.

I tried to look for emotion in her eyes. Regret. Anything. But I saw nothing.

"On the night in question, were you wearing this negligee in the room that you accused my client of raping you?" Mika asked.

"Not that I recall," Isabella said.

I shook my head. *Why, Iz?*

"Well, what *do* you recall that night, Ms. Rohnstein?" Mika asked her.

"Objection!" the DA yelled before Isabella could answer further.

"Sustained," Judge Beekman said. "You need to stay narrow, Mr. Mika."

"What *do* you recall wearing that night, Ms. Rohnstein?" Mika asked.

"I was wearing a formal dress at the party."

"And is that what you recall wearing when you entered the room my client was in after the party?" Mika asked.

"Oh, no. I don't believe so," she said.

Mika went back to his table for notes. "I'm confused, Ms. Rohnstein. If none of your clothes were recovered at the scene, then were you naked when you ran out of the room yelling 'rape'?"

"No, I wasn't naked when I ran out of the room…"

"Okay," Mika said. "We have now established that you don't recall wearing the negligee, and that you didn't have your formal dress on, and you testified that you weren't naked. So, what *were* you wearing?"

"It must have been my robe," she said.

"Are you sure, Ms. Rohnstein? Because you seem confused."

"Yes, because Ray had asked me to bring him a drink before he went to bed. So, I was just being polite when I brought him something to drink because he had been drinking all day. After that, I kind of blacked out."

Mika's eyebrows went up. "And what about you, Ms. Rohnstein? Weren't you drinking and doing drugs all day?"

"Objection, Your Honor!" the DA yelled.

"Sustained," the judge said, annoyed now. "Mr. Mika, we are not going there right now. And you know this. But you insist on making me upset, don't you?"

"I'm sorry, Your Honor," Mika said. "But the witness opened the door."

The judge couldn't argue with him there because he was right. Instead, with a wave of her hand, she allowed him to move on.

"Ms. Rohnstein," Mika said, "it seems like it was a long day, and night. It also seems as if your memory was shot, as you said you 'kind of blacked out'. So, is it plausible that you could have possibly been wearing this negligee underneath your robe?"

"Like I said before, I don't recall wearing it at all that night," she said.

And with that, the DA stood up. "Your Honor, I think the victim has now answered the question twice in two different forms. I ask that Mr. Mika finishes up with his testimony since he has fully examined the witness from his side. And I ask if we can follow-up?"

"She is *your* witness," Mika said, seeming confident that he got what he needed out of Isabella.

I was in a state of shock. The lack of remorse in her tone. I never saw this side of Isabella before. It was like she was a completely different person. I knew she was lying. Hell, *she* knew she was lying. But she seemed like she couldn't care less. I bowed my head in disgust, unable to look at her anymore.

Alexandra pinched me, and as I lifted my head, the DA began his line of questioning.

"Ms. Rohnstein, thank you for your testimony today," he said. "We don't have much to ask you, but these are important questions, so please try to refresh your memory as best you can."

"Okay," she said calmly.

"When was the last time you saw this negligee?" he asked.

"It was in my walk-in closet hanging up."

"And was the defendant ever in that walk-in closet?"

"Yes," she said.

"Can you tell us when?"

"During the night of the party," she said. "I showed him

my separate apartment in the penthouse because he wanted some privacy so he could do some coke."

"And what drugs were you doing that night?"

"We both dabbled in a little cocaine just to keep us energized. It was a long day. It's really not uncommon in this industry."

"And Ms. Rohnstein, did you and Mr. Jansen snort cocaine in your walk-in closet?"

"Yes, we did," she said.

"And did you leave Mr. Jansen in the apartment alone at any time?"

"I did. I went back to the party and told him to come about five minutes later so it didn't look like we went missing together. Ray and I were never an item, so it wouldn't have looked appropriate if we were missing together for too long."

I couldn't believe what I was hearing. Before Isabella could even finish her testimony, several media members ran out of the courtroom. I wanted to, too. It almost made me sick, just hearing her speak. Hearing her lie about us, pretending we were never involved.

She might as well have looked me in my eyes and told me she never gave a fucking shit about me.

CHAPTER THIRTY-SIX

AP

NEWS OF THE ACCUSER'S TESTIMONY HAD ALREADY SPREAD. Judge Beekman ordered a break and a 2:30 recall for oral summations. Online, reports were being spread that Isabella Rohnstein's testimony was "bombastic".

Anthony ran back to the office to do some quick research on the case law, while Ray and I went out for lunch at the *Roxy Hotel.* We sat in a private corner booth, and he barely spoke other than when he ordered our drinks. I tried to talk to him, but he just shut me down with a shake of his head. When the beers came, Ray took a Xanax with his. I'd never seen him this down before, even in the depths of despair in isolation on Rikers Island. He was acting as if he'd already been found guilty.

"We got her to admit she doesn't remember," I reminded him. "We can still win this."

"You don't understand," he said quietly. "She lied. About everything. It's like we had nothing together. She *never* left me in her apartment alone."

"I know it hurts. I'm sorry. But I also know she was wearing that negligee, and that's all that should matter to you now. I know the truth, and the jury will too when I'm done with her."

"Do you know what it's to like to love someone and have them do something like this?" he asked. "In all my life, I never even could have imagined this…"

"Ray, look at me," I said, grabbing his forearm tightly. "We are getting you off. I won't let her win."

Then he surprised me. He leaned over in the booth and kissed me gently on my forehead.

"I love your conviction, AP. I just don't know if you understand what we're up against," he said.

It was the first time he ever called me AP. The two beers and Xanax must have calmed his nerves a bit. Then I checked the time and told him it was time to go.

The sunny brisk walk through Tribeca back to the courthouse seemed to wake him up a bit, and he put his best face on. I held his arm on the neighborhood backstreets where no one was around to see.

Then, we were back in the courtroom.

The DA got the first side of the oral argument. "Your Honor, in light of Ms. Rohnstein's testimony, there is no way that the court can ascertain that the negligee was not a product of crime evidence. In fact, it's very plausible that the defendant actually stole it. Very simply, it must be suppressed."

The judge looked at him sternly and pressed back. "I want the People to know I have some concerns about the victim's memory and I need to take more time to research the case law myself."

"Your Honor, may I?" Anthony said. "In these instances of admissibility, it comes down to credibility and prejudice. I don't believe you can ascertain if someone is credible or not when they have testified that they can't remember. However, what is indisputable is that if this key piece of evidence—

which could be the linchpin of Ms. Rohnstein's state of mind —is not admitted, then my client's defense would be greatly prejudiced. And the law is clear. If this is the case, then the garment must be admitted for the jury to consider the weight of it."

"The problem I have with your client is that he ran from the scene and caused a manhunt," the judge said. "Not to mention he is a convicted felon for manipulating stock prices. He has a high level of sophistication in him. I have no idea where or how he got this, but I cannot allow a piece of evidence to be entered if I think there could be a chance it was obtained fraudulently to possibly cover up his actions. Additionally, I need to be sensitive to the victim's recollection, which could have been severely traumatized by the incident. So, in that regard, I do find that her testimony *could* indeed be credible."

She then asked the lawyers to prepare final briefs and send them in by the morning, saying she would rule the following day after receiving the written arguments.

CHAPTER THIRTY-SEVEN

RAY

48 HOURS LATER WE WERE BACK IN PART 55 FOR JUDGE Beekman to give a final ruling on the negligee. I couldn't sleep so I took an early morning walk. The sun wasn't up yet, but I knew where I could grab the first newspapers in my old neighborhood. And no matter how bad KB's ruling would be, nothing could be as bad as what the papers were saying. *The New York Post* took the worst shot at me —"Judge to Rule if Stock Scum Stole Panties Too." Along with the headline was an unflattering picture of me on the cover. That wasn't nearly as bad as what was five pages in though, a huge article about the sexual assault crimes Bill Cosby committed, and how rape was up all over the city.

What a coincidence. I thought about ending it right there. Possibly getting in a cab and going to the GW Bridge and putting myself out of my misery. I could jump.

Instead, I went back to my apartment and cried for the first time in years. I knew if Judge Beekman hadn't already made her decision, the papers were just enough to swing her to the prosecution's side. Worse than a decision being overturned by another judge is a backlash of public opinion that she was soft on a sexual crime against a woman. New Yorkers were already incensed at Bill Cosby, so who better to take their anger out on than a convicted felon like me?

I didn't respond to anyone's calls or texts, other than a quick "yes" reply to AP when she asked if I was okay. I walked to court alone and waited for the judge's decision.

She made a brief statement suppressing the negligee as evidence that our defense could use, based on the credibility of the testimony of the witness, believing that her memory could have been severely hampered by the trauma of the event. "Now, we will start picking a jury on April 11," she said. "Make sure you all clear your calendars." And she tapped her gavel.

Before anyone could say much, we all escaped for the weekend.

ONCE SATURDAY ROLLED around I thought I'd feel better, but I still couldn't shake off the devastating blow. I had enough experience to know when a case had turned against me. But I forced myself to return some calls.

Andy seemed the most anxious to speak with me. When I finally called him back, I could sense a different tone in his voice.

"Listen, cuz, we gotta meet. You got my balls twisted over this shit now and as much as I love you, the perception out there is making me look bad," he said.

"I understand, but what do you want me to do? You know I didn't do this shit. I don't know how many times I have to say it..."

"Things are different now. Remember that big thing I

told you was gonna happen over Christmas?" he asked cryptically.

"Yeah," I said, imploring for more.

"Well, I got the promotion on the job. You know what I'm saying, *cugine?*"

I knew then that Andy was bumped up to a Capo, and there was now a higher standard expected of him, and the associates around him for that matter. "Congrats, bro, long overdue. I'm happy for you. I'll do whatever you want me to. Just let me know."

"I gotta stop by a couple of construction sites this week, to show my face. Once that's done, tell Frankie he has to meet us on Thursday night for dinner."

I could sense the change in Andy, mostly in his assertiveness not only to me but Frankie now too. "You got it. I don't want to put you in a bad spot. I can't thank you enough for believing in me. And when this is over, I hope there are no hard feelings," I said.

"You just gotta beat the case, kid. This whole negligee thing has everybody shaking their heads. I'm not in the business of sticking up for rape-os, but I told you I'd always be there for you. Unfortunately, things are a little different now, but let's just talk about it in person."

"I understand. I'll see you Thursday night." I hung up the phone, feeling like Andy was about to turn his back on me, too.

FOR THE NEXT WEEK, I tuned out the case. I barely talked to AP. The money issues consumed me. I spoke with my business partner and told him I needed more, especially with what I was expecting to go down with Andy. The idea of losing Andy as a friend bothered me, but I knew it had to be this way—for his sake.

Frankie called me Wednesday night and said Andy wanted to meet in Brooklyn the next day, but Frankie objected going into the neighborhood. We ultimately decided to meet at a quiet restaurant in SOHO, where no wise guys would run into us. It was a neighborhood place with a nice cocktail lounge, so Frankie and I decided to go early to talk about how to deal with Andy.

"You know this dude is gonna be coming here on some rah-rah shit, so be prepared," Frankie said. "I told you about him, but he's your boy. Even I'm outraged at all this shit in the papers, but I'm fully backing you at this point."

"Look, Frank, I know who Andy is…"

"No. You don't. Trust me on that. You're not on the street like me. And now I hear he's bumped up so he's pushing his weight around like he's John Gotti."

I didn't have time for the street politics. "He's been there for me. So, whatever he wants, I'll give it to him and move on."

"I'm telling you if you wasn't with me tonight he would come in here looking to push up on you, for real."

Before we noticed, Andy was already an hour late. Frank tried to text him, but got nothing in response. We called, but it went straight to voicemail. Before long, one hour turned into two and Frank was cursing him.

"You see what I mean about these Brooklyn guys?" he said. "Most of them aren't like us."

"I just hope something didn't happen," I said.

"Well I hope something did," Frank said. "'Cause there's no excuse for something like this. It's a slap in the face. Maybe not to you, but it is to me. When you set up a meeting with another crew, you better show or have a damn good reason why you don't. It don't matter if he's a captain now or not."

"I really hope he didn't get another parole violation," I said.

Andy never showed. We went home after dinner, not accomplishing much without him. Frankie called me before bed to let me know that he heard Andy was in a beef in Brooklyn. He'd gotten into a fight and supposedly got the worst of it.

"I don't know the whole story, but it sounds like the same bullshit he was doing upstate, bullying people around that were scared of him and someone tested him again. You think he would learn," Frankie said.

"I'm tired, Frank. Let's talk in the morning and we'll reschedule with him."

I GOT UP EARLY AS usual to go get the newspaper and stroll through the city. I brought my phone and noticed there was a text that came in from Frankie in the middle of the night. I figured Frankie was probably out partying, but the text was straightforward:

Andy got stabbed up. He's not gonna make it.

I dropped my phone. Andy was gone. Dead. It was more bad news that I just couldn't take. Forget about the case, this was someone who meant something to me. A friend. A good fucking guy I did hard time with. *Dead? No.*

I tried to pull myself together and picked up my phone from the ground. Then I got the papers and the story was already making headlines. "Live by the Sword, Die by the Sword" read the *Daily News*, chronicling how Andy went to prison for 17 years for stabbing and killing someone, and then had the knife turned on him. It was true, but that didn't make it any easier to accept.

I went home quietly with the paper in hand. The gravity of the news hit me like a ton of bricks. I walked into my apartment and threw my remote at a mirror out of anger, yelling "fuck!" at the top of my lungs.

Someone from Andy's crew reached out to Frankie, who passed the news to me. And they all agreed that I would take care of what I needed, and that the Balboni crime family would no longer have any involvement in my case. It was best for everyone, but I couldn't stop the thoughts that were plaguing me, of how Andy went out. And that he was gone. Forever. Just like that.

I WENT to Brooklyn to pay my final respects to my friend and his wife, Stephanie, whom I had come to know from sending packages up to Andy while he finished his bid. Frankie, on the other hand, refused to go into Brooklyn for the wake. Andy and I had some mutual friends from Brooklyn, and we all met up at *Scarpaci's Funeral Home* to say our final goodbyes. We went out to Bay Ridge after the service.

It seemed like no one was really surprised to see Andy gone, but it still hurt like hell. Andy was always there when I needed him most—a sign of a true friend.

I took a Fireball shot with everyone in Andy's honor and said my goodbyes, not knowing if or when I would ever see any of them again. I didn't care anymore. I headed out into the blistering cold night in the Ridge.

As I walked toward my car, I could see the green lights of the Verrazano Bridge not too far in the background. The brutal wind blew on my face just like it did when I was walking the yard up in Attica. And just like that, I felt like I was back there again. All alone. The eerie silence in the neighborhood around me took over for a moment and I felt like I was back in prison. I shook my head at the memory. And as cruel as it felt, I knew I had to be selfish and try to forget about Andy. I had to focus on my own problems now. And before I got into my warm truck, I let Andy go.

CHAPTER THIRTY-EIGHT

AP

IT HAD BEEN MORE THAN A WEEK SINCE I HEARD FROM RAY. Anthony was becoming impatient, but he'd heard about Andy, and told me we had to have a little consideration. Give him space. Time to grieve.

I couldn't help myself from checking in on him, though. With all that he was going through, and now losing a friend, my heart ached for him.

And then, when I was losing hope, he finally texted me back.

I promise I'll be ready to go on Monday. I've just been through a lot these last two weeks.

I'm so sorry. Why didn't you call me to talk?

I don't know. Don't take it personally. I didn't want you to see me like this. But you have been on my mind.

Really? I asked.

Really. I'll be in the office Monday. And I promise you and I will have dinner and catch up.

Okay.

. . .

All I could do then was wait. And patience was never one of my strong suits.

CHAPTER THIRTY-NINE

RAY

I WAS SURFING THE WEB A LITTLE MORE THAN TWO WEEKS before the trial date when another email popped up from Jane Doe Glow. My hands shook as I clicked to open it. It was a line I had told Isabella before:

I'll always be here for you.

I replied, no longer caring about the order of protection. *Who the hell is this?*

I waited for a response and poured myself some red wine.

And then finally, it came. The name "Bianca Sori" was typed, followed by a non-descript address in Argentina. I didn't know what to make of it, especially the end, that read: *Goodnight, love.*

Regardless of how jaded my mind had been, I knew this was a lead. A big one. Whatever someone was up to, Isabella or not, they wanted the defense to have this address.

WHEN MONDAY CAME, I handed over the address to Jay

Johnstone.

"Where'd you get this?" he asked.

"Don't worry about that. Isabella had told me the only connection she had to South America was her aunt that she lived with in LA. I'm pretty sure this is her. I'm also pretty sure she knows about the adoption. I have a gut feeling she knows something."

Anthony overheard and came over. He looked at the address, then looked at Jay. "I need you to make another trip down there. We need something. Get there as soon as you can."

Jay nodded and booked a flight. The earliest he could do was the middle of the following week. It wasn't as soon as any of us would have liked, but it would have to do.

In the meantime, I worked closely with AP on trial preparation, giving her as much background on Isabella as possible. We were getting closer, but not close enough for me to trust telling her about the emails I was receiving.

THE FOLLOWING WEEK, Anthony got a call from Jay Johnstone when he checked into his hotel in Argentina, telling him service was choppy and we might not hear from him for a few days.

"I don't think we have a few days," Anthony told him. "We need to prepare an opening as soon as possible. Plus, if I'm going to present anything new to the judge, she'll want it before the trial actually starts."

This led to growing tensions in Mika's office. Our stress levels went up as the trial neared. AP kept me in the loop, on everything. I texted her back.

Thanks for the update, AP. I've been meaning to tell you something. I need to see you tonight in person.

CHAPTER FORTY

AP

THE BOTTLE OF WINE AND QUIET DINNER BETWEEN RAY AND me had moved onto cocktails at a local bar. We were both feeling a solid buzz at this point. Neither of us were in a rush, with no one to go home to. My boyfriend had broken up with me just before I took on this case. He wanted me to move out west with him, but I decided to stay here for the firm. For my first big case. It was an all or nothing decision, and so far, I hadn't regretted it.

Something about that night was different with Ray. I wondered what was so important that he had to see me in person. So far, he wasn't giving me any inclination as to what it was. As a woman, I started pondering maybe he just *wanted* to see me for no real reason at all. Professionally, I knew it was wrong. But personally, I couldn't help my mind wandering there. He was attractive—I wasn't blind. There was chemistry there. Between us. We worked well together. We got along. He was the kind of person I could relate to.

He looked at me differently that night. I don't know if I opened that door or if he did. But neither of us closed it. He complimented me in a forward way, and I accepted it.

"Wait, what's up with you tonight?" I finally asked him. "You never told me why you wanted to meet."

"I just wanted to see you, AP."

He laughed, making me wonder if he was being serious or if he was playing with me.

"Awww, really, Ray?" I asked, squeezing his cheek in jest.

"Yeah, I'm doing better. How are you doing with everything?"

"I'm not the one on trial," I said.

"I know, but we're always talking about me. I wanna know how you're doing with all this. I know it can't be easy for you."

He was right about that. I had many people question me as to why I was defending a felon, a rapist. A scumbag, as they called him. But they didn't know him. They only knew what they read. What they heard about. What the media told them he was.

"To be totally honest with you, I'm so engulfed in this. I've never been so involved in a case like this before. As emotionally draining as it can be, it's also invigorating. I want to stop them from trying to destroy you. I saw my uncle get railroaded on a drug case in North Hills when I was in high school. It ruined my cousin's family. I was too young then to understand, but not now. You know, my boyfriend left me a few months ago, and the saddest part is that I don't even miss him because I've been so distracted with the case."

He grabbed my hand. "I appreciate your efforts in all this. I want this to turn out good for you, too. I'm sorry about your boyfriend. I want the storybook ending where you get to be the big celebrity lawyer."

"That's not why I'm doing this. Do you know how

embarrassed I was when I was on the cover of the *New York Post*?"

"Oh, come on, you loved it. They made you look so sultry, too!" he joked.

I laughed and shook my head.

Ray ordered two shots for us, and after shooting down the Fireball, he continued. "Look, AP, I don't want you to get too consumed with this. It's dangerous for you. We're fighting evil forces here. These stories don't always end happily. I learned that in my last case when I lost everything without even being able to fight. I don't want you to be too disappointed if things go left."

"I will never stop fighting for you or believing that we can win this," I said. "Isn't that why we're all here? To do our best and persevere? All the time? Regardless of the circumstances?"

"You sound like me when I was younger," he said. "Now, I've turned cynical. Keep your innocence as long as you can. It's refreshing to see, really."

I circled my finger around my empty shot glass. "What was it like seeing her?"

He shook his head. "I could never describe it. It was beyond bizarre. I've never felt anything like that, especially in a courtroom, and that's saying a lot."

"I just don't get it," I said angrily. "It's like she's up to something. She lies and then has the gall to glance over at you the way she did."

"You saw that look?" he asked me.

"Oh yeah, and that wasn't the look of a girl who was raped."

"That's what I needed to talk to you about," he said. "If I tell you something, can you promise me you won't disclose it to anyone until I say so?"

I wasn't sure where he was going with this. "I don't understand the question."

He leaned forward and whispered to me. "I need you to promise me that your word to me is stronger than any ethical obligation you have."

"My loyalties are to you, not the bar, okay?" I said quietly. "Anything you say stays with me until you say so. I swear. Now tell me what the hell you're talking about."

"Isabella contacted me. I think she's trying to sabotage their case," he said bluntly.

My eyes widened and I almost spit out my drink. "Holy shit! What? How do you know it's her?"

"She copied an old email exchange we had, and I'm pretty sure she's the one who provided me with the lead in Argentina to her Aunt Bianca."

What the fuck is wrong with this girl? "I need some time to process this. This girl seems like a real psychopath, Ray. I hope you know that?"

"I don't know, AP. I still believe in her."

To this, I could say nothing. I looked at him for a long moment. He looked like a man who was still in love. And just like that, the door I thought we were opening had closed. I looked down and shook my head in disgust, wondering how someone could be so good at manipulating—and how a person could still love them despite knowing it.

CHAPTER FORTY-ONE

ISABELLA

THE INADMISSIBILITY OF THE NEGLIGEE WAS A MAJOR WIN for the DA in "our" case. Or what I should refer to as "their" case. I was simply a pawn to them now. Something they needed to win. To bury Ray. To make an example out of him. It made me sick to get on the stand and say what they wanted me to say. It wasn't true, but they didn't care. They just wanted to win. And the more I saw from them all, the more disgusted I became.

I was being standoffish in my cooperation with them, which only caused more tension at home with my "family" who claimed they were supposedly doing their best to *support me*.

"Isabella, I don't understand what has gotten into you," my mom said. "Don't you want to put him in jail for what he did to you?"

I looked at my mom, finding it funny that she was suddenly acting like she was a worried mother to me now. "At this point, I don't really care what happens. I just want some peace in my life," I said flatly.

My dad was standing there listening. "I have to warn you

here, honey, if you don't testify truthfully then they might charge you with perjury. Especially if you make the whole DA's office look foolish after they have gone out of their way to prosecute this guy for you."

"For me?" I snapped. "I promise to tell the truth. Just like the last hearing. But you seem to be the one controlling the case, so I'm sure you and the DA's office have everything under control."

His face stiffened. "You are the one that needs to testify about what happened, not me. That's why you need to go see the DA and have a briefing so you're fully prepared. This is very important. I'm not sure you get it."

"Important for who?" I asked, my tone even sharper.

My mom stepped in. "Don't you understand what the media is trying to do? They're trying to destroy our good name. If for some reason Ray were to walk, don't you understand we would lose all credibility, like your father says?"

I'd heard enough and laughed a little at how insane they sounded. "You know, Mom, maybe when this is over you'll understand." I started to walk out of the kitchen but stopped at my father's voice.

"Isabella," he said sternly. "You are playing with fire here."

I turned and looked at him. "You're not scaring me anymore, *Daddy*."

Then I turned back around and walked out.

CHAPTER FORTY-TWO

AP

OUR TEAM WAS WORKING AROUND THE CLOCK IN preparation for the trial. Anthony especially was getting tense, with now just hours to go before jury selection and no word from Jay Johnstone. My paralegals and I were preparing an adequate defense on the merits of the case, but Anthony thought we needed more, insisting we needed some sort of shock value that could sway the jury and make them either not like or not trust Ari Rohnstein and company. But as of now, we had nothing.

On the Saturday before the trial, Ray texted me, even though we were both in the office.

Jane Doe is back. Let's go have lunch, NOW.

I was curious, for obvious reasons, to see what more she had to say and *why* exactly she was reaching out to him in the first place. I cut Anthony off mid-sentence when I got Ray's text. "I'm sorry, Ray and I have to meet a potential late character witness for a quick lunch. Can we pick this up when I get back?"

Without waiting for an answer, I walked out of his office and motioned for Ray to leave with me. We put our coats on quickly and were met with some questioning stares from a few associates as we rushed out of the office.

Before the elevator door could fully close, I turned to him. “What did she say?”

Ray showed me his phone. The email read: *I know for sure you are getting these now. I’m here for you if you need me.* And it ended with a heart emoji.

“But how does she know for sure?” he asked. “You’re the only one I’ve told about this.”

“What about the lead?” I asked. “Maybe Jay was able to make contact with her aunt?”

“Who knows?” Ray said. “He’s been unreachable for days now according to Anthony.”

We went to a quiet place for lunch and had a quick sandwich. But I was feeling more uncomfortable with this the more it progressed. “Ray, we need to tell Anthony. We’re playing a dangerous game, here. You are not supposed to be in contact with her. She could be sabotaging you on purpose. Who knows if she’s showing anyone at the DA’s office, or if they put her up to this?”

“No, AP, not yet! We are *not* telling Anthony anything. And I don’t know, I don’t think she would do that. She’d be hurting herself and killing their case at same time.”

I backed off, sensing the emphatic tone of his response. But I wanted to make my point calmly. “I’m just saying we’re getting close to trial, here. There could be consequences to this. But I’ll do what you want.”

“I appreciate that. This is my life. If she hands us the case and no one knows except me and you, then no one can say shit. It’s over, no double jeopardy. We need to see what fruit it will bear. We need to be patient, at least until we hear back from Jay.”

“Fine,” I said. “We’ll do it your way.”

When we got back to the firm, Anthony summoned us

into his office and closed the door. Before he could say anything, I asked him if he heard from Jay.

"No, I haven't, and I'm starting to get worried on many levels. I didn't want to scare his wife, but there's been no sign of him for days. It's problematic to the defense of this trial," he said.

"I think you might be hearing from him soon," I said, unable to catch the impulsive words from slipping out.

"What the hell is going on with you two?" Anthony asked.

Ray and I looked at each other, and simply responded with, "Nothing."

THE PROSECUTORS ASKED ANTHONY—AND me, by association—to come back to their office one last time to discuss a plea. We obliged, mainly because we hadn't heard from Jay. Plus, we were interested to see what they had to offer. The DA's office called Judge Beekman's clerk and told her both sides needed a little more time before picking a jury.

"Look," the male ADA said, "it's already been a war and we haven't even picked a jury yet. We think we can offer your client a great deal."

"Let's hear it," Anthony said.

"Two flat. That's the lowest we can possibly go. And just remember, if he loses at trial we are recommending nine years," the ADA said.

"What's the charge?" Anthony asked. "Does he have to register as a sex offender?"

The chief stepped in. "Yes. That still needs to be a stipulation of the plea. If he doesn't do that then we will take our shot with a jury."

"Then I don't think it works," Anthony said. "First off,

he's been adamant that he won't cop to anything involving a sexual charge of any kind, so I think it's a non-starter. Plus, there are a few residual issues with some of the assets tied up."

The chief made a face. "Do you know how many guys were adamant about not pleading to a sex charge, but when we started to pick a jury, two years instead of nine looked too good to pass up? And by the way, as far as his financial assets go, we aren't prepared to discuss any of that yet."

"Chief, you've frozen financial assets that are typically only seized in white-collar cases. I've been working for free, here," Anthony said.

"We feel we have a right to protect the assets for restitution," the chief answered.

Anthony shook his head, not wasting energy with a response.

While they were bickering, I noticed Ari sitting there, with a contemplative look on his face. I'd also noticed his company stock dropping precipitously in the weeks leading up to trial, so maybe this case was affecting his business more than he was letting on. I was just waiting for the bribe from him at that point.

Ari stood up and joined the conversation. "Look, maybe there's a way we can squash this whole thing and have everyone walk away with something," he said.

I shook my head and tried not to roll my eyes. *I knew it.*

"Hold on, hold on," the chief said. "I don't know where you guys are going with this, but we cannot be privy to any private deals. I suggest you think about the legalities before you rush ahead in the direction I think you are going. For Christ's sake..."

"Well, I'm sure we can get creative here," Anthony said, looking at Ari for a reaction.

"Let's be clear," the chief said. "Any deals must include strict confidentiality clauses."

"You're right, chief. Before we get ahead of ourselves, let me speak with my client regarding the sex charge," Anthony said firmly. "Are you *sure* we cannot somehow make that go away?" he asked, looking at Ari again.

"Let me make this clear," the chief said to Ari. "If there is *any* tampering with the case, I don't care how much of a donor you are to our office, we will have no choice but to charge you. We will not allow anyone to compromise the integrity of this office. Do you understand?"

"Yes," Ari said. "Of course."

If I didn't know better, I'd say Ari *almost* looked ashamed of himself. Almost. At least, he looked somewhat deflated over this. And everyone in that room, including me, knew that even though this was a sleazy proposition, there was just too much at stake for the loser at this point. And the trial was approaching. Rapidly.

We were all running out of time.

CHAPTER FORTY-THREE

ISABELLA

My therapy sessions with Dr. Morgan became more like strategy briefings, with her becoming my senior advisor on how to proceed with my testimony. Our conversations, at my insistence, remained completely private. And I trusted her more than anyone else in my life. I needed her. I was flying by the seat of my pants, not knowing how to approach any of this. She had experience with court, testimony, all of that. I didn't.

I could hardly grasp the reality of how deep I'd gotten myself. I just followed my heart and intuition at this point, remembering what Ray had told me.

You're doomed for failure if you try to make everyone happy. It never works.

I reminded myself of that on the hard days, when things felt impossible. When I was close to giving up hope for good. I told myself I could do this.

The problem with my grand plan was that I had already given testimony on the record at the Grand Jury and in statements to detectives. Dr. Morgan warned me about this and told me I needed to be careful, just like my dad had. But coming from her, it was a genuine concern. Not a way to get me to do what she wanted.

"Isabella, I hope you have a plan to figure a way out of this mess," Dr. Morgan said.

"I may need you to back me up with your medical testimony at some point," I told her.

"I know, I just need to keep researching. I've never come across this type of issue," she said.

Issues. I was full of them. I just hoped she could come through on this.

CHAPTER FORTY-FOUR

RAY

On Monday afternoon, AP and I were called into Mika's private office.

"There's an offer on the table," he said. "And as your counsel, I need to present it to you."

I tried to cut him off, but Mika seemed annoyed for some reason.

"Let me finish," he said angrily. "They're offering you a two flat. It's just a general concept with a lot of stips to it, so let's get through it. You need to plead to Rape 3 and register."

"I can't do it," I said, then I looked at AP who sat motionless and quiet.

"Just hear it out," Anthony said. "When a plea is agreed to, it usually means no one is happy. Everyone has to give a little. If you are willing to cop to the two flat, then we can concurrently sign a separate settlement and confidentiality agreement with Ari to ensure none of us can speak about the case in the future in any manner whatsoever. In exchange for signing the confidentiality, Ari is willing to make a cash settlement. However, it needs to be mutually exclusive to the plea."

"Ah, I get it," I said. "So, Ari is paying me to plead so he can save face for his family and the DA's office? And as long as the DA doesn't have their hand on the private agreement then they're gonna look the other way?" As gross as it all was, I knew it was a reasonable deal. "How much, Anthony?" I asked dryly.

"I don't know yet," Anthony said. "But let's just say I think Ari is pretty motivated to get this done. I think he was made aware of the emails and texts that I finally got between the two of you. And I think we could get all of our firm's fees paid with whatever he does decide to offer. Then I think you can cover your friends that helped you out and still have enough money to get your business jumpstarted again. Plus, most of your remaining assets would be unfrozen."

I hung my head low and for some reason, Andy came to mind. I wondered what he would tell me to do here. The moment lingered, becoming heavy. AP grabbed my hand to show her support.

"So, besides the money, what's really in it for me? I'd have to live my life as a scumbag rape-o. Really, who would want to do business with me after that anyway? And how would I live with myself, knowing I copped out like a sucker to a sex charge I'm not guilty of?"

"You're facing nine years, Ray," Anthony said softly. "If you take this deal, you'll be home in a year or so with your Rikers credit. By the time you get upstate, you'll be heading back down."

I weighed the probabilities in my head. If this was a poker hand, I knew I'd need to fold and take the little two as opposed to the nine. But this was something I had to risk the whole stack on: My reputation. My life.

Mika took one more stab at convincing me. "I don't have an alibi defense here. The DA has you at the scene of the alleged crime. All I have are some racy texts and emails. But the only thing that matters is that moment in question, and this quickly becomes a 'he said, she said' case. Even if she teased you they could still say in that moment that it was rape. You want to risk nine years of your life on a coin flip in Beekman's part?"

I looked up at him, beginning to get a little irritated at how hard he was trying to talk me into this. "Anthony, do you remember why you took this case? What did we say? We are going to trial. You know how I feel about lawyers who force pleas."

"I'm not forcing you. Every situation is different. A good deal is on the table, that's all. I would feel horrible if you had to do nine fucking years over this bullshit. But you're not a novice, you know anything can happen in Manhattan," he said.

"I'm not pleading to a sex charge of any kind. I'm not going into those SOP programs and living with those rape-os. That's not me. Tell them to find something else, and *maybe* I'll consider."

"That's the problem," Anthony said, voice low. "The head DA made it clear that there has to be a sex charge and you would need to register. They also made it clear that Ari cannot influence that in any way. It's too important to the integrity of the Sex Crime Unit. If you don't plead, they will try the case, Ray. And you know they'll be playing to win."

"Yeah, at all costs," I said. I got up and shook Mika's hand, looked at AP, then walked out of the office. Just before I made it through the door, I turned. "I'll get back to you on it. I need some time to think it through."

And down the elevator I went.

CHAPTER FORTY-FIVE

ISABELLA

My father told me we needed to have a family discussion that night. So, I agreed to go have dinner with them in the penthouse. He got right to the point, telling me there was a deal on the table that Ray's attorney was considering. For him to plead to Rape 3 and do another year or so in upstate prison. I was shocked that they were sinking to this, especially when my dad said he would have to pony up some money to make it happen.

He softened his tone. "Honey, we just want to get this deal done to spare you from having to go through the pain of all this. Plus testifying. The DA doesn't think your heart is in it, especially with your refusal to be briefed. They don't feel you are cooperating. That's why I reluctantly agreed to consider this from our end. But ultimately, it's your choice."

"He'll never take it," I said, hoping it was true. "But if that's what you and the DA want to do, then I don't object. I'm ready. Either way."

"Okay, well, we just needed your approval. I'll let them know first thing in the morning that it's a go. Either way."

"Okay," I said, getting up, suddenly having a loss of appetite. "I'm gonna go to the movies with a friend. Please excuse me."

"Which friend?" my mom asked in a questionable tone.

"Just a friend," I said—like she really cared anyway—and left.

I wanted to vomit on the elevator down to the lobby. *Is Ray really considering this?* I never thought he'd consider a deal. Ever.

I slipped into a movie by myself, just in case anyone was tailing me. I made sure to buy popcorn and candy, for receipts. Then I walked down to the front of the dark theater and instead of taking a seat, I walked out of the fire exit at the front and headed to Dr. Morgan's, with no warning.

I pounded on her door, which she answered with an alarmed look on her face.

Before even saying hello, I blurted it out. "They're trying to make Ray take a deal."

"If that happens, you won't get to testify," Dr. Morgan said.

"I know. And my dad is so worried about his business interests that he's willing to pay to cover Ray's attorney fees. But no one in the public can or will ever know about that part of it. There'd be some sort of confidentiality agreement that my father is known for—AKA a payoff."

"Do you think Ray might take it?" Dr. Morgan asked.

I shrugged. "I don't know anything anymore."

I got my cell phone out and called my Aunt Bianca to confirm—again—that everything was provided to the private investigator.

"Of course," my aunt said. "But you know that already. Is everything okay, sweetie?"

"Yes, Auntie, thank you," I said. "I love you."

"I love you, too, *mi corazón*," she said.

I hung up the phone and looked at Dr. Morgan. "I need to do something. Fast."

CHAPTER FORTY-SIX

RAY

I MET FRANKIE FOR DINNER TO EXPLAIN THE PLIGHT I WAS in. With Andy's crew out of the picture, it only came down to what Frankie and his bosses wanted.

"There's a deal on the table for me to plead to Rape in the Third Degree," I told him.

"After all these years of being upstate around us, why would you even bring this up to me?" he asked.

"I'm not here because of me, I'm here because there's a money play in this," I said.

"Well, you shoulda said that first. Let me hear it."

I knew when it came to dealing with wise guys, money was paramount. No matter what the rules said on the street, they could always be broken when convenient for the bosses' wallets. "Okay, this is confidential what I'm about to tell you. I take the two flat and register, but we sign a confidentiality agreement with Rohnstein not to comment about the case. Mika gets his fees, and we can all take our money out of the deal and then some, without trial risk."

Frankie considered it. "Ray, did you do it?"

"No," I said. "You already know that. I don't want to

take it, but if you guys want me to, I will. I mean, a year sounds a lot better than nine joints anyway, you heard?"

"Whatcha wanna do?" Frankie asked me in his thick Bronx accent.

"I want to go to trial and clear my name. I'm confident we can win, cuz. Very confident. That's all I can say for now."

"Well, I could never ask you to take a deal for me on a charge like this. So, there's nothing left to discuss," Frankie said, folding his hands together. "Ride out."

CHAPTER FORTY-SEVEN

AP

AT THE OFFICE, OUR TEAM CONTINUED TO PREPARE FOR ALL directions. Anthony himself was working the phone with Ari's brash attorney—Jimmy Jacobs—reiterating that the deal wouldn't work with the Rape 3 charge, trying to gauge if there was any wiggle room for them to push the DA.

After overhearing some arguing between them, Anthony got loud. "Look, you may work for Ari Rohnstein, but I take offense at you taking shots at my client when you don't know all the facts. I won't negotiate with you if you take that approach again."

After another brief moment, he hung up.

"Are they willing to budge?" I asked him.

"Not yet," he said. "But my sense is that Ari will get aggressive at some point to get this deal done. He wants it to happen."

"Of course he does," I said. "It's bullshit."

Before we could continue, Anthony's private line rang again. I thought it might be Ari's attorney again, but Anthony looked at me and motioned for me to come in.

"It's Jay," he said. "Close the door." Then he picked up and put Jay on speaker.

"Anthony, I dug up some important information. I don't know how it could fit into your defense, but you need to hold off on your opening until you hear this," Jay said.

"We haven't started the trial yet," Anthony said. "Are you okay for Christ's sake? We haven't heard from you."

"I'm fine. I was out of civilization for a while. I told you I might not have cell service in the mountains. I'm rushing to catch a flight now. Hold off on everything. I'll be back in the city tomorrow night since I have a layover. Once I get in, I'll come to your office. I gotta go now."

Then the line went dead.

CHAPTER FORTY-EIGHT

RAY

I WAS JUST FINISHING UP MY DINNER WITH FRANKIE WHEN AP texted me saying Jay had something positive to report. It seemed like he came through, but we wouldn't fully know what it was until tomorrow. Or if it would be enough to proceed to trial now, or possibly use the info to leverage a better deal. Either way we were going to have to delay Judge Beekman and tell her we were still discussing pleas again.

I could tell by AP's texts that the roller coaster of emotions was becoming commonplace for both of us at this point. We agreed to speak at 11 o'clock that night once we both got home.

After meeting with Frankie, I was feeling good about things. If I lost at trial, at least I had put the deal on the table with them and they couldn't hold it against me. And my kids wouldn't have to watch their dad accept a shitty deal for a crime he didn't commit. Now, with the text from AP, things were looking up. My gut told me to check my email and sure enough, Jane Doe Glow was back. The email was succinct.

Don't take it. Be patient...

Things were not always as they seemed, but my gut told

me I was right about Isabella. For whatever reason, she was helping me now.

By the time I got home, AP beat me to the punch and rang me up a little after 11. She told me about the news Jay had. I decided to wait on telling her about the email. But after we caught up, the conversation shifted.

"Are you okay?" she asked.

"Yeah, I'm just relaxing in bed feeling good about everything," I said. "Why don't we meet in the morning and I can catch you up on my side of things?"

"That works. Anthony wants us all to meet before court. Why don't we meet first for breakfast at eight at our spot?" she asked.

"Works for me," I said. "You know I love any chance I get to spend time with you."

She giggled. "You know, Anthony made a comment to me earlier, questioning if you and I were getting too close. As if something was going on between us…"

"And what did you say?" I asked. I wasn't surprised Mika had his speculations. I was used to this, especially from other men. I guess there was something to it, since I did love women.

"I told him the truth," she said. "I said of course we're getting close, but only because I'm doing everything possible to win the case. Isn't that what he wants from me anyway?"

"Oh, you are a good girl, AP!" I said, laughing.

"If you only knew, Ray, if you only knew," she said in a confident voice that almost had a wink to it.

But I was not about to go there with her. I just laughed. "I think we'd better say good night now. I'll see you in the morning, sweetheart."

CHAPTER FORTY-NINE

ISABELLA

Breakfast was being served at the penthouse, so I went down to have the chef prepare my favorite omelet so I could get the latest scoop on the direction of the trial.

"It looks like Ray is seriously considering pleading guilty. The attorneys were talking last night on how to resolve this so we can wrap this whole thing up for everyone's sake," my dad said.

"Is that what they're discussing today?" I asked.

"I don't know," he said. "All I know is jury selection is planned, and everyone needs to see where the plea deal stands. I'm heading down there now."

"If it doesn't get resolved, when would I have to testify?"

"I'm not sure, but I'd say another week or so at least," he said.

I felt relief knowing I had a little more time. "Tell them I'm ready."

"Well, no offense, but no one thinks you're ready. You wouldn't be briefed. What do you expect?" he said. "I told you this was serious."

My mom sighed and tossed in her two cents. "I just don't

understand why you would even consider paying the rapist," she quipped. "What if the press ever gets a hold of that information?"

"That's what a confidentiality agreement is for, Michele," he said, and I could hear the roll of his eyes in his voice. "I'm just trying to make this all go away. So maybe our family can have some peace. It seems no matter what I do, I can't win here. Somehow I'm always the bad guy."

At that, I bit my tongue so hard I almost bled.

CHAPTER FIFTY

RAY

DOWNTOWN, I WAS DRESSED MY BEST FOR COURT. AP looked like the professional, sexy lawyer she was, and I gave her a big hug and kiss on the cheek before we sat in our private corner booth.

"I got another message," I told AP. "It said, 'Don't take it, be patient.'"

"She must be referring to the plea," AP said.

I nodded. "I need you to back me up from a girl's perspective. I love Anthony, but I know lawyers, and he's gonna try to sell this deal one last time."

"Okay, I'll do it, but I'm sure at that point he's going to fully expect that we are fucking," she said.

"I like the way you said that," I said, laughing.

Then, we both ordered our food and ate.

JUST BEFORE COURT, Mika was running late, so he huddled us all up outside Part 55 before we started. "Okay, gang, here's where we are," he said. "I'm still waiting on Jay's info when he arrives tonight, but it sounds promising. The DA is trying to force my hand today with the deal though. I spoke with Ari's attorney last night and they seem receptive to putting a nice package together."

I cut him off. "I won't plead to the rape, Mika. I'm sorry."

"I understand. You don't have to be sorry," Mika said. "But we could all wrap this thing up and you could be home in 14 months. I did the math."

"Then what?" I asked. "I mean what type of girl would ever want to date a convicted rapist? I'd be scarred for life in every aspect."

"I agree with Ray," AP said, looking at Anthony. "I signed up to fight this case, not to take a deal. And now we have the upper hand. I don't think Ray should have to be branded with that on his record. It's not him."

Anthony gave AP a hard stare but said nothing.

As we stepped into the sealed courtroom to keep the press out due to the nature of the plea discussions, Judge Beekman seemed anxious to hear about the deal. She directed her first question at me.

"Mr. Jansen, are you prepared to accept the plea that is on the table today or are we going to start picking a jury?" she asked.

"Your Honor," Mika said, "my client has not gotten all the facts. We had some late discussions last night and it is a complicated situation. I ask that you give us another day with this."

"Mr. Jansen is a grown man and doesn't need another day on this. How about we take a recess and after lunch you decide what you want to do? I don't need to hold up this court another day for *you*," she said to me harshly.

Now, I felt compelled to answer. "Well, Your Honor, if you prefer, they can withdraw the plea talks right now."

"Your Honor," the male ADA said, "Mr. Mika is correct. This is a little complicated and I do think another day would do everyone well."

Judge Beekman sighed. "Very well," she said, with irritation apparent in her voice. "I will see everyone back here in 24 hours. And Mr. Jansen, be advised that this will be your last chance at a deal this good, because remember, any pleas must be approved by me. I'm very hesitant as it is to let you plead to a flat two on a charge of this nature with your extensive criminal history."

"Right, Your Honor," I said quietly to no one in particular.

CHAPTER FIFTY-ONE

AP

On our way out of the courtroom, Ari grabbed Mika and pulled him to the side. I rushed over to see what he had to say. Ari gave me a quick glance and looked back at Mika.

"Call my lawyer Jimmy back and try to get this thing done," Ari said aggressively.

"Ari, my client is not a rapist. He's not pleading to that charge," Anthony said.

"Look, there's an extra bonus for you and your team if you can make this happen," Ari said, softer. "I feel like I owe you for what happened years ago with the real estate deal. Just tell your client not to be too piggish and he'll walk away fine, too."

"I think the deal makes sense for a lot of reasons," Anthony said, "but it's not my call."

Ari's face twisted in anger. "Then talk some sense into him, damn it!" Then he glanced at me. "And from what I'm hearing, she'll probably be here waiting for him once he's released. And that's coming from good investigative sources, not like your worthless guy down in Buenos Aires."

"My PI is just doing his job," Anthony said.

"Well, you tell him to never try to use my name in vain in that city. I'm revered there. He went barking up the wrong trees," Ari said.

And with that, he walked away, and we went back to the firm. One of us seemingly more offended than the other.

Within minutes of being back in the office, Anthony received a phone call from Ari's attorney. He put it on speaker.

"What do you want Jimmy?" Anthony asked.

"To discuss the deal, which is very straightforward. Ari said to offer you and anyone associated with the case non-disclosure agreements, with a compensation package of $1MM for you to distribute as you see fit, provided everyone signs off."

"I cannot force my client to do something he doesn't want to do," Anthony said, sighing. "Is there room to go higher on the compensation?"

"Quite possibly," Jimmy said in a rather cocky tone now. "A lot of people say that money talks, but what I've found is if you get to the right number it stops people from talking, too."

The nerve of this guy.

But Anthony was undeterred and began entering numbers into his calculator. "I'll discuss it with my client and get back to you shortly."

"Okay. Ari wants me to get a memorandum of understanding together so worst case we're prepared in the morning, even if your client doesn't take the deal."

"I understand," Anthony said, then ended the call.

Then he immediately got Ray on the line and told him we'd all have a private lunch in the office to discuss the next direction, to which Ray agreed.

The conversation was direct.

Anthony looked at Ray as he sat down. "Rohnstein is

willing to put a substantial package together for you, me, Alexandra, and your friends to take the deal and sign the non-disclosures. It's over a million dollars, Ray," Anthony said.

Ray shook his head in disbelief. "Unbelievable."

"Now, no one is putting a gun to your head," Anthony said, "but as your lawyer I have to advise you of the deal and tell you my thoughts."

"I know your thoughts," Ray said. "You want out of the case."

"That's not true. I just want you to understand your risk and reward here, and that this isn't only about you," Anthony said. "You can take care of everyone who has been there for you and even Alexandra can get a very nice bonus. You would have everything you lost and a little more in less than a year. It's an equitable deal and you should strongly consider it."

"It would be equitable if the Rape 3 was gone. Don't you see how desperate they are? They're making Rohnstein pay me off to take a plea to save face. The fucking hypocrisy that goes on in this city," Ray said, irritated.

"I don't know if this is coming from the DA or Ari, but it really doesn't matter," Anthony said. "All that matters is the deal on the table."

"I would do it for everyone, but Frankie doesn't want me to. And neither does Alexandra."

I shifted in my seat at this and watched Anthony's reaction.

"Do you think Alexandra wants to see you do nine years if they pull some stunt in there?" Anthony asked him. Then, he scribbled some financial figures on a piece of paper and handed it to Ray.

Ray looked at it, seeming to consider it momentarily, but he flipped the paper back on Anthony's desk. "I'm sorry, I can't do it. If you want to withdraw from the case, I'll go forward with Alexandra."

"Come on, Ray," Anthony said. "Give me more credit than that. I want to try this case. I just thought the deal needed to be fully considered. Now, we go to battle. I just hope Jay has something strong for us."

He then told us to take the afternoon off and come back at 7PM to begin going through the information Jay was about to deliver, letting us know he expected it to be a late night for all of us.

CHAPTER FIFTY-TWO

RAY

I SHOWED BACK UP AT MIKA'S FIRM AT 6:45PM TO SEE what Jay had for us. AP, Mika, and I took out our pads and Jay got started right away with his narration of what he found out.

"Okay, we got some interesting stuff. Ari adopted Isabella from Argentina after her mother was murdered. The reason for the adoption being that her family believed anyone who took Isabella in could also be murdered. It was during a time of political unrest and violence in the country, and Ari adopted Isabella because, well, Isabella's mother was Ari's mistress."

"Wait, what?" I asked. "His *mistress*? I didn't know this. I don't know if Isabella even knows that. If she did, she never told me…"

"There's more to it," Jay said, pulling out a folder of material.

The story Jay portrayed based on Isabella's aunt's point of view—with physical evidence backing it all up—was that Ari was madly in love with Isabella's mother. They took trips together around the globe that initially started for business purposes, but turned into romantic getaways once Isabella's father mysteriously left the family one day. Ari had the pleasure of spending some time with Isabella, after her mom introduced them by saying Ari was a business contact from the bank. Ari fell in love with Isabella almost right away, and teased her mom about having a miniature clone.

He never had children with Michele; whether it was because he didn't want to, or she couldn't, no one knew for sure. But Ari was supposedly planning on divorcing Michele to marry Isabella's mother, adopting Isabella, and moving the new family to LA with the hopes of having children of their own.

"Hold on," AP said. "What happened with Isabella's real father?"

"Good question," Jay said. "That's where I'm going with all this. There seems to be a major scandal and cover-up going on here, but a lot of it is unsubstantiated."

"Just tell us what we know for sure first, then we can fill in the blanks from there," Mika said.

"We know this. Isabella's mom wanted to get off the cow farm. She wanted to live a cosmopolitan lifestyle for her family, mostly for her daughter. She was very ambitious. The father was a simple guy, but he went along with it and when Isabella was about five years old, her family moved to the big city where her mom secured an entry-level job in banking. Her status changed rather quickly, and she moved up the corporate ladder as a customer relationship liaison to a private banking group. This is where she meets Rohnstein, and he at some point instructs the bank to have her become his personal account executive."

I laughed. "And the bank wants to make sure Rohnstein is happy, so basically she becomes extremely valuable to the bank."

"Correct," Jay said. "From there, Isabella's mother

becomes cozier with Rohnstein, her husband gets jealous of the relationship and instructs her to quit the job. Now the family is fighting, but the mother believes she's finally on track to provide the life she wants for herself and her daughter and tells the husband she won't quit the job. That's all I got. The rest of the info is all open for debate as far as why the father really left after that."

"Okay," Mika said. "Give us the aunt's version of what occurred. And then we have to formalize a theory on how to make this work into some sort of trial strategy. Alexandra, take notes with this in mind, please."

"The circumstances and the dates are all fuzzy," Jay said. "But basically, shortly thereafter the dad left for a trip to Brazil and didn't come back for a while. It wasn't uncommon for something like that to happen in that country. There were rumors that Rohnstein's political and underworld contacts got to this guy in some regard and either threatened him or paid him off to leave, again unsubstantiated. He eventually came back, showed up at the bank one day in an outrage to speak to his wife and caused a big stir. The bank's security guards had to get rid of him and they roughed him up on the way out."

"And the bank couldn't care less as long as Rohnstein's money stayed at the bank," I said, rubbing my head. "Poor Isabella," I mumbled.

"It gets worse," Jay said. "Things seemed to be calm, but Isabella's dad was a prideful man. He *also* had contacts that were in the underworld, just like Ari did, and back then it didn't take much to get a job done. The word is that he felt so disrespected by his wife and destroyed over losing his daughter, that he vowed to get back at Isabella's mother. She was murdered less than a month after he was kicked out of the bank. The aunt said her sister's dedication to her job made her an executive, but it was also what got her executed."

I shook my head, trying to wrap my mind around all this.

Jay took a sip of water and continued. "Now, here's where it gets even stickier. Rohnstein was devastated, and supposedly took it especially hard because indirectly, he was involved in the murder. Regardless, he lost the woman he loved and now Isabella would be all alone. Rumors were swirling that anyone who took in Isabella could also be in danger. Rohnstein insisted on adopting her right away, and he had the political clout to get it done. He felt he needed to protect her at all costs."

"That's it!" AP screamed out. "Protect her at all costs. That's why he's using his power and media contacts now, to bury Ray. He's obsessed with protecting her, because it was *his* fault her mother and family were destroyed. Because he was having an extramarital affair. We make him out to be the biggest scum of all, willing to destroy Ray for the sake of his own conscience."

"I like it, Alexandra," Mika said. "But we need to really research the rules of evidence regarding relevant testimony for a witness. I think this has the potential to really bring doubt into the jurors' heads and make Rohnstein look like the bad guy pulling all the strings to convict Ray, especially with his personal comments to the press about the case. We add in the college incident, and Isabella looks like a girl who has been through a lot, but incredibly unstable because of it. And her credibility goes out the window with the jury."

I shook my head, still trying to take all this in. "No wonder Rohnstein wants to settle this up so badly." Then I looked at Jay. "Wait, when did Isabella find all this out about Ari basically destroying her family?"

"It seems that the aunt enlightened her to most of this when she moved to LA. I don't know about all of it, though.

Isabella lost touch with her during her early years until they both wound up in the same city. The move was tough on Isabella at first. She'd initially wanted to run away, but once her aunt moved there full-time to watch over her, I guess it made the situation more agreeable. Running away was no longer an option. Because let's be honest, they needed Ari's money to live."

I glanced at AP at the mention of this. I didn't need to speak. I'm sure we were both thinking of Jane Doe Glow, and how this was all starting to make sense. Why Isabella would be helping us. But what still didn't make sense to me was how we got here in the first place. And why she freaked out, yelling rape.

CHAPTER FIFTY-THREE

AP

ANTHONY CALLED ME INTO HIS OFFICE AND HANDED ME A folder. "I need you to read over this memorandum of understanding."

I opened it up, seeing what looked like amended terms of the deal. US$1,500,000.00 read the settlement figure in the document. "What the hell is this?" I asked.

"It's a draft agreement with Ari, just in case Ray changes his mind and decides he wants to plead in the morning. We never know what they might hit us with, so we need this in place just in case."

"I thought we all already agreed that we're going to trial," I said.

"We are, but Ray needed to approve a compensation package as a plan B, that's all. Which he did over the phone with me. And as you can see, if he takes this deal, you would walk away with a nice sum of money."

I shook my head and tried not to explode. "This is fucking unbelievable. After everything we're going through."

"Look, I understand that it's not what any of us want, but

let's just see how things break in the morning, okay? You never know what the DA has up their sleeves. I don't know how many times I have to tell you that."

"But aren't you feeling more confident with what Jay brought back?" I asked.

"Just review it quickly and get back to doing your diligence on the aunt's file. I'd like to feel even better about it in the morning. Who knows, maybe we can get them to drop the Rape 3 after all," he said.

"Fine," I said. "I'll review it."

I left and went back to my office, ignoring Ray's repeated texts. I immersed myself in the aunt's file, amazed at the pictures of just how much Isabella looked like her mother. Her mom truly was beautiful, and the resemblance was uncanny.

Finally, Ray called the office.

"What?" I answered.

"What the fuck? How come you aren't answering my texts?" he asked.

"I can't talk right now. I'm tied up reviewing your proposed memorandum with Ari." And I hung up.

I eventually answered him later, agreeing to meet at a local diner at 11PM when I got off work.

Prior to our late meeting, I found some positive case law on rules of evidence that I felt would be enough to get the Ari adoption issues in. But, like everything in the law, it was ambiguous and based on the judge's discretion. I showed it to Anthony to get his approval before I left.

"I like it," he said. "But you know what they say about discretion. It is the mother of corruption. Either way, good work, Alexandra."

I was starting to get it. The more I delved through the information, the more I was able to form my own opinions on how to defend the case. But I continued to keep my thoughts mostly to myself.

I showed up 20 minutes late to my meeting with Ray, and I wasn't happy to see him either.

"What's your problem?" he asked me. "Did I do something wrong?"

"I read the documents, Ray. Did you really think that giving me money for you to plead to *rape* would make me happy?" I asked, raising my voice as I underscored rape to him.

"We aren't taking the deal, so this is a moot point," he said.

"Well I just want you to know, if you plead to this charge, I don't want anything. Not even a red cent of that million and a half. And I find it insulting that you would even think of doing that."

"Geez," he said. "It was just coming from the heart. If anything were to happen, I wanted to make sure you'd be good. And knowing that, at least, would make me feel just a little bit better."

With the way he said it, my face softened. I realized my thoughts were misguided, since he was actually thinking of me. "I'm sorry," I said, squeezing his arm. "If you want to do something for me, then let's stop talking about deals once and for all. I'm in this for *you*, not money. Please understand that."

"Okay," he said. "Now order a glass of wine and try to relax. We have a big day tomorrow."

After we ordered our drinks, I could tell Ray was holding something back. "She emailed you again, didn't she?"

He nodded. "Yep. But it was kind of personal, this one. I'd like to take some more time to think about it before we talk about it if that's okay."

"I understand," I said. Although inside, I was dying to know what it said.

"Let's just get through tomorrow and discuss it over the weekend. But I just can't help feeling like I'm letting her down."

"That's just crazy, Ray. *You,* letting *her* down? After what she did? She started this!"

"I know," he said. "But I had this dream that's been bothering me. It was like she had this look in her eyes that I could help her, and I didn't." He finished his drink and saw mine was about empty, too. "Let's just get out of here. It's late and we could both use some sleep."

I agreed and we left, walking a few extra blocks as the night air was warmer than usual. After a little while, Ray hailed me a cab and we said goodbye, giving each other a long hug after a long day.

"Now go get ready for tomorrow," he said. "You never know what the day will bring." Then he gently kissed me on my forehead, and I went home.

THE NEXT DAY IN COURT, it was crunch time—either time to plead or go to trial. The DA's office was left in the dark about what direction Ray would go in. And they seemed desperate to wrap the case up.

The formalities were simple and on the record.

"So, do we have a plea agreement in place?" Judge Beekman asked.

"No, Your Honor," Anthony said. "My client has told me that he will not plead to a Rape 3 charge under any circumstances. He wishes to defend the case at trial."

"Okay," the judge said, then she looked at Ray. "Well, Mr. Jansen, I don't need to remind you of the risks you're facing. The deal on the table is a very good one based on the charges. But you have a constitutional right to a fair trial, and that is what you will get in this courtroom. You do understand, that if you lose on all counts you are facing nine years in state penitentiary?"

"Yes, Your Honor," Ray said. "You have explained this to me already."

"Okay, then it's time a pick a jury. The testimony will start right after that," the judge said.

Ray and I looked at each other, and I gave him a silent nod of reassurance.

JURY SELECTION WENT SURPRISINGLY smooth over the next couple of days, and once completed, it left us a long three-day weekend to finish trial prep. Behind the scenes, Anthony was trying to work his media contacts. His long-time publicist pulled some strings to get a story printed that Ray Jansen turned down an even lower plea deal. He had this done in order to imply Ray's innocence and show that the case overall was weak.

Meanwhile, the DA's office staff were using their last-minute tactics of character assassination in the press with a new slew of items directed to pollute jurors' minds about Ray.

Anthony gave the team off on Friday, but asked us to come back on Saturday so we could start working on the defense opening. I continued to map out a defense strategy involving cross-examinations, and how to incorporate any possible testimonial issues with Ari.

I was working from home on Friday when I accessed Isabella's Facebook page, which was still active. I kept looking through her pictures, trying to see if I could pick anything up in them or her posts. I needed a cohesive defense as to why Isabella accused Ray of rape in the first place. At times, I became overwhelmed. It was a difficult task, trying to correlate pictures, documents, and timelines for it to make sense to a jury.

On Saturday, we were back at it again, together. Trying to put a full plan in motion. However, it mostly fell on my shoulders and I just wasn't there yet. I didn't have enough. I needed more help from Ray, which I mentioned to him in the office.

"We need to spend some time in private brainstorming about this opening," I said. "I'm having a tough time with it and could use a little more insight."

"That's funny you asked because I was gonna see if you wanted to go to dinner with me tonight," he said.

"Wait, are you talking business or pleasure?" I asked him.

"A little of both?" he said.

I smiled, unable to help it. "Okay, where do you want to go?"

"Let me decide that one," he said. "I'll pick you up at eight."

Why is my heart doing things inside my chest? I pushed the butterflies aside, and got back to work, knowing damn well I should not be going on even an almost-sort-of-date with my client.

But I was about to do it anyway.

CHAPTER FIFTY-FOUR

RAY

I SHOWED UP WITH A DOZEN YELLOW ROSES FOR AP, TO which she responded with a big hug and kiss before putting them in a vase in her apartment. We had a quick drink and then AP showed me some pictures.

"Look at this," she said. "This is Isabella's mom and Ari in Curacao."

I took the photo in my hand and studied it. "Wow, you were right. They look so much alike. Her mom looks so young here compared to Ari."

We sat and talked a little more about the case, but I could see she needed a break. Her apartment looked like she was a mad scientist, with sticky notes and documents littered everywhere.

I touched her arm. "I know you've been working hard, so I want to take you to a special place tonight, just you and me. I know we have a lot to go over, but can we just try to have some fun for once?"

"Sure," she said, smiling. "That sounds nice."

When we got in the cab, I lost any desire to keep things professional. This was not work anymore. I leaned over to her and told her she looked gorgeous, then let her in on my secret that I'd secured us reservations at *Beauty & Essex*, one of the city's hottest hot spots that I knew she'd been dying to check out. I had owned a Tapas restaurant down that way and used my old neighborhood hookups to get us in on this Saturday night.

"Shut up!" she squealed.

I just laughed, glad to make her smile.

After we got there and had a cozy drink and some small talk at the dark trendy restaurant filled with lit candles everywhere, the ice was more than broken. We were both comfortable by the time we sat down to eat. We shared our stories, talking about how and why each of us were alone right now in life. AP opened up a little more about her ex-boyfriend and then turned the questions on me.

"What are you feeling inside?" she asked me.

She didn't have to elaborate. I knew what she meant. "I can't identify with it all to be totally honest. It's really hard to wrap my mind around. Trusting someone, loving them, and having them switch on you like *this*."

"I can't imagine," she said. "Wait, what did the last email say? You never told me."

I pulled out my phone and read the email to her, verbatim. "I'm here for you. Doing all I can and holding out hope for us. I need a sign from you. Anything." Then I put it back in my pocket.

"Wow," she said. "I don't even know what to say to that."

"You know, I've been through so much in my life, and usually I can find a way to resolve things internally, like make some sense of the things that make no sense, but I'm really fucked up over this. And I don't really have anyone to talk to about it. This is the only girl I've fallen in love with since my wife and I split, and practically the only girl I even dated since I was released from prison six years ago. The craziest thing is not only did she leave me, but she accused me of the most heinous crime. Do you know I fear dying in prison? I saw so many people die in there and it's like if I blow trial, I may never come home. Andy used to say to me all the time that home is never guaranteed. The whole thing can drive you insane." I took a big gulp of my drink and let all that sink in for her.

"Well, I'm here for you," AP said. "Not only with this case either. I will always be here for you."

"Yeah?" I said, laughing a little. "Does that mean you'll come visit me upstate for the next nine years?"

"Stop talking nonsense," she said. "Seriously, I think we need to bring Anthony in on all this. I'm pretty sure if we can trace the IP address to her then we have enough to dismiss this right now."

"No, he's the lead attorney. If we disclose this to him then he's gotta disclose it to the court. And what if she's handing us the case? She obviously has some agenda so why fuck that up? And I know what you're gonna say, that she accused me of rape, and I shouldn't care about throwing *her* under the bus."

"Nope. I'm not anymore. I feel we are missing something. It's your dream you told me about, that she's calling out for help. I've been analyzing all the documents and listening to what you've been saying about her. How you said the two of you were so solid. And the truth of the matter is that I just can't see her hurting you in the end. I can't explain it."

"Really?" I asked her, surprised to hear this. "Why the change?"

"I don't know. I can't see her doing it. Not with the way you make a woman feel. It just doesn't add up."

"What do you mean?" I asked her, not following where she was going with this.

"You make a woman feel so special when you get close with them, like you think the world of them. Especially for a woman who is insecure, who craves that sort of acceptance. You do it in such a sincere way. I know if Isabella was lucky enough to get that close to you, she would have also felt this without a shadow of a doubt."

I didn't like being complimented much, and hearing this put me at a loss for words, especially when I was used to people thinking the opposite. "That's probably the nicest thing anyone has ever said to me, AP. Thank you for that."

I had to break the all-of-a-sudden awkwardness that I felt by her compliment. "I'm thinking of responding to her email. I don't know though. What do you think?"

"Well, you know if you respond then it's an acknowledgment that you believe it to be Isabella and it's a point of no return," she said, putting her lawyer cap back on.

"That's why I'm talking to you. You're the only person I trust right now. This is killing me inside. Tell me what to do," I said.

"Do you still love her?" she asked.

I wanted to be honest with her, but I also felt like an ass for wanting to say yes. "I don't know," I said, looking down.

"I've been looking through all her social media pages and she really is a beautiful girl. It's such a shame that she's been through so much, losing her family, all that. I believe she may have been victimized at USC, but I don't know for sure. I'm not done with all my research," she said. "It's coming along slowly, but I have a gut feeling on how to present our defense that could be a game changer. But it could also be a risky approach, so I really need to discuss it with Anthony first."

The inevitable case talk ended, and I took AP's hand to escort her to the lounge which was even darker and hipper than the main restaurant. The DJs were the best in the city and the A-list crowd was lightly bouncing to the beat. AP and I found a quiet corner table and ordered another round of drinks, which led to us touching each other more than usual. Tonight, I could feel it, we both wanted more. But it was already early Sunday morning and we knew there was work to be done for the trial.

Better judgment got the best of us, and we decided to walk out and hail separate cabs to our own apartments. We gave each other a kiss and long hug and said goodnight. AP said it was the most perfect night she had in as long as she could remember. And I admitted I felt the same way.

CHAPTER FIFTY-FIVE

AP

TEAM MIKA WORKED ON LAST-MINUTE ITEMS ON SUNDAY. We were all pretty much ready for the trial to start. Anthony suggested we all meet early Monday morning at the office so we could be on the same page and show a united front while walking into the courtroom, which was sure to have full media coverage.

I got up early Monday morning, and after I got out of the shower, I noted that Anthony had been blowing up my phone. A wave of anxiety rolled over me as I called him back.

"Good morning, Anthony," I said. "Is everything okay?"

"No, actually everything is *not* okay!" he yelled. "Great job entertaining our client on Saturday night, Alexandra. Real professional. There's a photo of you two in the *Post* looking real cozy coming out of *Beauty & Essex*. God damn it, don't you know there are celebrities and paparazzi all over that place?"

I covered my mouth with my hand and felt embarrassed tears building. I couldn't cry, though. I wouldn't. Not so he could hear me anyway. Part of me knew he was right, but another part of me was enraged. I could have a personal life, too. "Why are you yelling at me? We went to discuss the case. Nothing else." I said.

"Because it looks like much more than that, and it's going to hurt your credibility in front of jury members, who by the way love to read that gossip bullshit! I'm sorry, I may have no choice but to pull you off the case now," he said, hanging up on me.

I immediately dialed Ray, panicking. "Anthony wants to pull me from the case!" I yelled.

"Calm down," Ray said already aware of the situation. "It's gonna be okay. Remember there's nothing to this. It's just the New York media. Let's just get to the office a little earlier and I'll calm him down, okay?"

His words soothed me, slightly. The fact that he was so calm about this meant maybe I was over-exaggerating. Maybe Anthony was, too. But I wasn't convinced. I was about to potentially be pulled off the biggest case of my career. "Are you sure everything is gonna be okay? I'm scared. I fucked up. Big time. We should never have gone out."

"Don't say that. It's going to be fine. I need you to relax and be strong, okay? I need you focused. They're trying to get you off your game, that's what they want. I need you with me today. So, clean yourself up and I'll see you in an hour."

"Okay, fine," I said, hanging up. And I wiped my tears away like they were never there at all, then got dressed to impress the jury and put my makeup on.

ONCE I GOT to the law firm, the three of us went into Anthony's private office for what I knew would be a serious discussion. Anthony was still visibly upset with me. Disappointing him was never part of my plan. But Ray was trying to be the voice of reason.

"We're talking crazy, here," Ray said. "We cannot pull her off the case, Anthony. We need her. *I* need her!"

Anthony shrugged. "Well then she can work in the background. You don't know what damage this could have done. I don't need to lose a case of this magnitude in this type of manner. Fucking Rohnstein..."

"We can't have a knee-jerk reaction to the gossip page," Ray said. "Everyone knows that it's all a bunch of bullshit."

"Not the idiots that read it," Anthony said. "Some of them could be on the jury!"

"Look, he's the client, Mr. Mika," I said. "And our relationship has been nothing but professional," I said. "Yes, we are close, but this is not a hindrance. It's been a huge help in our preparation."

"She's 100% correct," Ray said. "And she's got the best instincts of any lawyer I ever had. That, along with our chemistry, is exactly what we need to win a case like this. This is a blessing and we can't let the media make it a curse. I'm sorry, but it's my life, and I'd much rather lose knowing I had her fighting with us. And another thing, the jury is gonna love her. All of them. There's nothing not to like about her and you know it, Anthony."

"I know, Ray," Anthony said. "It's easy for you to say, but I'm the attorney of record on this and I'm running the case."

"I'm not telling you how to run the case," Ray said. "I'm just saying I never listen to what they're saying in the papers, ever. I just stick with what I believe in. And I believe in Alexandra."

Anthony let out an exaggerated sigh. "All right, fine, but whatever you two are up to, you better tone it the hell down.

No more kissing in public. I guarantee that Rohnstein is gonna try to exploit this now, especially if he knows our plan to try and impeach him and his whole family. Hell, we already got a courier-delivered letter from him before all this crap, threatening us that his legal team would be keenly aware of any attempts to defame him or his brands at trial."

"All I'm focused on is the case," I said softly.

My boss looked at me, trying to see a lie in there. Instead, he just gave me a disappointed look. "Okay then. Let's go downtown and get to war."

I WAS RELIEVED to get into court and out of the tension in Anthony's office. I didn't want to miss this trial but walking into court had a new kind of tension of its own with all the cameras and media—and knowing what they were all whispering about me.

There was a different kind of buzz around the court now, with the potential "affair" between Ray and me in the news. I tried not to let it distract me, but I saw it. In their eyes. On their faces. I could almost hear the judgment being passed through their lips. The only relief was the fact that the DA was giving their opening first.

The DA had a short and quick opening statement that focused on a simple "he said, she said" case. They had Ray's DNA of hair and semen. They had the rape kit results. They had him running from the scene. That was about it. But they also had the victim—Isabella—who was going to corroborate it all.

Before I could become consumed with my own self-doubt, Anthony was doing his opening statement. My anxiety started to hike. Ray, on the other hand—the one on trial here—seemed like this was all so normal. He was taking notes as if he was another lawyer on the case. Anthony's opening was longer than the DA's, but he was crisp and to the point. He charmed the jury from the get-go, and his statements were a direct rebuff to the DA's factual claims in the case—specifically the medical reports. It was simple and convincing.

He asked the court for a lunch adjournment so we could make the second part of our opening in the afternoon, and no one knew what they were in store for.

When court started again at promptly 2:30PM, everyone in the court took notice when it was *me* who took center stage. Judging by the stunned and confused faces, they were all surprised that Anthony remained seated, especially the jury who seemed to perk up even more, anxious to see what I had to say. I braced myself for the attention. For the eyes and ears that would all be on me. But now was not the time for cowardice, for giving up. I was here for one reason. I thought back to the advice that Ray and Anthony had both given me. To ignore all the bullshit. To focus on what mattered. And I dug up some inner strength and stood before the room, praying to whatever god existed not to let me fail now.

I tried to give an emotional delivery coupled with the precision of a corporate presentation. I wore my hair up, and a business skirt that was conservative in nature but short enough to catch everyone's attention—especially jurors #4 and #8. Those were the ones Ray wanted me to focus my attention on, the ones he suggested I try to appeal to. I listened to his instincts. I trusted him, especially since it was his ass on the line, not mine. I gave them the perfect amount of eye contact and maybe a little more, just in case.

Ray was watching me. I could feel his eyes on me. I tried to speak eloquently and with conviction, which wasn't as hard as I thought given the passion behind my speech. I was almost running off his energy then. It was my first major opening in such a high-profile case, but it was my client I was doing it for. This is what you do when you believe in the client you are representing. The way I spoke, the way I moved, even the way I looked at him, it was all for him. And out of everyone who was watching me, I knew he took notice, because when I finished my last line and walked back from the jury, he gave me a distinct look. A look that contained something more than a typical glance between client and lawyer. I just hope no one else noticed it, since it would only fuel the illicit rumors of a steamy affair between us.

CHAPTER FIFTY-SIX

Ray

JUDGE BEEKMAN HAD SOMETHING SCHEDULED FOR THE NEXT couple of days, which gave us all a break until Thursday. And once AP had finished the second part of our opening, the judge dismissed the jury.

AP and Mika designed a two-pronged approach, where Mika would stick to the basics of the defense, and AP would get a little more aggressive with her own theory. A dangerous strategy, but a good hedge.

But with AP, I was almost mesmerized. I couldn't stop thinking about her. It dawned on me that I was falling for her. And fast. She did a five-star job in her delivery. And here she was, fighting for me like no one ever had before.

But in the end, her performance still had a lot of theories and what ifs. The strategy was pretty risky since she had taken aim at Ari—and his resources that were provided to help convict me. She also touched on the complexity of Isabella's adoption and Ari's controlling nature. But the highlight was the shockingly similar sexual assault claim that Isabella made at USC, and how the Rohnstein father/daughter relationship became strained thereafter.

After court, Mika offered to take us all out—the entire defense team—for an early dinner at Acapella in Tribeca, one of my favorite restaurants. But tonight wasn't about me when Mika raised his glass for a toast.

"I've been a trial lawyer for a long time," he said, "and I think we have them on their heels, all of them. But most importantly, I thought Alexandra's performance was one of the best openings I've ever seen. Cheers to that. Nice job, Alexandra."

She blushed. "Thanks guys, but we have a long way to go. I do feel relieved that it's over with, though. At least for now."

As everyone broke into their own side conversations, AP leaned over to me and whispered. "Now we have to initiate contact with her."

"Okay, but how?" I asked.

AP took a sip of her wine. "I don't know. But we need to put our heads together and think of something, fast."

"You know the paparazzi are going to be all over us," I said. "Maybe we should get out of the city. What do you think?"

"Ohhh like a secret rendezvous?" she joked.

I smiled even though I was being serious. "If we're gonna make contact with her, we need to find a remote location where nothing can be traced back to either of us."

"Okay, I'm in," she said.

And with that, we made plans to meet shortly after dinner. I thought quickly and called Frankie on the burner with a plan. He was the one guy I could trust now with Andy gone.

LATER, and three blocks from her apartment, I picked AP up in my black Rover.

"Wow, nice truck," she said, sliding her hand along the smooth black hood as she made her way to the passenger seat.

"You can have it if I blow trial," I said, laughing. "It'll be my gift to you!"

"Shut up," she said, slapping me on the arm and hopping in the front seat. "Where are you taking me?"

"We're gonna head out to the Hamptons. My friend Frankie has a house that he and his friends rent for the year."

"Okay," she said. "I didn't bring anything extravagant to wear, though."

"Don't worry. Besides Frankie and his girl, it's just gonna be us for the most part."

"Whatever you say, master," she said.

"Please don't say that to me," I said, half-serious and half-joking.

During the ride, I explained to her that I had already begun opening a dialogue with Isabella, stopping at a public computer on University Avenue by NYU. I made sure that the IP address couldn't be traced back to me directly, and told her Iz was expecting to hear from me later that night.

AP listened intently. But to all of that, she just responded with, "Okay, good."

WHEN WE GOT to the Hamptons, Frankie had a nice buzz on and a big cigar in his mouth when I greeted him in the billiards room out by the pool. It was now April and the Hamptons scene was dead. But Frankie had the Mets game on the tube making it feel like summer, and his girl had taken the ride out east with him.

Alexandra and Frankie's girl mingled while Frankie and I went out back to speak privately.

"So, what's going on with you and the lawyer?" Frankie asked.

"Nothing," I said, smiling. "Didn't I already tell you to never believe what you read in the papers?"

Frankie shrugged with a smirk on his face. "Well, she's some hot piece of ass all right. And she did a great job with that opening, but you guys gotta tone it down. The whole city thinks you two are fucking."

"That's why we came out here, to get away from anyone watching us. Plus, there's something big going on. I need that information about the public internet access."

"Something big?" he asked. "You know I got my ass on the line here, so tell me what the fuck you mean."

"It's good, that's all you need to know. I may need your help, but right now I just need the internet location. It's too hot in the city."

Frankie made a face that said he wasn't quite convinced, but that he'd let it go—for now. Then, he pulled out a piece of paper with an address and gave me his phone to use for navigation, also handing me a set of car keys so I didn't have to drive my own car. "This is a 24-hour laundromat. It's kinda remote, so it might take you a half-hour to get out there, but no one will find you there. Do you want me to go with you?"

"Nah," I said. "On this one, I gotta handle my own biz." I chuckled, talking like we were back in the prison yard. "Just do me a favor and make Alexandra feel comfortable while I'm gone."

He nodded. "Of course."

By the time I went back in and found AP, she was on her first frozen margarita with Frankie's girl. No stranger to the Hamptons scene, even in the spring, she was already having a good time. I told her I had to go. Before I left, I brought her bags to the room that Frank had assigned to her for the night.

"I don't know how long this is gonna be," I told her. "I know you're tired, so don't wait up if I'm out too late."

"Okay," she said. "I'll be here."

CHAPTER FIFTY-SEVEN

ISABELLA

My parents urged me to meet them for a private dinner, saying we really needed to talk. To me, it was just more of the same bullshit coming from them, but I went seeing as how I needed to stay up-to-date on the status of the trial.

My mom started the conversation with a soft tone. "Honey, we've all been through so much as a family. We need to address our issues when this is all over. Your father has agreed that we should all get family counseling to try to pull us all together somehow."

I raised an eyebrow at this and looked at my dad. "Really? *Now*?"

He didn't answer at first, until the awkward silence was thick and growing even more uncomfortable. When he realized no one else was about to speak for him, he talked. "Isabella," he said, "I'm willing to do whatever it takes. You're in a fragile state after this incident, and everything that has come along with it. We need to put our issues aside now and focus on giving you all the support you need to get through this. And if therapy helps you, maybe it can help all of us. I want us to be close again."

I nodded my head, taking in his words. I could count at least half of them that were most likely bullshit. "I can handle it. I've been through worse," I said, looking at him. "I told you, I'm ready to testify against him."

"I know you are," he said. "I was just trying to protect all of us, I hope you know that. With that deal. You don't know what Anthony Mika might try to do to you, but I do."

I was still listening to him when my mom jumped in.

"This is big, Isabella," she said. "You're probably still in a traumatic state without even realizing it. We want—no, *need*—to be there for you, even if you want your space. You can't just keep shutting us out completely. Not after this. You've been even more distant lately. Even more so than before."

I found it almost hilarious, the way my mom was stepping in now to play the concerned mother. Where was she all those years? She was playing the role now because the whole world was watching. At least, that's how it felt to me.

Ari nodded. "I want you to know that I am willing to do whatever it takes to keep us all together. Anything. That's why I agreed to the counseling. You know that's never been something I believe in, but I'm willing to do it. For you. For us."

I sat there for a moment, silent. I had a hard time believing my dad would ever change. Why was he coming around now? Who was he trying to convince here? Regardless of the sell job he was laying on me, I wasn't buying it. A huge part of me wanted to move on with my own life, always had. But there was a small part of me that was so afraid to lose my only semblance of a family, forever. Despite how dysfunctional it was.

So, I went along with the idea of keeping us all together

for now. But regardless of what he said, I didn't think that man would ever sit in a chair in a counselor's office and really put work in to fix himself. To fix any of this. He may have been too far gone for that.

But I wasn't.

CHAPTER FIFTY-EIGHT

RAY

On the dark drive along Eastern Long Island, I felt a sense of peace. I almost wanted to drive all night, just to think and clear my head. But I got to the laundromat and walked in with a hoodie on, holding a basket of towels and old T-shirts in my arms. Before washing my clothes, I went to secure the internet kiosk and put cash in to get to my email. There was already an email from Iz.

Your lawyer is good, but her theory is not exactly correct. And what is going on with you two? I need to know...

I was glad to see she was ready to engage, but concerned about her jealousy with my relationship with AP. After thinking about it, I realized I needed to squelch the flames, not spread them.

C'mon, you know the media is playing that up. It's all for entertainment. There's nothing to it. She's my lawyer, nothing more. More importantly, tell me how her theory is wrong?

I put the towels and T-shirts in the washer, and by the time I got back, Jane Doe Glow had already replied.

Well, if she's that good, she'll figure it out.

I wasn't in the mood for fun and games with this. I was

tired as hell. Plus, the fact that she never told me about the other sexual assault claim at USC was still burning me inside, though I didn't let on to that. I responded simply and to the point.

If you are playing games I will NEVER forgive you.

To which she replied back quickly: *I'm sorry. I'm not playing games, at all. I promise. I can't get into details right now, but the family dispute occurred before the USC incident. Just tell her that for now. When we have more time, I plan to explain all the details about when I found out what my dad did to my family. Just be patient and trust me with the process. But I need to know, are we gonna get through this somehow? Together?*

I responded quickly as well. But with trepidation. *I hope we can both get through this. Let's plan to talk to each other again soon, when we both have time.*

And with that, I logged out of my email.

I STEPPED into a small local tavern on my way back to the house. It looked like a log cabin in a secluded forest out west. I ordered a craft beer and sat there pondering what was all occurring, somehow finding a sick thrill in the gamble that I was taking with my life on the line. I wondered if I was a masochist. And why something inside me was telling me to be patient with Iz, despite what she'd done to me.

When I finally left and got back to the house, the girls were sleeping. But Frankie was still watching ESPN and drinking.

"Your girl had a good time. We had a few drinks, a few laughs, then she went to bed about an hour ago. She said she was exhausted," he said.

"Okay. Let me go see her," I said. "I'll be back down to hang in a bit."

When I entered AP's room and sat on the side of the bed, she rolled over and her eyes fluttered open.

"Hey," she said sleepily. "How'd it go?"

"It went okay, but let's talk in the morning. I just wanted to check on you. Did you have a good time?"

"Yeah," she said. "We got a little crazy. I wished you were here."

She put her hand on my thigh when she said that and I looked down, wondering if she had too much to drink as I watched her rub my leg. "I wished I was, too," I said. I put my hand under the blanket and started gently rubbing her back.

As AP slid her hands nearer to my midsection, I did the same, with neither of us saying anything. I could feel myself start to get hard as she grazed the front of my pants, but I stopped her.

"I love being with you, I just wish it was under different circumstances," I said, moving her hand.

"I know," she said, disappointment in her voice. "What can we do, though?"

I touched her face and started caressing her hair. The room was dark, but the moonlight was just enough for me to see the look in her eyes. It was clear, she didn't want to wait any longer. And neither did I. I knew the right time for us—if ever—was now, and I wanted to grab her and take her right then and there.

But I fought off the feelings. I couldn't do it. Not now. Not with everything going on. It wouldn't be right, no matter how I tried to rationalize it in my head. "I can't tell you how much you mean to me, and what I'm feeling for you, but I'm just so confused with everything."

She sighed and rolled on her side. "I know. Just know

that I'm here for you whenever, for whatever you want. I'm not the one with all the traffic in my head."

"You understand everything that I'm going through?" I asked her.

She was slow to respond this time, her eyes closing. "I think so…"

And with that, she fell asleep. I stayed a little longer, just looking at her, stroking her hair. It was hard to get up and leave her there alone, but I had to. I bent down and gave her a kiss on the forehead, then started to get off the bed.

AP grabbed for me as I started to stand, eyes still closed. "I love you," she said effortlessly.

I smiled. "I love you too, AP." And I left the room to go back and hang with Frankie.

CHAPTER FIFTY-NINE

AP

AFTER RAY AND I GOT BACK FROM THE HAMPTONS, NEITHER of us brought up what had almost happened between us. Instead, I focused on working with Anthony to prepare for our defense and witness testimony. And before court, Anthony pulled me aside.

He said he liked my thinking and preparation, but he did try to warn me. "It's clear that Ari has tried to influence this trial, and we have plenty of ammunition on that. But you need to be careful not to lead the jury down a path that you can't deliver on. So, keep things somewhat open with doubt, and then as we get through some of the testimony we'll try to slam the door on them with the closing arguments."

I nodded my head. "Okay. Got it. I just wish I could find a link that could give me free rein on this guy…"

"Just be careful," Anthony cautioned me. "Even though *we* know he's behind the scenes pulling strings to get Ray convicted, his lawyers are no dummies. And if you cross the line, this guy will have you practicing immigration law for the rest of your career, and that's *if* you're even lucky enough to keep your license."

It was a scary thought, that maybe Ari had enough power and influence to make something like that happen to me. But I was from Pittsburgh. And I wasn't afraid of him.

ON THE FIRST day of witness testimony in the case of the People vs. Jansen, the court was packed. It felt like a normal spring day, but the body heat inside the courtroom made it feel almost sweltering in there. Between my nervousness of being in front of the crowd, and the electricity now hot and brewing between me and Ray, it was a lot. I tried to remain calm, pushing all the different manifesting butterflies away.

There weren't too many fireworks at first that day, except that Ari was taking every opportunity he could to stare at me in an obvious way, trying to intimidate me.

At first I ignored it, but when I realized he was doing it on purpose, I stared back. I could see that his undershirt was wet with some sweat forming under his tie-less button-down shirt. And after a good look, I thought how unflattering he looked. He disgusted me. It was the first sign of what was to come during the showdown between the two of us. I felt it.

That night after court, I had a horrible nightmare. Ari was chasing me with a meat cleaver in his hand. He had his shirt off. His hairy body made him look like a monster, which is kind of how he looked in the picture on the beach in Curacao with Isabella's real mother. I woke up sweating, realizing that the pressure may be starting to take a toll on me. In reality, a simple girl from Pennsylvania taking a shot at a man of this stature was pretty overwhelming.

I called Ray the next morning and asked him to meet me privately so I could tell him about the dream and see if he had any more contact with Isabella. He said he hadn't yet.

He listened intently to my dream description, asking for

every detail. He took notes, searching for what each symbol in the dream could mean. "You know this dream is telling you something," he said. "It's our job to find the meaning."

"We're running out of time," I said. "We need to find a connection here as to why Ari is so motivated to protect her and convict you. I'm not coming up with anything concrete. We need more from Isabella than just to trust her."

"Let me see what I can do," he said.

"My strategy can only be deployed on him if we can assert that in some way, he was involved with witness tampering and/or obstruction of justice to manipulate the outcome of this case. And I need a real reason why."

"You're skating on thin ice," he said. "But I think the judge will give you some latitude because everyone on the jury will want to hear this. If they object, you need to grandstand in front of them. It will make you look sympathetic to the jury if they think she's favoring them."

"I think I have enough to get this in, but if I get some help from her then I got him," I said. "We all know there's some agenda against you, but we need a theory that is plausible to the jurors."

"Trust me, I get it. The jury could look at it as if he was just doing what a good father would do to protect her," he said.

"Right, that's why I want to go in a totally different direction with this," I said. "We can't leave anything to chance, Ray. You need to re-engage with her. I'm serious. Get me something tangible."

Back in court, the People got through the testimony on the factual parts of the case in two days, and Anthony did a solid job cross-examining most of the medical experts and discrediting them the best he could before the weekend. In particular, his cross regarding the lack of semen content found on the inside of Ray's boxers was getting rave reviews in the tabloids. And the key points would be driven home in our closing statement. The next week would bring in the most important testimony. Salerno, Ari, and of course Isabella.

Although the original female detective who interviewed Isabella was on the prosecution list, we weren't sure when or if they would take the lead and call her on their own. It was really strategy on their part, the timing of it, because I'm sure they knew it would be bad. Regardless, it was time for Anthony to prepare me for my cross-examinations—and for Ray to get Jane Doe Glow to finally talk some substance.

Anthony listened again to my two-pronged approach in attacking Ari's credibility. And while he thought some of it was ingenious, he also found it flawed. He didn't sugarcoat it.

"You bring up some great points, but at the end of the day, this is a theory that you have. This is not *A Few Good Men* where the witness is just going to admit on the stand that he committed some sort of crime. Especially Rohnstein," he said. "And what makes you think Judge Beekman will give you free rein on him?"

"I believe with the adoption stuff there's some relevancy to his behavior of cover-ups and manipulation. I think the jury will want to hear it, and if she shuts me down, then it plays into our theory that Ray isn't getting a fair trial. The jury will see it, too. I know it," I said.

"I don't disagree with you there," he said, "but what you're talking about could really land you in some hot water with the bar. I mean, where are you even coming up with this stuff?"

I shrugged. "Call it women's intuition. Plus, I had a dream about him. Trust me, I *know* he's bad news."

Anthony shook his head and let out a short laugh. "A dream? You can't base anything off a dream, Alexandra. I know we've been through this before, but you need to listen to me on certain things. This is starting to become your case more than it is mine, so I'll give you some latitude here since you've put in so much work, but I want you to be cognizant of what you're doing here. Ari Rohnstein is one of the most powerful guys in the world."

"Well, if I can't practice law the way I believe, then maybe immigration law will be better for me," I stated. "And anyway, that sad excuse for a man only scares me in my dreams."

"I just really hope you're not pinning your strategy based on a goddamn dream," he said in all seriousness, expressing how ridiculous it sounded.

"Give me some credit," I said. "Ray and I have been working nonstop."

"Okay. I'm going to start rolling up my sleeves even more now that the trial is underway. If you're really hell-bent on going after Rohnstein, then I'm going to have you prepared for the most important part of any criminal defense strategy. The art of the cross-examination."

I smiled. "Now you're talking."

CHAPTER SIXTY

RAY

WHILE MIKA WAS CRAFTING A MASTERFUL CROSS FOR AP, I went to the *Ritz Carlton* downtown to see Frankie, who got a room there so I could use the business center and email Isabella. I knew I needed to heighten things up and try to get AP what she needed, especially since the clock was ticking away. I was direct now.

How can I have hope for anything if I could be put away for the next decade?

She responded quickly. *Please don't worry about that. I'm not letting you go anywhere.*

How can I be sure? I asked her.

She emailed quickly again. *All I ask for is patience. Please.*

It's hard to trust anything after all this insanity. Don't you understand where I'm coming from? I asked.

I do, but I need to know that you still have hope for us. Please tell me.

I read her email several times before replying, conflicted on how to respond. So, I hedged my bets. *I can assure you that although I'm skeptical, I'm still in love with that girl I met at Nick's party. True love is the strongest emotion in the universe and it cannot be broken. I haven't lost hope, but time is running out on me.* I waited for her response, my heart beating inside my chest. And then it came.

The truth needs to come out with what happened. To me. To you. I'm going to tell it.

Now I was direct. *What truth? And are you fully committed to doing that?*

She answered fast. *Like nothing before in my entire life, and you know this is the real Iz saying this. You just need to be a little more patient. I can't tell you what that truth is yet.*

We were having a little breakthrough, but I needed to resolve one major thing. My concern for AP. *I'm worried about my friend. She's fighting for me and she needs to be protected. I need to make sure of that.*

She replied yet again within moments. *You should be. They have her in their bullseye. But if she is important to you then I won't let her down.*

I shook my head and typed. *Do you promise me, like we used to promise each other?*

Her response came. *Yes, babe. With everything I have in my heart. I have to go. Goodbye for now. Love, Iz.*

I HAD an early room service in the room with Frankie so we could speak ultra-privately. I showed him the printouts of the email exchange from the business center, indicating what was going on with the alleged "victim".

Frankie finally understood. And now, he had reassurance for the bosses, so he could let them know their loans—or investments—were looking good.

On the way back uptown, I checked in with AP so we could update each other, and we decided to meet after court on Monday to discuss particulars with respect to the emails between Isabella and me.

After some serious talk, I was honest with her. "I miss you. I don't really wanna wait until Monday to see you."

"Well, if it's any consolation, I probably miss you more," she said. "Why don't you take me away on another rendezvous? But alone this time."

It had been a few days since the Hamptons, and not a word was spoken about what happened—or rather, didn't happen—in that room that night. But it never meant I stopped thinking about it. We just didn't need the extra complications right now. "Let's just get through the next week and maybe we can find a way to get out of the city for a day or two. If we get a break in the case."

"I would love that," she said. "And don't worry, I know you're conflicted about things. It's okay. I understand."

I didn't respond to that and just said goodnight, thinking to myself that she had no idea how conflicted I truly was.

IT WAS JARRING for me when Nick Salerno took the stand on Monday, watching as one of my oldest friends readied to give his testimony. The People delivered a long history of background information detailing his separate associations with me and the Rohnstein family, as well as his link between me and Isabella.

The jury seemed bored, and I didn't know where they were going with any of it.

After lunch, contrary to the overdrawn and direct examination of Salerno by the People, Mika's cross was short and sweet.

"How long have you known Mr. Jansen?" Mika asked him.

"Over 30 years now," Salerno said, looking at me briefly.

"Is it safe to say that in order to have a friendship that long, you must hold Mr. Jansen's character in high regard?" Mika asked.

"Yes, I think that's fair."

"And after hearing your earlier testimony, I'm assuming that you are not a psychologist of any sort?" Mika asked.

"No, I'm not," Salerno said, adding a chuckle to lighten the mood.

"So, I'm going to spare the jury some time and not discuss anything with you that involves medical assertion of any kind," Mika said. "Is it safe to say, Mr. Salerno, that you're pretty much like the rest of us and really have no clue what was truly going on within the relationship between Isabella and my client—or better yet—what happened in that room?"

"Objection!" the DA yelled. "He's leading the witness."

"Sustained," the judge said. "Please rephrase, Mr. Mika."

Mika took a moment. "You were the one that was closest to the both of them, correct?

"Yes."

"Do you have any opinion that you want to share about what you think happened between your two friends?"

"To be truthful, I stopped trying to figure it out a long time ago," Salerno said.

But Mika drove the point home. "So, although you basically set the two of them up, and they were both clients of yours, and both long-time friends, the reality is that you are just like the rest of us here, still trying to figure out what really happened that night?"

"Objection," the DA yelled again.

"Sustained," Judge Beekman said. "Rephrase, Mr. Mika."

"It's okay, Your Honor," Mika said. "I'm going to move

on. Mr. Salerno, I want to go back to the day of the alleged incident. Where were you that day?"

"I was with Ray. We got massages and finished getting ready in his room in the *Four Seasons Hotel* on 57th Street."

"And where was your wife?" Mika asked.

"She was with Isabella, shopping."

"So, it was just you and Ray that day, alone?"

"Correct," Salerno said.

"And isn't it true, that before the massages you two engaged in some conversation while taking a steam bath?"

"Yes…"

"And you also went into the hot tub as well?" Mika asked.

"Yes. First we hit the steam, and then we went to the jacuzzi after. Before showering for our massages."

"And, Mr. Salerno, during the time you and Mr. Jansen were in the steam room and then the hot tub conversing, what were the two of you wearing?"

"What were we wearing?" Salerno asked curiously.

"Yes, can you tell me exactly what the both of you were wearing from head to toe?" Mika asked calmly.

"Both of us just had a towel around our waists. Nothing else."

"Thank you so much, Mr. Salerno, for your brief time with me today. You have been extremely cooperative. I have no more questions for you at this time." Mika gave Salerno a subtle smile, then turned to face the judge. "However, Your Honor, I would like to reserve the right to call Mr. Salerno again on a re-direct if needed."

"Duly noted," Judge Beekman said, and she dismissed the jury for the rest of the day.

CHAPTER SIXTY-ONE

AP

AFTER SALERNO'S TESTIMONY ON MONDAY, THE DA'S office decided to put their initial female detective on the stand the following day.

Anthony took aim at the female detective, and there was no hiding that she openly admitted on the record that she did take personal notes, and that the DA's office failed to provide them initially. It was a procedural mishap, bigger than conveyed. And the entire cross-examination was nothing short of pummeling, not only on her but the entire detective work on the DA's side. It looked exactly like what it was: A cover-up.

I was more focused on some of the details in the final incident report, but I let my boss ask the line of questioning.

"So, detective, can you provide clarity to exactly what Ms. Rohnstein said in her initial report about trying to push the defendant on his chest?" Anthony asked.

"Yes. The girl was somewhat dazed but she said she initially pushed his chest and then scratched and pulled his hair as hard as she could but he was too strong, and then he began raping her," the female detective said.

"But detective, the report says that she did manage to fight him off, correct?" Anthony said in a questioning tone.

"Yes, I'm told that she changed the report at some point to say that she only managed to fight him off after he penetrated her," she said. "I guess she was traumatized at first and not so sure as to exactly what happened."

"So, what you're saying is that you were not aware that your initial report was later altered?"

"That's correct," she answered matter-of-factly.

Mika walked back to the table to let that one hang in the air while he scribbled some notes.

"Detective, in the initial report, there is no mention of the defendant ejaculating, only semen samples found later. So, I ask you if the victim ever said in your initial interview whether the defendant ejaculated or not?"

"She said she was unsure," she replied.

"So, the hair follicles that we're talking about that were found were not consistent with the pulling of any hair on the head, detective. In fact, many were pubic hair and leg hair follicles. Did Isabella explain to you in your initial interview what hair she actually pulled?" Anthony asked.

"No, not specifically. However, she was very clear that he was overpowering her and she was too small in comparison to do anything other than push off his chest and she tried to scratch and pull whatever she could get her hands on."

"Thank you, detective," Anthony said. "No more questions at this time. However, we might like to recall you later."

But he wasn't done there. In light of the testimony from the detective outlining the clear mishaps in the case—in which the original statements from Isabella could've been coerced or altered—he was going to file a motion to dismiss the indictment. While the jury was dismissed, he spoke on the record.

"Your Honor, I request a day's adjournment so I can file my brief by Thursday morning, along with some additional evidentiary items that we would like to add to the discovery list," he said. "But I would like to review the transcripts tonight before doing so."

"Very well," Judge Beekman said. "In light of this information, I'm going to give the jury the rest of the week off until the lawyers and the court can sort these issues out."

Public sentiment was shifting in the case. The tabloids were underscoring that it was now making sense why Ray Jansen turned down a plea. But the DA's office remained steadfast in trying to convict him.

Ray and I went back to the office beaming with confidence and a plan to get more information from Isabella as soon as possible—to hopefully slam the door on the DA's case, for good.

CHAPTER SIXTY-TWO

RAY

THE UNSEASONABLY WARM WEATHER CONTINUED EVEN though summer was still months away. And AP seemed to be dressed more provocatively than normal the next morning, seeing as the jury wouldn't be there. I smiled when I saw her, noticing she obliged my request when I had asked her in jest to look extra sexy today.

For the last few days, we could barely contain ourselves. The grazing of each other's legs under the table during parts of the trial and the texts to each other during breaks just kept crossing more and more lines.

The only thing hotter than AP in the courtroom was the heat being turned up on Ari. As court started at 9:30AM on Thursday morning, Mika dropped two bombs on the DA. First was the expected motion to dismiss the indictment. Second was a file of newly acquired evidence regarding background information about the Rohnstein adoption of Isabella Martin from Buenos Aires circa 1996.

The ADAs immediately objected to the admittance of evidence as not being timely, as well as "purposely withheld". Ari's lawyer was taking feverish notes in the first row, while the court seemed to turn into mayhem within mere seconds.

Mika played to the media again. First, he handed a huge red weld file over to the clerk. Then he walked to the prosecution table with another copy for them. He dropped it on the table with a nice *thud* for theatrics and without missing a beat, responded to the ADA's objection. "Your Honor, we needed to check the veracity of the documents first and foremost. We are now sure that they are authentic, and we included relevant case law that we believe is in line with granting us the admittance of this as evidence. This information is essential to our defense theory and cuts to the credibility of the prosecution's witnesses."

"I know all about rules of evidence, Mr. Mika," the judge said, sounding perturbed. "I will take a look at what we have here and make a determination along with the Brady Motion to dismiss."

I watched media members run out of the court, trying to be the first to break both stories even though no one knew as of yet what the contents of the material were in regard to Rohnstein.

The young ADA addressed the judge. "Your Honor, what is going on here is preposterous. We are seriously thinking of filing sanction motions against Mr. Mika and his entire firm if he doesn't voluntarily withdraw this evidence, as we were not properly delivered any of this during the allotted discovery period."

"Hold on there," the judge said. "Keep in mind we now have a new motion to dismiss the entire indictment for sanctions within the DA's investigative unit. I have concerns about the Brady breach in and of itself after your detective's testimony. However, we are not going to have this thing drag out. So, go back to your offices, prepare any oral arguments on both issues, and we will have a 2:30 recall. I will rule from there. If you want to file your frivolous sanctions motion then you can do so after my ruling." Then she banged the gavel extra hard before retiring to her chambers.

"But Your Honor!" the ADA yelled.

It was too late, though. The entire court got up and moved out as if the building had suddenly caught fire.

Team Mika went back to his office to work on the final touches of any oral arguments. It was great lawyering by Mika, and the media was giving him props with breaking news reports from reporters all over Centre Street.

The 2:30 afternoon recall was short and sweet, and Mika's tactical move worked to precision. The judge split the baby; Mika lost the motion to dismiss again, but he won the evidentiary request to allow the documents on the Rohnstein adoption to be admitted.

The DA objected, but for now, Ari Rohnstein would be called to the stand on Monday to testify. It was a big win for the defense team, and everyone knew it.

I felt hope now in a way I hadn't in a long, long time. And I looked at AP who returned the smile and excitement. Legal experts were calling for the DA to just end it already. All I could think of were my kids, and having their full faith restored in me once this nightmare was over.

WITH THE LONG WEEKEND OFF, I invited AP out for drinks downtown by the *Ritz*. Frankie had agreed to get a room for me there so I could use the internet in the business center again if needed. AP implored me to reconnect with Isabella before we resumed trial on Monday, and I agreed to try.

We met in the hotel lobby. AP was wearing a skin-tight black dress that showed all her curves. We skipped the hotel bar in case anyone was watching, and I took her up the elevator to the room so we could have a drink. But when I opened the room door, she saw the huge bouquet of red and yellow roses intertwined in a large glass vase sitting on the table.

Before either of us could process anything, she grabbed me and kissed me as I closed the door and pinned her up against it. We kissed deeply for the first time. I started off slowly, but she wasn't having it. She pushed for more, kissing me even deeper and more passionately. There was an intense rush in it all, especially with the build-up from all the waiting. I slid my hand up the back of her thighs, under her dress, feeling how wet she was already. She was barely wearing panties at all, just a string of a thong, exposing her bare ass in my hands. She breathed as I touched her, moaning. Feeling how wet she was, I instantly got hard. She grabbed me, and I began to undress her right there. Her breasts were perfect. Not overly big, but perfectly shaped. I put them in my mouth as she grabbed me and rubbed me while I did so.

"Baby, I want you so bad," I said. "My head is just still so confused right now. I don't want…"

But she covered my mouth. "Don't talk. Just take me, however you want."

With my conscience now clear, I grabbed her hand and took her to the bed. The room had a romantic view of the New York Harbor and the vibrant red and yellow flowers made the room look like something out of a dream. I grabbed two of the stems as I laid her on the bed. We took our time now, undressing each other, until there was nothing left on either of us. She had her own desires and took me in her mouth.

When she took a break, I pushed her on her back. Her hips and thighs felt so nice and tight, her body—perfect. She had an ivy vine tattoo from her rib cage that spiraled down her stomach to her inner thigh and I could only think how sexy it wore on her.

I grabbed one of the rose stems and dragged it down from her breasts to her clit as she tilted her head back and moaned. I began to peel off the petals and littered them all over her naked body. Then I kissed her stomach gently all the way down to her pussy. I could feel how fast and hard her heart was beating. She was soaking wet. She moaned and gyrated her hips hard into my mouth. I loved how aggressive she was and how sweet she tasted. Before long, she was moaning louder and louder, until she came, and I felt her body go limp. I loved pleasing her so fast, but we weren't nearly through yet.

She pulled me on top of her and then inside of her as she started moving her hips against me. She pressed me for more, to go faster, so I obliged, and kept going harder, waiting for her to come. And she did, harder this time with me inside her, scratching her nails down my back as she let out a visceral moan.

I couldn't hold out anymore at that and pulled out, but she grabbed me and jerked me off until I came directly onto her breasts. I felt like I came for so long, and she stroked me until the very end, sucking whatever was left from the end of my cock, swirling her tongue around the tip and sides. *She's good,* I thought. And just like that, I fell in love with the sex immediately.

But it was more than that. I think for the both of us.

And even though we just finished, she wanted more. She turned to me and draped her leg over mine, leaning against my naked body with her own. She ran her hand down my stomach and rested it there. Her breasts were against my chest. And we lay there together, both out of breath, but comfortable. Like it wasn't our first time. Like we had been together so many times before. Like it was so normal to us.

She kissed me. "That was amazing," she said.

"It was," I said, kissing her back.

But for some reason, I started to think about Isabella. I didn't want to, but I couldn't shake it. And I couldn't tell AP. Not while we were still here, naked, after *that*. So, I kept it to myself. The guilt. Wondering why I felt like I just cheated on someone I wasn't even with anymore.

We held each other, lying there naked for a while with the smell of sex and fresh roses in the air. We ordered room service and drinks. And then we had a little party, just the two of us, lying in bed and watching TV.

We had sex another three times by the time we checked out in the morning.

And then we left in separate cabs. No strings attached. Or at least that's how we played it.

That's what we both pretended, anyway.

CHAPTER SIXTY-THREE

ISABELLA

IT WAS SATURDAY MORNING AND MY MOTHER WAS OUT AT the Hamptons house. She and my father were basically not talking at this point, as he was focused on dealing with the lawyers. I left the penthouse for my final session with Dr. Morgan before testifying.

It was less about therapy at this point and more about strategy. Dr. Morgan had assured me that her research indicated that my past sexual encounter could have played tricks on my mind the night I was with Ray. Or rather, the night I *tried* to be with Ray. It was amazing to me. How your mind could play such tricks on you, how it could betray you like that. How a flashback to a past encounter—a horrible one—could ruin one that had the potential to be beautiful. Dr. Morgan said my reaction came from that. The fear. The panicking. The screaming. It was all still a blur.

But Dr. Morgan even went a step further and assured me that she could testify to my condition, if I needed it. That she would prove this was plausible. She was confident from a medical standpoint that her expert testimony would be enough to clear me of any potential perjury charges down the road, which made me feel better.

It wasn't fair to Ray. For him to be a pawn in this dysfunctional and warped chess game. But I had hope he would be cleared of all charges. And how couldn't he be? The world could not be as corrupt as he always said it was. I refused to believe that. There had to be justice. There had to be goodness out there. Even if there was just a little of it.

I gave Dr. Morgan a hug and thanked her for everything. But one last thing was bothering me. "Do you think he's having an affair with his lawyer?"

"It's tough to say for sure. Anything is possible, especially in an instance like this," she said. "But remember, you need to worry about clearing your own demons first. Before you can share any of his."

I nodded. She was right. I left her office. The mission was my own at that moment. Mine and mine alone.

CHAPTER SIXTY-FOUR

AP

AT THE OFFICE, ANTHONY AND I WERE INTENSELY PLANNING the cross on Ari. Anthony was the screenwriter and I was the actress. We would role-play the questions. The traps, the diversions. The possible answers. I was getting it. But I realized now more than ever just how aggressive my theory was, and I knew I had to walk a fine line in my delivery of it.

I met Ray at a local coffee shop near the office to fill him in on my final defense strategy. It was something I had been developing for quite some time now, but this was the first time I revealed it to him in precise detail.

Ray didn't say much. He sat there quietly, like he was thinking about something. Like maybe it was too much for him. Too risky. Too cruel.

"Well, what do you think?" I asked him, breaking the silence.

"Look, AP, this is a slippery slope," he said. "I gotta get some answers from her first. I'm sorry. I gotta go." He got up to leave.

"Are you okay?" I asked. "What's wrong?"

But he didn't answer. He was already halfway to the door.

"Ray!" I called.

But he never even turned.

And I thought I could do this. This hot-and-cold thing. Be his lawyer one moment, his lover the next. One in public and one in private. But it was beginning to get harder to separate the two. To distinguish who exactly he wanted me to be, and when.

And I couldn't pretend that didn't hurt.

CHAPTER SIXTY-FIVE

RAY

I had been in touch with Isabella even more than I was before. I put the questions out there for her. And she promised she would give me what we needed from her. What AP needed. What I needed. For my freedom.

Just not yet.

I had a quiet night in my small apartment and couldn't sleep much, but I kept my eyes on the clock on the night-stand, tossing and turning every few minutes. When the clock read 3:20AM I sat up and stared at it for a moment. Then I got out of bed, put on my jacket and baseball hat, and ventured outside in the pouring rain to take a walk alone. To hopefully resolve some things. In my head. In my life. All of it.

The beautiful spring weather had turned gray, cold, and rainy as Saturday night seeped into Sunday morning. It was 3:28AM and the city was eerily dead, mostly due to the weather. Especially on the neighborhood blocks that I was strolling on.

I took a turn up the long block going east. My phone read

3:29AM now. And I walked up the block of apartments to the north side of the street—just as planned.

A person was standing ahead with a large umbrella. But the winds and the rain began to pick up and it blurred my vision from seeing clearly, even though the person was only about 30 feet in front of me.

I focused my eyes and my heart started racing as I got a better look. I surveyed the area behind me, then across the street, but there wasn't another soul in sight.

Time stopped then. I looked at the figure ahead of me, and as she came into focus, I almost couldn't believe what I was seeing. It was her—Isabella—waiting for me. Just like she said she would be in her email—at 3:30AM on the dot.

Once we could fully discern the other, we ran the last few feet that separated us. No words were spoken. None were needed. The only sounds that were heard were our hurried footsteps and then her umbrella dropping and splashing as she took her final steps into my arms.

Our embrace was tight, close, with an intensity I could never explain. The cold, pouring rain pounded atop our heads and instinctually, we kissed. For the first time since that infamous night. But it was like no other kiss I'd ever experienced. For me, it was the kiss of freedom. And right there in the rain, I felt born again. I felt like *we* were born again. Given another chance to do this right.

But we had no time to waste. I grabbed her hand and rushed her back to my building, straight up the stairwell to my apartment.

CHAPTER SIXTY-SIX

AP

I TRIED TO FALL ASLEEP. TRIED AND FAILED. KNOWING THE biggest week of my life was coming up had me tossing and turning. I awoke in the middle of the night, going back to my work. Reading through the questions that Anthony and I had gone through earlier in the day. Sitting alone in my apartment, rehearsing the questions and visualizing the multitude of possible answers was helping to prepare me. But reciting them early Sunday morning to myself while the rest of the city was sleeping also scared the shit out of me.

Ray wasn't here. I didn't know where he was. And for some reason, it was bothering me. I checked my phone again. For the hundredth time. There was still no goodnight text message from him. No call. No email. Why? Where was he?

I never liked this. The waiting. The wondering. The worrying. And the insecurities were creeping in on me. About Ray. About my ability to pull off an incredibly dangerous cross-examination. My confidence was officially shaken. And my lover—at least in private—was not even pretending to care.

CHAPTER SIXTY-SEVEN

RAY

I CLOSED THE DOOR SOFTLY BEHIND US. ISABELLA'S HAIR was soaking wet, but somehow her makeup was untouched. The light in my apartment illuminated her face as I looked at her. God, she was gorgeous. Flawless. Her brown eyes were big, beautiful, desperate. For me. I didn't say anything. I just wanted to stare at her.

Finally, I moved closer to her. My hand gently touched her face. A tear began to roll down her cheek and mixed with some of the raindrops, all beading up on her skin perfectly.

"It's okay," I said. "I know what you've been through."

"Ray," she said, her voice shaking. "Can you ever forgive me?"

I looked down, not wanting to say anything because I wasn't sure I even knew the answer. I wanted to. But could I? Could anyone forgive something like this?

She lifted my face with her finger to make me look at her. "Do you love me?" she asked.

"I do," I said. "I will always love you, but…"

Before I could say anything else, she kissed me. There was an impatience to it, a passion. A desire.

I tried to slow her down. Especially after how she freaked out on me last time. And all that I knew she had been through. All *we* had been through. "Iz, it's okay. We don't have to do this now. There's so much going on. I think we should just talk."

"I understand how you feel. And I'm not asking you for anything right this second about our future, but you said you loved me. And if you do, then you'll understand that I need this right now," she said.

And with that, she pulled me to the couch and began undressing herself. She was wearing a sexy bra and her beautiful breasts were popping over the top of the cups. I was turned on but hesitant. "Really, babe. Let's take it slow. Please." I tried to back away, but she wasn't having it.

"I am asking you to *please* be with me. Don't you understand this is the only way for me to heal? To get better?" she said.

She started to get emotional again. And I questioned if she had a hidden agenda. One she wasn't being honest with me about. Was she trying to frame me? Get my semen? DNA? But then I realized her being here, in my apartment at 4AM, at *her* request…consummating sex would guarantee my freedom. I still wasn't sure though. The sheer paranoia made me doubt everything.

She got on her knees and undid my pants.

I stopped her. "Iz, please."

But she didn't listen. She began to take me in her mouth. I wasn't even hard. Until she started. But she was unsure of herself, seeming like she was doing this for the first time.

"Are you okay?" I asked her. "You should stop."

But she didn't. And I tried to back away. Again.

"We don't have to do this," I said.

"Yes, we do," she said, peering up at me with a pleading look on her face.

I held out my hand and picked her up off the floor. If this was what she needed, I would try, despite not wanting to. The entire thing was uncomfortable. And that's when I realized this is how it must feel for her. Every time. And no one should feel that way. I led her into the bedroom.

She was still holding my hand when she looked at me. "This time, I need to feel you inside me. Please promise you won't stop. No matter what."

"I promise," I said.

She lay on her back and I got on top of her and told her how beautiful she was. We kissed, and I kept stopping to ask her if she was okay; each time, she responded with a nod. The heavier we got, the more vulnerable and hesitant she became.

And I stopped. "Baby, I want you, I do, but this doesn't feel right."

She was tense as she kissed me again. "Keep going. Please," she whispered.

She took off my pants. My shirt. Everything. Then she grabbed my body and pulled me as close to her as she could. She froze at first, prompting me to find a way to make her more comfortable. I got on my back so she wouldn't feel so trapped this time. So she could be in control. She straddled me and we slid together in a perfect fit. She squeezed my shoulders tightly while on top. And I stopped, frozen. Unwilling to move. I didn't want to spook her in any way.

"If this is what you want, Iz, then don't stop," I said softly.

"I'm not. I need this," she said, maneuvering to position herself comfortably.

"It's gonna be okay, baby. Just take your time," I said.

And even though it was uncomfortable to start, as soon as I said that, it seemed to calm her. Her body relaxed. And her pain seemed to turn to pleasure as her shallow breathing turned to moans of wanting more.

Before long, she had a rhythm going on top while riding me. We were deeply kissing at the same time. It didn't last long, as it was too intense for both of us. I tried to pull out but she asked me not to.

"Stay with me," she breathed.

And so I came, right there inside her. Both of us breathing heavily as she collapsed on top of me. As she lay covering my body, I pulled the sheets over us both. Tightly, so she felt secure.

"Are you okay?" I asked her.

Tears filled her eyes. "Ray, please don't ever leave me. I can't ever imagine being with anyone else. I've never felt better in my entire life than in this moment right now. It's so hard to explain. I'm so sorry, I told myself I wouldn't cry…"

"No, it's okay," I said, wiping her tears and then squeezing her as close to my body as I could without hurting her. "Tell me. Tell me everything. I need to know."

WE LAY THERE TOGETHER until the sky outside began to lighten, the sun piercing into my apartment from the east window.

She told me about certain things but said she couldn't tell me everything. Not yet. And when I pushed for more, the more emotional she got. She couldn't even formulate sentences.

"I'm sorry, baby," I said. "Try to relax."

But she got anxious anyway. "I have to go. I'm sorry," she said. "This is too much right now. Please just give me a little more time and I promise, I'll tell you everything."

I watched her get dressed quickly, and then she was running for the door.

"Wait!" I said. "Iz, I need to know why you yelled rape that night. I need to know."

She shook her head, tears filling her eyes.

I stood up, needing to shift gears quickly to at least get something from her. "In the police report where it says you pulled my hair. Did you mean the hair on my head or somewhere else?"

"I pulled his chest hair," she said, between sobs. "I have to go. I'm sorry. I love you, Ray."

And with that, she was out the door.

I eventually fell back asleep, waking up at noon. I hadn't had a deep sleep like that since my arrest. I turned on my phone and there were three text messages from AP. A pang of guilt hit me, realizing I neglected her last night. Especially after we just had a wild night together 48 hours prior.

I called her, apologizing for being out of pocket. She said she understood but I swore I heard hurt in her voice. I told her we had to meet.

"I was emailing Isabella yesterday and I have good news for us," I said, half-lying.

"Okay," she said. "Why don't you come over later? I'll cook us a nice dinner and we can talk about it."

"I would love that. I'll see you around four," I said.

WHEN I GOT to AP's apartment, she had some light music playing in the background. Candles were burning, and the roses I bought for her were the centerpiece in her cozy apartment. She looked beautiful, hair up in a messy bun. And when she saw me, she kissed me on the lips as we hugged. I said nothing, not knowing what to feel, never mind say. I couldn't tell her about Iz. I couldn't break AP's heart like that for no reason.

"I missed you last night," she confessed. "I could barely sleep. I haven't been able to stop thinking about the *Ritz*."

"I can't stop thinking about it either," I said. "You're amazing, all around, you know that?"

But I escaped the embrace and broke off to pour us each a glass of wine while she started cooking. Then the talk shifted to the case.

I didn't know how to tell her what transpired between Isabella and me last night. I didn't want to lie to her. But I couldn't be totally honest with her, either. I couldn't. I shook my head and looked down.

"Are you okay?" she asked. "You're being weird."

"I'm just confused," I said. "It feels like all these big things in my life are converging at once."

"What did she say?" AP asked.

"She wanted to talk about the two of us getting back together. She didn't go into too much detail with me on your specific theory. She said it was too tough to discuss right now. But she did confirm Ari's indirect involvement in her mom's murder, and said that she will testify to that. She seemed to be emotional in the emails but I get the feeling that your theory is dead on."

"Do you have the email printouts?" she asked me.

"Nah," I said. "I couldn't get them where I was at. But the bottom line is she confirmed that she meant she pulled *chest* hair, which I think is huge."

"Oh my god, Ray! That's great! We have them now," AP said. "Knowing this, I can now go after Ari, full bore."

But I wasn't excited. Or happy. I really didn't know what the fuck I was feeling. "I don't think any of this matters now to be honest. I don't know how the hell this whole thing will be resolved, for anyone..."

AP was quiet. She got up to clean some dishes and brought more food out. We ate less and started drinking more, eventually snuggling and then kissing passionately. We stopped talking about the trial altogether and before we knew it, we were in AP's bed, fooling around. Her room was lit with more candles, and we lay on the bed kissing as I slowly started to undress her. And she did the same to me.

The sex only intensified from the first time, but this time it was more like lovemaking. I could only think that I had gone years without having sex of this nature, and now within two days, I had two of the most beautiful women I could ever desire. It was most men's dream, but right now, for me, it was a fucking curse.

We lay in bed under the covers for a while, naked and close. Talking. And she rolled on her side and looked at me.

"When this is all over, I don't want to lose you," she said. "I'll go wherever you want. If you want to move and get out of here, I'll go with you. Just name the place. And I'm not trying to pressure you, but I want you to know that. I want you to know how I feel."

I sat up a little. "Babe, you're flattering me too much. You know this thing is so damn complicated, I can't even look ahead right now. I'm still on trial and I feel like my head is gonna explode."

"I know, I know all of this," she said. "But I know I want to be with you." She paused, keeping her eyes on me. "Do you feel the same? At all?"

"I always feel good with you, whenever we're together. I love you to death, AP, but I don't know how practical things will be with us after this is all over. How do we know what will change?"

"Do you love me? Really?" she asked.

"I do. I am in love with you. I don't question that in the

least," I said. "But you know you're not the only one I have feelings for. You know that, right?"

She looked down. "I *cannot* hear about you having feelings for a girl that would do what she did to you. And who cares what everyone says after this is over? *I'm* the one fighting for you. I'm the one that would lie for you, do anything for you. I'm not the one who put you in prison." Then, she sat up and pulled the covers over her chest. "Do you really still have feelings for her? After all this?"

I never saw this side of AP before. And I already knew that no matter what a girl says about no strings attached, very rarely was it ever fully true. But her courage to lay it all on the line was brave, endearing, and it made me love and respect her more. It didn't scare me. I knew the trial was bringing a closeness to us that made this almost inevitable, for both of us. "AP, let's not go there now. Please just know that I love you. There is so much to this."

She hugged me as she spoke, her voice cracking. "I want you to know that no matter what happens between us, I will always cherish our time together. And I will always love you, Ray."

I hugged her back and closed my eyes, thinking that was one of sexiest things a girl had ever said to me. My heart melted even more for her after that. I knew it was something that would always stick in my mind forever as quintessential AP.

I woke before dawn and looked at her when it hit me: I was in love with two women at the same time. I realized that this was possible now, regardless of what any old adage said. I kissed her on the forehead, then went back to my apartment to get ready for court. I knew, leaving her that morning, that soon my heart would have to make a decision.

But it wasn't ready yet.

CHAPTER SIXTY-EIGHT

AP

As if things couldn't get worse, the DA's office filed a motion to dismiss me from the case for "misconduct" based on evidence they had of me and Ray having an inappropriate sexual relationship. It had a ripple effect throughout the media almost immediately. All eyes were on me as rumors flew about the young promiscuous lawyer who was having an alleged fling with her convict client. The only thing worse than the idea of being pulled from the case was being pulled away from Ray.

The judge convened all of us in a side bar even though the jury was not present, wanting to speak ex-parte with both sides due to the sensitive nature of the motion. She was perturbed, to say the least. At me, for my actions. And at the DA, for making such allegations.

"I'm going to read the allegations, but absent Ms. Peterson telling me that she's having an affair with her client, I am not removing her from the case," the judge said. Then she looked at me. "Unless, of course, you'd like to recuse yourself?"

"I am appalled by these allegations, Your Honor," I lied.

"My client has been wronged and I am here to defend him. That is all. During the course of our time working together, we have become friends. Nothing more. I take my oath to the bar very seriously and I..."

But Anthony cut me off. "I've seen some dirty things out of this office, but this is a new low. And what relevance does this have at this point? This is not a matrimonial case." he said. "I'm telling you right now, whoever is behind this, whoever is going to try to defame this lawyer's reputation, is going to pay."

Judge Beekman tried to calm him down. "Okay, okay, Mr. Mika. I understand where you're coming from. Let's just all calm down and try to finish this trial with some civility. We still have a way to go. I am going to look into this a little more and let the dust settle until the morning."

She called the jury in and gave them brief instructions to refrain from watching the news or reading the papers. And then she dismissed them for the day. Who knew if any of them would listen, but the ones who didn't would hear all about the DA's claims of a steamy affair with me and Ray, the accused rapist. There were enough cozy pictures of us—undoubtedly from Rohnstein's private investigators—littered all over the media to make me look guilty as charged.

My credibility took a hit in the court of public opinion. I just couldn't let it throw me off my game. But I will admit I was shaken. And embarrassed. And part of me kicked myself for getting as close to Ray as I had. But it would never be something I'd regret. Regardless of what would come from it.

Ray felt horrible. He tried to console me.

But I played it off. "Remember what you said to me?" I told him. "Don't get concerned with what they write about you in the papers? So, that's what I'm doing. And I know who planted this, so let's see who gets the last laugh."

"Yep," Ray said. "He who laughs last, laughs loudest."

COURT RESUMED on Tuesday morning promptly at 9:30AM, and after the city got more than their fill of the story, Judge Beekman took it easy on me.

"The motion to disqualify is denied," the judge stated. "The People can call their next witness."

The young male ADA stood up as confidently as could be. "The People call Mr. Ari Rohnstein to the stand."

The DA tried to paint Ari as a great father who saved Isabella from a horrendous childhood in an impoverished country with no family. And it seemed to be working. I watched the jurors' faces. They were *moved*. Compassion, it lived in them.

The DA outlined Ari's incredible accomplishments and all his charitable work for the city. *What a guy.* That's what they wanted to portray. The DA got through with Ari rather quickly, and then it was our turn.

Anthony took the initial cross, which seemed to surprise many. And although the DA had already covered much of the stuff Anthony was going over, he made it much more gruesome to the jury. Told it more like it was, not like it seemed. It wasn't only about the issues related to the adoption, and the bad business deals that were a direct rebuff of him being a great philanthropist, but also the shocking truth that Isabella's birth mother was Ari's mistress.

He set Ari up like a bowling pin and then asked for an adjournment so I could finish the cross afterwards.

I was dressed more conservatively today than usual. My hair was pulled back, and I had little makeup on. I meant business. And I did not need anyone looking at me thinking anything more than they already were. Even though I was about to go up against one of the most powerful businessmen in the world, I would control the action, which liberated me to the point of fearlessness. A dangerous thing for Ari Rohnstein.

Anthony had given the jury a history lesson of what occurred decades ago that led young Isabella to come to America. And now I would pick up on the more recent history, first by laying some ground work and then directing the action toward the first sexual assault claim by Isabella while she attended USC.

Needless to say, the jury was a little taken aback at the mention of the incident. It was addressed in the defense opening, but a lot had transpired since then that it was almost forgotten. And instead of trying to speculate as to what occurred in the frat house that night, I wanted to focus on how Ari handled it. But I would save the gory details for my cross with Isabella herself.

I looked at Ari. "Isn't it true, Mr. Rohnstein, that the first time Isabella did something like this, you wanted it buried because you cared more about your companies growing in Los Angeles than bringing unneeded attention to you and your family?"

"Absolutely not," he replied firmly.

"What about this time?" I asked. "Why were you so insistent on pressing charges against my client?"

"I just wanted to help Isabella stick up for herself," he said.

"But my question is, why not the first time? What was the difference between supporting her now but not then in LA?" I questioned.

"I don't know…"

"Well I think the jury would like to know, don't you?" I asked.

"Objection, Your Honor!" the young ADA yelled as he

stood. "She is leading the witness. He answered the question that he doesn't know, and I don't understand what relevance this has to whether or not Mr. Jansen raped his daughter."

"Sustained," the judge said. "Move in a relevant direction, Ms. Peterson."

I nodded. "Don't worry, Your Honor. I'm going somewhere with this." I looked back at Ari. "So, Mr. Rohnstein, may I ask you, did the guilt of not supporting your daughter by filing a complaint in LA come to mind? Meaning, did you feel guilty that you didn't support her the first time, so now you wanted to right that wrong?"

"No," Ari said.

I smiled. "I actually believe you. See, I believe there is something even bigger going on here. A much bigger, deliberate scheme to frame my client, so I ask you…"

"Objection!" Ari's lawyer Jimmy yelled, standing up from the crowd. "Your Honor, as Mr. Rohnstein's lawyer, Ms. Peterson is insinuating that my client may be involved with some sort of nefarious activity with no basis whatsoever, and I must object to my client answering any further questions at this time. Don't answer, Ari." Then he looked at me. "And you better watch yourself, young lady."

Just like that, the court became a temporary circus again, with both sides standing up and shouting things toward the bench. The media members seemed stunned at the sudden chaos, especially over what seemed like such normal questions to the victim's father.

The judge was now visibly enraged, desperately seeking order in her court. "Before we go any further," she said, "let's dismiss the jury and meet privately in my chambers. I demand order in this court, now!"

In the judge's chambers, Judge Beekman was as impartial as she could be. And Anthony took control on behalf of his law firm.

“Your Honor,” he said, “we believe that Mr. Rohnstein is directly involved with witness tampering and other items in connection to this case, and it is imperative that we have this examination. Our client is on trial for *rape* and is facing nine years in state prison. The law is very clear in this regard, if it’s relevant testimony then there is no disputing that we must be allowed to proceed.”

“This is preposterous,” Ari’s lawyer said. “She’s trying to smear my client in the hopes of polluting the minds of the jurors to get her client off. And in doing so, she is damaging him and his business brands, all so she can make a name for herself.”

To that, I laughed out loud.

Judge Beekman considered this all before speaking. “So far,” she finally said, “I haven’t heard anything that tells me Ms. Peterson cannot proceed. But I also understand where Mr. Rohnstein’s lawyer is coming from.” Then she looked at me sternly. “He doesn’t want to allow you to get started on this fishing expedition. So, I’m warning you, if you cross the line, you could be opening yourself up to ethic charges.”

Rohnstein’s lawyer jumped in and looked at me. “And be forewarned, honey, you *will* be facing civil defamation from us regardless.”

“I’m not your honey,” I snapped at him. “And if your client is such a solid citizen, then he should complete his civic duty and testify truthfully.”

Then, just as it seemed that the trial would finally go on, Rohnstein’s lawyer had one more question.

“What happens if I advise my client to take the Fifth from here on out?” he asked, directing his question to the head DA.

“We will have no choice but to request that the judge hold him in contempt of court for impeding the investigation and trial,” the head of the Sex Crime Unit said.

Judge Beekman chimed in. “And I will have no choice but to have Mr. Rohnstein detained until the trial is concluded.”

Ari’s lawyer considered all this, then spoke. “But you won’t grant him immunity?”

The Sex Crime Unit chief let out an exaggerated noise at the ridiculousness of the request. “Immunity for *what*? We have no idea where Ms. Peterson’s examination is even headed.”

But in the end, it didn’t matter.

Ari refused to wave the white flag, ignored their advice to take the Fifth, and decided to proceed with taking the stand.

CHAPTER SIXTY-NINE

ISABELLA

DESPITE MY FATHER'S INSISTENCE TO TAKE THE STAND WHILE the sky was falling down on him, his lawyers and the DA were able to postpone the testimony until the morning, giving him a chance to *try* to create some sort of plan. The penthouse was madness, with so much speculation going on that there had to be *some* sort of key information getting to the defense.

In an effort to prevent any more leaks, especially within his own camp, my father put everyone under intense watch. He even hired additional security staff and implemented new surveillance measures.

That night, they called an emergency meeting at the penthouse. Everyone was there, from his personal legal staff working on the case, to any and all witnesses or hired help tied to the situation. The ground rules were simple. If they wanted to win the case, there needed to be strict guidelines to protect my father.

This went for everyone. Especially me. And they drilled it into my head. How bad things could be for him if things went left. How bad things could be for me. But regardless of their threats, some sick part of me was enjoying this. Watching him squirm.

CHAPTER SEVENTY

RAY

I MET AP IN THE EARLY EVENING AT HER APARTMENT AFTER she and Anthony went back to the office to re-craft the cross. I stayed the night with her, again. Despite the chaos, we couldn't get enough of each other. And with the stakes so high, we were *knowingly* risking everything. But neither of us cared about that. Our passion was like a drug, giving us energy to keep pushing forward. Giving us a *reason* to.

I had tried to reconnect with Iz again after court by email, but I got nothing back from her. And for some reason, I had a gut feeling I wouldn't be hearing from her again. I even left AP's apartment to run to a nearby *Dunkin Donuts* around 10:30PM, just to log onto the public internet kiosk there and see if I had anything. But there was nothing from Jane Doe Glow.

I tried to downplay it to AP while we lay in bed watching the evening news, but AP could sense something was amiss. The 11PM news reports on the case only added to AP's growing concerns.

"Ray, we have the biggest day of the trial tomorrow and all I have from her is that she *said* she would back me up.

Back me up when? I need more *now!*" she said, getting frantic.

"I know, I know," I said, shaking my head, my concern growing too. "What can we do? We've come this far already."

"You understand that they're going to be watching me extremely closely, right?" AP said. "And without any clear indication whether our theory is right or not, I am heading into a fucking lion's den. I'm getting scared here." She looked at me for answers.

But I didn't have any. I sat up. "I'm sorry. She gave me her word that she would explain everything. I didn't think she would go dark, especially after our last exchange. I got a sense that we were on the right track and I didn't want to push her. I don't know. I think we still have enough with the emails, god forbid this goes bad."

"My ass is on the line now," AP said. "Yeah, we can probably get you off at some point if we subpoena the email trails, but what about me? My career is on the line, here."

I tried to calm her down, but I knew she was right. "Now isn't the time to be scared. They're just as scared of you. They're trying to put the pressure on you, hoping you back down. You said it, this is why you signed up for this case. So go get 'em tomorrow. Be your best when the lights are brightest, and finish him."

She took a deep breath and let out a long exhale. "You promise we're gonna be okay here?"

"Yes," I said. "With everything I got."

CHAPTER SEVENTY-ONE

AP

I LOOKED AT ARI AND STRAIGHTENED MY SHOULDERS. "MR. Rohnstein, yesterday we heard about an adulterous affair between you and Isabella's mother dating back to the 1990s. Did you ever discuss the affair with your wife prior to her agreeing to adopt Isabella?"

He seemed unshaken by this as he sat completely still. "No, I did not."

"And you have testified that you're in the media business," I said, "so, isn't it safe to say that you are constantly involved in cover-ups and manipulating facts?"

"No," he said, sounding offended. "We simply try to report accurate news for the people on what is relevant."

"So, are you saying that it *wasn't* relevant to discuss with your wife that you were going to adopt the daughter of your slain mistress?"

"It was in the past," he said. "I didn't want to lose my family…"

"And can you clarify what 'family' that is, because we have evidence that you wanted to leave your current wife and start a new family with Isabella's mother, Ms. Martin." I said.

Ari looked unsettled now. "I meant my wife Michele and Isabella, obviously."

"So, after the news broke yesterday and the cat was out of the bag, did you at least discuss the affair with your wife then, finally?" I asked him, with a hint of sarcasm.

Ari moved in his seat. "That's a personal family matter."

"I'm sure it is," I said, fighting back a smile. "And I'm sure you didn't seem to have time for it yet either, but if you haven't noticed, you are under oath, sir, so please answer the question."

"No, I did not discuss it with her," he said quietly.

"So, even though the information is quite apparent, you are *still* trying to manipulate the truth to your own wife, is that correct, Mr. Rohnstein?"

"There's nothing to manipulate," he said. "It was a long time ago, and it's all over the news now anyway."

"So, let me ask you, Mr. Rohnstein, did you use your media contacts to directly or indirectly put out news items that were not favorable to my client in an effort to manipulate the public's perception of him?"

"I had nothing to do with any of that," he said. "This case is not about *me.*"

"I'm sure you didn't," I said, smiling briefly. "Now, once the DA had decided to charge my client with a crime, is it fair to say that helping secure a conviction would be beneficial to you, and that you set an agenda to ensure it would happen?"

"No." Then he raised his brow. "Why would there be a benefit for me?"

Judge Beekman then instructed Ari not to answer a question with a question, to which he nodded out of respect.

"That's exactly what we're trying to figure out here," I

said to him. "It sure is a good question, isn't it, Mr. Rohnstein? Because if there was no benefit for you then why did you hire private investigators for countless hours to try and convict my client?

"I'm just trying to find justice for my daughter and help the DA's office do its job effectively," he said. "It's no secret that I've been a big donor toward organizations that fight crime here in New York for a very long time. It doesn't matter if it were my own daughter or someone else's." He looked into the jurors' eyes when he said this, apparently trying to score some brownie points.

"Well, thank you for your service to our great city," I said, with just a touch of sarcasm as I flipped my hair and took a look at jurors #4 and #8. I paused then, going back to the defense table for some notes. I wanted to make Ari uncomfortable, and by the time I faced him again, it looked like I succeeded. "Well, Mr. Rohnstein, then I assume if you are a man for justice, you can respect that I'm just trying to do my job and get to the truth."

"Objection, Your Honor," the ADA said as there was a break in the action. "This whole line of questioning is not appropriate. I understand that Ms. Peterson has not tried a lot of cases, but can we please stop the dialogue with the witness and focus on direct questions?"

"Sustained," the judge said matter-of-factly. "Ms. Peterson, as you should be aware, your job is to ask questions only, please."

I didn't let it get me off my game, though. And I wouldn't let that stop the way I was going to do this. *Let them keep objecting*. "Mr. Rohnstein, do you seek the truth like the rest of us here?"

"Yes, of course," he said.

"Mr. Rohnstein, I ask you to unbutton your shirt please and expose part of your bare chest to us."

Judging by the noises and gasps, everyone thought I had lost my mind by asking this question.

"Objection, Your Honor!" the young ADA yelled.

The judge quieted everyone down and looked at me. "Before I rule, Ms. Peterson, please tell me you have something very relevant in mind to make such a request?"

"I do, Your Honor, very much so," I said, my heart pounding in my chest now.

"Overruled then," Judge Beekman said. "Please open your shirt to expose part of your chest, Mr. Rohnstein."

"This is preposterous!" Ari's lawyer yelled out.

Judge Beekman banged her gavel. "If we have any other outbursts in the courtroom, I will hold the individual in contempt, no questions asked."

Ari looked at the judge like he just got his hand caught in the cookie jar as she signaled to him to do the deed.

With that, Ari unbuttoned the top few buttons to expose part of his chest—a chest full of dark hair.

With the exception of a few whispers, there was silence in the court.

"Thank you, Mr. Rohnstein," I said. "I will come back to this later. I'd like the record to reflect that Mr. Rohnstein has shown that he does not shave his chest hair."

I then admitted into evidence the picture of Ari with his mistress in Curacao 20 years ago, which showed him to be just as hairy.

Ari seemed angry now as he spat the words at me in front of the jury. "You're no angel. We all know the truth about you and your client."

The judge snapped at him. "That is *enough*, Mr. Rohnstein."

"Objection, Your Honor, move to strike," Mika rose in my defense.

"Sustained." Judge Beekman then instructed the jury to strike Mr. Rohnstein's outburst from their mental record.

I took it in stride though and looked back at him confidently. "Well, thankfully for me we aren't discussing my sex life today, but we will be discussing yours."

The people in the court began to laugh in unison. The ADA stood up, but before he could finish, the judge ordered a side bar to quell the commotion now going on.

"Please approach, all of you," she said. Then she looked at me. "Ms. Peterson, I'm not going to warn you again about your examinations anymore. Questions only," she said angrily. "Do you understand me?"

"Yes, Your Honor," I said.

She then let the ADA speak who was clearly chomping at the bit.

"Your Honor, Ms. Peterson is about to embark on a smear campaign on this witness and I'm letting you know now we have a major problem with relevancy to the crime in question."

Without undermining me this time, the judge politely asked me where I was going with all this.

"We intend to make a claim of possible criminal activity that cuts right to the heart of this case," I said. "The testimony is mandatory to our defense."

"Okay," Judge Beekman said calmly. "You've been warned already."

"This is going to pollute the jurors' minds and we are going to object on the record to this line of questioning," the young ADA said. "And if this is a smear campaign, then the Mika Law Firm will be the target of a separate investigation when this is over."

It started getting ugly at the side bar, with the low talk now escalating and echoing out to the jury and spectators in the courtroom. We were sent back to our table to take our places, and the ADA made a brief statement on the record for possible appellate rights.

I resumed my questioning and looked at Ari again. "Exactly how many mistresses did you have over the last 20 years since Isabella's mother was murdered?"

"She was the last one," Ari said. "I changed my ways."

"Can you please take your time before answering, and be sure that you never had another indiscretion with another woman in the last 20 years?" I asked him, carefully.

"No. I didn't. Something happened to me after that. It was life-changing, gaining a daughter," he said.

He was so good that I was almost leery to proceed with all the threats from my adversary. And I figured the jury might be thinking the same. But I kept plugging away in spite of his convincing responses. "Did adopting Isabella help you fill the void after your true love had been murdered?"

"I wouldn't say she was my true love," Ari said. "And I don't know if Isabella filled the void of someone tragically being murdered, I just felt the need to ensure the little girl had a family. She had no one to take her in back in South America."

"And you felt responsible for her mom being murdered and ultimately breaking up her family with your affair?" I asked.

"I don't feel responsible for things I have no control over, Ms. Peterson."

I nodded. "Let's go back to your wife then. Did you feel guilty holding all this in your conscience for almost 20 years?"

"Yes," he said after a moment, and a flash of honesty seemed to shoot across his eyes before he looked down. "In a way, I'm glad this has come out now." Then he looked back up at me. "Even though it has absolutely no relevance to your client raping my daughter."

I glanced at the jurors, who seemed to agree with him by the looks on their faces. I felt like I was losing them now.

Anthony shot me a look that said *get to the point.*

I looked back at Ari. "So, you had all this on your conscience for 20 years and you felt guilty, yet you still hid the truth?"

"Well, obviously," he said, clearly frustrated now. "We've been through this already."

"Are you sure that the reason you didn't have any other mistresses was because no one else could ever live up to Isabella's mother?" I asked.

"No, I told you, I changed. I was still in love with my wife Michele. I still am. We're a good match."

I gave him a slight nod and looked at the judge. "Your Honor, the defense would like to submit into evidence a letter from Mr. Rohnstein to Ms. Martin before her death, written close to 20 years ago. We have taken the time to have it authenticated, and I want to show this to Mr. Rohnstein and remind him that he is under oath. May I proceed? "

"Proceed," the judge said.

"Do you recognize this letter to your mistress—Ms. Martin?" I asked him.

"I do," said Ari sheepishly.

I took the theatrical approach and asked Ari to read the letter to the jury.

It was cringeworthy stuff, especially the part where Ari professed his love and desire to be with her and start a new family. And even more so the part where he professed his obsession with her.

Then I turned away from the jurors and looked at Ari, whose face was red now. "Now tell me, is that your writing?"

Redness flushed his cheeks. "Yes."

"Did you ever get over losing her?" I asked.

"Yes, in time."

"I just want to clarify, having Isabella around didn't help you with coping with the grieving process?" I asked.

"Of course, in some regards it did," he said. "We loved having Isabella in our lives. But as I said, it was more about me changing my ways internally."

"Interesting," I said, as I looked toward the jury before facing him again. "And looking at Isabella, would you agree that she looks very much like her mom?"

"Yes…"

"So, do you also find her to be attractive like her mother?" I asked.

Ari's face changed and it was obvious he didn't know how to answer the question. "Well, yes, even though she is my daughter I do think she is a very attractive young lady…"

"And isn't it true that when Isabella wanted to go out on her own that you were very protective of her around boys?"

"I think I was the same as most dads are," he said. "Cautious."

"So, you wanted to protect her, especially since it was you that adopted her, correct?" I asked.

"Yes, of course."

"Objection, Your Honor," the ADA said. "Ms. Peterson is going in circles here. She has already covered most of this information."

"Overruled," the judge said. "Keep your examination moving, Ms. Peterson."

I nodded. "Mr. Rohnstein, there was obviously a strained relationship between you and Isabella, even as recently as just before she started her magazine, correct?"

"Yes, you could say that," Ari said.

"And was the whole USC incident the reason the relationship became strained?"

"I don't know what it was," he said. "Isabella had a tough childhood and we did the best we could for her, but she always seemed to have a tendency to shut down."

"So, what was the point in starting the magazine project together if the relationship was so strained?" I asked.

"I thought it was a good business idea, and as a family we were really trying to make Isabella happy," he said.

I knew I had to cut to the chase. "Mr. Rohnstein, with all that was going on with Isabella from the tough childhood to the alleged sexual assault incident at USC, why didn't you recommend that she seek counseling at some point?"

"I just never believed in therapy. I'm from a different generation, and looking back, maybe I was flawed in that thinking," he said.

"So, it had nothing to do with you not wanting to reveal to a stranger anything about your life that could make its way to the media?"

"No, I just don't think shrinks help."

I made a face. "I'm sorry, I'm confused. You testified that you were protective of her and she had a tough childhood, but you never even *considered* getting her professional help?"

"Like I said, looking back, maybe it was a mistake," he said.

The jury seemed to sit up now with this line of questioning, as if I was onto something.

I narrowed my eyes as I looked at him. "No, it wasn't a mistake at all, Mr. Rohnstein, was it?"

"Objection!" the ADA yelled again. "Ms. Peterson is leading the witness again! What is the point of this, Your Honor?"

"Sustained," Judge Beekman said. "Rephrase."

I didn't need the answer to that one, I was moving on and going right to the crux of the case. I looked at Ray for a brief moment to try to get the balls to spit this out. Then I moved closer to Ari and stopped for a few seconds, staring at him until he became visibly uncomfortable. "Mr. Rohnstein, you testified today that you wanted the truth, is that still the case after the recent line of questioning?"

"Yes, of course."

"So, the cover-ups to your wife and everyone else are now over?"

He took a sip of water, a bead of sweat forming on his forehead. "Yes, they have been for quite some time."

I watched him and waited. The court was quiet. I took a deep breath and resumed.

"Isn't it true, Mr. Rohnstein, that the reason you never let Isabella see a therapist during her childhood was because it was highly possible that she could have revealed to her therapist that *you* were sexually abusing her?"

CHAPTER SEVENTY-TWO

RAY

NOT A WORD WAS SPOKEN IN THE COURT FOR ABOUT A HALF a second. It was as if time had stopped and everything was moving in slow motion. You could hear a pin drop in that instance.

My heart was pounding in my chest, echoing in the walls of the room surrounding me. I watched Ari's face go pale.

AP was suspended in the moment, watching his face, staring into him almost like she was daring him to speak, move, to do *something*. Along with everyone else, I waited for his reaction. A look. An admission.

Then the chaos erupted. Like never before in this case.

Ari's lawyer stood up and began to shout to Ari, distracting him from AP and the question that was hanging in the air. "Don't answer the question, Ari! Don't say anything else!"

Ari's stunned face turned to anger as he stood up in the chair and looked at AP menacingly, rage apparent on his face. "How dare you accuse me of something like that!" he yelled at her. "I promise you, I will do everything in my power to ensure you never practice law again!"

Judge Beekman was banging her gavel, but no one seemed to care.

There was no order in the court. The DA objected—but to what, they didn't really know. The media reporters were basically trampling over one another to get out the door. And the jurors, judging by their faces, were in a state of shock—mouths agape, eyes wide.

I turned my head to look at AP just to witness the look of triumph on her face. And there it was.

She was beaming. And in that pivotal moment, I felt that same triumph running through my veins, too.

CHAPTER SEVENTY-THREE

ISABELLA

I FELT LIKE I WAS BEING GUARDED IN MY OWN APARTMENT, watched by my father's security staff under the notion that he was actually "protecting" me in some way. I only found out what was going on in the case when there was a breaking news alert from Channel 2 on the television we had on in the room.

The lead trial reporter was the first to get on the air and report "another wild scene" at 111 Centre Street. "When Raymond Jansen's attorney, Alexandra Peterson, accused Ari Rohnstein of sexually abusing his adopted daughter, Isabella, the judge immediately sent the jury home and had an adjournment. Now, the lawyers are meeting yet again to try to figure out how to deal with this new development. No one knows if this is a bona fide accusation or if Ms. Peterson is merely throwing another theory out there to the jury. In either case, it was a bombshell."

All the staff in the penthouse were silent as they looked at one another with shock and questions all over their awkward faces. No one knew what to say. But I felt my stomach bubble up to my throat and get lodged there. A permanent sense of nausea overcame me, and I needed air. I wanted to run, to get out of there. I stood up and was immediately ordered to sit down and stay put.

My father was just accused of raping me on national television. But they didn't report on what was important. They didn't mention his response. How he reacted. The look on his face at the mere allegation. A moment I did not get to witness. A moment I would never get back.

CHAPTER SEVENTY-FOUR

AP

BACK IN THE JUDGE'S CHAMBERS AT THE COURT, JUDGE Beekman seemed in over her head and at a loss for what to do, trying to get answers out of me. She instructed everyone to be on their best behavior, stating yet again that she would have no problem arresting someone for contempt if they got out of line. Then she looked at me.

"Ms. Peterson, please explain to me where your examination is going?"

"Your Honor, we believe that Mr. Rohnstein raped his daughter at a young age and as a result, she has been emotionally scarred by it. This is what we believe led to both the USC allegations as well as the allegations against our client. It is likely that Isabella had a psychological flashback of some sort the night in question," I said.

Judge Beekman looked at me with hesitation. "Ms. Peterson, you can't just accuse someone of a crime of this nature as some theory without any basis. Do you understand this? Please tell me you do?"

I nodded. "It's more than a theory, Your Honor. We feel that the testimony of the initial detective indicates that what

Isabella described in her report precludes Mr. Jansen as the perpetrator. And through more witness testimony we will prove it out."

Ari's lawyer jumped in. "Your Honor, how do you allow her to just make this accusation of my client when there's no basis for this whatsoever."

Anthony stepped in before the judge could answer. "Your Honor, this is not just *someone*. This is her adoptive father, the man who had an affair with her mother before she was murdered. And I can assure you that we have taken extreme measures to investigate this case before throwing out such an accusation. As we continue to present our case, maybe the DA will actually search to get to the person who really caused the psychological damage to this young woman."

The judge listened and then permitted Ari's lawyer to speak again at his request.

"We understand the court has a job to do," he said, "and our issues are probably best served in a civil complaint against the Mika Law Firm, but my client denies these allegations as nothing but a publicity stunt. Regardless of what you allow or not, Judge Beekman, I believe Mr. Rohnstein has legitimate Fifth Amendment rights now."

"Okay, and what is the position of the People on that?" Judge Beekman asked, facing the department head directly.

"We are in agreement," he said. "Mr. Rohnstein does have Fifth Amendment rights and we are not offering immunity of any kind at this point. We are seeking the truth, and without the victim taking the stand yet, we don't know what to make of any of this."

"Well, that's the problem," the judge said. "If I let this go on and the victim doesn't corroborate the defense theory, then the People's case is compromised."

"How so?" Anthony asked. "Judge, we are only offering another theory of what might have happened. No different than in a murder case when there are theories of killers other than the accused."

"It is more than a theory!" the judge snapped. "The comments by Ms. Peterson were so inflammatory that if the victim doesn't corroborate this in some way, then I would almost certainly have to declare a mistrial." She paused then and looked at Ari. "And if she does corroborate it…well, Mr. Rohnstein, you'll have a big problem on your hands." And with that, she dismissed everyone until the morning, deciding that she needed the rest of the day off to figure out the legal mess that was now on her hands.

Meanwhile, our entire defense team went back to the office even though there was nothing to work on until the judge decided how to proceed with the trial. The media reports were all over now, flashing not only on the local New York stations but nationally. The stakes were getting higher, and I needed some help or I would be in hot water with my career.

I pulled Ray aside. "Will you please try to reach out to her again?"

"I've been trying through Frankie," he said. "We've got nothing."

CHAPTER SEVENTY-FIVE

ISABELLA

THE DA'S OFFICE CALLED ME. BUT WHILE IN THE MIDST OF being watched closely and being stunned at what was going on to thinking the phones were probably tapped, I kept it short with them.

"I'm sorry, I found out what Ray's lawyer said about my dad and I'm in shock. All I can say is that my position hasn't changed. I intend to testify against Ray when called. I just need some time to discuss this with my family. We'll be in touch soon." And I hung up.

I heard the door open and shut. The quiet that took over the penthouse told me what I needed to know before even turning around. My father was home. I couldn't bring myself to turn around to face him. To see his face. The potential disappointment or sadness or anger in his eyes.

But I heard him dismiss his driver for the evening. I heard him ask the head of security how I was doing. If I had seen the news.

He went into his room.

But eventually, he came out. And I had to face him. He straightened his shoulders and walked into the main living room area where I was watching TV. I felt a sense of safety with the head of security there but when my dad dismissed him, my heart started to race.

My dad, dressed casually now, spoke politely to me. "Honey, can you come into the kitchen? We need to resolve some things for both our sakes."

I swallowed hard. We were about to be alone for the first time since the summer that I left to reconnect with my aunt. There wasn't even a single staff member in a distant room that I could call.

And then, he apologized. He confessed how sorry he was for all his past actions but told me that he needed my help now. And that my helping him would be better for everyone in the long run. He waited to see my reaction but I had none. I had nothing left in me at this point. I stayed silent.

I was confused. Scared. Angry.

And then there was a brief knock on the door, and someone walked in unannounced. I heard the stomp of a man's walk, and my heart dropped. Instantly, I felt as though I were about to faint.

CHAPTER SEVENTY-SIX

AP

THE LOCAL NEWS TRUCKS WERE LINED UP ON CENTRE Street early the next morning, and the national media was there making it that much more of a scene. None of us knew what direction Judge Beekman would take, but Anthony instructed me to make a brief statement to the press while walking in.

"We feel confident in our position and are seeking the truth to clear our client," I said. I kept it short and sweet to try to show that we were undeterred.

Judge Beekman came out at promptly 9:30AM while the jurors waited in the jury room to see if they would be called at all today.

She got right to the point. "This case has become complex on many levels. In these situations at trial, I try to deal with each question in the order of legal priority, meaning I ask myself, 'Where does the strongest legal issue reside?' And I have determined that the strongest legal issue right now is that Mr. Jansen cannot have his defense prejudiced. I did not see anything up to this point that justified a question of that nature to the witness. However, I have to have faith in Ms. Peterson as an officer of this court, and I must let her conduct her examination regardless of the witness' rights. The witness and his legal team can deal with that on their own when the time comes. So, with that said, we will proceed with the trial as we left off yesterday," she said.

She called the jury in and informed the People that an objection was made yesterday that was not ruled on.

"So now I'm going to overrule the objection on the record that Ms. Peterson's testimony was not relevant." And she looked at me for the first time with some respect. "Ms. Peterson, you may proceed."

I felt butterflies swarm at the win. And I approached the witness: Ari himself. "Mr. Rohnstein, yesterday I asked you a direct question, and I will ask you again now, isn't it true that shortly after you adopted Isabella, you repeatedly sexually abused her?"

He hardly flinched. "Under advice from my counsel, I have been instructed to assert my Fifth Amendment right from self-incrimination at this time. However, when legally appropriate, I hope to clarify any open questions directly related to me."

His response was robotic, practiced. I was not surprised by this at all. But the jury certainly looked confused. It didn't matter though. Asserting his Fifth Amendment right made him look guilty.

I did my best to present the remaining questions to Ari, even though he answered each question with the response "Same answer" instead of saying the full rehearsed statement each time. He had an air of confidence today, I could sense it. Even the jury felt it. It seemed like no one knew anymore who was getting railroaded here—Ray or Ari.

I quickly put the finishing touches on my defense theory in my supposed cross-examination. The jury was following, but without any indication from Ari if any of this was true or false. No one could really know how effective it was with them.

Ari got off the stand and walked right out of the courtroom like he had somewhere important to go.

"Would the People like to call another witness?" Judge Beekman asked.

"Your Honor," the male ADA said, "we plan to conclude our case by calling Isabella Rohnstein to the stand as our last witness. We spoke with her yesterday and she assured us she would be ready to testify. However, in light of the circumstances, we request an adjournment until Monday."

The judge nodded. "I think that a long weekend would do everyone some good. And jurors, I want to warn you," she said, facing them, "you must not, under any circumstances, read or watch any reports in the media on this case or you will be disqualified. Do you all understand me?"

The jurors nodded. And just like that the courtroom filed out.

However, the circus was not over just yet, as crowds started gathering across the street in the park for what appeared to be an impromptu press conference by Ari's legal team.

There was a media frenzy going on instantaneously, and the court officers were unable to control the crowds rushing out of the circular doors of the old courthouse. Police enforcement was being called in, but with so many things happening so fast, there simply weren't enough of them. Everyone seemed interested to know what Ari's lawyer, Jimmy Jacobs, had to say.

I rushed over to hear just as he began speaking.

"My client vehemently denies the baseless allegations that were hurled at him in court from a young, inexperienced lawyer doing whatever she can to try and get her client off.

Neither Mr. Rohnstein nor his media brands can stand for this type of reckless conduct. We are compelled at this time to protect our shareholders from vicious attacks such as this, and that is why we will be walking over to federal court right now to file a lawsuit against Alexandra Peterson and the Anthony Mika Law Firm," he said, holding up what appeared to be fresh lawsuit documents. "Mr. Rohnstein will continue to aid his daughter in the pursuit of justice in this case. She remains prepared to testify against the defendant when called upon."

Then he stepped down and started walking toward the federal court steps with the famous media tycoon as throngs of people followed them. I watched Ari walk up the stairs one by one to file a lawsuit. Against me. And Anthony's firm.

Because of me.

CHAPTER SEVENTY-SEVEN

ISABELLA

I OPENED MY EYES AND SAW THAT THE ROOM WAS DARK. Softly lit. I had no idea what time it was, where I was. Nothing looked familiar to me. I finally came to, slightly coherent, suddenly aware of what was going on. It was then that I recognized something. Someone, rather. A familiar dark-skinned man sitting there, armed with the same gun that I saw right before I passed out.

Out of instinct, I tried to back up. Retreated against the wall as much as I could. It was what I did best. Retreat. Hide. Sink into some version of myself that was nearly invisible. I couldn't move my hands, my feet. I couldn't tell if I was harmed in any way, but it didn't seem like it. I was still groggy, but then it started coming back. The sweet odor I smelled right before I passed out and woke up here. Whatever they put over my nose and mouth knocked me out, I knew that much.

I started to fully open my eyes, tried to focus them. I got a glimpse of a building through one of the drawn blinds and realized I was still in my family's building. But this room?

This room was not something I knew. I closed my eyes and tried to piece it all together.

The man spoke to me gently in a non-threatening tone, trying to reassure me. How ironic when he was sitting there holding a gun. I could hear the South American accent in his voice, and I believed him when he promised he wouldn't hurt me. Then a revelation came to me, and I recognized his voice. I remembered the man and my dad speaking in the kitchen. I didn't remember specifics. I went to speak and realized my mouth had been gagged.

"Isabella," he said. "I promise I won't hurt you. But you cannot testify at that trial under any circumstances. I don't want either of us to get hurt here. I'm just trying to protect you and your family. If you let this go away, your dad will provide you with an early inheritance to start your life over. But you can never speak about the past again. Not to the media, not to the cops, not even to your friends. Do you understand?"

I looked at him in disgust. This was a new low for my father. Locking me away, keeping me from even speaking. So inhumane. Here I was, caged like a rabid animal. Tied up.

"You'll be safe with me until the trial is dismissed," he said.

Then he held up a document for me to read. It was a settlement agreement. $100MM for my silence. And a clause stating that I would agree to a statement to be issued to the press. I read it through tears, blurring my vision.

"You are a pretty girl. I don't want to hurt you," he said, "but if you ever speak about this to anyone, I won't think twice about killing you. And your boyfriend, too."

I was just old enough to remember the violence of the Argentinean gangs. I closed my eyes again and remembered my mother. The violent death she faced. And I knew, I knew this man was not bluffing in the least.

CHAPTER SEVENTY-EIGHT

RAY

Back in Mika's office, things were beyond tense. The old lawyer had gone ballistic.

"Did you hear what the DA said?" Mika shouted. "They talked to Isabella and she's prepared to testify! She's not giving any credibility to our theory that Ari raped her! Do you both realize we're fucked now? Do you realize that not only could Ray be going to prison, but we could be filing for bankruptcy if we have no basis for this theory we threw out there? Ari will sue me for everything we got!"

He was shooting from the hip, but AP and I just took it in silently. We both knew he was right. There was nothing we could say for ourselves. We got played. But Mika wasn't done there.

"I am so sick of both of you," he said. "Sneaking around all the time like you guys have some grand plan! Well, I hope you do, because Isabella is going to hit the stand on Monday. And by the looks of it, she's going to tell the jury you raped her, Ray. It's going to be your word against hers, and if the jury thinks that this pedophile stuff was some stunt, guess what? That could very well undermine the great defense we had just on the flimsy facts alone. Do you realize that if you can't prove this, we lose *all* credibility? They could even declare a mistrial! We have now pigeon-holed our defense into this hokey theory! Neither of you have a clue about trial strategy! I should have never gone along with this." He then went into his cabinet, mumbling under his breath. "Fucking Rohnstein, gonna bury me again." He pulled out a bottle of whiskey and took a swig straight from the bottle.

I motioned with my head for AP to leave the room. I needed to talk to Mika, man to man. When she was gone, I stood up to console him.

"Anthony, calm down. Please. I'm sorry for what happened today. You're right about everything you're saying. But trust me on one thing, look me in the eyes. *Ari* is the one who raped her. I told you the first time I sat in this office, I never penetrated her. Let it all play out before we get crazy." Then I took a swig from the whiskey bottle myself and sat back down.

Mika took another large swig and plopped down in his executive chair. "I'm sorry. I'm getting old, and this is a young man's game. I don't have the power or the resources to go up against Rohnstein. I had no business taking this case in the first place. I took it for the wrong reasons. I hope you don't take this personally, but it was a poor business decision on my part. And Alexandra, I can't control her anymore. She's smart but she doesn't understand trial law. Not yet, anyway." He reached for the bottle again.

"You're only saying all this because you're down right now," I said. "But we can still win. Please just let AP and me take it from here. Enjoy the weekend. We'll be ready for Isabella come Monday. I'm pretty sure she's going to corroborate most of our story, if not all of it."

Mika sighed. "I just hope you two know what the fuck you're doing, for all our sakes."

I stuck my arm out and shook his hand like a gentleman. "We won't let you down." Then I took another big swig before leaving his office, hoping I could keep my word.

CHAPTER SEVENTY-NINE

ISABELLA

THE WEEKEND WAS UNDERWAY, AND ALL I COULD THINK about was getting away from these monsters and starting a new life. When all this was over. I didn't care about exposing my father anymore. I knew I could never beat him. He forced me to accept that. I was more worried about my life. And Ray's. I couldn't put him in danger by going against my "dad". I couldn't. I had put Ray through enough as it was.

I looked out the window. After having warmth and sunshine recently, the weather pattern had turned cold and wet. El Niño was coming from the west and it made the room even darker and drearier all day while I sat in there, mostly alone. They did their best to keep me "comfortable".

Ari's henchman would come back in the morning to bring me food and drink. It became normal to me in some sick way. I almost understood that my dad had no choice but to do this. At least I started to believe that. I still hated him for it, but I knew he would free me once this all died down. After I promised not to expose him.

I remembered the man's words.

"In a few days the case will be dismissed, and I will never disturb your life again. Plus, after this, you'll never have a single financial worry for the rest of your life."

As if finances were my problem. As if money would make any of this better.

CHAPTER EIGHTY

AP

THE CITY HAD SHIFTED GEARS OVER THE WEEKEND AS THE big media story revolved around the surprising, surging poll numbers indicating Donald Trump's substantial lead to be named the Republican candidate for president. But for me, the weekend seemed to last forever. Ray was desperately trying to make contact with Isabella, to no avail.

I became increasingly frustrated and started to truly hate her. I had to confront Ray once and for all about her.

"Did you ever think that this girl could be such a psychopath that she was just playing some sick game with you the whole time?" I asked him bluntly.

"Unfortunately," he said slowly, "I have."

WHEN MONDAY MORNING CAME, we were all refreshed and ready for battle. But we were not all agreeing on how to cross-examine Isabella. Anthony wanted to retreat and stick with the facts of the case. We decided to wait it out and see what direction the People took with their direct on her.

But now the problem for the DA was that Isabella was not answering their calls, from what I was being told secondhand. And she was a no-show at 9:30 in Part 55. They tried to play it off to Judge Beekman that they believed it was just a miscommunication, but no one was buying it, including me.

Judge Beekman was stern in her remarks to the DA. "You know how I feel when victims don't show up in court to testify in these cases, right?" she asked the young ADA, not waiting for an answer. "I have no issue dismissing this case tomorrow morning if you do not locate her."

CHAPTER EIGHTY-ONE

RAY

I COULDN'T SLEEP AT ALL ON MONDAY NIGHT. I COULD sense that something more was going on with Isabella, despite what AP said about her. I was exhausted, but anxious that the case might be dismissed soon. Everything had been so crazy for so long, it almost felt normal now. Like nothing could surprise me at this point.

I strolled into court that Tuesday like it was just another status hearing. But Isabella, she was nowhere to be found. Again.

The judge told the ADAs that she had no more patience and was prepared to dismiss the case right then and there. But they were clinging on to all hope, pleading with her not to. There was a side bar talk about something nefarious going on, and the DA's office began to insinuate that their team was investigating a possible witness tampering case involving me and some organized crime figures, according to AP.

When she told me about this, I could only think of the Jane Doe Glow emails, and that Frankie and I could face charges for breaking the order of protection.

"Fuck," I said. "I hope they aren't trying to give me a new one."

"No," Anthony said. "Relax. I don't think the judge is buying it. I say we make our motion to dismiss the case when she comes out from her chambers."

"I don't want to do that just yet," I said.

Mika's eyes widened. "Why not? Are you insane? I think I can end this right here, right now."

"I have my reasons," I said. "I don't want to look anxious and piss the DA's office off." I left it at that, unable to elaborate, not wanting to tell him about the emails or any other concerns floating around in my head.

The judge came out and got back on the record. "Well, I've thought about this, and I'm inclined to dismiss the case today, but I'll hear what the People want to say."

The male ADA stood up. "Your Honor, we have come a long way with this case and if we were to dismiss it prematurely, I feel like you *could* be aiding some potential witness tampering activity that is going on. I beg you to give us one more day to investigate."

"I've heard enough," Judge Beekman said, motioning for him to sit. She then requested a response from the defense. "Mr. Mika, do you have something to say?"

I looked at him and shook my head before he spoke.

He shot me a pissed off look and faced the judge. "Well, Your Honor, we understand the DA's position and if they feel there is something nefarious going on, then we don't want to stand in their way of investigating."

A hush filled the courtroom then, and Judge Beekman's eyes widened in surprise. When she finally spoke again, it was in disbelief.

"Only in this case," she started, "would a defense attorney *not* want to put a motion in to dismiss." She shook her head. "Okay, fine. I'll see you all here tomorrow. But I don't care what the defense says, the People better have their witness ready at 9:30 sharp or I *will* be dismissing this case."

Everyone went their separate ways after court. As for me, I went back to my apartment to finally catch up on some much-needed sleep.

I was in a deep daytime sleep when I started dreaming about Isabella.

She was in trouble again. This time, Ari had a knife to her throat and was going to rape her. She yelled, "No, Papa!" just as he slit her throat.

I woke in a cold sweat, bolting upright in my bed. That was it. That was what she said to me right before I was about to penetrate her.

No, Papa!

There was no question in my mind then that it was Ari who raped her. She must have had a flashback. AP's theory was dead-on. And I now knew that Isabella meant it when she said she would protect AP.

The dream also made me realize the likely reason Isabella wasn't showing for court. I believed my instincts were right in keeping this thing going, even at my own potential peril. I called Jay Johnstone immediately and told him about the hunch I had. And he promised he was on the move to do his own private investigation—just as the media was reporting that investigators were inside Ari Rohnstein's penthouse.

Soon enough, a loud knock rang out on my apartment door. I had heard *that* knock before. It could only be one thing. Cops.

Before I even opened the door, I yelled out to them. "You got a search warrant?"

They did not. And I told them they couldn't come in.

"Well, if you don't let us in, we'll just run back downtown and get one. I can promise we'll have you in central booking, too," a brash detective said.

I laughed at the young cop's tough-guy talk. "You better check my jacket before you start with the threats, pal. Let me call my lawyer if you want, that's the best I can do. Or you can go get your fucking warrant. I got nothing to hide."

An older investigator stepped in, trying on the "good cop" act. "Ray, we don't believe you did anything wrong; we just need to make sure the girl isn't here."

When I opened the door, I recognized the older guy from my last case. "I don't know, man. I don't trust you guys, you know that."

"The past is the past," he said. "We don't have any agenda here. That's the reason why I insisted to come myself. Just let us do a quick run-through. As long as the girl isn't here, you got no issues. You have my word on it, kid. No playing around this time." He stuck his hand out and looked me in the eye through the slight opening of the chain-locked door.

We had a mutual respect for each other even though there was great disdain in our history. I put my guard down, undid the chain-lock, and let them in.

"Thanks," he said. "I'll put a good word in for you when we get back."

"Thanks, but I needed you to do that ten years ago," I said with a laugh.

CHAPTER EIGHTY-TWO

ISABELLA

I HEARD WHAT SOUNDED LIKE A STAMPEDE COMING THROUGH the building, until I realized it was the police. I could hear from somewhere above me that they were looking for me. The man that had been keeping guard over me ran down the stairs and came into the room anxiously, and I knew this was bad. For them. And maybe for me.

As the shuffling of feet and faint sounds of loud police radios and people calling my name were heard from the floor above, the henchman put his hand over my mouth to make sure I didn't try to yell or scream. Then he put a knife to my throat for good measure. *Afraid* was not the word for what I felt in that moment.

I knew it was bad now that the police were looking for me. It meant that my father's plan wasn't working, and he could do something even worse out of sheer desperation at this point.

I didn't know if I wanted the police to find me. I could only imagine that if they did, my throat might be slit right then and there. It was the way the South American gangs operated.

The noises got louder. Closer. My hearing was now impeccable after being blindfolded, arms and legs bound. I could swear they were heading closer when I heard the door to a nearby stairwell open. It sounded like they were making their way down the stairs as he pulled me closer to him, putting the knife closer to my skin.

But then the stairway door above slammed shut.

And the noises faded.

CHAPTER EIGHTY-THREE

RAY

I STOPPED BY MIKA'S OFFICE IN THE AFTERNOON TO GIVE MY lawyers a rundown of what happened with the cops earlier at my apartment.

"Ray, you should have called me!" Mika said. "But I wouldn't worry about it. I think the investigation is geared toward Rohnstein now, especially since we didn't go for the dismissal. I do have to tell you, though, whatever little game you're trying to play here, it's over tomorrow if she doesn't show. I *am* dismissing the case, whether you want me to or not."

"I'm okay with that, and I agree," I said. "This is it. We'll see tomorrow."

"Good," AP added. "I've had enough of her," she said.

My phone rang. Jay Johnstone. I said goodbye to AP and Mika, telling them I had to take the call.

Jay told me he got information from someone who was in touch with Michele Rohnstein. The unnamed contact said that her relationship with Ari was faltering, and so Jay was getting ready to head out east to get some information straight from the source. I insisted on going with him to the Hamptons.

"You know we can't do that," Jay said. "You cannot confront her."

"Jay, I want to be there," I said. "I have a feeling there's more to the story than just a missing-in-action Isabella. Mrs. Rohnstein knows how much I cared about her daughter. Don't argue with me on this."

"If Anthony finds out…"

"Then he finds out. This case is already as corrupt as it can be. Come get me," I said.

WHEN OUR CAR pulled up on Dune Road, the sun was starting to make its descent for the day. I walked with Jay down the long path to the front door of the Rohnsteins' Hamptons home as my heart started pounding. Maybe this wasn't a good idea.

Jay put on his usual charm when Michele answered so she wouldn't slam the door. But she took one look at *me* and lost it.

"What is this?" she snapped. "*He* has no right to be anywhere near me!" Then she looked at me. "You're disgusting and I hope you rot in hell for what you did."

I looked at her as sincerely as I could. "Mrs. Rohnstein, you know how close Isabella and I were. I would never hurt her. She hasn't been showing up to court and no one can reach her. I'm worried about her. Genuinely. You have to know that. And I wanted to come here to tell you that myself."

She eyed me suspiciously. Listening, but maybe not truly hearing me.

"All I'm asking is if she's okay," I said. "Please, I need to know that she's okay."

She crossed her arms. "I haven't heard from her. But you don't know my daughter the way I do. She's stubborn. And at times, unpredictable. She might just be blowing this all off because she doesn't want to deal with it."

I cut her off. "I don't think she's blowing it off," I said. "I think there's something wrong. Please, if you can, just try to reach out to her and make sure she's okay. That's all I'm asking. I can't talk to her. I need to know that someone who can, someone who cares about her, is making sure she's okay."

She sighed, seeming bored now. "Look, the bottom line is I have absolutely no interest in speaking with either of you. Especially you, Ray. I'm sorry. Get off my property." She closed the door without anything further.

"Mrs. Rohnstein," I called.

But there was no answer. I leaned my head on the door and stood there for a few minutes before Jay peeled me away. I couldn't help but wonder why she was here, instead of with her daughter.

"I told you this was a bad idea," he said.

"God, she's her mother!" I yelled loudly, hoping that Michele would hear me.

"Let's go, kid," Jay said, grabbing my arm and pulling me away.

LATER THAT NIGHT, the 11:00 news had nothing to report in the case, except that Ari Rohnstein had finally filed a missing person's report on Isabella. There was nothing else, and no signs of her anywhere. I continued to email her, hoping that she would eventually respond. But I got nothing.

And I went to bed not knowing if the drawn-out trial would finally come to a close in the morning, with or without Iz.

CHAPTER EIGHTY-FOUR

ISABELLA

My father came to see me after the cops left, assuring me that tomorrow it would all be over. No matter what. And that once the case was dismissed, he would issue our statements. He won again.

He left me after that brief conversation.

Alone.

The city was unusually quiet as the misty-rain-sounding conditions continued for yet another day. This was what I did now. Think. I couldn't imagine how this would play out with my relationship with Ray. Me, not showing up. Me, not testifying. Me, not keeping my word or helping his lawyer friend. At least without me testifying, he would be freed.

But everything had backfired. For me. In the worst possible way. And I kicked myself for ever thinking I was smart enough to pull this off in the first place.

It was the middle of the night when I heard the door suddenly open, causing me to sit up in a panic. No one ever came in the middle of the night. When I turned around and waited for my fate, the blindfold was pulled down, and I gasped.

"Mom?" I tried to ask, the gag muffling my voice. The "mother" that was never there for me. The "mother" that never nurtured me. Not even once. Why was she here now? Was she in on this?

She was in front of me. I could see tears filling her eyes. Terror. Shock.

"Oh my god, honey. I'm so sorry. I'm getting you out of here right now," she said frantically, turning to look behind her as if she was afraid someone was trailing her. She took the gag off me and began helping me get loose.

Once I could speak, I whispered to her in fear. "If this guy finds you he'll kill us both." I didn't know if he was still there sleeping or somewhere else. But his scare tactics worked. I was afraid. Perpetually.

"Fuck them," she said. "No one will hurt us, do you hear me?"

I nodded. "Wait, what are you doing here?" I asked.

"I looked the other way far too many times. It's time I did something. For once," she said.

I felt tears well up in my eyes. But now was not the time for this conversation.

She pulled me to my feet. "Now let's get the hell out of here."

We took the escape stairs to the bottom of the building and went out undetected. In a sense, we were both used to this by now. The fleeing. The escaping. Without my dad knowing.

She had a warm car waiting for us. And we drove aimlessly for a bit, just to make sure no one was following us.

"How did you know where I was?" I asked her, still in shock.

"Your father told me no one could ever know about that

apartment. Why, I don't know. But I had a feeling you were in there."

I nodded, then I grabbed her hand. "Thank you. For coming. For *caring*."

Then the dam burst. Tears started falling from her eyes and she pulled over before grabbing me and wrapping me in a tight hug. "I am so sorry. I am so sorry for everything. I should have been a better mother. I should have done more. I just didn't know what to do. I didn't know how to be a mom to you. I just went along pretending everything was perfect because that was what your father wanted. It was hard to live with at times. Resenting you, jealous of you. Angry. God! What's wrong with me? You were just a child. You were just a…"

"Shh," I said, hugging her tighter. "Stop. Please. You've done enough. You came to save me when no one else could have. That's all that matters now. Everything else is in the past."

She sniffled and wiped her face. "It was Ray," she whispered.

"What?" I asked.

She shook her head, tears still streaming down her face.

"Mom, *what* was Ray? Tell me."

"He came to see me at the Hamptons house last night, when the cops started looking for you. He told me he felt like there was something more to you not showing up for court. He was worried. I brushed it off at first, but the more I thought about it, the more I realized what a shit mother I've been. Not even reaching out to you to check on you. To see if you were okay. And you were in this fucking apartment, alone. Tied up. Kept from seeing anyone. This is just unbelievable. Your father, he's a monster. I didn't know. I didn't know."

I looked down, taking this all in. Ray, going to speak to

my mother. I couldn't believe it. "He really came to see you?"

"Yeah, he did. And we've had that apartment downstairs for so long, strictly for emergency situations, as your father put it. He had it in someone else's name so even the co-op board wouldn't know about it. And he told me to never tell you or anyone else about it either. When the cops were looking for you, something just hit me. And I knew if you were anywhere against your will, it'd be in there. I wanted to be wrong. I swear, I wanted to be wrong."

We were both fully crying at that point. "Thank you, Mom. Thank you for finding me. I love you."

"I love you, too," she said, grabbing my hand. "From this moment forward, I want to help you in any way I can. I mean that."

And looking into her eyes, I could tell she meant it.

For the first time since my birth mother died, I finally felt connected to a parent again.

"Well, if that's the case, I'll tell you how you can help me," I said.

CHAPTER EIGHTY-FIVE

RAY

THE CITY WAS AWAKE AND RUSH HOUR WAS UNDERWAY. THE breaking news reports started on 1010 WINS Radio and began to trickle down to other media outlets. Everyone was reporting the same thing: Isabella Rohnstein was confirmed to be testifying today in her case against Ray Jansen.

I was just happy she was okay. Whatever she had to say about me, at least she would be there to say it.

When I got into the courtroom, everyone was shocked to see her. Mika. AP. Me. But when she didn't look like her usual glammed-up self, I knew something was up. And now it was Ari who was missing. It was a bizarre turn of events, but the circumstances of this entire case had been so strange, no one knew how to deal with any of it at this point.

Out of instinct, I almost walked over to Iz to see if she was okay. Mika was annoyed to see her, knowing this all could have been over yesterday.

The DA requested a quick moment with Isabella, which Judge Beekman granted. They had a quick chat at the prosecution table, and from the distance, I could see Isabella nodding adamantly, passionate in whatever she was saying.

Before the jury came into the room, Judge Beekman addressed Isabella. “Ms. Rohnstein, are you prepared to testify today?”

“Yes, Your Honor,” Isabella said.

“And you came here today on your own free will?”

“Yes, ma’am,” Isabella said firmly.

“Okay,” the judge said. “Let’s call the jury in and the People can begin their questioning.”

The trial was still being held in balance between the two sides when the DA finally had their chance to steal it once and for all. The DA’s tactic seemed to be a short and direct examination, to get her on and off as quick as they could, and she didn’t disappoint them. Although her answers were very curt at times, she gave an impassioned performance detailing how I forced myself on her. She seemed like she was telling the truth from her heart—even though the story was a complete fabrication. Some of the women on the jury were crying.

I knew this only meant one thing: They believed her.

Judge Beekman called an adjournment afterwards, just before lunch, with a 2:30 call back for Alexandra to cross-examine Isabella.

Mika lambasted Alexandra and me at lunch again. He was becoming more and more erratic with each setback. I tried to calm him down, but he’d had it.

“Ray, do you realize that every move you’ve made in this case has been wrong?” he asked. “I’m done listening to your opinions here.”

I’d heard this before from other lawyers and didn’t appreciate it. “Right, I know, every move we made was wrong, Anthony. You lawyers know it all.”

We could all feel the case slipping away and tensions were getting high.

Mika tried to take control of the conversation and said he

was taking over the cross of Isabella and getting off the Ari stuff to focus on the core defense that we had. At this point I didn't care if we got into a heated exchange. It was my life. And it was AP's case.

"We are not doing that," I told him.

"I'm the one with the experience here. We lost all the momentum with her implicating you this morning, Ray!" he said.

"You don't know what's going on!" I said, raising my voice. "And you don't want to know!"

"What the fuck is that supposed to mean?" he questioned, looking at AP for a response.

She was expressionless. She didn't want to say or do anything that was going to escalate things even further between the two of us.

"Isabella wants AP to do the cross, that's what it means," I said simply.

Mika let out a short, sarcastic laugh. "And explain to me how you know this exactly? Are you a mind reader now? This girl has accused you of rape. You realize that, right?"

"Anthony, this is my case and Alexandra is my lawyer, too. I am not asking you this. I'm telling you, she is doing the cross."

"Fine," Mika said, throwing up his hands. Then he looked at AP. "Are you even prepared for this?"

"Yes," she said. "I am."

COURT RESUMED PROMPTLY at 2:30, and Isabella's cross examination was set to begin.

"Okay, we're back on the record," Judge Beekman said as the jury was seated. "The defense can begin their examination."

And before long, AP was firing questions at Isabella.

I was doing my best to get a read on Iz who seemed much more comfortable now than she did in the morning. And she also looked refreshed and pretty. It was strange, it seemed like she trusted AP for some reason.

The early questions were easy, but I knew AP was setting her up for the kill. And I didn't know how Isabella would respond to that. I just hoped that after all this, she wouldn't let us down.

CHAPTER EIGHTY-SIX

AP

I LOOKED AT THE YOUNG, BEAUTIFUL WOMAN ON THE STAND, still trying to understand how we got here, with her accusing Ray of rape. And I would try to assess this with every juror watching.

"So, let's shift gears now and go back to the incident in college that we have come to know about," I said. "Can you explain to me exactly what happened that night?"

Isabella responded in detail about what happened to her, in her own words.

"Ms. Rohnstein, I'm now going to read back to you your statement from the night in question when you also claimed that my client sexually assaulted you." After I read it into the record, I looked at her. "Doesn't it seem eerily similar to what happened at the frat house in college?"

"Yes," Isabella said, her voice low.

"So, now I ask you to clarify something in the report. You said that Mr. Jansen forced himself on top of you, and that you initially tried to stop him by pushing against his chest, but he was too strong and powerful. So, you pulled his hair as hard as you could to try to get him to stop. Were you referring to the hair on his head or his chest?"

"My hands were on his chest, pushing him off," Isabella said. "He had his shirt off and he was just too strong for me. All I could do was clench my fist on his chest hair and squeeze as hard as I could. And then, I pretty much blacked out."

I walked back to the table and pulled out the testimony from Nick Salerno. "Ms. Rohnstein, I want to read back the testimony of Nick Salerno who was with Mr. Jansen at the *Four Seasons* spa just nine hours before you alleged that my client raped you. When Mr. Salerno was asked what they were wearing, he said 'Both of us just had a towel around our waists. Nothing else.' So, Mr. Salerno testified that he saw Ray Jansen with only a towel on that day. And I'm pretty certain that if I call Mr. Salerno back, he's going to testify that my client, Ray Jansen, doesn't have any chest hair."

I walked over toward Ray and put my hand on his shoulder, then stopped and stood there, looking at Isabella as a hush filled the courtroom. I let it hold.

Isabella's head bowed.

"So, I ask you again, Ms. Rohnstein, was it the chest hair of Ray Jansen that you pulled that night, or could you have been mistaken?" I asked.

Isabella looked ever so slightly at Ray, and I turned just in time to see him give her a slight nod, like it was okay to say whatever she was about to.

"I'm not sure what happened," Isabella said.

"Ms. Rohnstein, how long have you been seeing a therapist?" I asked her.

"On and off for the last few years since I moved back to New York," she said.

"And has your therapist discussed with you the possibility of having some type of psychosis where your mind could play tricks on you, particularly on the night in question?"

Isabella swallowed and looked at someone in the courtroom. "Yes, she did."

My tone softened when I spoke again. This was not an easy subject. Judge Beekman could sense it too, and was giving me more latitude with my dialogue because of it. I took advantage of her leniency, especially because the ADAs didn't seem anxious to object and wanted to hear it all as well.

I finally saw Isabella as a human. A girl, with a very sad and traumatic past. And my heart broke for her in that courtroom while I held it together and maintained my composure. "And Ms. Rohnstein, I know this is very hard on you, but we have a potentially innocent man facing serious charges," I said, walking closer to Isabella. "A man that I know has professed his love for you, and I'm certain would never hurt you. So, I ask you, is it possible that the rape you've accused my client of was merely a flashback to some traumatic sexual experience you encountered while you were just a child?"

Streams of tears were now falling down Isabella's face. "Yes," she said, looking down, voice cracking.

"Ms. Rohnstein, it's okay," I said. "Please look at me and answer the questions so that we can hear. Is it possible?"

Isabella sniffled and looked up at me. "Yes," she said. "It is possible that I had a flashback."

"And isn't it true that the person who did all this damage to you, the person who repeatedly raped you at a young age, was none other than your father that adopted you from Argentina, Mr. Ari Rohnstein?"

Isabella had her head down, now crying hysterically.

I stood there waiting, wanting to hug her, but not

moving. The entire court seemed suspended in time in that moment. Judge Beekman was waiting for an answer. The entire world was waiting for this answer.

"Yes," Isabella said. "He began sexually abusing me shortly after I came to America."

CHAPTER EIGHTY-SEVEN

ISABELLA

My mother, who was in the front row, stood up. "Oh my god!" she yelled, then she covered her mouth like she was going to be sick from hearing the words actually come out. Even though she turned a blind eye to it for so long. Even though I thought she had known, or at least *should've* known.

And then the hysteria began.

The commotion in the courtroom was spreading like wildfire. A bunch of people were yelling for the judge to dismiss the case right there on the spot. The media members were flying out of the court, undoubtedly trying to be the first to break the story. The ADAs requested an immediate recess. The jurors began commenting to one another.

But Ray's lawyer, Alexandra, did not move. She moved closer to me and held out her hand to take mine.

"Are you okay?" she asked me.

I nodded that I was and squeezed her hand. "I am. Thank you. For everything."

Before we could continue speaking, the judge started yelling. "Order in this court, order in this court!"

Once things finally settled down and the room became quiet, she continued.

"I'm going to grant the ADAs a short recess to talk with their witness. In fact, you can use my chambers to do so privately, if Mr. Mika is okay with that?" the judge said, glancing at him.

"Yes, Your Honor, of course," Ray's other lawyer replied.

"First, let's dismiss the jury for now," the judge said, then she looked at me. "Then you can come to my chambers, okay, Ms. Rohnstein?" she said compassionately.

I nodded and wiped at my eyes, the tears still falling. "Okay."

Once we were back there, the DA's office staff were questioning me along with my mother to confirm what she knew. The questions were direct. I answered as honestly as I could, explaining that my father had raped me, that the excruciating memory came back whenever I attempted to get intimate with someone. That I was confused that night with Ray, which was why I had tried to leave the hospital the first time. I told them I felt that my mind was so damaged, unsure what was real, what wasn't, that I didn't know what was true or false anymore.

"So, when everyone kept pressuring me to admit that Ray hurt me, I assumed it was true."

"We would like to interview you as soon as possible regarding these allegations against your father, but now is not the time," the head DA said. "For now, we are going to go back in there and request that Judge Beekman dismiss the case against Ray Jansen. Do you understand this?"

"Yes, of course," I said. "I feel horrible for what I put him through. He is completely innocent in all this."

"It's okay," the department head said. "I just have one

more question for you. Where were you the last few days when you didn't show up to court?"

"I was staying with a friend," I lied. "I didn't know if I had the courage to testify again."

My mom didn't say anything about this, but instead grabbed my arm and told them we were done for now before leading me out back through the courtroom to the street.

The media frenzy was incredible, but my mother had enough savvy to ask them to please back off and respect our privacy.

Before long, we disappeared into a waiting SUV and headed uptown.

CHAPTER EIGHTY-EIGHT

RAY

Once the door shut behind Isabella, there was a massive celebration in the courtroom. Part of me wished my kids were here so I could hug them, but I knew none of that testimony was anything I ever wanted them to hear. My heart broke for Iz. Kids should have their innocence preserved as long as humanly possible.

I turned to AP and hugged her, pulling her in close. Tears welled up in my eyes. "I can never thank you enough for everything you've done for me."

Even Mika was content now, more than satisfied. And we all hugged one another, happy that this was over. Finally.

My mom and sisters came to the front row, also with tears of joy. The judge allowed us to celebrate for a moment, but as more and more people began approaching me, she motioned for the guards to put an end to it, sending out a quick vocal reminder that the case was not fully over yet.

After a brief recess with both parties in the judge's chambers, there were still formalities to take care of. The judge decided to bring the jury back in so that they could wrap it all up at once.

"Do the People wish to make a statement into the record?" the judge asked.

"Yes, Your Honor. After a brief interview with Isabella Rohnstein, we can no longer proceed with prosecuting Mr. Jansen."

The crowd wanted to explode, but the judge would not let them.

"Hold on, we're not done here yet," she said. Judge Beekman then looked at the jury. "I want to thank all of you for your great dedication and service throughout this trial. This case is now concluded, and you are all free to go home now."

I stood there with AP and thanked each of them as they walked past.

As the jury left, the judge glanced at the court reporter to ensure she was ready.

AP grabbed my hand under the table, and we both squeezed.

I watched the judge, waiting to hear the words.

"In light of the statement from the DA's office that they cannot proceed, and in the interest of justice, I am hereby dismissing all charges in the indictment of the People versus Raymond Jansen."

And with that, a roar came from the spectators in attendance. KB allowed it to go on for a moment longer than necessary, and I swore I saw a slight smile forming on her lips as she banged that gavel. Then she looked at me and spoke politely for the first time since I stepped into her courtroom.

"You are free to go, Mr. Jansen. Good luck to you from here."

CHAPTER EIGHTY-NINE

ISABELLA

THE INITIAL SHOCK OF WHAT HAD JUST OCCURRED PUBLICLY did not wear off for quite some time. I was still processing everything. Still grasping the weight of what went down. There is something strange people don't talk about. The mourning you feel when grieving a monster. A father. Someone you trusted, someone who was supposed to protect you. Take care of you. The guilt you feel when you say the things out loud. The things they did to you. The things they took from you.

No one tells you this will hurt. That you'll feel bad for speaking your truth into existence. That you might even wish you could take it back.

I had to start separating him from the idea that he was ever a father to me. An idea he drilled into my head.

Ari was holed up in his penthouse, all alone. He hadn't tried to contact me. What would he say? What did I expect? Did I expect remorse from him? An acknowledgment of some sort? An apology? A reason?

The media reports had two common themes splattered

everywhere: The dismissal of Ray Jansen's case, and my testimony that I was sexually abused by my father, mogul Ari Rohnstein. "Mogul or Molester?" was one of the headlines flashing across the screen as I watched, staring in contemplation. Accepting.

I saw Ray's lawyer, Alexandra Peterson, being interviewed on television. I watched her face closely. Her voice.

"The system failed because my client should have never been charged with a crime in the first place. It shouldn't have come to this," she said with conviction.

Ray's other lawyer, Anthony Mika, also commented. "Ari Rohnstein needs to be charged with obstruction of justice and investigated for sexual abuse against a minor. Period."

Channel 2 News was leading the local coverage, with a reporter stating they'd obtained a statement from the DA's office. The reporter read it: "The DA's office has confirmed that they are actively pursuing charges against Mr. Rohnstein for potential crimes in connection to the case. However, any case for a sex crime against a minor gets a little tougher in respect to Statute of Limitations issues in New York. So, that case or investigation is just starting and could take some time, assuming that Isabella Rohnstein wants to pursue that after this entire ordeal."

The reporter kept reading from his notes, live outside the mayhem of Centre Street. "And one other thing the DA's office told us was that Isabella Rohnstein said she was absent from court the last two days because she was hiding out with a friend, unsure if she could go through with the testimony. We can surely see now why it was so tough for her. The case against Raymond Jansen has been dismissed. I repeat, the judge and the DA have dismissed all charges against Raymond Jansen and he has been freed to go. However, in one of the most incredible trials I can remember in a long time, criminal charges are just potentially beginning for none other than Ari Rohnstein."

I looked at my mother, who had been crying since we left court. "I think you should call him," I said to her.

Her face twisted into something unrecognizable. "Call him for what?" she said. "I never want to speak to that pedophile again."

"This is a lot for anyone to go through. And he's still your husband."

"I'll do it if you want me to, but not because I want to," she stated simply.

"I do. Please," I said.

She got out her cell phone and dialed Ari, putting it on speaker.

"Michele? Baby?" he answered, sounding deflated. "I am so sorry, I am so fucking sorry."

Something in his tone broke my heart and I wished I didn't feel bad for him.

"I don't want to hear you're sorry. Even though you should be. But no apologies will ever undo what you did. Only god can forgive you now. I just wanted to check on you to make sure you don't do anything stupid. Are you okay?" she asked.

"No, I'm not. I'm thinking of ending it right now. I can't take it anymore," he said.

I looked at her, stunned into silence. She shrugged her arms at me as if to tell me she didn't know what to say next. But she didn't have to say anything, because he spoke again.

"I've done bad things. I don't belong in this world," he said. Then he started to sob.

"I want a divorce," my mom said to him.

I closed my eyes, knowing that was probably the last

thing he needed to hear right now, even though it was a given.

"I have to go," he said. "I love you. And please, tell Isabella I love her. She has to know I love her." And with that, we heard a loud bang and the line went dead.

CHAPTER NINETY

RAY

AFTER ALL THE HUGS AND KISSES IN THE COURTROOM, I JUST wanted to go home and be by myself. Just for a little bit, to reflect. As I started to jump in the shower to get ready for the evening, the TV broke to a shot of Ari's Sutton Place neighborhood, where they were reporting that the NYPD wasted no time in arresting him on charges of tampering with the case. I took notice, but I couldn't care less tonight.

I threw a party for myself, one for the ages, and I invited as many old friends that could make it out to the city for the night. I knew it was me that disconnected from most of the world, but with such short notice, there was still a great turnout. I realized more people loved me than I thought.

The only important one missing was Andy.

The first toast of the night went to Anthony and Alexandra, and then AP spent the rest of the evening pretty much glued to my side. Our chemistry was obvious, electric. No one asked us any questions about our closeness, which wouldn't have mattered anyway seeing as neither of us had to hide it any longer. The fact was she wasn't my lawyer anymore.

The night didn't end until the sun came up. And then AP and I finally went to bed in the presidential suite at the *Dream Hotel*. There was no serious talk that night, but our relationship and where it was headed was stuck in my mind.

In the morning, I had an email from Iz, who wanted to reconnect. I didn't know how to feel about it in the moment, but with everything happening with Ari, I knew I had to talk to her. For various reasons.

I saw a statement that was issued before the weekend, a joint statement from Michele and Isabella. It was short and sweet, but indicative that if Ari messed with either of them ever again, there would be hell to pay—worse than what he was already facing. But the world wanted to hear from Isabella. That much was obvious.

I didn't just have Isabella to worry about, but AP as well. Our situation was complicated, to say the least. Instead of dealing with it in New York, we hopped on a flight to South Beach on Saturday and spent a few days in the sun, relaxing and enjoying our newfound, stress-free days. We spent the days in the sun and the nights partying away.

Neither of us knew how much time we'd have together, so we simply tried to enjoy it. With constant lovemaking and solid communication, our relationship ran the gamut of friends, colleagues, and lovers. It was beyond dangerous, and we both knew it.

Our few days in Miami were devoid of drama, but it was impossible not to discuss the elephant in the room, with both of us wondering what lay ahead for us.

Despite not wanting to, I brought it up as we were out on our hotel balcony, smoking a joint as the sun was coming up over the ocean.

"I don't want to think about the future," AP said. "I just want to enjoy my time with you. I know it's complicated, but

I know I love you and I wouldn't want to be anywhere else right now than here with you."

I looked at her, unable to help thinking that she was one of the most perfect girls I'd ever met. Someone I had great chemistry with—and passion, too. We had a history now after this trial that would never leave us. But even though I didn't want to admit it to her, or even myself, I still had feelings for Isabella. And I had to be honest with AP about that. I felt so torn, and she deserved to know.

"I'm sorry," I said. "I wish I didn't feel this way, but the bottom line is that I do. I'm just so confused."

"So am I," she admitted. "My ex wants me to go to California to spend some time with him now that the trial is over…"

"Wait, are you serious?" I asked her, kind of surprised.

"Yeah. I never really told you the full story, but I had a job lined up for me in San Francisco working at a firm connected to his family's practice. Unfortunately, it wasn't in criminal law, so I decided to stay here instead and work on your case. That's when he gave me an ultimatum."

"I didn't know it went down like *that*," I said. "I'm sorry."

"No, don't be," she said. "And then after meeting you on Rikers Island...god, I don't even know what it was. I just fell for you. And I couldn't stop thinking about us being together. It was so crazy. And it's still crazy to me that we're here together right now."

I let her confession sink in before speaking. I wanted my words to come out right. I grabbed her hand and looked at her. "I owe you everything. And I've fallen in love with you. It's just hard to think what our relationship would be without the case, you know?" I caressed her shoulders. "Listen, baby, I'll do whatever you want me to do. If you tell me that you have no doubt that you want us to be together, and you want me to end everything with Iz, I'll do it. I promise. And I won't look back. I'll be all yours."

She looked into my eyes and a sad smile crossed her face. "You don't owe me anything. I'm grateful for all of this, what it's done for my career. For me as a lawyer and as a person. I could never pay you back for that. When it comes to *us,* I would go anywhere you wanted to go. I would be your wife if you wanted that. But if you even have to think about that, or ask me to make that decision for you, then you'd be doing it for the wrong reasons. I could never force you to choose me. That would be so selfish. And I love you too much to ask you to do that."

"But I'm in love with you, Alexandra," I said, kissing her on the lips.

"I know, Ray. But you and I will always be strong no matter what. Isabella needs you. More than I do, anyway. I can't stand in the way of you two anymore. I've been feeling guilty about it."

"Why?" I asked.

"Because I was only supposed to be your lawyer, and here I am, fucking *her* man."

I laughed at her bluntness. Then I grabbed her close in the warm Miami air, and took her back into the bedroom one last time.

CHAPTER NINETY-ONE

ISABELLA

RAY AND I HAD BEEN IN TOUCH, PLANNING TO MEET OVER the weekend when he got back from Miami. In the meantime, I was scheduled to go on a major network for a prime-time Friday night interview. I wanted a platform to tell my story, not just for me, but for all the other victims of sexual abuse. And even though it was just over a week since the trial, it was time. The only stipulation was that I couldn't legally discuss anything regarding the current pending charges against Ari.

When I was asked about Ray, I was honest. "I know this sounds crazy, but Ray gave me the courage to come out and face the fact that my father had raped me."

In the interview, the host asked me the million-dollar question. The one the entire world was probably wondering.

"If you loved Ray so much, then why would you do this to him? Why would you put him through all of that?"

"I knew the only way we would have a chance to be together was if I spoke up about what had happened to me. If I didn't testify, no one would have ever believed me. My dad would have found a way to spin the story through the media. So, as crazy as it sounds, Ray was my inspiration."

"What if the plan backfired and you sent the man you loved to jail, then what?" she asked me.

"I never thought that would happen. I was confident it would work itself out. I just didn't know how," I said.

The host seized the moment. "Tell me, what is your message here tonight, Isabella?"

"I hope that my actions give others the courage to stand up against sexual abuse, in all forms. It doesn't matter how you do it, just find some way to do it. That's part of the problem. It's so hard for people to come out and speak their truth. The guilt, the shame, the embarrassment...it's all so strong. And you don't think anyone will believe you. But I'm here to tell you that I believe you. And others will, too."

"Well, what a circuitous route you took to get here. Is there any hope left for you and Ray to find love again?"

I thought about it before answering, and then responded honestly. "I hope so. I really hope so."

WHEN RAY GOT BACK to New York, he agreed to meet me and my mother for lunch at the *Four Seasons Hotel*. At first he was hesitant, but he finally agreed. We both apologized for what we put him through, and thanked him for helping me throughout this entire ordeal. He said he understood what I needed, and just wanted to move on now. Both my mom and I felt relieved to hear him say this face-to-face. And I was reminded why I fell in love with this man in the first place.

We also told him about Ari having me kidnapped, and Ray was incensed.

"I fucking knew it," he said, shaking his head. "That's

why I insisted on going with Jay to see you, Michele. And I want to apologize for showing up like that, but I just felt like something was wrong."

"No," my mom said to him. "Don't apologize, I'm the one who is sorry for not inviting you in. I'm grateful you came to me that night. Otherwise, who knows what would have happened? After you left, it started to hit me that maybe something really was wrong. I knew I had to go see where she was, no matter the risk."

Ray shook his head in disgust. "What are you guys gonna do about this? You have to do something."

I grabbed his hand. "It's okay, Ray. I'm fine. It all worked out for the best. I just feel blessed that my mom found me and I got to testify and get this all out in the open."

"You mean you're not going to bring this up to the DA?" he asked, confused.

I shook my head in silence.

"Isabella doesn't want to," my mom said.

Ray seemed to think about it for a moment, but then he turned his eyes back on me. "Isabella, are you okay?" He was still holding my hand.

"I think so," I said. "I will be if I know you'll be here for me. Even if it's only as friends."

I looked into his green eyes and watched him consider how to respond. There was still a softness there. He still cared. I could tell.

"Well, I can guarantee you that I'll always be your friend," he said, looking into my eyes. "But I need to be honest with you. I have feelings for someone else. It's just complicated. I'm sorry."

Someone else? The lawyer? I wanted to ask him who. I wanted to know if it was her. I saw the way they looked at each other. The way they interacted. I saw the photos of them in the papers. And gossip tabloids weren't *always* a bunch of bullshit. Sometimes, they stemmed from truth. And hearing him say this now just confirmed it.

But I needed to know something. "Ray, do you still love me?" I asked him, flat out.

"Yes, I do," he said. "Very much, actually."

"Then it's impossible to love another person," I insisted, hoping whatever he felt was not love or even close.

"No, actually it isn't," he said, looking at me. "I wish it was."

It hurt to hear. How could it not? But I put him in prison. I accused him of rape. How could I expect him to wait for me, to stay faithful? I knew, logically speaking, that it wasn't realistic to expect his undying fidelity. But I still wanted it. Selfishly, I only wanted him to love me. No one else.

"Listen, that isn't what's important right now," Ray said. "What are you guys planning to do about Ari?"

My mother responded. "We aren't exactly sure yet. I have a divorce proceeding underway, though. That's for damn sure." Then she looked at him. "What are your thoughts on all of this?"

After a moment, he responded to my mother. "If Isabella is okay and can move on with her life, I think we should all move on. I can tell you if you bring up the kidnapping charges, it's going to cause a whole new stir and open up the potential for a lot of jail time for Ari. It'll get really messy. I think he's got enough to deal with, just with his ouster as CEO. I mean, don't get me wrong, personally I think he deserves to rot in hell, but that will likely happen regardless of how the system works him. I think we should just try to work out a global settlement that we can all live with."

My mom thought this over. "That makes sense, but ultimately, it's up to Isabella." Then she looked at me. "What do you want to do, honey?"

"I trust Ray. I want to do whatever he thinks is best," I said.

"Okay," my mom said. "Why don't we schedule a meeting to get all of our lawyers working on the same page early next week then?"

"Sounds good to me," Ray said.

He picked up the check and walked my mom and me to the valet on the 58th Street entrance, where there was more privacy. He whispered to me that it was the same exit he raced out the night that changed everything. I felt guilt hit me yet again, picturing him running from the police. Being chased. Being hunted. When he never did anything wrong. And then, what he said next surprised me.

"Isabella, do you want to stay here with me tonight in the hotel, just like we planned before all the madness?"

I smiled and felt tears coming. "I'd love to."

And there it was. In the form of an unexpected invitation. My second chance at love with Ray, the man who believed in me. The man who loved me despite all the darkness I brought with me. The man who singlehandedly changed my entire life. For the better. And I knew then, I could never lose him again. And I also knew victims of sexual abuse didn't need to stay victims forever. Just as Ray was vindicated, I felt like I was, too.

I was not a victim. I was a survivor.

Just as he was.

CHAPTER NINETY-TWO

RAY

WITHIN A WEEK, ARI'S TEAM OF LAWYERS—ALONG WITH Isabella's, mine, and Michele's lawyers—had put a compensation package together that worked for everyone. In addition, Ari's lawyer had called the DA to relay the message that documents were being drafted to resolve all of Isabella's issues civilly. The key point was that the family had no interest in pursuing any of the sexual abuse claims. There was never a mention of the kidnapping to the lawyers or courts. For this, Ari was "eternally grateful", according to Michele. And he made sure Jimmy fast-tracked the legal documents before anyone could change their mind.

Under the given circumstances, the DA allowed Ari to plead to a reasonable two to six year bid for perjury for lying to the Grand Jury, which was a first time D felony. The plea also included a seven-figure fine that went directly to the DA's restitution fund. And due to the financial exposure for Ari on the civil arrangements, all the agreements were done in a concurrent closing with all parties present.

It was a win for everyone, especially Ari, who would be able to retain enough assets to live the rest of his life lavishly in the South of France where, also according to Michele, he planned to relocate. Most importantly, he wouldn't have to face the sexual abuse or kidnapping charges that Isabella could have pressed against him. He would have his life back in less than two years if he behaved, all of which he owed to Isabella—the one person who could have crushed him the most. I saw Iz in a new light. Over and over again, I was reminded why I fell in love with her in the first place. And I realized that instincts never lie.

After officially signing all the documents, the entire story took a backseat in the press— finally. Something we were all grateful for.

I finally reunited with my boys, able to spend some extended time with them for the first time since all of this went down. And when I did, I didn't see what I feared most looking back at me. The possibility of them believing any of this could have ever been true. I could tell they viewed their father with the same eyes as before. Knowing the kind of man I was. The kind of man they could look up to. They confirmed they never believed any of it. Not even for a second.

During the break between the signing of Ari's plea and his sentencing, AP spent a few weeks in San Francisco. We remained in touch, both completely honest with each other as to what we were doing in our lives, romantically and otherwise. We missed each other but we knew being together was not realistic. And we agreed to spend some time together when she got back, both of us determined to never allow anything to come between our friendship.

Iz and I got close again, and fast. We picked up right where we left off. And somehow, the intensity of the ordeal strengthened our relationship. I didn't have any resentment toward her. I still thought of AP, but I knew in my heart that Iz was the one for me. I loved everything about her—her mind, her heart, and now, her body. And her fears of intimacy were washing away with each night we spent together. And the closer we got, the more she realized how much she actually enjoyed it.

The closing of all the settlement documents and assets were finally transferred before the Fourth of July. The closing went as smoothly as possible. Ari would be sentenced the next day, with little fanfare before the holiday weekend. He was a beaten man, but he still had a net worth north of two billion dollars, as well as a new lease on life to look forward to. He just had to go do his time like a man and come home.

Since he was a high-profile inmate and accused sex offender, he was sent to protective custody in the Manhattan Tombs holding facility, where he was waiting to go upstate to serve his sentence. In protective custody, he didn't have to go into general population, which meant he'd be safe from other inmates giving him the beat-down he truly deserved.

But it didn't matter. He didn't last long in there.

On his third night in protective custody, Ari Rohnstein hung himself.

EPILOGUE

RAY

Michele Rohnstein's pre-nuptial agreement only guaranteed her $500MM, even though Ari's net worth was estimated to be close to $10BIL just a few months before the trial. At Isabella's insistence, Ari threw in the sports franchise, the properties associated with their Sutton Place penthouse, and the Hamptons house for them as well. But there were still formal divorce proceedings that needed to be resolved to transfer all the marital assets. Due to the complexity, Michele had no choice but to wait until after he was released from prison to finalize the divorce.

Isabella got the $100MM Ari had promised her while in captivity. In the settlement agreement, she agreed to an iron-clad confidentiality agreement that she could never speak about the sexual abuse or kidnapping. It was yet another hush agreement from Ari and his slime-ball lawyer.

All of that became moot once Ari tied his bedsheet around the vent, slipped the knot around his neck, and slid off the sink of his cell. Since Ari had killed himself before officially finalizing his divorce, half of his estate went to

Michelle, who was still his legal wife. And per his will, the other half went to Isabella, making her an instant billionaire.

Anthony Mika rebuilt his name through my case exposure, but the stress of it all zapped his energy for good. Claiming he was just happy to have cemented his legacy, he ended up selling half his practice to a young, aggressive lawyer, a guy eerily similar to the Anthony of the past. He ended up retiring in Charleston, SC where he spent most of his time on his fishing boat.

AP left the Mika firm—and New York City altogether—to move to Los Angeles. Before she left, she insisted on smoothing things over with Iz and me.

Isabella would always be jealous of AP in some way, but in the end, she got her man and freed her soul. Or at least took a big step in her healing process. Part of that was due to AP, whom she learned to accept in my life, agreeing to respect our friendship.

And AP may not have gotten *me*, but she got a slew of successes flung her way following the high-profile case. She was a hot commodity and was hired at a top law firm in Century City. She also signed a lucrative TV contract with a Los Angeles-based network to be a legal personality. She reunited with her ex-boyfriend, and they had plans to get engaged in due time. However, the heavy travel between San Francisco and LA put a strain on their relationship again at a time when they were trying to rebuild what had broken down over the last year. The distance wasn't the only issue. The bigger problem was the very public relationship she'd had with her infamous client.

My associated specialty finance company received over $50MM in stock compensation from Ari prior to him being sent to prison. He'd been charged with damaging the company's reputation as well as my own, what with all those defamatory statements to the press in his attempt to convict me. It was a deal Ari's lawyer, Jimmy, and my partner in Scottsdale worked on since it wouldn't totally deplete Ari's cash on hand.

In the end, I went with my partner's gut to take the stock, and it couldn't have worked out better, especially when the stock doubled after Ari's death. Our company was back on the map like never before, but the truth was that I didn't have the passion to work five days a week any longer after what I had been through.

I made sure to take care of Mika and his employees, as well as Jay Johnstone, Frankie, and Andy's wife with all the money I made in the settlement. They were all so appreciative. I went the extra mile for AP though, presenting her with a very special piece of jewelry just for her. I also gave her an exquisite painting by a famous artist of her first cover shot in The *NY Post*—the photo taken while she was fighting for my bail, the moment that put her on the map. She would take it with her to every office she'd ever work in.

My life, and Iz's, finally calmed down, allowing our love to fall into a comfort zone for the first time. We were basically living together in the city, still working on joint projects, but without the stress this time around.

Once she overcame her sexual insecurities, I couldn't slow her down in the bedroom. She said she wanted to make up for all the years she missed out on. And truth be told, she satisfied me like no woman ever had before.

She was hell-bent on changing her name from Rohnstein back to Martin. Ironically enough, she had to go downtown to Centre Street to make it all happen.

I agreed to go with her as a show of support, but we never made it inside to file the official paperwork.

Instead, I proposed to her outside that state building—mere months after she testified against me on the other side of the block. Her name would be legally changed from Rohnstein to Jansen.

We eventually moved to Newport Coast, California, after both my boys graduated from high school and decided to head out west for college. My kids loved her, and she formed a close relationship with each of them over some time.

Once we got settled out west, we had a small wedding ceremony at *Pelican Hill Resort.* Dr. Morgan was Isabella's maid of honor. And my sons were my best men.

Before we knew it, Iz and I had a boy and girl together—Christopher and Jaclyn. Michele was thrilled to be a grandmother and finally have babies in her life, and our new family just got closer as we grew.

Isabella finally had a relationship with her mother, something she always yearned for. And with Ari out of the picture, there were no more secrets.

I REMAINED CLOSE WITH AP, occasionally driving up the 405 to meet her for lunch or dinner in Beverly Hills when I had business in LA. The brief times we spent together made us realize how much we missed each other over the years, even though our lives had gone in different directions. It was still tough for Iz to accept our closeness, but it was one battle she couldn't fight. Eventually, I requested that AP work on a project with me so we could see each other more.

AP agreed, and in partnership with me, wrote a tell-all story about the Ray Jansen trial. It was a steamy page-turner about the torrid affair between Alexandra and her client, the scandalous inside-info emails and taboo meeting with the victim, and the never-before-told kidnapping portion of Isabella's story. It was a *New York Times* Bestseller for weeks on end. We eventually parlayed it into a movie deal. Ari was long dead, so there was no one to challenge the confidentiality agreement except his lawyer, Jimmy. Regardless, Iz never publicly confirmed any of it or spoke of it in the press.

However, the author described in detail the uncomfortable sexual abuse at the hands of Ari Rohnstein, with the young girl desperately trying to fight off her predator by grasping and pulling his chest hair in her tiny fingers. Dr. Morgan prodded Iz to work with me and AP on the book project, and she agreed. Ultimately, her input was both difficult on her emotions but also therapeutic in finally closing that chapter of her life for good.

Alexandra Peterson became a star amongst stars after the smashing success of the book and movie deals. At 33 years old, she finally found love, marrying a Los Angeles professional athlete in a very large celebrity-filled reception. Isabella and I couldn't have been happier for her.

Isabella would always be my wife and true love, but my friendship and bond with AP would never be broken.

ACKNOWLEDGMENTS

First, I want to thank my family. My mom, Joanne Janish; and my wife, Jules, who put up with me at my darkest times and held our family together. And for my sons, Joseph and Nicholas, who gave me just enough time and space—not always quietly—to write this book. I hope you all know that your love and support was what helped carry this project through to completion. And I love you all for it.

There would be no *Vindication* without Christina Hart. I think I could write another book about the whole process of how this one came about, and how many times Christina wanted to stab me. Literally. She pushed me to get the first draft out of the closet. She believed in the story as much as I did, consulted with me, understood the characters intimately, edited, re-wrote, and re-edited. In short, she was dedicated from start to finish. In the most simplistic way to say it, she *is Vindication*. And I could never thank her enough for working with me, dealing with me, and making it the best novel I could've ever hoped for. She is a hidden gem in the writing industry, and I have been blessed to have had the opportunity to work with her before she hits it too big to help out a first-timer like me. Please check out her amazing work at: https://amzn.to/2GY3Zua

Dr. Vera Anselmi. I had no scientific understanding of the sexual abuse laid out in these pages and consulted with her to educate me on the dynamics. However, she went above and beyond. And whether she knew it or not, her input drastically altered the entire plot and provided the much-needed realism surrounding the circumstances of childhood sexual abuse. It was hard to grasp, and even harder for me to write. However, I believe in my heart that the artistic value of *Vindication* is in the authenticity of these psychological aspects of the story. Thank you for your help and for lending your brilliant mind to this project. (And for talking me off the ledge a few times, too.) There is no one quite like you.

Tina Torrest. Already an acclaimed author, her consultation was instrumental during every aspect of completing this novel and bringing it to market. Her editing, cover assistance, and publishing insight made this transition so much easier for me than it would have been otherwise. She was genuinely dedicated, professional, and also at times a quasi-therapist while talking me through this daunting self-publishing process. Thank you. You are a true friend and pro's pro. To view her extensive list of successful romance novels, please go to: https://www.ttorrest.com/

Marco Laracca, Esq., Super Lawyer. A talented attorney in every way, but his most outstanding quality is how he shares his limited time with others. (Free of charge, mostly!) He took the time to consult with me on the trial scenes and overall legal aspects of the book, which were also instrumental in creating a realistic feel to the criminal proceedings throughout the story. Thank you for your time and expertise.

Marilyn Church, a world-renowned sketch artist who has covered some of the biggest trials in U.S. History, including "Son of Sam". Some of her work is in the Smithsonian

Museum. She was instrumental in getting the cover exactly how I envisioned it by evoking the gripping emotion of the key trial scene better than anyone else ever could have. I am honored that you've contributed your talents to *Vindication*, and I thank you for taking on this project (even though there was no way I was going to let you say no). To view her work, please go to: MarilynChurch.com

Kat Savage, thank you for your creativeness in making the cover work just as I intended and dealing with all my little changes of font, colors, scale, etc. etc. etc.

Thank you to my inside marketing team led by Jim Alamia of *Route 72*, and Joe Giordano and Rob Smither of *Reclaim Digital* who provided me with a great website and a platform to promote the book. And to my book publicist team who brought me the true expertise on how to get the exposure that I felt this novel deserved—thank you.

Thank you to all my beta readers and consultants, including—but not limited to—Rob Lombardi and Rob Fox. Rob Fox was brutally honest with me as a first-timer, which was what I desperately needed in order to be taken seriously. Sam Gallucci who helped with printing and answered many of my annoying questions along the way. Mark Ganton, my media consultant and best friend (in town), who gave me priceless advice along the way. Also, Jason Cocuzza, who provided great insight and was responsible for coming up with the title of this novel. Lastly, to all my other friends and family who helped give me encouragement and inspiration in those moments when I thought about quitting: All of you played a part in making this book a reality. There are too many of you to mention...Thank you!

The NY DOCs. Yes, I want to thank the Department of Corrections for their dysfunctional ways, whether deliberate or not. I applied for Work Release for two years and was repeatedly denied. Just when I asked to be removed from consideration, they decided to "force" me into the program. They basically put me on lockdown and made the last two months of my bid miserable. However, if it wasn't for those last 40 days, I would've never had the time to handwrite this story, a sign that there are no coincidences in life.

Last but not least, the people at my day job. To my business partner and best friend, Dr. Peter Caravella, who provided me the opportunity to thrive in a new career nine years ago when opportunities were scarce. Thank you for believing in me and allowing me the space I needed—sometimes at a detriment to our funding business—to complete this project. And to my "Legal-Bae's", Silvana Lopez and Melisa Pagan, and all the employees and consultants at *Legal-Bay* that held down the fort during those times when my focus was on this book. I know that you didn't always see what was going on behind the scenes, but your immeasurable patience was vital to the separate successes of both Legal-Bay and *Vindication*. Thank you for your loyalty and dedication.

CONTACT THE AUTHOR

ChrisJ@Legal-Bay.com